LARVA

Julián Ríos

LARVA

Midsummer Night's Babel

Translated by Richard Alan Francis
with Suzanne Jill Levine and the author

Dalkey Archive Press

Acknowledgments

The translators would like to thank the National Endowment for the Arts, the Fulbright Commission, the Spanish Government, and the University of Washington for their support.

Originally published by Ediciones del Mall, 1983
Copyright © 1983 Julián Ríos
English translation copyright © 1990 Richard Alan Francis, Suzanne Jill Levine, and Julián Ríos

Library of Congress Cataloging in Publication Data
Ríos, Julián.
    [Babel de una noche de San Juan. English]
    Larva. Midsummer night's Babel / translated by Richard Alan Francis
with Suzanne Jill Levine and the author.
    Translation of: Larva. Babel de una noche de San Juan.
    Includes index.
    I. Title.
PQ6668.I576B313   1990   863'.64—dc20   90-3773
ISBN: 0-916583-66-X

First Edition

Partially funded by grants from The National Endowment for the Arts and The Illinois Arts Council.

Dalkey Archive Press
1817 North 79th Avenue
Elmwood Park, IL 60635 USA

Printed on permanent/durable acid-free paper and bound in the United States of America.

Table of Contents

Pluck the Clover

1. The trifolium of our Roman à Klee?:
Three-partying through our folie à deux: do I, don't I, he loves me he leaves me
not, leaf by leafing through the nocturnotes of our bacchantes, back hunting buck-
beans in the back cuntry. ((Seek, Dartful Lodger, your tarts in Hyde Park . . .))
Living in clover . . . [Sauberes Klee! Awesumptuous trio! This summer sum of
some of the . . . There's no threesome folía a dos? he would calculatedly ask
himself one night, that highest bidder of a thousand aliases paperilously perusing
papers with his babelic beauty ((: Sing, sing, christening after christening)) in the
Tower of Paper. Babelle, Milalias and . . . Herr Narrator. Qui? she inquired.
Who? A sort of ventriloquacious nut who misproduces our voices, he explained. A
cunning conning cofounder and confounder. The Echommentator who dubdoubles
us and tries to root in black-and-white everything we live and write en route . . .
Twice as crazy for being split, Narr and Tor, so I Germangled him into Herr Narrator. Ah bon. You'll get to know him . . . In his deliriums he thinks he's the author
of our feuilleton, our surreal serial . . .: Au! Tor! let the doubler be doubled . . .
Anyway, here they have me, the aforementioned nut, trapped between brackets,
making me Herr Narrator.] And now, King of Clovers! Roi de trèfle! Kleekönig! in
ah-one ah-two ah-three to trick or treat you with PILLOW NOTES 1, p. 453.

2. Chemise de nuit? Black gown of night?:
Ah, don't exaggerate, salaud montreur de marionnénettes! My nigh-gone night
gown, of A Thousand and One . . . Vaporous and so tempting . . . La roba, mumma
mía! the robe of my dreams, all in raptures in those Oxford Street department
stores! that I would pay for so dearly . . .

3. Slyly sweettalking? Wily seekwalking?:
Scratch, Old Scratch!: The devil will take the hindmost!

4. The Villa of Mysteries . . .:
That's right, Mr. Pompeii. And circumstance!

5. Don what . . . ? Who?:
A man without a name. Yes, because he has them all. Let's call him, for short: Don
Johannes Fucktotum . . .

6. Giovannitrio! always neighing, never nay-saying:
Hyhnhnm!!! Call me hoarse. Sometime a stud I'll be . . .

PLUCK THE CLOVER[1] . . . PLUCK THE CLOVER . . ., harped black-haired Sleeping Beauty in her vaporous black nightie[2] as she pushed her way through the thicket of serpentwining masks in the Hall of Mirrors, PLUCK THE CLOVER . . ., smilingly sleepwalking[3] with arms extended toward the three glass doors open to the bosky night: in the background, among the shadows in the rear garden of the villa,[4] a bonfire gleamed.

Pluck the clover . . .

((On the night of Saint John? Yes, in the masquerade of a dark Don Juan night, with a harpy ending! prepared by filmmaker Bob "Hitch-Cock" with so many hitches in that rambling nuthouse or Villa of Mysteries across from Bishop's Park and the Thames, Midsummer Madness at Fulham's Folly! on orders from his boss Mr. "Napo" Leone, the Napoleon of Porn, to celebrate the publication of a salacious magazine, *Clover Club,* whose emblem was a cockeyed ace of clubs suggesting various forms, depending on your point of view.))

Pluck . . ., she looked around, . . . the clover . . ., as if to orient herself in the uproar, wavering for a moment, Pluck the clover . . ., before going on her way.

And a few steps behind her, a dark Don Giovanni[5] (: wide-brimmed black hat with white feathers, black velvet mask, black cloak) twirling an index finger at his temple: È pazzerella! She's nutty! Loca . . . ((Giovannitrio! Tritone tenor! Don Juan Trenorio![6]))

Pluck the clover . . .

1. Interpolation/interpellation of the Commentator, alias Herr Narrator:
Heels! Heal the heel! as he goes over the hill. To be content, a long-distance reader must always be in form. Be exhaustive, not exhausted! A kill, easy readers, will be faster than the tortuous! Keep after the high-stepping heroine, tracing her steps step after turtling step . . . (And in the meantime the fallen angel Don Juan fearlessly treading her heels. In search of his bedder half? Nox Mirabilis! Every donjuan seeks his Belle-de-Nuit . . .) Ah, and forgetting to note that the faithful transcription of her litany would be: Pluck the clo-vair . . .

2. What's she saying?: Pique des clos vers?!?:
Almost how it sounds in the frankly galling repetition of that Belle au Bois Dormant. In the sleeping forest? For rest. Stopping in the woods on a showy night, our bore arboreal sleeps like a log. Irked, encircled. A tree truncated under the two fairy fellers in this choppy tree-sea. Making kindling out of their kind, out of the frying pan and into the firewood. / Emil, a meal. / Fallacious traitors / Fälla! Fellatio!: See Pillow Notes 2 and 3, pp. 457 and 459.

3. Tes blondines! Your blondines!:
Blondon. Blonding. Blinding. Blending. Blond dona. Sandy blondunes . . . Quick-sanding, la donna è mobile! sandwenched in that dark night of a Thou-sand Nights: See Pillow Notes 4, p. 460.

4. Notte matta!:
Yes, that luny night as mad as a hatter . . .

5. Refrain from ruining the refrain . . .:
Buried in the hexceedingly exxed Magnuscript (: . . . XXX . . .) are the short-tempered curses of your shortstuff, Cunty Concha Cota! the Madrilenian maid from the Nomad Hotel who made it with you and didn't unmake the bed. For conscience's sake? Cramped concupiscence in that cubicle. standing against the sink, panting and prompting . . . losing consciousness in the prompter's conch box . . . Concha! She wouldn't take it lying down.

6. Wise man in a dunce cap:
Wise guy, ready to make a fool out of you . . .

7. Apeshit! Apa! Nobody makes a monkey out of me:
Plump! he falls. And rises, Plump! and falls in the tub. So! Inkognito! murmuring in mid-metamorphosis. Cold? Sweating ink. Sinbad in his Swedish bath . . . / Suédois? / Suée d'oie, mon gosse. Lapsus calami . . .: See Pillow Notes 5, p. 461.

Wacky woman, she's a nutty nude majesty! Little lost lamebrain . . .
I'll follow in her footsteps, yeah, I'll tread on her heels[1] as long as
she doesn't put her foot down. Like she did that other night, a
jealous fit and off she stamped, completely buzzed. Lost in
London, all night in the rain. Lightly dressed this time too. A-ha,
and with high hashpirations. This hi-fi vamplifier flying high . . .

Pluck the clover . . .

Vad säger hon? Qu'est-ce qu'elle dit?[2] asked at once two blondulat-
ing undines[3] (: with wet hair, and wrapped in big bath towels)
pressing against a Merlin the Magician with long cotton beard and
starry cloak. Att plocka klöver. A la cueillette du trèfle.

Pluck the clover . . .

No te mata![4] You'll get over it. Enough of this crap.[5] Clam up, butt-
head! What a bore that bimbo is with her babbling . . . Hey you,
wise Merlinguist, you know who that broken record is, that loopy
windup soundbox?

No idea,[6] he said turning toward the maja in her black Spanish
shawl, plump and dark, fanning herself with theatrical exaggera-
tion, leaning one shoulder against a mirror. Earlier she was flitting
here and there incessantly, looking for someone. But it looks like
she's already flipped out.

Hoopla! Apa! Sinbad . . .,[7] the two blondies come clapping behind
the bathrobed blackamoor, blackened and turbaned Sinbad . . .
who was volleyballing with shouts, Rock and ball!!! a big white
globe.

Pluck the clover . . .

1. Cape of sinners?:
Escape!

2. Soulstice! Yes. Dark night of the soul . . .:
Soûle! Soûle! Spirited souls on this dark Saint John night . . .

3. Mask carillon:
Tong! Tong! . . . till all hours. Tongs and bones! And when the erring tongue says
Tong! lovers, to bed, 'tis almost spherical time, a fairy ring . . .

4. La Traviata?:
The strains of Verdi will come back to you tonight at the opera. Ah fors'è lui . . .
What? Semper libera! Come, brother marksman, let's drop a brick into this bric-a-
brac bacchanal. Tamper, temper, tempest. Storm und drunk, don! Thunder the
bog, the crazy memories intertwine, arousing the wild ire, Mireland! Erinring.
Erin, yes. Mad. Furiouser and furiouser! With all the sound and the furies, the
poor thing is lost and out of her mind . . .

5. Salvation!:
Salvo. It's every man for himself in an infernight . . .

6. God natt! (: Swedish, echoed):
Ecco: noce e noche . . .

7. You're carrying the triumphal palm—of martyrdom! Pass it on to another:
Evolve, love dove!!! Palm, pall, pal . . . He dies for her and is born for her. The
phoenix and the turtledove! Pounding palms . . . / Saint Esprit! you'll see when the
pigeon shoot begins. Palm by napalm, young dove, you will . . .

8. Milalias of a million flights, alas, we'll have to clip your wingcognitos . . .:
A millennium passing; yes, mariachi, more than a thousand years . . . / See the
simurgh! Go fly a kite! Wax your wings, Dedalias!

9. Saint dessein Cezannien . . .:
Blanc-seing, zinzin!: Another of your tête-à-tits, hardheaded esthete! / A teetering
stumbling blockhead . . . Pluck! Like a dove, bloodied . . . Plummeting . . . Pum-
meled . . . Reanimamation . . . Tremorous, timorous . . . Trembling, twinning . . .
Dadance mamacabre . . . Mummy bubs . . . Let big ones by bygones . . . Eh paumé!
Elle est tombée dans les pommes, ta vieille nounouille . . .: See PILLOW NOTES 6,
p. 463.

10. Saindoux!:
Mamargarine mammaries, Agh!

Trébol . . . treble . . ., and Don Juan covered up with his cape.[1] Treble clef: in the key of summer solstice[2] . . . Have to put it in a light tone. And when the hall clock strikes the last stroke of midnight . . .[3] If she doesn't cause a fuss, kick up a fa! this soapoperatic soprano.[4]

The clover . . . Not again! hummed over and over. This high-sounding prima donna is gonna wear out our ears this long night. Such a silly refrain, and so catchy. Shit! Another trick? Better to play dumb than wind up an echo of this sweet dish . . . Ja! Yeah! C'mon! pushing ahead. I'm gonna lose her (and he elbowed his way) in this tumultitude. I'll be her shadow 'til I can unmask myself. Not so fast now . . . (already catching up with her), there's plenty of night left. This hardheaded hannah, a tough nut! still hasn't heard her Masker Voice. Pluck . . . Sing on with the sing-song!—in an arrogant tone with three fingersnaps. Much ado, crack! skräck! about nuttin' . . . Hell![5] raising his right hand to his hat: Good nut![6]

((Her ravening-mad shadow encroaching? And her echo, almost. But she was out of it or hypnotized and didn't realize, at least at first, that the cawing black baron, aspetta il corvo! was following her all the time.))

Pluck the clover . . .

A bird in hand is worth two in the bash . . . And that voluble violator flew away. Three months' rent and then some! he left owing me. The best room, with rights to the garden. All those bushes, and he had to pick . . . Eek! Help! Look at my hand: a wounded dove[7] that he covered with kisses and dressed with his handkerchief. Hanky-panky! Young man! . . . I lost my senses in his arms. Then he sacked me on the sofa, Mr. Alia! Emill!!![8] manhandling my love-apples, Saints seins . . .[9] my gallant with his french kisses that pork cochon: Seins doux![10]

1. Retorting distractions? Mirage?:
Mere image . . .

2. To the pyre, vampyromaniac . . .:
Yes you peered and pyrated from vamp to vamportunity, vampiranha! Vampirandello in search of his shady little characters! Go up your torrid tower of silence, parsimonious vampiroman! No, I won't shut up, traditore! even if you keep pointing at me with your menacing index! / Povera sventurata! i passi suoi voglio seguir, non voglio che faccia un principizio . . .

3. Hell? to beat all hells!:
Gelatine and gelignight / Hehl? / Hell! hell-seher, hell-sayer . . . Es wird hell. Let's get the hell out of here! Dawnward drawn: NONWARD HO! OH DRAWN ON . . . Daybreak, into little pieces! The night watchman's last lullaby . . . There's still a lot of night left, devil!

4. Schlaf?:
Falsch!

5. Flush! Have a splash in the pool-bash!:
Enough pooling around! Just pool off, buddy. ((A whole poolfool of duck soup . . . unceasing swantonness in the cesspool. Bob and Milalias pool forces with the chicks . . . Oh yes and cheep champagne. Milalias leaping and firing foam from a champagne bottle. What, sauce for the goose? Shampooling, sploshing, stammering. And the silly goose with his cantus firmus: Yearning houri to the urinal . . . Pooh-Poop-Poule mouillée!)) POOL LOOP. Pull out.

6. Flimflam?:
Soflaming.

7. Which stain? Lots of spots in your first drafts:
And all together they make one great and free one. The natural indivisible state of our corrupt stage hacktress. Maid in S^p_tain.

8. You've played out your bellows, accordionanist!:
Nanay. Blow below, bellower. Give us an accordionysian aphrodiscordant chord, a record of that record-breaking performance with sharp hellish infernotes in your oneironymous bosky rhapsodamusical.

Pluck the clover . . . And she went right by without even a glance at the plumpish middle-aged chatty nanny in white starched uniform who kept her bandaged hand cradled to her breast. Pluck the clover . . .

((Perhaps she went out to clear her head? And to shake herself free from the distorting refractions.[1] Still sleepwalking she dreamily droned her spell—her abracodabraxas! her talismantra! her reincantation!—seeing herself and the others, the other masks, being distortured in the mirrors that nearly covered the walls and ceiling of that dizzying hall.))

Absorbed, in the doorway, looking at the chiaroscuro: fleeting silhouettes running to hide among the trees and hedges and bushes and statues, pursued by laughs and shouts. Bonfire beams[2] beckoning, yellowflickering among purple blue black fronds.

High! High! Hell![3] shouting and clapping and splashing in the distance, Schlaf![4] Schlaff! from those leaping over the bonfire (: crispy crackling strippers) and into the lily pond. Schlaf![5]

Behind the blazes, rearing up: incandescentaurs! And the two tousled blondies, saddled on the shoulders of their also-naked shaggy-haired mounts, let out whoops as they jumped with their steeds over the bonfire flam![6] plash! into the shallow pool.

There under the weeping willows, and glowing, behind the pool: a wide milky stain,[7] stretching toward the fronds in the river's darkness. Reptilinearity slithering. Wriggly-winding, hanging down. Stretching out, like an accordion, faster now. Accordiondulating.[8]

1. Fleur de lease, Novalis?:
No valise in that portmanteau. Lyrical delirium, lily incarnation. Madonna lily, Callas lily, Jersey Lily . . . Deflowering and proustituting your blooming girls en fleurs-de-lease. Keep scanning, scam artist. Ciana a ciana, trovatore. As you ask, so shall you receive your good piece of aspiration, asinine assessor. Popoetaster! Plucking your pretty pickup girls. Keep sifting for your all-purpose flower, Heinrich von Afterdingen!

2. Sizzling thistles . . .:
Aperi oculum!

3. Crowporeal bodies?:
Ja. Jaha: Korporation!

4. Figments? Indeed! Fruit of his imagination:
Feverish. Yes, flaming fig bonbons in front of the bonfire. Can't figure it out? Oh that indigo blue summer night in Holland Park: hippies and gopis swinging on branches of the great fig tree, krax! krax! while flames rose dramatically with the sitar scratches. Ragatime! The great fig tree, ignited in the night. Fire it was, and ashes it will be. Ashvatta!!!

5. This fiery rood will conquer . . .:
Ignuminous!

6. Fawkes? Guy Fawkes?:
Please to remember the Fifth of November, Punpowder Treason and Plot, in the Phoenix Lodge attic, when the conspirator Fawkes or Focs lighted all your speeches and Parliaments. In his Auto da Phoenix.

Centipede!!! ((Or almost one hundred.))

Now the thread of nudes on all fours was closing on itself, forming a circle of high-held butts around the upside-down gymnast rigid as a fence post, his legs forming a V. But still more difficult: his hands hiding his genitals.

One fellow with blue flowers ((a bunch of lilies?)) stuck between his buttocks, kneeling with his back arched and his head between his arms. While his floriculturist, also naked and kneeling, took aim and planted bullseye! another blue flower.[1]

((Another osculation?! . . .)): the Wolf-Man buried his hairy face in the white rump of a Valkyrie in horned helmet, as she crawled cat-scratching and meowling on the grass. While he continued to lash her with a handful of thistles.[2]

Bodies[3] in the branches. Bunches of bodies, black, balancing in the branches of the great burning fig[4] tree.

To the left, toward the purplish woods of Bishop's Park: white blobs, and torches. Silent procession of hooded white forms. And leading them, a burning cross.[5]

((Fox!? Focs?!: Fires?)): furious uproar rising with the flames of a blazing rag-and-straw effigy stuck in the center of the bonfire. ((Focs!?[6]))

It is better to marry than to burn, better wed than dead . . ., a bride fluttering her white veils around the fire, chased by a friar in a chef's hat, clutching a skillet.

1. Fry!:
Yes, fryer. Fried . . . ((Poor Fray, even after he was fried, he kept dreaming of that pluperfect mate . . .))

2. Fire . . . ?:
Fie, Falla fallacious. Please, no more fuel on that ritual fire dance. Burning lovers' flame, flame of living love . . .: See PILLOW NOTES 7, p. 463.

3. Son! in the Land of Nod, Don . . .:
Dreams are dreams.

4. Son son?:
Oui! The same old son. And dance!

5. Band of cobras?:
An all cobrass band!

6. Pap! Pap with a hatchest?:
Papist! Just a few piddling tit-hits . . .

7. O Felix pulpa . . .:
Culpap! Skinny, yes, but papa is part to blame. Charity and beating begin at home.

8. Stern sternum! Harsh and untuneful are the notes of love . . .:
Break this sterne consternation.

9. Din?:
Yes, dean. When religion sounds right . . .

Ay! Fray! Fray! . . ., she cried at full speed. Things are getting hot around here . . . And with a half-turn she suddenly raised, in a wave of frilly petticoats, her dress up to her head. And hurled herself through the flames, Fray!!![1] and into the water.

Fire ball . . .[2] The Fire Dance . . ., and Don Juan peeped out on the porch. The flame that inflames. Cherchez la flamme! spying from his corner in shadows. Flamenco flame? Yes, such a fine fire, a flamboyant flame . . . He continued, delighted, Such sultry contortiondulations (: bracelets flashing in her jingling snaking gesticulation) by that Hindu ballerina.

Ring! Son! . . .,[3] smilingly nodding in time with the tinkling of the rattles circling her shapely arms, her hands hooked like cobras. Son son . . .,[4] she nodded in slow motion, as if sleepy. Son sonata . . .[5]

Pap! Pap! sharply smacking hand against breast, Pap! Pap! now frantically twisting. Pap![6]

So tender . . . ized she'll be, turned to pulp[7] if she keeps on meaculpanegyrating like that. Skinny, but how she makes her sternum resound . . . Almost stereo. On she goes, turn[8] after turn, pap! pap! giving herself a sound thrashing, like a chest-beating penitent. And to top it off the jangling din! din![9] of all that scrap brass she's wearing.

That sweet little noisemaker. She really drove me wild with her bangling jangles as she slinky-slithered, our nudeness knotted. Pretending to resist no no nanette! right to the end, Ooh la la! that afternoon in the red-hot nest of Phoenix Lodge. Purring in ecstasy and curling, coiling, climbing. Biting, and dying. How that dark woman could bite! And slip away with a wriggle. Marks, from beatings? on her back.

1. Rubify!:
Oui, il faut franchir le rubis con . . . You've got to cross the ruby, conman!

2. Currying flavor . . .:
With Madame Curry. Caress, careless . . .

3. Axiliary elixir?:
Ambrosia. Elixir, sir. Indian nectar, amrit! from that panicked girl, an Amritsar native.

4. Silk skin, like watered silk?:
Springing forth thread by thread . . . Mana emanating . . . Venerable venery, forbidden fountain. Mana, a spring in summer. Skinny-deep, deep unfathomed lake, abysmal font. And you drowning in her arms. Until you touch bottom, in pleasure.

5. Mana Kaur . . .:
The slave-princess of the Indian shop on Shepherd's Bush Road where you used to buy your evening supplies—and the apple, the only one, of discord. Distant and different, your Mana . . . So exotic in those clothes. In a sari and always so serious, tied to the cash register. And constantly watched by the gray-bearded guy in the turban. His eyes threw sparks the time you tried to talk to her, while you searched your pockets for the remaining pence. Until you had the opportunity to approach her alone, in the Brook Green phone booth, in front of her school.

Her bronze body aroused, her eyes like coal. Jewel[1] of fire in her humid hollow. Savoraciously tasting her everywhere. Afternoon Indian delight. Pungent flavor—clove?—on the tip of her tongue. Ah! ah her hot breath, of curry[2] and tea. Hot feverish gypsy skin. Caress after caress, simmering in her own salsalacity. Cool sweat flowing under her arms.[3] Down her valleys: five rivulets down the anointed body of that daughter of Punjab. Moist silky smoothness.[4] And the slippery seductress slid away. Silk soothing the senses . . . Succulent slipperiness! then off she slipped, licketysplit. A cool fleeting kiss and fear in her glance. Time already!

A-ho! that characteristic sound of her bracelets. With nervous caresses and endearments. Always watching the clock. Qué será, what must be, must beat the clock. All those bracelets din! din! on her right arm. Brushing her rebellious hair. Slipping away barefoot in the reddish shadows. That fornicating room like an oven. Agile, making her shadow on the wall colossal. Clothes scattered around the floor. Sinuous and jingling as she wraps up in her sheets. Eight o'clock!? she would get to the shop too late. Slave to her uncle, the long-handed sikh. Pap! Slap for sinning. Pap! Pap! up one side and down the other for disobedience. India without independence.

Until her nose was swollen. After the last beating. Sudden start in the middle of the night. Croakcroakcroakcroak . . . Hey! frogcroak through the front-door intercom. It's me . . .,[5] in a moan. Oh yes, it was her, the unexpected Indian. And almost unrecognizable. Her face swollen (: moon face!) and covered with bruises. She had run away from home, at that hour, from the grasp of the psychopathic sikh. Seeking refuge in my lair.

1. Alu-cination?:
Quelle patate! With pap for brains, no potentate. Enough of this pulp and patter, of pat answers and palpable lies, of elusive allusions, of yanging and yammering. Et patati et patata, pathetic pal, you'll see when she goes out like a light . . . Like a marionette with those jerky jolts . . .

2. Savage salve:
Fiery lubricity, lubricantlapper . . .

3. Fall?
Fall, guy. Fallen fruit. (Punjabi pun: punjabberwocky!)

4. Morsecchiatura in punto di morte . . .:
Qui sta il punto. That's the point. (A certain Mr. Tod, a real cynic, will arrive in good time, at the designated hour on the dot. Mr. Tod is waiting for God-Dot . . ., waiting, a fine pointer! for what must come.)

5. Hasan al Sabbat!:
Le maure s'occulte . . . Point.

Hey! Is that her or a hallucination?![1] The dancer or some other answer? . . ., searching the shadows. The Bayadere!!!

Illuminated in the gleam: an enormous golden apple for a head, in an iridescent sari, the elusive exotic ballerindian belly-swaying at the flames' edge.

Tallowy, well anointed with oil. For the burns?[2] And with such a shiny gleaming apple. Ready to bake. Or to melt on the spot . . . Is she trying to knock her block off? ((Better wed than beheaded?)) Bopping her own head. Hey! She's going to bust her skull doing that, in her steady epileptic fit.

Then she shrieked in falsetto, Fall! Fall! all trembling, with tin-tinkling convulsions, and raising her hands to her apple. Fall![3]

Malum! the short-order friar Latinized, shaking his head. Malum prohibitum. From the apple came the evil of the world. The apple of evil. Of discord. Forbidden fruit, and he pinched his Adam's apple. Sharply. A-ha, that Edenbite, Agenbite of Inwit, mordant remorse of conscience still gnawing at us . . .

Mors . . . Morse?[4] and Don Juan stretched an arm to his right, toward the flashes. (In the background, next to the ironwork and half-hidden by a sycamore, a phantasmal white sheik[5] insistently turning on off on his lantern.) Morse and remorse . . .

What?!: — · ? — — — ! — ? · · · · !? · · · :
Dash dot. Dash dash dash. Dash. Dot dot dot dot. Dot dot. Dash dot. Dash dash dot. Dot dot. Dot dot dot. Dash. Dot dash dot. Dot dot dash. Dot. Dash dash dash dot dot dot. Dot dash. Dot dash dot dot. Dot dash dot dot. Dot dot. Dot dot dot. Dot dash dash dot.

1. You're dotty, dash it all!:
That dottering old fool dashing my hopes. More's the pity. Don't distract me, wise guy.

2. Note from the script-girl:
Article by article, getting them down . . . Have you seen the Emperor's new clothes? A costumed Don Juan, figged out! Down to the last detail, each article of clothing (: black felt sombrero with white feathers, black satin half-mask, doublet with ruff collar and slashed sleeves of white lace, black kid gloves, jerkin and black velvet trunk hose and black leggings with silver trimmings, Spanish cape) and their rental prices (: Total: 13 guineas) on a receipt from Emperor Clothes Ltd., 5 Emperor's Gate SW7.

3. Sic, sycophant!:
C'mon to the forbidden fruit stand, hypofigliac, to our figlibuster . . .

4. Still more prohibitions?:
From Veda to vedette, more forbitten fruit in that branch of the Tree of Knowledge.

5. Such flaming! Such phlegm!:
Agh! Gagging gag by gag . . .

6. Sikh up!:
Yes. Hiccuping fire, this heat-seeking sikh.

7. Eternal? papyromaniac?:
C'étaient des follets, mais ils avaient cette flamme qui ne s'éteint pas.

8. With his forked tongue . . . Serpentecosthesaurusizing . . .:
A great feast of slanguages . . . A movable feast! and so moving. Yes, you're in the great buffeting buffet of languages, a jumble of jargons . . .

9. Pipe that in your schtick . . .:
Down where the sun don't shine . . . Like that night in the Park Walk smoking den, with the Queen of the Night, that pipe wench! when she tried assiduously to buttonhole you into one of her caprices . . . Olisbos-pipe dream? Pipe nightmare. Gaude mihi.

10. Hash it out!:
Put that in your pipe, Monsieur le pipeur, and smoke it. Fume ta pipe!

Dot. Dot dash dot. Dash dash. Dot dot. Dot dot dot. Dot dot dot. Dot dot. Dash dot dot dot. Dot dash dot dot. Dot.[1]

Farewell remorse . . ., and he turned around to cloak himself in his cape.[2] Good-bye to the remorse-ridden commandments. And to the garden of the malicious gardener. Din! Din! la midinette (Bon appétit!) is served in the Eden snack bar. You shall not eat from . . . (As if we cared a fig! Or a syconium . . .[3] Yes, eat. The forbidden fruit of her womb. Rubrub, such fun. Rubrub, fruit so ripe . . .) That rogue-savior only savored the fore-bidden[4] fruit of that tree . . . Ag! Ag! he sputtered,[5] Gag! Ag! Fallen. Yes, fallen. So ripe . . .

Agg! A light! a leaper in the night belched a flare-up. (That fire-spewing fakir[6] in turban and loincloth had moved close, a cigar—or pipe? in hand, to the scarlet-cloaked devil chewing on his pipe in front of the glass door to the garden. Give me a light? An ever-lasting hellfire?[7] With his forked tongue of fire.)

From slang to slang . . .[8] My turn now, said the Dutch woman in a nun's habit, a red rooster hanging from her belt, going klomp! klop! in her clanky clogs. A match, Lucifer? and with a wooden match and a curtsy, she lit the pipe of the stupefied devil.

Pipe down,[9] shaking out his glowing pipe toward the garden. Peace pipe. Sh! Hush up![10] Don't play with fire. You know what happens. Someone will settle your hash. Want me to tell you the shaggy pipe story? and he turned to face (: the Dutch peasant had gone up in smoke, into the turmoiling crowded ballroom) the empty doorway.

1. Dream dream dream . . .:
Languid airs rising, voluptuous aromas . . .

2. Or conversely, The Pipe of Desire, passing from hand to hand . . .:
And from mouth to mouth, down the pipeline.

3. Plus ça change . . .:
C'est du kif!

4. Floggy mountain blakedown?:
They've dropped their drawers of perception!

5. Ja! Rasen!:
¿Arrasen? Arse-raisin'! Raze to the bitter end.

6. Ilumina oculos meos!:
Careful with that griegorian chant . . .

7. Volume voluminous! Éléphantiastique!:
Notre bouquin émissaire . . . [The scrapegoat and his defile cabinet. Summammary of his Magnum Opuss. The Black Book. The Book of Changes. The Wandering and the Book: Deambularvagabounding through London, reading on the run the book of their more or less imaginary lives. Or wandering blindly and randomly on his parodyssey, waylaid in search of adventures. His graphomanionanism made them err; airy erotic errata. Living the written and writing the relived was one of the paraphrasisyphean tasks of his Londonerous novel. They called it (w)rite to life, or writ(h)ing, without realizing they would ever overspend themselves in the undertaking.] Our old phony book . . .

8. Icebrigantine?:
The Flying Dutchman, between cumuli and cirri.

Pipe dream . . .,[1] Don Juan muttered into his beard. Oneiric kaleidoscopium of a summer night. If it's possible, let it pass me by . . . Is it the same one?[2] Calumetamorphosis, yes. All the humor in a joke goes up in smoke? Kif-kif,[3] it's all the same. Oui. Seems like everyone's passing the pipe tonight. Except the two of us . . ., spying Sleeping Beauty from his hiding place.

Moving stealthily, little by little, along the porch. Then she stopped between two columns and faced the garden. Again she took a few steps and at the top edge of the steps, she stopped again.

Forming, gangling up, a naked nexus. Bareskinned, butting together then busting apart, buzzing blooming confusion,[4] bare bums bumble-tumbling in the fireglow. Embracing shadows over the coals. Intertwining, the team teeming and swarming in the sparking smoke-cloud. Fiery twisting nudes. Giant snake slithering in the high grass. Laying down the lawn.[5]

There on a carpet of light, between the bonfire and the fig tree: nudes knotting in agreement. And farther back, in the weeds, amalgamating rituals. Trickle of purple points along the opposite bank. Thistles[6] and nettles, pricklebushes. Smoke, and between the statues, shadows. Rambles and entanglements in the blackberry brambles. Rustling and cracking of distant branches, near the river. Red eyes in the shrubs.

That milling swirling scramble, impetuous and tipsy. And squatting in the center of the ring of witches wrapped in their black shawls, the coal-black Lecherous Goat from Goya's *Witches' Sabbath,* holding a big black book[7] over his shaggy groin. (Mouths agape and eyes shining electric, hanging on every word from his whispering lips: reading that powerful old tome?)

The phantom ship!?: with its dark hull and tattered sails, adrift in a sea of ice floes.[8] Toward the high white cliffs on the horizon, over Putney, where big thunderheads were building up.

1. Dies Irae? Get out of your cell, annotator:
Yes, the Erinnyes! the Furies with their sound . . .

2. Kay! Kay! Kay!:
Cake ache, eh? The *K.K.K.* (Kinder, Küche, Kirche: Kids, Kitchen, Kongrega-
tion) by which the subjector subjects the feminine subject, viewed as object, to
speak objectively, in abject absentia.

3. My uncle!? in penjabi?:
Cacacowering with fear after only a glimpse of him . . .

4. One beats the bush, but another has the harem . . .:
Hare! Hare! Hare Krishna, dance with your gopis, and make a tabula rasa of
everything. Yoga! Yoga!

5. Another ambush?:
Almost. When we were waiting for the bus in Shepherd's Bush, one afternoon
when Mana was playing hooky. Almost immediately she spotted his turban across
the Green. All upset, paralyzed with fright. Good thing it started to sprinkle and I
thought to hood her with that big plastic bag someone had left on the sidewalk. So
tempting: a golden apple, and bitten, shining in the black plastic. Had to use some
imagination. He headed straight for us, the bearded face under the turban, and his
eyes were shooting daggers. Did he recognize me? a nightly customer in his little
hole of a shop, who paid compliments to his slave . . . The sikh stiffly stalked the
length of the queue for the 88, glanced at the bag, a bitten apple of temptation, and
continued on his way without suspecting whom it covered. (Good bag! In the bag!)

6. To the empyre!:
Ha! Sh! Go up your torrid tower of silence, parsimonious vampiroman! Here in
the Phoenix Lodge attic. The Tower of Babel will burn. Close cover before
striking?

Fireflies winking in the fronds of that riverbank. The procession of hooded figures with burning candles began to leave the clearing illuminated by the bonfire. (Singing the Kyrie Eleison in a whisper?) Women's voices, muffled. (Dies irae?[1]) Murmured monotone jeremiad (Ora pro nobis?) and whispers. At the front, fluttering next to the burning cross, a white banner with *KKK*[2] in big red letters.

Caca! Caca! she with the apple head clucked squatting close in the bushes. Mere caca![3] and pointed at the fakir who ran about bellowing ag! agg! and breathing fire from his mouth.

What cachaos . . ., mused Don Juan. Merdier! That pyromaniac will wind up catching her, no matter how well she hides in the thicket.[4] A close call that afternoon in Shepherd's Bush.[5] He spouts fire as he goes and lights up the darkest corners. He's sly like a fox! And she with her cacackles of disgust, and goosepimples no doubt, hasn't picked up on his little ruse. That's him all right, that flamethrowing sikh. I give the orders, you listen. That tyrant will drag her from the party, and it's off to clerk that run-down shop till the time comes to offer her in holy martyrmony.

Ag! Agg! Casting about for his daughter, to chastise her. Unworthy of her caste? Indomitable Indian, chased, unchaste, and miscast. Damn! Who would pluck that brown chestnut from the fire? Not that indolent fiancé back in northern India, who couldn't quench the burning passions with letters. Better to marry than to burn? Better wedded than breaded . . . Pushing the poor Punjab to the pyre,[6] Sikhrifice! To flames: salamander? red man, alas . . . And she praying fervorishly. Until she finally expires . . . Is he still looking for her? Agg! Going around mad enough to spit fire. And to top it off, they still haven't started the fireworks. Crack, crackers . . . And this other reveler there completely in the dark.

1. Crux? Crossly!:
Get to the point . . . of racking your brains!

2. Black shadow that will cover it all . . .:
Inkubus! O yes . . .

3. Fou? Fu? Fooey!:
Go back and consult your book of changes. Without stopping to screw, you sinic (sic), since it will soon be your turn for the Chinadoll . . . In yet another of your cock-and-bull-in-a-china-shop stories . . .: See PILLOW NOTES 8, p. 464.

4. Fu fu, fuliginous!:
That loudy cloud clawling about, lolling in the lushes. Hiding. Almost can't see. Lobbers? Who'll take the lap for all that lot? Lending each other. My loyal wife, with legal status down in the locks! Should I flee or stay? The election difficult at my age. Things getting lank, at this late better leave lickety-split. Look at those lakish women, in the law? what lumps! going down to the blackish pond, that wicked blue. This is all long.

5. Like a riddle, very arduous!:
Centipede? Mille-pattes? / Or put it another way, NAME MAN: When it's odd, it's odd; and when it's even, it's even odder!

6. . . . VOI CH'ENTRATE . . .:
Enfermés: trapped in hell! (Enter through the exit? With so many false ways in and out you'll end up finding, Leapin' lepers! leppe! the fire escape . . .)

7. Blind Alice?:
ALICE IN WONDERLONDON!!! The blind Alice of your London Romances: See PILLOW NOTES 9, p. 465.

She, quiet and immobile (lightning flashes, among the black foliage, towards Putney) at the edge of the stairway. ((Deeply inhaling, exhaling?)) Taking the air (trickles of flames, along the other bank, up the Thames) of the burning night: charged with electricity. And the storm growing ever closer. Acrid odor, crackling crepitations— growing, approaching. Krax!!![1] She turned (: a shadow[2] stretching, a rearing animal, along the columns) hastily toward the ballroom.

((Uncertain? Yes, and surely fearing something. And maybe startled too. The timid are scared by a shadow . . . But it's still not time for the great stampede.))

Foo![3] sulked Fu Manchu in his big blue robe with golden dragons, continually tugging on thin mustache ends, over in the doorway, squinting at the wooded darkness of the garden. Fu . . . Fu . . .,[4] he kept grumbling with a scowl.

Stationed on the porch, next to the stairway, so provocatintedly painted: butterfly-winged sphinx with all kinds of insects painted on her body from top to toe. And she was silently presenting, her spider-hands clutching a blackboard, a riddle scrawled in chalk: What animal has feet that grow when it changes its tongue, and when you look closely, you can't make head or tail of it?[5]

Blind alleys! No sallying forth . . .[6] the blindfolded one in the creamy gauze costume, dirt-stained and ripped at the shoulder, a little blind chick so pale groping at the air, Blind alleys . . .,[7] tottering toward the door.

1. Pretty Penny!:
A penny, as I said, in her throat. Reddened eyes. And lips, very red, trembling.
(Touchy, at the first kiss . . .) The blonde in the red anorak looking teary-eyed
((But this is no time to cry . . .)) at the resounding platform. Posters, placards,
waving flags, over the tumultuous breaking waves. Almost as tall as you, but
crouching the better to see. And sticking to you in that crush. Steady, without
budging an inch. Little Red Riding Hood picked up by the Big Bad Wolf (riddle-
led writing hood) that fourth of November in the multitudinous meeting,
ALLENDE LIVES, in Trafalgar Square.

2. Miss Grey-"Hound"!:
Face and ass of a greyhound. So narrow-hipped. And you had to see her on all
fours, panting, tongue hanging out. Don't let the prey go. Want more, Artful
Dogger? C'mon, fox derrière!: See PILLOW NOTES 10, p. 466.

3. Angela María! And stop this dispute about the sex of angels!:
Angelus Novus. What a blonde she was! Or he. With a permanent, and tight
tailored pants of fuchsia satin. In Angel, on the most dangerous corner in
Islington. Winking at us—at you or at me? Look at the wrong angel from the right
angle!

4. Blot out!:
Blotto. Chivalrous Spaniard, fearless and stainful, who bit by bit broadens the
original sin . . .: See PILLOW NOTES 11, p. 467.

5. Ja! Kleecks! We're moving through the trifolium of the Roman à Klee . . .:
Leaf by leaf, page by page (: recto verso to the back and start over again!),
unbinding, defoliating: See PILLOW NOTES 12, p. 467.

Penny for the Guy . . .,[1] a lanky Little Red Riding Hood shaklink-
ing a cap full of coins, Penny for the Guy . . ., next to the little toy
car occupied by a worn-out rag doll with red scarf and smoked
lenses.

Time for scars and scares, Scaramouchard! a skinny Harlequin
shouted at the musketeer who, sword at his side, was bowing
obsequiously, his right hand out as if begging, his eyes imploring or
questioning, before a damsel in dazzling silver-gray vestments and
black half-mask, who held her gaze unperturbed, leaning back
slightly against a mirror.

The case is such, Milady, murmured the musketeer, that your
scornful lower lip, those steely clear eyes, your ringlets so black,
and that delicate profile of a greyhound,[2] tell me something . . .

No one knows himself, said the Harlequin, half hidden among two
fierce swaggerers in cloaks and big conical hats, now busy observing the courtly coquettish scene. No one knows who he is, he
insisted, because no one recognizes himself . . . Let each and every
one identify himself with his role! and he started to make faces in
the mirrors.

Lost edentity . . ., that angel ((or Angela?[3])) with drooping wings
and blond ringlet wig brandishing a sword at the door to the
garden. Looking for the first fall from grace. We angels carry the
mark of the beast too . . . And every saint his cross. Everybody
crisscrossed.

DRY BLOT![4] Don Juan yanked the glove from his left hand and
stopped to examine on the back of his hand, near the base of the
thumb, a black ink spot (: in the shape of a clover). Let bygones be
drag-ons . . . So! DREIBLATT!!![5] ((Without further defray . . .
Rorschach test!))

1. Which? Whose? Who's figure?:
It's not so easy to figure out. And you know that when nothing is gratuitous, everything costs something. No such thing as a free hunch . . .

2. Remains to be seen . . .:
To see and knot to see, perchance too here.

3. Chanson de Gestalt . . . Canzone di gesta . . .:
Alt! Cut a figure. And bond appétit . . .

4. Fig . . .? Figa . . .?:
Bella, o yes! Figure . . . When you get right down to it, I don't give a fig / The Knight of the Woeful Cuntenance! Indiscreet hieroglyphs with vicious pun / Don't dote on those dotty erotic drawings. Sing those broken sirventes . . .

5. Manche à Manche!:
The laconic Don Quixote sans show, puffing up with la cantata, in the midst of the lunatic mirror phase . . .: See PILLOW NOTES 13, p. 468.

6. Quichette de la Manchette . . .:
Yes, and don't forget that all our notes are marginal.

7. Où sont les Blanches Neiges d'antan?:
The Snow Whites of yesteryear? Your white goddess, older each night?

8. Like a Quixotic spot? (Inky shot in the dark!):
SPIRT TRIPS!

9. Marked card? Queer card?:
Or acephalous, as assumed:

Pluck . . . ((startled?)) . . . the clover—deftly ducking.

((The clover, her only field of endeavor? A one-track trill to try our patience? Broken record with a fixed idea? More likely an association of fixed ideograms, revolving around a moving center. Tangles. Bonds. In action. Lassos, knots. With a sliding slipknot upshot, to finish that ultra-private party on a dark solstice night.))

In the background all is figure.[1] Making faces in the spaces, form and ground: the figure on the carpet![2] Triste Figura, Night of the Sad Countenance . . . Stuck with the same face and disfigure, till the grave![3] All is fig . . .:[4]

In front of a large concave mirror, Don Quixote in a straitjacket and house slippers, rocking, watching himself grow paunchy in the turbid mercury: Wide is La Mancha, and here's a self-made mancha![5] With widened eye? Widen, I? Why deny . . .

Meanwhile an immaculate lady impatiently tugging on his sleeve, Kitschotte!!!:[6] svelte time-honored beauty (sexy sexagenarian!), with tunic (: open at the sides) and hair white as snow.[7] Come on, do it quick. Like a quick shot!!![8]

Pluck the clo . . . ver . . ., and she held up to the light the black envelope ((a letter or card[9] inside?)) that she had just picked up from the floor. (Over her head, slowly turning, iridescent Chinese clover-lanterns.) She secured it in the black bag with sequins and jet ornaments hanging from her shoulder, and headed in the opposite direction, making her impetuous way toward the agglomeration on the far side. Pluck the clover . . .

1. Ta soeur à la con:
Sorcière ensorcelée. A baconnoisseur transforming old swine in new bottles, from Boardeaux to Sauternes. And searching, any pork in a storm, for his sow-bellied Mother . . . Saufeerei!

2. Save your bacon, nella guerra di Troia!:
And your brazen head . . . Time is!

3. From soeur-praise to surprise, O Grand Inquisitor, in your prison of loves . . .:
Silence! Big iron chains and iron bars do not a cage make! [Prosecution by Herr Narrator: Writing his night mare . . . I too am one of its big bad characters. And you? Hypocrite reader, break these brackets, free me from these fetters: the Blessed Sisterhood will set us free . . .]

4. PART ASS, PART TRAPS: SATRAP:
Either way.

5. Prière de ne pas toucher le riche lieu du cardinal!:
With sarcasm and sore wit, your sordid Sister, Sor . . .: "Sor" Dinah, the Deptford organist . . .

6. Libertine adventures require various agendas . . .:
Keep it under wraps: questo non picciol libro è tutto pieno dei nomi e telefoni di sue belle . . .

7. Babelle au bois dormant . . . (Bois de lit?):
Tour à tour . . . Les tours de Notre-Dame de la Nuit de la Saint-Jean! (In her black forest. Inside. Would she, wooden she, in her nocturnal desperanto. Can't see the bosky forest for the treatises?) Les tours de Babelle! around and around . . . And sighing all night for her sly familiar stoner. Who knows what Lady Luck might bring. Tempting blind luck? That devil on the lam as usual, from bed to bedlam, or bedevilment, and all to add new adventures to the Wild Joker's novel. But you are the prima donna assoluta of my bad-penny opera, the tenor would declare to any warm body he introduced himself to. (Surmenage à trois.) You're the protagonist I've been looking for all over, he had told her in illo tempore when they bumped into each other by chance in Paddington station. The first Saturday of a crazy little February. Was she flattered with the idea of becoming a novel character? He christened her Babelle, perhaps because in her dreams she often stammered a polyglot litany, in multiple languages and nocturnal dialects.

Next to the grand piano covered with a sheet, to the right of the door to the Hall of Murals, a scrawny cardinal listened as a heavy-hammed nun[1] with a pig mask[2] whispered in his ear; she swaying on a swiveling stool, he with a music book open on his lap.

Yes, yes, I know, he answered, pressing the skullcap to his crown, I already know where the surprise[3] must be. But we must pull out all the stops . . ., he added, lowering his voice and his hand. Ah yes, my virtuosa. Rather like when you used to play the organ in your Deptford choir. Ah oui, ma sage . . ., and he slid a finger, glissando, down her back. Et ma soeur cherche masseur?

Part, satrap.[4] Get thee hence, the nun mumbled dumbly. And spinning completely around she caressed, in passing, his crotch.[5]

Prick the clover . . .

Hahahey, wait . . . (Don Juan nervously leafing through a black notebook.[6]) Wait! trailing after Sleeping Beauty,[7] still sleep-wandering and humming the same old refrain. This is getting hallucinatory! And still she continued the search, droning her mesmerizing chant. Change the record! and the needle. How tiresome! Zitto! Shut up! Enough already of this, you're cloverdoing this damned clover business! Quit your wandering . . . You're wasting your time looking there again.

Pluck the clover . . .

1. Hookah! Hooker!:
Things were piping hot in the Park Walk smoking den . . . Want me to tell you the Apache storia of the war pipe?

2. Mandrake the Magician or Merlin the Enchanter once again?:
Mandrake, if he makes a beau gesture . . .: See PILLOW NOTES 14, p. 469.

3. Clutching the cut card, she cannily countered . . .:
Tut tut, quit trifoling with that triple play, that goading gordiaknot . . .

4. You were too cloever by half . . .:
Some parts were clever, but some parts were not.

5. Clunky clover!:
And almost stone-age primitive, the little scrawled drawing and inscription discovered by our scrutinizing protagonist in the Ladies' Room in the Hammersmith Broadway alley, which she had copied faithfully:
THE CLOVER OF MY LOVER

6. The night of the long knives!:
And dressed to kill. But the knife dance still hasn't started . . .

7. Pigsty!? Poor Chile! Porcile . . .:
Già da molto tempo. So it sounds. Some future biographer will write the diary of the war of the pig, the biggest swine in this pignorant police state or sty.

8. Alla Lotta, Lothario . . .:
Lotta sanculotta, Carlotta the Garibaldine!

Don't you have any other weed? the pampered Pompadour pompously pouted in her polished Argentinean, between puffs from her long long porcelain pipe.[1] And after a doorway dodge around the potbellied dark-lensed Napoleon who came swaying with a glass in each hand, she poked her head into the next room: Hey you silly thing, the act I'd really like to check out is that great magnetic Mandrake.[2] Like check with mate to follow in two, know what I mean? I'd like to give him what he merits, right here . . ., she sighed, taking a few flamenco steps.

And she smiled maliciously, Look for more adventures with your maids and servants . . ., examining closely the ace with cleavered clover[3] stretched to her, very stiffly, by a Dick Turpin, masked and wearing a three-cornered hat. Vivacho! What a smart aleck—! Aren't you too clever . . . Cloever Dick![4] (On that jaggedly cut half-card, the crude outline of a testicular-phallic clover.[5]) An unconcealed, clovert attempt to . . .!!!, in a feigned fit of rage.

Pluck the clover . . .

Ay-ay-ay! Yira! Gyrate in the carniwaltz! and spinning like a top or a whirling dervish, she swirled back into the madding crowd.

Pluck the clover . . .

Por Chile! an SS man, simian and sinister in his dark glasses, raised his cup. For Chile!! the toast echorused by a Chaplinesque Hitler, drawing his machete[6] and clicking his heels. Porcile!!![7] came the screech, accompanied by an obscene gesture, of a red-shirted Garibaldi soldier,[8] a red handkerchief knotted at her neck.

1. Bottom out! And don't forget Bottom means Ass . . .:
Bless thee, Bottom! bless thee! thou art translated.

2. And plenty horny!:
Copious cornocopycatscratch fever . . .

3. Bottom line: Brass music, in the don-key of A minor disaster:
Pianotto! Stepping into the dubious light of a Portobello day, still in the clouds
after a whole night of surrealism with Babelle and Catherine the Great in the
Electric Cinema, it occurred to Milalias, still doing verbal spins on the "piano-
asses" of *Un chien andalou,* that the perfect "dalirious" image would be an
onager on an organ. Groan.

4. Nodding off, down to the bottom stream:
The eye of man hath not heard, Aye! Oyez! the ear of man hath not seen, Audio-
visibility! man's hand is not able to taste, Palpalatability! his tongue to conceive,
Irrumination! nor his heart to report, Tick! Talk! what my dream was . . . ((: Deep
sopor in the Villa of Marvels.))

5. Pin the tale on the donkey? A dumb mule-driver drives a crazy ass . . .:
And don't forget that the Assnotator receives Herr Narrator's treatment . . .

6. With a silver lining, or lie?:
Yes, speech is silver, but silence is golden. Parlez d'or! and don't talk with that
silver spoon in your mouth. Silver sounds, mais l'or dure . . .

7. Intercontinental trunk of the Continental Drifter:
With all of his faults. Letters, albums, records, vouchers, agendas . . .

8. Puck marks . . .:
Freckle by freckle . . . Face like a grater. That's just great! When a little boy lies, an
imp marks his face while he's sleeping . . .—the Portuguese nanny Chona
"Choninha" had warned Milalias when he was a boy. A little nib for every fib?
One morning when he went to wash up, he found his whole face covered with black
dots. And the sardonic "Choninha" laughing . . . Milalias would say those black
dots (his face puckered up) marked him indelibly.

Bottoms up![1] the donkey-headed drunk raised his foamy cornucopia, Ch-cheers! and stagger-stammered around. Sh-sheers! and draining the horn o'plenty,[2] the tippler trip-toppled over the sheeted piano.[3] Ohee! Eeho! tottering and hanging his heavy horsy head. My head's coming and going . . .[4] Is it on straight? Heehaw!

((Heehaw! Heehaw! Who is this braying madman? It's the Assnotator who burro-burrows into these nocturnotes, neither clear nor there! the malefactitious cardsharp who shuffles the aces, asses to asses, bust to bust! He's the brains and gray eminence, the donkeynote speaker, critical of and to the story, who at the moment prefers to remain assnonymous; our mentor and fomentor,[5] the drunk craftsmaniac of Plateresque intricacies in search of the final asnamorphosis and lowest creature in a form as pure as good gold, The Golden Ass![6] it's him, Haw! Haw! our Echommentator of this carnovelesque jumble of a Midsummer Night.))

Pluck the clover . . .

Can't make head or tail of it . . . A piece short, that's for sure. A fine mess! The most important one. Unfathomable without it. Or perhaps it can be deduced. Yes, good, patience and . . . To recompose it. Piece by piece. And the best part for the whole. All scrambled. Foiled again. At least one hundred. This centipieces. Patience and . . . more patience. And that's the end of it! in pieces again.

Sitting spread-legged on the floor next to the trunk,[7] an impish Puck[8] (all in scarlet, from half-boots to peaked hood) absorbed in sorting through the pieces of a jigsaw puzzle.

Pluck the clover . . .

1. Trumperies . . .
Tr$\frac{e}{o}$mpe l'oeil! In a moment, in the twinkling of an eye, at the last trump . . . / From tramp to trap . . .: See PILLOW NOTES 15, p. 469.

2. Her rosy gums of chicle . . . (Agh! Hag!):
Chewing gums!

3. Cataracts! Cut a rat:
Catherine the Great, the boiling Brazilian sculptress, a real scalder! always ready to cull derelict objects, call derrière cri! Creator of the "Mobile Dick" . . . ((In a cossack's coat when the Don met her in Le Troubadour. They drank like bottomless cossacks . . .))

4. Acha! Kata!:
Cut! Cut this catalog of shaggy-dog stories . . .

5. Gin bottle? Genie bottle . . .:
Sip after slip, gobble after goblin, gin after jinx in search of the genie of inspiration.

6. Chupa?:
Suck on this!

7. Abba, if it be popossible let this cup papass meme bye-bye . . .:
Kuna joto kali . . . Firewater! Eau de vie! Usquebaugh! Acqua di Vita—and so strong . . .

8. Her agility in lingua franca:
Yes bwana, sue a healer. And so musicaliginous . . . Oh la la! . . . PITAPAT!

9. Maté? A bottle of saliva?!!!:
HE TIPS SPIT, EH? Sip maté, and swallow your pride. And don't forget that the goddess-bottle Chew-pah! goes around from mouth to mouth.

10. La dive fiole est vide . . .:
Evidemment! A bottle of mere words! / C'est la bouteille à l'encre!

11. Kwa-kwa!:
Bye-bye, silly battler. The battle of the bottle has ended.

Clubs are trumps! . . .[1] ((They're painting clovers!)), the blackened bag lady, bundled in rags and shawls, slyly baring her teeth in a rosy smile,[2] Club together! . . . ((Pair up, pet!)), as she raised and lowered her 'alf an ace of clubs with both hands, then right and left making crosses in the air, Dicky Dicky! . . . Dirty Dick! ((Dirty Turpin-up boy!)) Stooped, hoarse and hobbling, she followed Dick Turpin through the jostling jamboree. There's a jenny for every jockey! . . .

Pluck the clover . . .

Hot! . . . Quente! . . . He spies her but he doesn't try her . . .,[3] interposed the gigantitted tamer in a red cossack coat and black boots, as she cracked the whip, Get it! Acha! Aicha! . . ., and clumsily raised a bottle, Taste it! Cata! Cat o' nine tales![4] Catatau!!!

A terrible tangle . . ., Don Juan caped in his cloak, attentively observing, What a thickly knotted plot . . ., the tattered ragged witch, A fine mess we're in now . . ., and the colossal tamerette, still whip-cracking and brandishing, C'est la bouteille à l'encre! . . ., her black bottle. It's the bottle of the battle . . .[5]

Chew, pa![6] a lithe painted warrior in African mask (: rimmed with raffia flowers and geometric goldfinches) snatched the bottle with a leap. Till then she had been hurling her plumed assegai straight up and catching it in flight. Mama! stopping to upend the bottle anxiously. Baba![7] drooling and licking.[8] Chupa ya mate![9] she spit out, knocking over the bottle.[10] And off she went with exaggerated slips and slides in samba rhythm, Qua! Qua![11] with a nagging nasal twang.

Pluck the clover . . .

1. Roll and rock! Rock of ages, my top lady!:
Oh yeah! diamonds are forever . . . But I prefer Rocks and Rolls . . . [Hermenaut, you owe us an explicaution. Jesus, I demand an exegesis! / Just this once, and don't think it will set a precedent, but with a great deal of summarizing: Roll can mean copulate in slang. Top lady could be a woman of noble ancestry and also the spinning toy; and a Toplady wrote the famous hymn to Christ, "Rock of Ages" . . ., composed in a rapture inspired by a playing card, of diamonds. Diamonds, in American slang, can mean testicles. Rocks is slang for diamonds and Rolls of course is the famous car. Did I miss anything? Oh yes, Sinbad, on his second voyage, is transported by the bird Roc to the Valley of Diamonds . . . / What a rocococktail of . . . / Until you understand the book of good love, say nothing about it—neither good nor bad. Because you understand one thing and the book says something else. / Not a word.]

2. Sinbad egg! Ab ovo . . ., egghead! Go to bed! Ab ovo . . .:
Ay! I can't, Hempty Dempty, because I'm already on the second voyage . . .

3. SHAMROCK!!!:
Irish rock, from the band of four . . .

4. The Roc and its egg? Rock and ball? Rock and bawl . . .:
ROC and BOL, Russian ball-et and roll-ette! . . ., bolshevik. FATALITY and ay! PAIN.

Ooh la la! here comes Sinbad the Mooriner . . ., and she went back
to launching her lance. Simba, Simbad!

Rock and roll![1] Rock! the egg-globe clinging to the outflung skirts
of the gyrating Pompadour. Rocambolesque rock ma rococotte!
the turbaned Moor rasped as he rock-and-rolled the white globe
along. Dance, egg,[2] dance!

Shilly-shally that empty shell, Spinbad! the Pompadour jumped
and pipe-jabbed the balloon to keep it aloft. Sambad, Simbad! And
then she rubbed it, belly to belly, dynamic static, and scrambled off
faster still, Ayay! making a face. Now don't you rock and don't
you roll . . .

Pluck the clover . . .

SHAM ROCK! ROCK! . . ., soundwaves grinding out across the spree
of the ballroom and the Hall of Murals, on came the exploding
screaming guitar chords of the apopcalyptic four, the rock and roll
band SHAM ROCK![3] writhing as if electroshocked up on the stage.
ROCK!

Roc-and-ball![4] a stout Russian pope with tangled beard shouted,
pointing with his crozier at Sinbad leaping to volley the balloon.
Roc! he insisted, turning an attentive ear to his left: now from the
hall came thunderous blasts grom! grom! pogrom! of the electrical
storm. Rock! with a hoarser caw, and he rolled his eyes heaven-
ward.

Pluck the clover . . .

1. Mallet! mauliciously mouthed. Gathering nuts in May? You're still very green . . .:
Damn it to shell!

2. È dura! that enduring derring-do . . .:
Hard and dense as that wrinkled up nocturnote, wadded into a ball, that our Miss Magpie rescued from the wastebasket and hid as a souvenir in her Pandora's box. (Una noche in un sacco fa rumore . . . Hit the sack! Nocevolezza! Our thousand nights in una noce . . . In nuce! Wrapped and tied in a nocturnal nodyssey . . . Noutis! Note by note, wherever the wind blows your nutty fancy . . . Notturnot! Crack this hard nut with a Portemartaud Word . . . Nuts! Give it one with the mallet. Tret a tret, bit by bit. Drop by drop till we're slanguished. Nucta de San Xuan! The sphear of music . . . Nocekowsky! No! And the sfear of our sorrow . . . Nutshelley! Noz e nozze de Nozferatu . . . Noce nocente! Fais la noce, Nosferatu . . . No! Naughty knotty argonut! I know now . . . Argotnoutàmbul! Ce sont des noises, tes notes à la noix . . . Nuts to you! Relinquere nuces . . . Enough of your no-good nugacities . . . Argonnotateur! Ou veux-tu te noyer avec ta coquille de noix? Leave your shell, argonout! king of infinite space. Espai de cap. Spy the cup . . . Skoal! Skull! The cup under the cape. Kapala.)

3. Fou-fou! Flee fly foe fun:
I smell the pun of an Inkishman. Fu fu, ciacco. Fuliginous inkquizitor.

4. Keep the wolf from the door!:
Hungry for love? Lycanthropy? / A hungry man is an angry wolf-man. NO, WOLF: FLOW ON!

5. Farouche? Bette?:
Fou! Rage!

6. Spyashchaya krasavitsa . . .:
Russo russo!

7. Treffas:
Treffpunkt!

And it never lets up . . ., Don Juan grumbling at the rear, not to be left behind. Going like mad and it never stops . . . What a night. Cackling and crackling without showing her face. Malo![1] Eeh! What a night . . . Hard day's night![2] Until finally she can't take any more, and crack! But I'm afraid there's still a good amount left. Will she keep pulling my leg, this scatterbrain? And so stubborn. Ufuf! spitting, fu fu![3] what a night . . . And under his breath: A lot of crack for a few nutcrackers . . . ((Nussferatu!))

Pluck . . .—cut off, suddenly sucking in her breath: in the doorway, ferocious, the Wolf-Man.[4] (: His red eyes narrowed to slits in the dark furry mask.) He stepped aside and (: devouring her with his eyes!) let her pass. She, now out of his reach, still peeking at him from the corner of her eye.

Pluck the cl- . . .—again she lost her voice.

Lost the -over! Don Juan quickly following her to the Hall of Murals. Bad luck. Beauty had finally come across the Beast of her dreams? Bête farouche . . .[5] Et Belle farouche! To each her onus. Sleeping Beauty[6] already hoarse? Or hoarsing around. ((That Jollicking Joker!))

Treff ist Trumpf![7] Clubs are trumps . . .

((Was she finally changing her jingle-litany? For the moment, but she kept talking to herself, mumbling her half-words doubled in faltering sibilant whispers, barely audible, as she resolutely pierced that pandemonium—loud coarse shouts and babellicose baabling, diverse lingue, orribili favelle . . ., and scraps of misheard mumblings—as if guided by an invisible thread.))

L'atout est le trèfle! Quit groping about in the dark . . .

1. The balloon goes up!:
And the chaos hasn't even started yet . . .

2. L'ou! L'ou brau!???:
A bold egg? A gold egg? Or a bad egg! A cock and bullshit story . . .

3. Cap d'olla!:
Pot head. Your catalunatic Sor Olla . . . Another in your sequence of nun sexiturs.
The high-sounding Sònia (Sor Olla) with her Catalan headgear. Pom! Pom!

4. Sou?:
So! Sònia sona si la bossa és bona . . .

5. Dream dream dream . . . Les sones sones son! A minuit sonnant!:
Somnia in Somnia . . . Somnipotent! Somnia Sònia . . . Somniénie. Niét.

6. Son son? Dream on?:
Son son! So! So!

7. Pit? The Pit and the Pen—:
Pou! pendululations. Get out of that black pit. And change your Poegrom.

8. Pit off!:
Pitof! Pit i fora: Pitonissa!

9. Pitter pat!:
Pet, petulant? Petit apetit . . . Pit apart!

10. Pop!:
Undulant as an octopus . . .

11. Your bag or your life . . .:
Calemboursicoteur! Testiculations 'round the family jewels! Scrutinize some
other secret will and testesament . . .

Lo! Lo and behold! Sinbad leaping, bounding higher each time, over the crowd, Look! Look! loudly chasing after his white balloon.[1] Lo!

Low! Lowbrow![2] a jumbo Carmelite nun helmeted with a dented pot down to her eyes,[3] hop-dancing her big body about and kicking up a devil of a ruckus, Low! a string of pots and pans hanging off one shoulder. So! So![4]

Well done, Sister Insister, bravo . . . A nunsensical nonesuch . . .

Bang bang! brutally beating her kitchen drum set, son son! with a ladle. Son son sonant![5]

Son son?[6] Muckingbird without sound judgment . . .

Pit![7] Pit![8] banging the pans against her breast, Tip! Tip! reeling, drumming, Tap! Tap! and stamping.

Pit-a-pot . . . ,[9] Don Juan stamped in front of the crazy-costumed Carmelite, What a din, a one-nun shoe-slapping slapstick scuffle, as she went on with her claptrap tapdancing and gongbanging, with each sway swinging her breasts. Another heavy titanic thunderbust, potaplum! in this pompous saturnalia, pompataplum! and to top off the pot, it pans out she's here to put on airs.

Pop![10] Popmusic potpourri! slithering and snaking her arms and jolting about. Oh yah, already to a different drummer . . . Bossa nova,[11] moving like a mad maenad, and as if gauging the weight of something. Au! Roc! and she struck out, up at the white sphere, Roc!

1. Meet?:
Potted meet! There's more to beat than meets the eye! Go to Pott! Can it! As if it had been canned, that fortuitous encounter. So dazed by hunger, Ham! soon! looking at all those hanging hams, that harem of herrings, those salami columns, those foodpaths, that whole orgy of gourmet tidbits in the Harrods Food Hall, le Palais du palais! when you ran smack into the appetizing Mrs. Pott . . .: See Pɪʟʟᴏᴡ Nᴏᴛᴇs 16, p. 470.

2. Ababa!:
Aba! Pappy, poppy . . .

3. To each kook his cucaracha . . . Cuca—:
Cuca . . . Look for your nightshade, your uniquely inappropiated poppy. Careful with the veto, Papa, verboten! she's still in the gawkward age.

Potted meet![1] puffed a slight sprightly maid of honor (her low neck-line, trembling and fleshy, adorned with pearls). She lugged an oversize handbag (: *Enter a Different World,* in gold letters on a black background) in each hand, and could barely get through. A brutal encounter, a real smashup, and she clasped a hand to her bosom. I bumped into him in Harrods, she turned to huff at a tall graceful blonde (dressed in pink, with silver lamé, with a poppy in her hair) who followed her with an air of resignation. Almost dead from hunger, and with a quick nod of her head she indicated Don Juan. This is the lout, practically flattened me. He was prowling around the Food Hall, famished. But a cheery smile with his sorry-sorry. And such beautiful sad Spanish eyes. So I let him carry my bags for me. Complete lack of breeding! as I found out too late. Very respectful at first, he called me Meesees Pott.

Poppet! Puppet! Nincompoop, nincompuppet . . .

Pap! Pappy! parroted the Infanta, blushing. Pup! Pop! Poppy! and she coquettishly caressed the poppy. Poppycock! He seduced me with his lips. He was only a son to you, and like a father to me. He took advantage of my innocence! Such a flatterer. Popping over here, when you weren't watching us, and Poppy over there. A poppy of blood ay! popped up in the bed. He'd say he was going to introduce me to the secrets of his tongue, and all sorts of things. He'd call me Amapola,[2] beautiful poppy. Oh Poppy.

Coq à la coquine! Coq . . .[3]

Kok! Koket! Kokotelet! that grimy cook pestered (: his face and hat sooty), and the well-fattened friar forced his way with frying pan swings. A cutlet for every coquette, a flank for every flirt! And something more to start. Jeune fillet d'église! (: his skillet beating on the string of pans carried along by the armored Carmelite nun, who danced along free and easy at his side, encouraging him). C'mon, let's ham it up, give us a hamily, a regular ham session . . . Non! De non! at the top of his lungs as he danced with the heavy-gauge canoness, Not in vain was I a short-order friar before being a busboy.

1. Czardanapalus!:
From Hungarian czarda to Catalan sardana . . . From czardas to Portuguese
sardas, polka dot! sautée a sarda, Sardanapalusitanian!

2. Foc!:
Hot fuck!: Nit!

Fray! Fry! Frei! he who laughs longest laughs loudest . . .

No frigid dishmiss here, Fred Astaire! she let out comically, her pots clanging. Dance another dance, a jota. Or better yet a sardana, Sardanapalus.[1] Come up close and embrace (shamelessly scratching her pubis), and watch out for the fiery braziers. Foc![2] Frock to frock. Let's go, hot buttered lover, I'm melting with passion. Pot on a hot tin spoof. Or perhaps you prefer boiled eggs? she twisted, bellyslinking, provocatively. Coc al cóc, cocksman? Or tortuous tart, twisting to guffaws. Viu! C'mon! Let's live it up! and swinging her rear end. Viu!

View halloo! Sleepy eyes sneakily spying . . .

The sly old fox, and she gave the cook a big shove, he deserved a good tanning. The great chef of Abbots. A bots! With hops! Every time I came into the kitchen loaded up to my chin with plates, he'd start to ti-ti-tickle me, Ha! Ho! Hey! rubbing me the wrong way. His device for getting his hands on me. Taking advantage of my full hands. And he'd say I had a guitar body, and plunk away on me.

Guitar! Guitar! Picking and grinning, flirting and frying . . .

Cooking and kicking! as she hitched up her habit and danced. Until I let one loose, potaplum! that sent him flying against the oven. Déu! He took off like a bullet in a china shop! boyoboy bedlam! I dropped the skillet on him, Zip! Zap! right where it hurts most. What a castratophe . . .

Loss of skill? Kill two birds with one skillet . . .

1. Octopolluter!:
Watch it, don't throw out the booby with the inkwater . . .

2. What's left? The sinster!:
But known to be righteous . . .

3. The purgations must be purged . . .:
A Venerable Bede, a bishop-to-be. Or beat . . . But our apprentice priest would try to hide the bodily (corpus delecti) crime. Until, for fear they would amputate the offending member (by the lopping of a peccant member the body is saved from decay), he wound up confessing and sought a curate.

A stage-cast ration! Yes a good-sized portion! busy wiggling her big body and waving her arms in front of the cook. Of octopus, if possible. With all its tentacles. Why, he had more arms than an octopus.[1] Or would you prefer something more refined? Caviar and wine, or for you, soda pop. Non! Non! Pop music. Pop! and she sinuously gesticulated arms and hands, inciting the cook. Sister Potshot looking, looking for, and she skilletfully struck out (deadpan accuracy) with a pan, potshot! looking for a pig in a po-po-polka! Or whatever panned out. Sònia és bona si la bossa sona . . ., and she roguishly hefted an invisible pouch. When they play the bossa nova . . ., off she went (va-va-boom!) thumping her dishwasher-safe drum set. Take the skillet by the handle, and she turns to point it at the cook. Right where it's burning! Whether they're fried or not, in the end they'll be frigid . . .

Frigid! Rigid! He's done for, his bird is cooked . . .

Now I'm really getting heated up, yawned the cook, rubbing his eyes and cheeks. Like during nightly worship. Six years in the seminary! A monastic life, with only one monomania. That the right hand, a left-mute! not know what the left[2] is doing. Tangible, tactful, tactile monogamy. But gamy.

Homme de main gauche! A southpawn? With a full hand . . .

Man is man because he's a manipulator, and he looked at his own hands open before him. They used to say hair would grow on your palms. Sign of the devil. Shameful. Gross and dangerous. But isn't it better for the monk to be alone? Perdition came from woman. Evanescent Eden. Healthier with the hand. Master of celibacy. Puritanical, even: I ab jure coffee! But confucionanism after each confession. Still not vitiated? Six years! Penitential psalms and penetrating penances. The devil in the body, the sickness of the sin. Try to find the cure, as curate?[3] Death. Incurable? The only known curate is death?

Salvarsenic and old lascivious! Salvitiation! Let sinners burn for their sins . . .

1. Peach on!:
Don't impeach a preacher for pinching peaches.

2. La Tangerina:
So they called the madam of the whorehouse where the seminarian jerk-off (after the sin comes the penetrance) knew, in the biblical sense, his first woman.

3. A rotter, dame!:
Where our friar-cook and good buddy scattered farts on all the tarts in that cheap Rotterdam diner.

4. Bul! Boule! Boulez les boules de pierre . . .:
Aflaatus vocis!

5. OK! OK!:
Koko! OK! OK! Basquetball!

6. Humpty Dumpty had a great fall . . .:
Tombe! dans ton automne. Ou . . . ou . . . outono!: See Pillow Notes 17, p. 472.

That's how it all ended, he monologued in a sleepy voice, fingering his rosary of onions. Better to live behind the altar than the plow, pristine farmer wisdom. A father's ambition: my son the priest. Resign-a-cure! Ha ha! But wait. I was looking for my better half in that lecherous bordelirium. For bidding fruits.[1] The tangy Tangerine![2] Papaya-as-you-go! Away with the rotten apple! And after the sexpulsion, no plow for me! better to emigrate to Rotterdam.[3] The world! Bacchanals in the canals.

Rotterdam! Rotter rotor rotate . . .

From Romana Rota to routed rotter. He looked all around with blurred eyes. Six years as a semenarist! he ejaculated. Six years! he repetered, and he opened his eyes very wide, raising the left index finger and holding his right hand open. All jerked away. Can you beat that? How many times per week? At least once a day. The habit didn't make the monk. Shouldn't be so hard on myself. The spirit was willing, but the flesh is weak. What's bred in the bone, er-erupts in the flesh . . . he went on with his ejaculations, and today is carneval day. As proclaimed by Brother Gil, who's gotta papal bull[4] for everything.

Bully! Bullet! Shooting blanks . . .

Oof, the friar cook puffed. Who wants a poached egg à la portuguese? Boursoufflé, eggcellent. Eggstravagant. A fried egg for someone? he bawled. Cocino, eggo sum. C'mon! getting testy. A boiled egg? Eggstraordinary. Jesus! A la coque.

Koko! Kokoko! Kokos! the coquettish chorus of a ruddy rounded redhead in a seam-bursting bodice and skirt, who approached laden with mugs of beer. Koko!!![5] she stopped sharply, look what's coming . . .

Humpty Dumpty[6] roundly reeling, really floundering (followed at some distance by Sinbad the Staler, who was calling him, shouting, Rokokot! Ay! Come back, tubby! in vain), using both hands to hang on to his vast detachable eggbelly.

1. Disguised?:
Kokostumed!

2. Broody hen clucking?:
Painter painting with love-hate, Ab ovo! Kokoschka! tempestuously painting with egg tempera, giving his all, Mal! Mahlerei! the two lovers enclosed in their shell in the middle of the wind-blast. ((That Kokoschka image tacked on the Chinese folding screen, Spanische Wand! they used to comtemplate, entranced on the bed after some stormy dispute. After the storm comes the *cama,* or bed . . . —quip of volcanic Milalias, always seeking bedrock.))

3. Go and catch a falling star . . .:
Stunted stardom, rising to stardoom!

4. Scrape, scrape . . .:
Sh! Done. That divine treasure disappears underground.

5. Polish woman or Hungarian doll?:
Russian doll? Baba, yeah, gaya, a real witch. Madame Starzinsky, Polish clairvoyant. With her ogre's or vampire's mouth, murmuring: I see a voyage . . . Reading between the lines, while pressing between her claws the hand of credulous Babelle. (What kind of trip? Droga? Drugs?)

Coco! Coco! Oeuf à la coquette! Eggregious eggoist . . .

Cocoricocote! he clucked, snatching a bock beer. Toujours cocottes!
he sighed, sliding down her neckline a paper bird (made from a
one-pound note). Go Dutch. Just my just desserts. A compromis-
sory note. That's what I believe . . . Very good for the nerves, and
he pushed the bird-bill still deeper. And they can be made anywhere and with any kind of paper. I would like to submit you to a
psychotechnical test, he smiled, peeping down her unfathomable
neckline. When you've got a little free time. My name and address
appear on that little aviary visiting card. Doktor Kot, at your
service. Specialist in Freudian psychoanalnesses. And I'm also a
doctor of kokotheology. Like a compatriot of yours, yes, that great
basque-kotologist.

Koko! Kokos![1] How he eats you up . . .

Kokoschka . . .,[2] clucked the old harpy in the black turban (crowned
with a star[3] of diamond sparks) looking, seated at a small round
table, into her crystal ball. Kokoschka! she repeated, winking at
Humpty Dumpty, who was absorbed by the poster of astrologic
signs placed on the table. That's right, him! He made a magnificent
porrrtrait of me. Cocotte forrr Kokoschka . . ., with all mine feathers
and jewels. Wedding gift from my Budapest Buddha, who always
called me doll, his Polish doll, and a doll I was. Oh jes I was so jung
then . . ., she sighed, tugging on her painted face. And bootiful . . .,
stretching the parchment of her cheeks, Bootiful! looking at herself
in the ball. Good-bye, ha! divine treasure . . .[4] My bewitching
eyes . . ., as he used to call them. Baba! Baba![5] he would drrrool
looking at me. Deadly doll, with that errrotic mystery, just as in my
porrrtrait. Masterpiece! Lost in war. Ha! It stayed in our house in
Warsaw. Ebrryting broken, rrrobbed, absolutely rrruining me.
Now I see, and she leaned over her crystal ball, naked blonde on
sofa caressing, black cat against her belly . . .

1. Kot? Won't you ever give a shit?:
With his scacatology and his scocotology. Drain the cup to the dregs! What's in a name? Doctor Kot's almost catlike jump when Milalias asked him: Doctor, your name is German, isn't it? / I was born near Danzig and my parents were German, but the origin of our name is Polish.

2. Rococktail stirred in this stream of consciousness:
Entre côte and cocotte, the game goes on.

3. Might-have-been . . . Maite Maithuna!:
No-more! Too-late! Fare-well.

4. Vox Dei?: (Mysterious call, according to Maite):
The telephone rings on the night table. Tink! Tink! Tiki! Tink! I wake up and gropingly grab it. Hello. No one answers. Hello. Silence. Hello. Anyone there?! —Test a—says a voice whispering like the wind. Just like that: This. Or perhaps Heste, barely aspirated. And hangs up. I've got this funny feeling with the receiver in my hand and then I realize that the telephone wire is all tripe, twisted intestines. And the phone is a beating heart on the nightstand. What could this dream mean, Doctor Kot? [Korollary: Take heart and show some guts?]

Kot![1] Kokotte! he drank, his eyes closed, holding onto the waitress's arm. Anxiously with great gulps, foam dripping down the lips and chin drawn on his eggshell. Mir ist kotzerig! grimacing, doubling up. Ugh, I feel sick. I've got stomach cramps, rubbing himself with a circular motion from his big head to his paunch. And a stiff neck! Alcocoholic miserere, my sweet cocoquette, my head's bouncing like a cococktail shaker . . .[2] I'm blatantly bloating, and he shook his eggbody from belly to head. Kokoterie! he belched, throwing up in the empty mug.

Jusqu'à la lie, bidon! Alibido ad libitum! Libe, libidinous . . .

Might! Might![3] crowed the coarse chorus in the rear, where a choir of clamoring drinkers clinked their mugs and staggered about. Maite is right! wobbling about with their pints. Beerish boorish bores, toasting Might! Might!

Fort! Da capo! All their strength moves through their mouths . . .

And even more daring . . . High! she sweatily gasped, embracing her crystal tower and struggling to raise it to her face. Come on! Go for it! Brain is better with brawn . . ., and she let out a loud grunt trying to blow away a lock of hair covering her left eye. Putiko!!! Bastard! she suddenly lashed ((pointblank!)) at sick Humpty Dumpty, who was wobbling whoa! trying to embrace her or help her lift up the tankards. Hey! Hey! You sonofabitch! brusquely pulling away from him. I don't need your help. Bock à bock, buck up . . . Yes, that dirty dream I told him alone. All his intestinal tests . . . This guy, and she bumped his belly with the beer mugs, this straight-shooting tickling tester[4] . . .

Testy! Teste! Oui, monsieur, finish the test. Tickle your fancy?

1. Kilimiliklik, iz ezpaduk nai, nik!!!:
If you don't want it, I'll take it. And that addled battling cabin boy finished off what was left in the mugs. As he did in all the beer joints, when all was said and drunk, scouring the tables even after he was completely soused. Decorated like an admiral, his breast covered with ribbons awarded one per pint. When he reigns he pours . . . Occasionally an irritated drinker would dish out a pointblank beerblow. Bier! Bière! Beer! bopping around beerserk and beerating everyone. And the waitresses would try to break it up and sometimes even had to call the big bouncer, Birro, birrone! If Milalias hadn't already stepped in by then.

2. Mouthing off? Moats of oaths . . .:
And getting a mouthful of the stairway. And then supported by Milalias, who tried to staunch the bleeding with a handkerchief and cigarette ash. Then while waiting for the last train, on the platform of the North Bakerloo line, the Basque samaritan walked by. (Keeping your Basques in one exit?) She recognized them at a glance! And offered first aid to Rimbaudelaire, in her house nearby. She had been a nurse, she assured. She and Milalias with the poor ecce homo in between. Sit up straight, jerk!

3. Where am I?:
A shadowy bedroom, a cubbyhole, with tourist posters of Spain. An island-turtle in a blue dove bay. Conch Bay? *Matelot,* a novel by Pierre Loti, on the night table.
  —¿Qué pasa?
  Sitting up he saw two naked demons, a fat one and a skinny one, panting, tongue-and-grooving away at the foot of the bed.
  —That you, Emil?
  —No! Let sleeping dogs lie . . .

Kilimiliklik!!!¹ glassping at straws in her mug-juggling balancing act, teetertottering, struggling to lift the quivering tumblers.

Click! Lick! Lik! Another toast . . .

Soyez fous! Let's get crazy! a scruffy drunken cabin boy piped up, Buvez! Drink up! picking up the near-empty beer mugs from the floor, Suck it down! and draining them. Voilà! voilà! bandits! shaking the last drops into his mouth.

Drop out! Drop by drop by drop by dro . . .

Gangway, gang! the cabin boy swinging his arms, clearing a path to the waitress. Click! Clack! he tapped his shoes, I'm slap-dashing, packed up and ready to split, chaps.

When a slap gets lost I find it. Move it, make way for the Good Samaritan! The very same, my charitable Basquette case. She healed me and rocked me to sleep. I almost broke my neck getting out of the Tube station!² That night in Piccadilly. Drunk and dirty, mucked with mud and vomit, full of beer to the eyeballs and foaming at the mouth. She dragged me out of the gutter and lullabied me and let me sleep it off, ma bierceuse! basking right in her bed.³ Oh! Ho!

De lit en lie! Délie! Fissionable fecesist . . .

Délit de lit . . ., Don Juan delirioustammering, wrapped in his cape. The dirty deed . . . Let go! All those relations . . . Knots, links as the knotted vipers writhe. On mattresses of fire. Barely put one out another flares up. Eternal will o' the wisp! The never-ending story. Keep adding chapters and you'll see. I was galloping on that vicious circling nightmare, a real backbiter! and I woke up soaked in sweat. In a soporific funk. Then I went back to sleep counting, until a thousand at least.

1. Let ILL be GRILL:
All a-boar for grilled porker. You still have lots of circean numbers left to spend,
sir. Lots of odd odysseas to cross, homers to hit.

2. Dabel check:
Yes. Ah no. Carry over your double entry accounts / Dábel entry? Give the devil
God's due, prorated of course . . . / Then you don't believe in anything, unbelievable unbeliever? / My creed is what I accrete, namely: Una and one, Dieu.
Deity and duo, —empat! / Tie? / Not Thai. Malaysian. Malaise of a bad addi-
tion . . . I believe in arithmythic. And in non-Euclitdian geometry. [The love of
geometry, Ea! Frisch auf! would lead Don Juan to try his luck with a white
Russian (: Asa!: Geomater with geometritis?) the kruquadrature of the vicious
circle. The geometry of my suffering . . . as his companion Mr. Teste would say.]

3. Le diable au corps, porcs:
Mot de guet. Ça ne vaut pas un radis!

4. Glose:
Vase vaseux.

Mets dans le mille! Go through the millennial mill! Don't lose heart, get a hold of yourself . . .

Up to one thousand five hundred. And still not able to fall asleep. All night long the window of that Paddington hotel room reflected the red neon of the restaurant across the street. ILL, turning on and off, ILL.[1] Like a bad omen. Burning with fever in the Nomad Hotel. No. Mad Hotel! the neon sign over the doorway broken here too. Swell crazy hotel, spleendid for a London nomad. Other noises, other rooms. Trademarks and time's marks. Stealthily marking time until the last seal is opened. A vacillating burning with each vigil. Impossible to count them one by one. Hold a candle to the devil and one to God, godspeed and go to hell.[2] From final dream to wake, pass the flame from candle to candle, burning both ends. What an inferno! Living flame tapering out. Terror! Till finally you're snuffed out. Burning the last pieces. A hundred or one, what difference does it make. The numbers are knots in your throat. Ga-gag-gordian knot. Sophistic phallacies and curses and invisible bonds, in infernal circles. Unraveling them, hardly anything remains.

Pow! Wop! Keep your power dry . . .

Just dust. Dust to mud, cooked with sweat from those rolls in the hay. Two lie as one, and their name is Legion . . .[3] Rolling, wallowing with bodies possessed. Face to face. Soiling and spoiling in the nocturnal mire, and then a toast. To each his vessel. Or vassal? Vase de nuit![4] Retire to the nightmire. Groping along. Till breathless. Gasping and urging and merging and screwing and soaked in bloodsweattearssemen. Miasma! The floodwaters rising higher and higher. To settle accounts, evacuate! or wait till we get a good don pour . . . ((Il Dissoluto punito, o sia Don Giovannish!))

Forced evacuation! Cote d'alerte, flood level . . .

1. Kosher?:
Eat it.

2. Koteletteen!:
Clay for the proto-potter . . .

3. Geraldo Ribera, report this rib risible:
In Eva Marx's cubbyhole in Queensway, after snaring a solid picnic of ribs and sweet-and-sour pork from the Chinese "Take away" on the corner. Chop chop! Adam Milalias and Eve in bed eating ribs, gnawing away and finally fighting over the last rib. A real porky pignic!

4. Your bag or your life!:
The bag of life . . .

Kot![1] Côte d'Adam! Adam's rib, buxom Eve in a leaf bikini ((: fig leaves?)) devouring, ripping apart! a pork chop. Koteletten![2] The best part, of my clay idol. Or clay-footed man who went to sleep on me when things were really cooking. Spare me a rib![3] adamantly carnivoracious, cleaning the bones. Guten Appétit! Oui mon p'tit petit à petit, bit by bitte. Bis bis, nibble nibble. Love by the mouth-ful in our Queensway Eden, side by side, eating ourselves up with kisses, kiss kiss rekiss a biss . . . A whole weekend without getting out of bed, and we were consuming, hag! and rooting between the sheets, hog! and rolling around, hug! arguing over those hard-to-gnaw chops. Rip! Rippe! and repeat. Ach! I'd like to measure that swine's ribs, and something else! in this Kotillon.

Care for cocostly cucutlet? stammered the fryer friar. Kok! End! and he jumped. Anybody want a plate of fried eggs? Then he writhed about, Pop! Pop musichaos! like a marionette.

Pop! Pop music! Pop! a hefty nun, that Cromagnun! zigzagging and arm-swaying and shaking like a person possessed. Pop! slapping her massive poopdeck.

Bacchanalia buckaroo! More bubblegum tunes in various rooms . . .

Bossa nova![4] with the movements of a mindless maenad, motioning as if testing the weight of something. Au! Roc! she struck at the air, toward the great ovoid globe, Oh yeah! and hitched up her habit, roguishly showing her buskins and sizable thighs. With her hip-wiggling and heel-tapping, Sambad ad hoc, Simbadabadoc! to rouse the flying sailor, Inbad the Ailer.

Au! From oral to aural oriole . . .

1. Oriol?:
Oriole! But I don't think we're talking about the same bird, Muscovite. Aquila non captat muscas! Rigolo! Rigògolo! Papafigo, piglia due rigògoli a un fico . . .

2. Pop off!:
Yes. And while you're up, orient the antenna the better to catch the waves . . .

3. Tot?:
Tod!

4. Tai?:
Swat, healer. It's her agile ability with the lingua franca once again. Here's the lance heading straight down.

5. This high man, with a great thing to pursue . . .:
Highbrownie!

6. And splashdown in the high seas! Aave Maaria!:
Aave meri. Finnish! To the dead sea / Don't fall . . . Better to ride out the storm and wait for another, less decandescent decade.

7. But not habits . . .:
Today's my tenth birthday! Milalias shouted in mad emboozlement, hurling a cup—lacking a glass—into the fireplace. And he finished the birthday party by tossing out the window of the Phoenix nest the secondhand portable Adler that Babelle had given him. The eagle's last flight!

8. Mórie búrna! In Russian?:
Yes, the sea is choppy . . . And go russoccitate a less dead sea!

9. Buffoon plume?:
Bufa bufâo! Mimus polyglottus, you mocking bird. You'll wind up without a sound to your name . . .

Au! Ow! Ern nest! Goldfilches and bald illegal actions . . .

Oriole![1] Oriole! warbled the loudmouthed Russian pope.[2] Tot![3]
and he aimed his crozier at the airborne Sinbad, Tot! who was
falling tumultuously amidst shouts, trying to catch the balloon.

Tie up! Forward, sneaking out for a pass . . .

Tie![4] and the African warrioress launched her assegai high. We'll
clip his wings, and then some . . .

High![5] Don Juan put his hands up over the feathers of his hat, and
began to wave his cape, as if trying to untangle himself. Hiiigher!
The eagles are reborn flying higher . . .[6] (Ikaarus!!!)

Rara Avis . . . Plunging! Into a stormy sea . . .

ORIOLE! ORI-OLÉ! intoned the tenor Don Juan, parodying the
parrot-pope, and he pushed his way through with whipcracks of his
cape. Changing plumage every ten years?[7] Froth and feathers.
Reborn, flying at the sun and then plummeting, METEORIOLE!!!
into the high sea. Yes. Aiming high the better to sink one's self . . .,
as he swam in the whirlwind of masks. Yes. Rejuvenated eagles fly
high. ((Don Juan Tenoreal!))

Mórie búrna![8] The choppy sea! The sea that is death . . .

Mourir? Mou rire! the white-faced Pierrot white as a ghost, who
tickled the passersby with a white feather,[9] especially the ladies.
Gai rire!

1. Pierrot Lunaire?:
Schönberg! Precious stone . . . The Moonstone! Hide it well. (Off the cuff: Fuck off!) Madstone. Faux lit! Folly? Stone-dead hath no fellow. Follow?

2. Honeyed!:
Not exactly sweet, this loudmouth with his problems vodcalizing . . .

3. Bufphoonetics!:
Shoot!

4. When the party of the first part parcels out the parts, he gets the biggest . . .:
Part! Ah the repartee, the best part of the partying is such sweet . . .

5. A chaque béguine son béguin . . .:
And to each Walloon her balloon. The two dancing lesBelgians in that Soho hovel . . . The Fleming and the Walloon.

6. Bête féroce?:
Bet fer os! Flemishmashed: Prey for us!

7. A movable feast! and moving too . . .:
They have been to an orgy of tongues and stolen the scripts . . . O! they have lived long on the alms-basket of words . . .

8. Fast break!:
Of Champions . . . Barmecide's Feast . . . Schacabacchanal . . .

9. Reborn? Renée? Who goes by that?:
The mysterious Renée (née Kleeman), Milalias's mother?

10. Pluck the clover . . .
Leitmotiv of his dark lady. (Dizzying anamorphosis?) Merveilleuse! Milalias exclaimed, after the initial shock, when he discovered the trefoiloid mark on Babelle's arm, the first time they took to the bed. Quoi? Clutch the clover, catch the lover . . . What? Amada, oh yes, love and lover fused.

Pieró the Fool! Lunatic,[1] the Russian pope parroted, sweetening somewhat his coarse booming voice.[2] And on a farting note as he dodged the feather held by the buffoon Pierrot. Shoot off![3]

Part![4] Hand out! The parts in pieces . . .

Begin the Beguine![5] a chubby gal and a lean one, with hints of beguile and touches of Beguinity, their jeans responding note for note to the rumba rhythm, kissing rapturously by the door. But they suddenly split apart, Bête féroce! at the sight of the Wolf-Man, his terrifying grimace almost on top of them. Bet fer os![6] echoed the skinny one with flamingo legs, her face showing her fright.

Red clover! Recover the clover . . .

His big hairy paw scared me! the plump Beguine pouted, pointing at the Wolf-Man, who clutched a red clover. He shocked me with his great fist . . .

A great feast of slanguages,[7] breakfast of sham peons . . .[8]

Labors of lost loves! Don Juan again thumbing through his black notebook. So so many that we've already lost count. Any old way, easy or hard, the ball bounces you . . .

Renée! Renée![9] gasped an alchemist in a checkered robe, his face covered by an asthmatic's mask, staring at the yellowing photo of a woman with a clover-polka-dotted parasol.

Pluck the clover . . .,[10] and Sleeping Beauty rubbed a mark on her right arm ((: from a vaccination?)), shaped like a clover.

1. Red actor!:
He was imagining Red and his busy little hands acting out each "to day I am tel ing yu" that he edited stroke by stroke ((at Emma's request? Cousin Emma, marredly married, now maddening, LEMA SABACHTANI, for the false lover. Emma masked behind the enlarged handwriting of the prodigious child. Laying her red net to bring you back to the fold. To the redoubtable role of incestuous adultery with the carnal cousin . . .)) for the great storyteller of London.

2. Retrace . . . a string of lies . . .:
Leave the abacus to Bacchus . . . Stop! and learn to count on your fingers . . . Tally by tally, notch by notch. With your ogamic or orgasmic writing, tally per dally! ink per dink, notch per crotch, that you marked down in your agenda. Stroke by stroke . . .

3. RED GRAVE:
Sic. Sick. The news of fate or fatality in the telegram that the nomad lover in London would receive after such a delay. [Three days without showing up at his den, pornocturnal wanderings in the lower depths.] A little after the last letter: "for days now the poor little thing has been burning with fever." LLAMA. [Call? Flame?]

4. Cancan, garoo!:
Catch-as-catch-cancan, to Kangaroo Court. Or Earl's Court, where you courted your Australian Kangaroo . . .

5. A shipment of contraband!:
Go see what your Ken Garou la Belle Mourner de Melbourne was hiding in her marsupial pouch: See PILLOW NOTES 18, p. 473.

6. Fruitless furtiveness . . .:
Mission aborted!

Renée! sighed the Alchemist, looking at Sleeping Beauty who sleepwandered by. Rise! come back to life again . . .

These hallucinations sure are getting vivid, remarked Don Juan, firmly repositioning his hat with both hands.

Revived! Resuscitated! a slender vestal blonde, her hair hanging over her face, came out from behind a red marble sepulchre and, convulsed and ghostly, advanced toward Don Juan with her burning torch. Ready! Alive!

No! She's trying to catch me in her red trap . . .[1] To enmesh me, get me in a tight spot . . . in her tights . . . Retreat,[2] and Don Juan took a step backward, hiding his eyes with his forearm.

His son has set! an old bald skeleton in a mailman's suit handed him a telegram.[3] O sir! It's too late . . .

Next to him a bizarre blonde in a kangaroo disguise[4] with a black veil over her face: Draw pupil's lip upward? Slip up, pupils! I lost mine too in Melbourne . . . My catch! O bit! with plaintive moans and pressing her abdomen: But I'm still carrying it here![5]

And what about me! the gypsy woman flying into a rage of clinking medallions and coins, E eu! brandishing a disemboweled rag doll. Boneco . . . Bonico . . ., as if she were lulling and doting on her dumpy stump of a doll. Heu! Heu! Eureka! Fruitless of my womb . . .[6]

Orbituary! Orbo del figlio . . . Change for a changeling . . .

1. Defects, of an economic nature?:
Effetto utile, fetishist! One hundred pounds that Portuguese au pair from Tras-os-Montes tried to squeeze out of gullible Rimbaudelaire by claiming he left her pregnant. Milalias straightened her out . . .

2. And Attic salt?:
Yes, a seasoned woman for all seasons.

3. Your golden legend:
Monte! A rebours. Reverised? Take another look:

M
И O   ((In the room of Devonshire tapestries in the Victoria and Albert
T   Museum, that diluvian Sunday afternoon, trying to copy the golden
Ǝ ɿ   hieroglyphics on the cloak of the belle dame presiding over the bear
Ǝ ɒ   and boar hunt. And suddenly (did she emerge from the enchanted
2   woods?) she made her appearance. Had he heard well? She deci-
I   phered the inscription for him, for his ear only. Her French accent
Я   was perfect, though she was Greek. Wife of a crooked magnate. She
       preferred a black sheep to a shipowner?))

4. Something smells rotten in Denmark . . .:
Dinmurk!

5. From Spain to heaven!:
Seven years of bad luck?

6. Parte! Take?:
And give. Break down your commanding madonna. And tame that erratic tongue. It's all Greek to me . . . Miliá! mil lalias . . .

Menina, my three-month baby. But so developed! I almost had a fit . . . and searching willfully and woefully down her glittering neckline: Somewhere around here I've got the statement from the doctor. A hundred pounds at birth! A real phenomenon! It was the biggest news story of the year. The end result . . .,[1] this anomalo-cephaloid.

Fetus! scowled a haughty lady with perfect Greek profile,[2] adorned with a pompous white wimple and a blue tunic bearing an enigmatic legend[3] in reversed gold letters down the left side.

I'll vouch for the fetus! cried the potbellied scrivener with gray periwig and green specs, pointing at the gypsy. He was all dressed in black, with a high lace collarband, a bulging briefcase under one arm and a goose feather behind one ear. As stockbroker and principal notary of the Kingdom of Fetilandia,[4] I thus sign and seal it in this the year of our . . .

Fatuous! once again, and the Greek madam monologued on: Cette année. C'est tannée! Year with a seven.[5] Year of longing. Years of tears, tears of years. And every hour counts. Tearminal! Consult the horoscope! But still surrounded by faithful girlfriends. Ton piston filon, so lucky . . . Tu as trouvé le filon, saoul teneur! You struck the motherloaded vein, you mother . . . And she majestically stretched forth her arms, with half a pound note in each hand . . . Split![6]

No! and Don Juan slipped the bill up his sleeve. Odds man out!

It's parting time! The parts are cast . . .

The Book of Numbers

1. One-man show? That's one for the books. Comptababilité!:
Cuntemptibility!

2. For who? Du masochisme, quoi!:
Oui, more or less, chacun doit payer son dû mathémétèquement . . . [Add it up and give an account of . . . Monte Cristo! Dantesque numbers to battle the outstanding bills of that great captain.]

3. They have proclammed their malefractions . . .:
Clam up!

4. Two to tangle. Let it ♍ :
Over then, come over, for the B has quit the clover.

5. Or knotty?:
MUST UNKNIT INKNUT SUM.

6. Néanthropologue!:
Will the Sect of the Phoenix disappear one day? Till the last performance of the auto-da-fé / Nix!: man's only crime is to have been borne.

7. Jeanne Dark!:
One of your darkest dames . . .

8. DROWSY SWORD? Steel away!:
Une feinte de grand style . . .

Count recount . . ., Sleeping Beauty softly sang, rubbing her right thumb and index finger together, as if saying the rosary or asking for money. Count . . .

We'll have to settle accounts! and Don Juan followed Sleeping Beauty through the Hall of Murals, glancing at the extravagant poses of figures painted on the walls, figures twisted and contorted into numerical shapes.

Count! Raconteur, recount . . .

Multistory of stories. With double-entry bookkeeping. Tossing out stories, all for one.[1] Count! One for all, and all for one . . .[2] One-upmanship! Everyone has his problems, more or less. Substraction before the multiploccasion of the sum of his sedition. In order to counteract the action of his malefictions?[3] Everybody here trying to do his little number, and go you one better. Then he impudently pointed at the corner: Fancy that one! someone sincere. Wunder-kind? One wonders . . . ((Moderato contàbile!))

Back to square none! Roundabout turn, smoothly spinning back to nought . . .

To be, O! or knot two be . . .,[4] with left thumb and index he made a zero, while his right hand weighed a skull, that ceremonious Hamlet with monocle and dinner jacket. To be . . . naught, or naughty.[5] Two being, or not to be . . .,[6] he continued. ((Will you nill you, zerroneous nihilist! A silly goose egg, a real nullbody . . .))

Ok! Ko! a Joan of Arc two-handedly swung her sword his way, a Jeanne d'Arc[7] in martial and mourning dress with a black-scaled coat of mail. And bending the blade of her double-edged sword: No steel![8]

Steel soared. Quick on the draw, to even the score! Consult the Book of Numbers . . .

1. The radio-recorder of Our Lady of the Night?:
Registering everything! from top to bottom . . .

2. Conn man!:
Hero of the hundred battles . . . Oui, Conn, unweakened. They must be counted and recounted.

3. Hunomatopeia?:
Hun dread!

4. Kippling! Kiplingo! Kip down!:
Oh, Twiddledum is a twister, and Tweedledee is a webstern, and never the twain shall meet . . .

5. Test-à-test . . .:
TEST SET! No contest, testy!

6. Remember Attila!:
Sic, sicarius, that white-chalked inscription on a black wall of the Victoria and Albert Museum, that set your teeth on edge . . .

7. Alt!:
Syringe!: Alcheringa: Dreamtime down under . . .

8. The right arm? Shot to hell!:
Junkie shot. Quixotic heroine, La Luzana Andaluza! with Andalusian soul. A delicate subject, this heroine . . .: We'll have to touch on it later, tactfully.

9. Hun or man? Hunooman?:
Hanumandrill! Monogrammarian, don't start up with your punorama, your cyclorama of a diorama of a cosmorama . . .

10. Wheel? Rueda?:
Ruhe da capo!

11. No splendor in her herb:
Mal! Herbe!: Elle a vécu l'espace d'un matin . . .

12. Rasen?:
Reissen! Brake the lawn, grass-kisser.

One two . . ., quick as a magician, Don Juan pulled a black box[1] from his cape and stopped to examine it quite closely, with meticulous myopic curiosity. One-two . . . One-two . . ., testing in droning monotone. Seems like it still works . . ., he said, stashing it under his cape. One-two . . ., and he made two wanton punches in the air, shadowboxing. One-two! Count to a hundred, connecting.[2] Cursing! Count a hundred . . .[3] ((A no-account to be contended with, if not counted on, a hundredfold lady-killer!))

Mask time! Murk Twain! Neither this one nor that one will run into each other . . .[4]

One-to-one-two . . ., Don Juan wobbled wanly with a waning, wanting voice. One-two-want-to, do-se-do . . . Overdose? Testing! Tasting! Test[5] for two . . .

A tila tea for two Huns![6] intoned a guy in a horned helmet, syringe in hand, speedily pushing a voluptuous Andalusian gal with thick blue-black hair and a charming Spanish dress, also brandishing a syringe,[7] incessantly murmuring Mi arma! Mi arma! and trying to slip away in the crowd. Mi arma![8]

Take it easy, hooking her by an arm. ((Hands, and build! of an ape . . .[9])) Then he twisted her arm, his repulsive grin sending shivers down your spine, flashing his wired teeth: Ruhe da![10]

Now dragging and jostling her along by the arm, towards the hall. The Hun is at the Gate! he proclamored with stentorian braying. Wherever his horse sets foot, and he stamped one boot, the grass shall never grow . . .[11] Herbe. Herbei! Ja! Yes. Erase it! Raze it![12] Yeah, the Hun's already at Notting Hill Gate. The other one (: and he stretched his wiry smile, staring at the dancer) will be here soon . . .

1. Overdose?:
A strong doze!

2. His won and lonely:
The Hunter of the East has caught the Andalusian Sultana in a Noose of Light.

3. As in abstinence?:
Abstenancy! [Oh, Nancy, don't take aversion to your tenant . . . Ann! Mrs. Page! . . .]

4. Indignant Page! Children of the future age, please, take no note of this indignant Page:
Paginate and evaginate this vaginal and paginal fucksimile! Pagination and imagination, power to the imargination . . . No! Something is rotten in the state of power: Pow(d)er. Back to the page, to the sweet country. And I turn the page, and I return the page . . . O Sweet Page! Ensuite . . . A la page!: We'll have to turn a lot of pages before we finally meet Mrs. Page.

5. Pong?:
Pig! Who gives a shit! Excrete that expurgated excreature . . . And then wash your labyrinth.

6. Dye?:
Extinct. Careful, tinter, with the tintinfabulation of the stars, and tune down the stripes.

7. Hypostatic hiccup? Alcoholic hiccup?:
Hick up. Hick, cop out? You hippo-critic. [Hypothetic postulate of Herr Narrator: Hypocrite rereader, my likeness, my brothersatz. / Brother. . . ? / He who writes, reads twice. And he who reads twice, writes . . .]

Whimsical! Wasted! Wing your partner, do-se-do.[1] A Hun and his hunted one . . .[2]

Just add one and one together! Fast![3] The old sturdy-busted gossip pulled from her petticoats a typed sheet[4] blackened with corrections and cross-outs, Fie! I identify your typing-pong![5] Your number's up. In the wink of an eye I sniffed it out. Your litters and letturds! First typed with one finger, and then inkorrected by hand . . . His orthografting. His cacography. I recognize your illegitimate lexicon, your bastard offsprinkstains! He used to type his dirty love letters, with so many typos! Worthless paper! and I put them he-knows-where . . . Watch me deal with this one! ripping it in two and tossing a piece at a fat flatulent hiccuping Falstaff with a cottony beard, throned atop a clothesbasket.

One plus one! clapping hands around Falstaff. Your courting letters, anything but curt! About this long . . ., as she stretched her arms apart. Trying to put me off? Some courtship, you knavish seducer, you tricked me with your letters, deceived me! Thieving Joker, stealing with your clever ploys . . . She came close and fluttered her piece of paper at the piece Falstaff still held in his hand, stupefied.

One! Plus one! the old midwife hopping mad now with her paper scrap. Two turns into three. Part! and she tore her piece into two. Divide and conquer . . .

((Divide? Join, or Die![6] everlasting motto of these U-knight-it States, You nigh-twinned Stakes, a devious device of these mutating multimashional corperforations, these polyfoam monopolies. De-part is to die a little . . .))

Hip! Accrete! Hip![7] Falstaff with interrupted hiccups. Manège à trois! and he leaped from his tall wicker basket. I hope good fuck lies in odd numbers . . . (False toff! Falstevedore!!!))

1. Santa Clause . . .:
Cut the Clause off! Klauswitz! Weinnachstmann!!!

2. Two in one?:
Twone, twin, entwined. Eyesore mummy kissing Santy Claus, underneath the . . .

3. Siren or libidinous sibilant Sybil?:
ALIBIS A LA SIBILA!: The Sibyl of Swiss Cottage. Sib . . .

4. I've won!:
The game is done!

5. What the deuce. . . ?:
Not so dicey. Two out, vices are loaded . . .

6. Alpipinist . . .:
Alp-pianist! To the Magic Mountain, Mann. Abfallbett! A Don Juan Night on the Bald Mountain of your succubist Venus. Alphabeatified with the beautiful illiterate Alphabeast. Alp-phabett! Ja! Ramp, page! I strauggled through the elfabet as if it had been a bramble-bushido.

7. Three in one?:
Pip! (Pir-RIP! but great expectations are the last things lost), Pip! (Get your second pip . . . Pequodlibet!), Pip! (Till the pips squeak!)

8. 'Tis a naughty night to swim in, he leered . . .:
Swim and keep your clothes dry? At least for one night. UN SOIR . . . A-ha! naked buffoon, quit paper-paddling against the currents in your river-novels.

9. Loopy alchemy, rimbaudelesque, verbally applied?:
Lucubrate! Act! Research! Vigilize! Annotate! And then interrogate your alchemystifier . . . Al Maestrino.

Santa Claus . . . Numerous clawses . . . Fallstaff turned into Old Saint Nick![1] and the merry midwife trying to hang the basket on his back. The two brace and embrace, both temptangled. And she, nervous, claptrapped against his broad kegbelly. One plus one. Unamored![2]

Woo night, unite: win one twin! Pattern sowing . . .

I've one! I've one! and three times the siren[3] sounded: that blonde femme fatale, seductive, with luscious fair skin and ruby-red lips, squeezed into a tight black silk dress, black gloves to her elbows. I've ONE![4] And shaking the dice cup like a maraca she shot a wily look at the gray-bearded twinkly-eyed old salt in a sailor's cap adorned with an albatross feather, who nodded assent in time with the dicey dancing dice cup.

Gimme twosies! Double, deal me double deuces![5]

Peep ace! Peep! Peep! the piping of a pipsqueaking buffoon in blackface as he followed a sturdy woman, a beer-blonde mountain climber[6] coiled in ropes. Three in one![7] and he started banging fiercely at his tinplate tabor. Pip! on the rampage, Pip! and off the rampage, Pip! Time to get down, summer urge submerged.[8] This night will twist us all up. Pip! Pip!! Pip!!!

Pip out! Pipeur, larron, joujoueur . . .

Unity and trinity! the Alchemist[9] with disheveled locks and a voluminous harlequin robe with red white black gold rhomboids,

1. Digital mathemagic:
We have four (IV), take away one (~~IV~~) and that leaves us with five (V). / Vae Victrix! A Roman work, your Penta-Tlön.

2. TRAZO M?! I trace M?:
The first of your five capital Ms, tantraversifying tantraveler? Tantragicomic tantract-writer? *M?!* Lang Slang, long of tongue? One of the thousand ems or fems of your erotickling mammothesis? / Trazo M. You know that magistral line better backwards. Ein Mussikalischer Spassage . . .

3. Je vous le donne en mille . . .:
Mets dans le mille-feuille!

4. In Londra mille e tre?:
Miles Gloriosus, Don Giovanquish!

5. Shoring up your fornification? Ten-four. Four scores, and several cheers ago . . .:
His four-bagger: her, ham-it-up, hymen, homer! 4-H Club? In the four-poster! Those numbers wherewith heaven and earth are mov'd.

6. Elle se tient à quatre!:
Four already? Le temps . . . Pax! Register your trademark. Peaced off! And head to the florid war zone of your sanguine Swiss canal: See PILLOW NOTES 19, p. 474.

7. Quatre de chiffre?:
Careful! Don't fall in the traps!

8. Edelweiss?:
Adèle Weiss . . . [Alpinist, climb the wild mountain where the hills are alive and trapp your flower . . .]

counting on his fingers. We have four, take away one, and that leaves five![1] and with the index and the middle finger of his left hand he made a victory V. As the Romans do . . ., gasping, he abruptly covered his face with an asthma mask. ((Asthmathematician!?))

Rythme à rythme, mes tics! Oui, mi-lettré, the numbers count . . .

Trazo M![2] I trace M! and Don Juan sketched a tall M in the air. That would make a thousand,[3] he added, straightening three fingers of his left hand. One thousand three.[4] An operetta operation . . . And with index and middle fingers of each hand crossed at a sharp angle, Keep your fingers double-crossed! he formed the Pythagorean square. Fortuitous? Let's see if we wind up paired up and squared up. Four. Play! ((A fore-golf conclusion . . . Tie up your four-in-hand, start up your four-psyche infernal combustion engine. Fournicator!!![5]))

Four o'clock, Don Juan! Catch that marvel . . . of millennial perennials . . .

Irrelevant! She's no prime number! Don Juan struck his chest. The thousand flowers of a bumbling drone . . . (How exhausting. And there's still mille to come, millipederast! seize the daisy miller, flit on to the next flower, pollynator . . .) Ah my wily divine lady, and he sighed, have them bring me the bill. I'm ready to pay, for a thousand loves. Waitress! The bill! Everything is totailed and re-tailed and consume-consume-consummated? He indicated, stretching his arms, the throng of masks: Everyone wants to double-check the check, without taking into account—how shall I put it?—the X fucktor! Here everyone insists upon strict accounts and by the end they lose track . . . Looking for the menu? Toss the old debts and deal a new meal! And away he strutted with a cackle: Gag! Gag! Gag! Gag! Gagargling number-gags . . . ((Gagaffeur! Gagoliard!))

On four! Quatre![6] Déchiffre![7] and she tapped the floor four times with her pike, she with the garland of white flowers[8] on her head:

1. Doux leurre . . .:
Atout à l'heur!

2. Allarm clock, digital style:
With Swish movement, and deadbeat escapement.

3. Bad omen:
Omen! O paws!: O men! O pause!

4. A kiss is just a kiss, a sigh is just a sigh . . .:
As time goes by. Now and in the dour of . . .

5. Enough of this clock-and-dagger story!:
Going at it tooth and clock? A timetrial of errors . . . I too have my timetrials and
tributariations . . .

6. Passe passe . . .:
Simpleton Pass . . . Adelapsus in the Swiss Adelta? Beware of the Swiss Canal . . .
Eden's furrow!

7. O! call back jesterday, bead time return:
I would it were bedtime . . .

8. Toga man? A magot!:
O tempora! O morass . . . Cicerroneus! Don't recycle your viscous cycles.
Tampon age! Le temps-pont, tournant . . .

that magnificent mountain lass in hiking shorts ((: baby dimples on her knees . . .)) and a white sweater, a coil of ropes slung over a shoulder and a pack on her back. Douleur à l'heure de plaire,[1] Pain at the moment of pleasure . . . Dans la petite heure de notre petite mort . . . Time for the shepherd and his shepherdess! as she dropped her backpack and pulled from its depths, Cuckoo! Cuckoo! a cuckoo clock. Histoire de coucouchage! she stuttered again, shaking the clock. Have you not forgot to wind the cock? What a wily bird! He tickled me, we split our sides laughing. But, remember, she added sternely, to wind up the alarm clock, waker of passions. Urgent. Breaking all the rules, completely ignoring them. A clock and bell story . . . of a cuckoo! Breaking them all, all the rules of conduct, without sexception, period. Has it stopped? putting her ear to the clock. Remember! Wind the . . .[2] And then he went so far as to try it reversed, to shoot the moon, my nervy bird. Oh! there is pain in this life . . . Moon dial! Yes. And me with the monthly curse.[3] You must remember this . . .[4] Four o'clock already? Going cuckoo, playing dirty at hide-and-seek, that scheming trickster. Fa cucú! Fuck cuckoo! So eloquent and what a mouth . . .

Cock a trice! Cock your eyes! Don't lose the thread . . .

The truth is we were too tipsy-foolish . . . And just feeling our way along. Cache-cache-tampon, catch-as-catch-cant! He was just passing time with me. Time against time,[5] tempus is fugiting! what must pass, must pass. Tic-tact! curfew bell. Le temps passe . . .,[6] the alpinist sighed, looking at her cuckoo clock. Le temps . . .[7]

Pax! greeted the Roman magistrate in fine toga[8] and sour face, and waving a white flag stained with blood. Pace rossa! A pax upun

1. Cyclonic cycle of mights and menses . . .:
Men's true action! Les Anglais ont débarqué!

2. O Vico nocivo . . .:
Vico chiuso! Vico fechado! Sh!

3. Ding-a-lingo! Het dingen! Ding!:
Dong! Dingue dindon! Ay my ding-a-ling. Ding! Chuckleberry finish by the
Passing Bellman. In sextremis . . . And therefore never send to know, Damn! Don!
Done! for whom the Bellman tolls, Dim! Dam! Dom! it donne told for thee. Dang!
Ding! Dong!

4. Foot note:
Feet don't flail me now . . .

thee. Then he fluttered his flag windmill-fashion: Corsi e ricorsi![1] ((É il Vicomagíster![2]))

Tresse! Détresse! Careful with the rule of three . . .

Cruel rule of three! shouted the bearded man in striped sailor's shirt and sleeping cap, who sped by energetically ringing a bell, heading toward the hall. Ding! Ding! Ding![3] I know my rules of three almost by heart too, stopping suddenly with the bell held high, and I say what I say. At three bells! But we're not going to give an extra bel to the Bellman, —are we? We'll see who wrings the last bell . . .

Big Ban. Bang! And all's well, very well indeed . . .

((What the hell do all these innumerable number-dodges add up to, when you get right down to it? Not a thing. Empty deciphrase-ologizing. Figures of speech . . .))

Telling! Telling! Telling! And that peal appealing . . .

Bestelling! Besteling! Beesteling! he rang furiously, like a mad-man. The most beautiful love story, the one about the beautiful beast, I tell you. Said and done, for a fact. For a feat.

FOUR FEET![4] Three's more than a crowd when it's four bare legs in a bawd to make beauty and the beast . . ., Don Juan imitated some minuet steps with exaggerated mechanical mannequin move-ments. Cuatro pies de amigos! and he made an intricate Old World bow, removing his hat with a flourish: Forfeit! ((Hoffmannequin! Hoofman? A manic Manichean!))

1. Countersign? Password?:
Painword! Mention will be made, if opportunity arises, of the Rubenesque pseudo-masochist.

2. Très sot!:
Fais le saut dans la sauterie. Fais le grand saut dans le Fête des sots!

3. Convincing without vanquishing?:
Mieux vaut un convaincu qu'un vaincu . . .

4. Fou, géronte!:
The shameful act of that screwball tramp . . . An old alcoholic asking for handouts in Hyde Park Corner. Contorting and exhibiting himself (his scraggly fly open) in the center of a circle of astonished tourists. I'm so repulsive I even disgust myself.

5. The fern-flower?:
Infernal fern! Fernkraut! There's a long way from word to weed. With ferns like these, who needs enemies . . . Feto? Feat us, cryptogrammist!

6. The Alp-King und der Manschenfeind?:
Rappelkopf! Misanthroped-up tight!

7. Three for a thrill?:
Three cots, and another quarter, and another bed, you would have needed to really band bend bond your messenger pigeon . . .: See PILLOW NOTES 20, p. 475.

8. Fourgive us our trespasses of fourtune . . .:
Thrice-passers! Tresplicers! Trespassers will be violated.

Three times three! the rat-a-tat-tat of the password . . .,[1] tittered a Rubenesque blonde, in chains and nearly nude straddling a tom-tom. Three equaled three . . .

Tressaut![2] Treasure! Buried threesures . . .

When gold talks, the tongue balks! and Don Juan ostentatiously put an index finger to his lips. Hush! You must have a real golden tongue, and then promise them the sun and the moon to convince them . . .[3] ((Don Juan Chrysostom!))

Détresse! Tresse! Stresse! Triple threat? Triple Clown!

Rear up, I'm rarin' to go, remember the rampage! The wild wanderer (: a clump of ferns poking out of his fly) twisting and waving his arms madly. Crazy memories, memorable crazies . . ., then coiling and uncoiling the pinup blond alpinist's rope around himself. Fou! Fou![4] he grumbled, rattling his change, hands in his hip pockets, and jiggling the fronds coming out of his fly. Catch the flower in its bed![5] looking grimly about. Rappel. Ah oui! Rappel. Ach ja! ((Rappelkopf![6]))

Strasse! Strass! Chockachock! all that glitters is not Golden Fleece . . .

Threedom of choice? Threemendous . . .,[7] a Columbine in white pamela and dove-white breast, gracefully frolicking, lifting her skirts. And she raised the ruffle of her dress to her waist ((: heaving a frothy foamy thighdal wave . . .)) and flitted away full speed with a flutter of frufrumpling frilly underskirts. Trespass![8]

1. Drei!:
Unbeschriebenes Dreiblatt! Too tonic for the mysterious white cloversion.

2. If at first you don't succeed, dry, dry again. Dry den?:
A thing well said will be wit in all languages.

3. Blot out!:
Swift as a shadow . . . Correct, insert, refine, enlarge, diminish, interline.

4. Fuss!:
Je refuss . . . J'accuse! Jacques is as good as his jaccusity.

5. Inkaleidoscope . . .:
Careful with your Kalidoscopilots and your Kaligrams . . .

6. Tintagelignite! Your castles flying in the air?:
King Earthur! Word-castles in the air . . . Verba volant . . . (Châteaux de mots en Espagne!: A little moat-castle of oathereal words, reaching high in the sky as if suspended there. Mere remains, Don Jongleur, ruined runes of a babelic tower of homagisterial isolation.)

7. Nitroglycerin ink . . . Trinitrotoluene?:
Or some more patent and plastic explosive . . .

8. Mark of the beast?:
Of the Antiscribe!

9. Blad! . . . Kladver! Klaveer!:
Klaverdietsing! Klaverdaaien! The Plying Dutchmaniac grins and spins. Aai. Draai. Het nummer draaien! And he's back spinning through his duchy of daft drafts. Wield your weathervane penhand through your cloveering swivellum manuscryptology, with its quashtions and answerves.

10. Blad!:
Blatt! Fliegendes Blatt! A flying sheet.

11. You're blotto! Blot your grand ol' coprybook . . .:
The last and greatest art, the art to blot, as our Quixote of La Mancha used to repeat: blot and begin again.

12. Gal op!?:
Hiel. Op! Full gallop! gall-raising gallant. And up with the Achilles heel!

Still more echoes . . . Dry![1] Dry up! Dry . . .[2]

Blot out![3] exclaimed Don Juan, brusquely ungloving his left hand. Wipe the slate clean. If your slate is the least bit stale, steal tales from the latest sale! he anagrammed.

Tick-tock-toe, three in a row . . . Dreistimmig! Dreist! Drei . . .[4]

Dreiblatt! Dry blot! stressed Don Juan, who continued to scrutinize the trefoil stain stamped on his hand. Schizzo frenètico! and he twisted his thumb about, absorbed in contemplation, watching how the blot changed form.[5] Think ink, and lay it on thick! he roared sarcaustically. Tentative tenet . . ., he muttered, and with a threatening gesture: Inkcendiary![6] And gesticulating, he continued his monologue: Night of ink, explosive. Already extinckt?[7] Detonate, denotate! and he began to gyrate his hand, faster and faster. Indistinkt stain? Clear and sharp? The cloverbial inkspot? Ja! Ja! Ja! KLEECKS!!! And still spinning circles with the marked hand,[8] he pushed through: Cloverevolution! Clovirulence and clovirility with musical airs . . . ((Three-leafed bolshevik! Left-handed cloverthrow!))

A new turn . . . Draai! Draai! Draai . . .[9]

Blot![10] interrupted Don Juan, Blot![11] and enough blathering . . ., regloving his hand. Blast it! BLAAM!!! with a thunderous clap. Fearless and flawed . . . Like it used to be, in the good old days. And suddenly, sta-stammering with teeth chattering, Bla-blat-blatantaranteller . . ., jigging about double-jointedly. What a time that was, penning unpent, wrioting away like a person possessed. Another sheet, another and another, three sheets to the wind . . . A sheetflood never to return? And all to recover the clover on the night of Don Juan, Klavermeestering! and galloping galop op![12] to pop on that pop music, Pop! Pop! already changing rhythm. Rhythm! ritmeester . . .

1. Err on, Pater:
Limitless arduodyssies rewriting voluminous almanacs. Keep on with your algorithms and musical numbers, because all constantly aspires towards the condition of music.

2. Flabulously wrought. Rot!:
Not just flightful, but reely threeling too! A three-for-all, a three-wring circus!

3. Ludicrass gordiancient knot-possible? Enigmagnus hitch, cock-a-doodle-doom!?:
A riddle rapped in a mysteery inside an enigmagnum opussum . . . and packaged as a Romanège à Klee. A threefold record is not quickly broken.

4. Dreiheit!:
Dry height! Dry as dust, man!

5. Ever-turning triple play. Dreitreffer! It's ternate!:
It's ternary? Tern plus turn, forward and sternward, eternal triplay . . .

6. Terminal leaves . . . ever taking leave. Unpoetic license of the scholiast and exterminator of these leaves:
Idle reader: If you don't have anything better to do, you might take another look at PILLOW NOTES 1, the first leaf of the thousand-leafed clover . . .

7. Traan! Larme à la bretelle! Easy the tear. Tris . . .:
Trammel! Drop it and tristrample it! Triste trame bien coupée . . .

8. Cabre! Braque!:
Martelé mortellement!

9. Trèfle et tri. . . ?:
Three of clubs! A trifling discard for the card sharpooner!

10. Your evashiva adventures!:
Sh! Shivaree! A dance in five-five time . . .

11. Sotin! Sot! Trisse, hautain!:
Mot à mot, lierre grimpantemime, enmeshing yourself with your pedantic women, wells of wisdom! in search of true knowledge . . .

12. Silence, insane partisan!:
Yes here we are split down the middle in this Mad Party of parties . . . This is very Midsimmer Madness!

((Now the Joker cloveering about at his risk, clovertiginously roaming, a wild clover cloverdoing it on a midnight errant?[1] Return and retwist, the better to rhetorque his fabulously fraught, his flighteningly flawed[2] free-for-fall? To what trifolio did they allude? An eluding ludifiction, some trefoil composed of nevarious trefoils, all clover-hitched[3] together by a triaddled[4] brain. Eternal[5] threnody sans remedy. Terminull allness[6] with no end in site . . .))

Triste! Triste! Tris . . .[7]

Coupé! Don Juan executed a spectacular slip, one foot in the air, and gave chase, his undraped cape flapping behind him, with bounding dance steps. Chassé! hurling himself herward, tense and alert. Pas de danse macabre . . .[8] Détaché! And he ungloved half a hand and stared with theatrical astonishment at the ink mark: Très flétrie![9] So withered! Faded stain . . . With a contemptuous slap he rushed off, again with a lively wiry step, toward the agglomeration at the back, to his left. He stopped, hesitated, then slowly tested with one foot, from left to right, the shiny waxed floor. Glissez! and he speedily slid off in search of Sleepwalking Beauty, almost over to the door. Any faster and he'll be airborne . . .[10] In a trip, in a tryptrick, in a tristich! ((Trickstickler!))

Triste! Tryst! Tris . . .[11]

((Are the participants of this particular party parting ways and means? First things first! All the partygoers participate in this midsummer party since there's lots of parts to be parceled out and all part ways to partake with their partner, to find that ideal parti. And in a very partycular manner Divo Don Juan and his Godiva rumbunctiously rumba-ing, roaming and rambling, rehorsing their musical numbler. Mambo after mambo jumbo, with a real slang-bang-tangled tango. Take two. But the best of this surprise party is yet to come undone . . .[12]))

1. Rose tendre de Rose La Rousse . . .:
Rose "Larousse"! A walking encyclopedia, that readheaded French professor Milalias met in Foyles. Bookish, but from her lips came honey . . . One of the smartest women he ever had the luck to come across. She was writing a thesis (prosthesis, Milalias would say) on Molière and Women (plus a Latin subtitle) and would instruct Milalias by murmuring to him, in culminating moments, the most enlightening passages. Milalias, in reply, recited poems by Bécquer. To forget the pleasure, in order to prolong it, that's the great secret . . ., she used to claim. She was also, thanks to yoga, a sexual contortionist. Or as she'd say, an ascetic of love.

2. So tan! Sot in!:
De sotie en sauterie, Trissotin . . .

Tresse! Détresse! Extortion with torsion . . .

Redhead in a leotard alone on a chair, a figure eight: her head peeping through the upper crosspiece of the chair back (: a red paper rose[1] between her teeth) and her feet over her shoulders, framing her face (: her fanny brushing the top of her hair bun), and her hands gripping the edge of the seat.

Artristic! Tristre! Tris . . .[2]

Trisse, hautain poètereau! she murmured through clenched teeth, and elastically untied herself with a quick flip. She advanced sinuously, hands behind her back, offering the rose with her mouth to the wanderer dressed in mourning, and a cravat, who paced back and forth with an open book in his left hand, gesticulating and silently moving his lips, pretending to recite.

Trisse! Saute! For a trys . . .

Saute! Hein? doing a backflip (: fiery flareup as her hair comes loose) and landing seated. Trisse! she repeated, tossing her head, Trisse! Poet, beat your wings. The darkness will return, my dark wanderer of London. Allò! do! la! à Londra . . . And come get swallowed up. From picks and pecks to explications. Veux-tu encore becquer? Rima a rima, my fashionable poet. Your pedantic feminists and other precious pretties! You would recite your chosen popoems. Your scheming rhyme scheme, stanza to dance, verse to perverse, rhyming something with anything, as long as it worked. My jay, bouncing from bough to bed, and from balcony to bel . . .

Condensé! Adventures in double-time, dancing advances . . .

1. Lime, Emil! Or emilfoil, milady:
Honi soit qui mil y pense . . .

2. Sei tu?:
Say two. Who. And I. Giving the note . . . / So! Sei! / You may well say so . . .
What a Japanese pen name she stuck on me: Don Genji. Your irony when you
discovered my notebook under the pillow. That you would soon traduce,
traduttore, traditore. Pour ton Grand Livre. Bon. And when you came home at
some hour of the morning, if I was sitting waiting for you, you always muttered the
same Italianish cantilena Sei tu? Is that you? Who else. The night-prowler in the
wee hours, and joking to top it all off.

3. Yes, Mrs. Rosenstein:
A diamond rose for the Stone Guest. And he rose for . . .

4. Furnication!:
Struggling bareback in the furs of the traveler who had made a "peltgrimage" to
the eternal city. ((Alice and Babelle dragged the furs, Quel fou rire . . ., off of poor
caveman Robinson. After the voyage to the center of the earth, audas viator! the
three stretched out on Mrs. Rosenstein's bed of poses cuntemplating that
vernereal adventure on television . . .)) This unique twentieth-century fox . . . In
the bed of rises, Milalias with the stole, tickling the dozing duo. Whose stole? Who
then stole away, only to give it back to the stolid stinker, his toll! when he was
exhausted . . .

5. Primum bibere . . .:
Thirst first.

Every man has his mania . . ., Don Juan went by, wrapped in his cape. Trick after trick. Each one doing his number. Nos numerus sumus . . . And again it begins again! brusquely uncloaking. Dancing all those musical numbers. One two three! executing a light sleepy step.

Condense! Oui! jig upon those musicaleidoscopic numbers . . .

Recontradance! and the acrobat put herself on all fours on the chair. Fourtuitously! curling elassstically. Je me mettais à quatre pour le servir. Yes sir, on all fours. Giddy up, Rossinante, ah! ah! ah! arrosse mes roses, whipping herself. See what rosy cheeks . . . C'mon, giddy up! Look what fleshy roses, effeuille mes roses en feu! Such a rosy flush. En un cinq sec, mon six mouillé! and she slipped up her slip, revealing her rosy ripe rear. From pent-up five to hexed six to septic seven. Nues mes roses d'Eros!

Numbers of Eros, eroded . . . Fi-filed![1] Cinque. Sei.[2] Sete . . .

La Rosetta must be made of stone.[3] Fondling the big rosy diamond at her flabby throat, a delicate lady in a mink stole with silver seashells arrived, leaning upon a pilgrim's staff. And the stone dinner guest, that Spanish Stoned Gate-crasher! She turned her vulture head toward the whitewashed Comendador who stood like a statue by the door. Don Giovanity and his accomplices will get their just desserts someday . . . They desecrated my tabernacle at St. John's Wood, read my most intimate epistles and my will, fornicated on my furs[4] and in my rosebed. But they didn't find the most secret rose. Eros is Eros is . . . corrosive! The savory rose sub rosa. Where the knight of the rose would quench his thirst.[5]

1. Cervus fugitivus:
The plush-suede bambi of your Bambi Bambina . . . The Colombian with doe-like fear of losing her treasure. Her roommate (close to Victoria Station, but don't sing victory yet) and compatriot, Angela, was her bodyguard.

2. Be it unto me according to thy word:
And you did unto her. You undid her.

3. Fallen Angel?:
Hell Angel! Fucking Ann. Ann the Word. Always with the Word, like antonomasia, on her lips. ((Yanquijotescalifornicator Ann the Word [((Fuck! Fuck the shit out of me!))] clamped on a burning Clavileño, a steed galloping at full speed, decked out with a breastplate black as night . . . Ann telling us [((Ensuite! Conte! Ann sweet cunt . . .))] in a little café on Fulham Road [Small Café] one of her recurring dreams or phantasmotorgorias: Decked out in a tight black leather suit on a motorcycle at eighty-something miles per hour on a nocturnal desert highway when she's transfixed by no less than Marlon Brando, pressed against her butt [Rimette il brando víndice nella vagina!?] and he clamps her hands to the handlebars, forcing her to accelerate with the right, runrun! zwee-zweee! until the climax comes when the motorcycle [Yamaha? Ya!] skids zwee! and smashes against a phallic pylon [Orgasmotor? Orgasmotto: ad astra per asfera . . .])) Fuck!

Sete! Seven-up! Mette sete, kill your thirst!

I've got seven years of bad luck coming to me now . . ., the Indian squaw with dark braids and big flustered eyes showed the rip in the back of her short chamois skirt, all the while clutching a tawny little fawn.[1]

Faun on fawn! Servus fugitivus! Here's the master's little deer . . .[2]

He tempted me and tempted me, and he swayed me into tamptation . . . His manhands burning to touch me. Promise me, darling, you'll be good? My fever went up and his hands went down. He took advantage of my guardian angel's absence. The cold disappears after a "Grog and Magrog." Of his invention. And he made me drink it and lose my head. My fever was rising. Rising! Before he gave me time to open my mouth, ah no! he had me snuggled in bed. Oh no! But it's only to be closer to you. Darling, you promise you won't put it in? Yes, but no. And he gave me his word that I would stay just as virginal as before. Pure for my princeps charming. He wanted to colonize me! Those Culombian girls are hotter than the sun, they give off fire . . ., while he hugged me and burned me. He scratched me and broke me and overwhelmed me. The anuswer is mine, heinous thief, and the rose of fire . . .

Sacrificial altar, feu de feud! Foc, follet! Foc . . .

Fuck! chewing gum, Fuck! a tall blonde in tailored black leather pants and fringed bomber jacket (: FA,[3] in chrome studs on the back), holding a white motorcycle helmet under one arm. Fuck! leaning against the wall, fists on hips, and she looked at Don Juan irritably. Fuck all!

1. Ou coito ou oitenta!:
Koi to! . . ., or something like that ((: Koitu!?)), the impatient quaver of your geisha right in the middle of coitus interruptus.

2. Roto? Broken eight?:
Mute eight. Mutate behind the eight ball!

3. Amor a Roma! Honeyball:
All roads lead to roam . . .

4. Baked eight? Vile eight:
Break date—violate?

5. Otto?:
Otto. Oh! Watch it!

6. Dame Murasaki?:
Or perhaps ginger was the color of her faded kimono . . .

7. A fly in the ointment! Che vedo!:
Lord of the flies! Bushed Boschmaster of the popoets, all devils, arses and flies.

8. Tuno!? To know Nipponese, kunnilinguist?:
Ja! Jaspanisch!

9. Careful with the cape . . .:
To the bullring, bullshyster!

What a faculty! exclaimed Don Juan, spreading his arms dramatically. She has a marvelous verbal facility. Always the same word! But capable of giving it a thousand different intonations. Though tonight it seems she's not in full command of her faculties. A mere shadow of what she was, a false facsimile. It's a shame I must leave right now for an urgent appointment, and he shrugged to the armored cyclist, but I'll return as soon as possible to continue rehearsing that Fuck sostenuto . . . ((Don Johannes Fucktotum!))

Coito! Oito![1] Oi . . .

Otto rotto![2] replied the brazen Messalina[3] in veils of blue muslin and a yellow wig, contemplating the fresco on her left: two yogis, male and female, with shaved heads, nude and knotted in a contorted posture that formed a stretched eight. I ate eight . . . otto cotto![4] a lanky Pinocchio with a long fake nose answered, wrapping one hand around her from behind, his free one covering her eyes. Intrinsicate eight . . . an underhanded slippery knot! Noose from nowhere . . .

Intrick-eight! Otto! Gordianude! Infinite knot, o . . .

Otto![5] a purple-kimonoed Madamu Butterfly sopranoed,[6] Careful! squatting and feeling the fly,[7] One two no! Tuno![8] Rascal! of the bullfighter in his gold and tobacco suit of lights, Lazy bum! exhausted on a sofa deep and white like a bathtub. Look! and she raised her head with the expression of a tragedian, at my mucho macho matador . . .[9] Look, me mine! making funny faces, My wise monkey! caressing his thighs with exaggerated mime movements. Me ray!

1. Numburlesque?:
Nu, merodorama. Melodrama full of musical numbers.

2. Oboe? Musical instrument?:
Harmonic and mnemonic. To play from memory, and without score.

3. Me, too bah? Me too, tuba . . .:
Pluck the clover. ((All kaput in Kensington Gardens, the three of them sprawled on the grass, Sei Shonagon, Madamu Butterfly and Don Genji, when Sei discovered (Naturally. Who else!) that magic clover right under their noses. What's it called in Japanese? the inquisitor Don Genji inquired. Mi tuba! or something like that, exclaimed the musical Madamu. Tuya es, it's yours, replied the generous Don Genji.))

4. Syringa?:
Wind instrument.

5. Sayonara?:
Hee! Sigh an aria! Bye! farther and farther with the little scores playing back; the siringa and the tamburinal . . .

6. Sayoonara, kamikaze!:
Kamikaze? / Divine wind. Beautiful image . . .

7. In fragrante delicto:
A la couillette du trèfle! Mellot smellot!

Rien! Rien de rien! Nay, naught. O, Ottoman . . .

Otto, robotto! purred Madamu Butterfly. Rub, you good-for-nothing robot! shaking the bullfighter. Osoo, what a clown. Prick! Suddenly with the little bull in the ring.

Ring to ring, and to another matter, matterfly . . .

Exuberant music, maestrino, Madamu Butterfly mused. Sing sing a song song that I only sing my sin to the one who comes with me. Another sigh gone . . .

Cancan, cantor, in this numerodorama,[1] Madamu Butterfly continued. Kuku-roku-ku! she sang. Yes yes my ray I know the numbers sing.

Her song tires and tries them in countless ways . . .

Me oboe![2] and Madamu Butterfly looked under the sofa. Me tuba![3]

Clover bolero! A sound of ravelry . . .

Hee! Hey! laughing, looking in the folds of the creaking, Hee! sofa, Hee! and under the rear end of the sprawled bullfighter. He! now my siringa.[4]

Hee! Ha! Don Juan interjected. Pee-yew! Più farte! Hee! otro do di peto . . . Hee! Sayonara . . .[5] Good-bye.[6]

Foul! Foul play! . . .[7]

1. Hero?! . . .:
Sh! Sh! Another bombard, dear!

2. Word by word:
Tango for tango.

3. Venetian dagger?:
Mesu-mesu-mesura! messere messo. Rimete el bisturí de la hurí nella vagina.

4. Mu? Moo boom!:
Cowched in nothingness. La vache qui rit, hein? n'amasse pas moos.

5. Ha! Hai! Haikupuncture! But what was she ha-ha-ing?:
Ask your go-go girl . . .

6. Bon! Bon! Oh! Bon!:
Les âmes mortes à la lanterne des morts!

7. The drowsy dozing torero . . .:
Dormitory for the matador in his moist dreams.

8. Tatti-tati-tatiiri!:
Tarai, kara, tarai . . . Tariru! Oi toru! Ooi tooru! Ee tooro! Ei tooroo! O tooro! Ue
tureru! Toreru!! Taoreru!!!: Chin! Pun! Chimpunkan!!! (Tauromaquiacchierata . . .
From the womb to the tomb, what a ruckus . . . Issa! Get up! and go to Pillow
Notes 21, p. 475.)

9. The moment of truth?:
Ai no korida! The Empire of Senses . . .

Your woodwind in my nest, in my windpipe, in my mouthpiece, in my diaphragm . . . And don't forget the breath control! I know, as the canonical readings dictate. Aay no-o, not so much! she continued in a low hum over the matador. Toot your horn, your corno piccolo, as I do. Almost there! Not keeping score. Like a chorus. Be gay, pian pianola gay, fat man! play it again, my hero . . .[1] Tani tan'i que tane . . .

Tango[2] after tangle, my lazy idling loafer . . .

Tang! Tang! Tang! the bearded sailor passed pealing his bell. And he hawked up and spit on the floor, Karai! a bunch of noise for nothing . . . Quel boucan! Beat beat, Madame Butterfly, beat your baton. And he went straight for the Flying Dutchwoman, who was recklessly swinging a kitchen knife: Mesu-mesu-mesura! she stuttered, scared: Don't make your mess here, messagère de malheur . . .

Tan! Tan! Tanken! careful with the dagger . . .[3]

Ah you! Too! Ai! Haa! Oohoo! Ay, my onnanista . . . Oh my ray . . . Fretfully yours already. You-you-united! Oo! with a tremulous voice, until moody death mu-mu-moves us . . . Mu! mu![4] Till the mool mold us. Ha! Ha! Hai![5] Oohoo! Oi! Oioi! Huuhu! Hu! Huu! Huun! Hun! Hui! exhaling and mouthing and slobbering facedown on the matador's belly. Ha! Cowardly loafer!

Hare! Hare! Dare-dare, full speed to the bullfight . . .

And all the while the matador busy humming. Oo tooroo![6] Toro-toro![7] Taratara tariru tarai tarari![8] in the rhythm of a Spanish pasodoble, as if inciting the bull. And jittering in a tortured fashion under the anxious Butterfly. Aay![9]

1. Goo then:
Sonsonnez les matines!

2. Uncrowned petit king:
For half a crown, the Japanese doll won a king, —without a crown. And as a tip,
his ruined queen. In check. Babel and Milalias were so serious and withdrawn in a
corner of the Marble Arch Wimpy's, it was no florid night for jeunes filles en florin
when the almond-eyed beauty asked them what the coin in her hand was worth.
That's how they met Keiko. They explained it was a half-crown ((Don't you like
her? Mais oui, surtout son air de gamine un peu salopine . . .)) and then after lots
of twists and a bit of hounding ((Ahoo, toroo! playing the matador with Keiko's
umbrella and her overcoat in front of each car zooming down Bayswater . . .)),
they took her straight to bed. King-size. (Ima wa mukasi: Now water under the
bridge.)

3. Rain, rain, go away . . . Come again?:
Ease up on the rains!

4. Starting from scratch with a gaggle of goose eggs:
Ab ovo!

5. Immoderato contabile . . .:
"Mr. Cantor," the numbers count . . .: See PILLOW NOTES 22, p. 476.

Gag a gag, gaga à go-go . . .

Go-go-go-goo-gogo-googo-gottago-go to my bed, tired wander-er . . .,[1] Madame goggling over her worn-out matador. A rich knowledge I will give you, a sweet little riddle that only I know. OK? More and more! The way I figure it, I've got some accounts to settle with you, me ray! Gogo, san of a gan! Go go my go-go booy, my ray, my king![2] Go! Goou![3]

Goo! Goolies . . . Ghouls . . .

Googolgotha! Cross and double-cross. Googolplex! These calcu-lations aren't working out for me but I'll do them[4] again, figure by figure, until everything comes out fine.

A gentlemaniac[5] from the City, emaciated and spectral in a dark suit and bowler, an umbrella under his arm, went through the mass of masks muttering as if praying, his nose and glasses stuck in a thick account book held with both hands.

Look, Mr. Rays . . ., he said, brusquely handing the unaccountable tome to the long-haired Alchemist. I don't know if it's a three or an eight . . ., he added, absorbed, indicating a scrawl on the page blackened with scribbles. I don't see so well lately. I'll have to get my eyes checked. You with your X-ray visions, don't you think it's an eight?

Otto rotto! Busted eight . . . Who ate the eight . . .

And you my king yes yes my lord yes, Madamu Butterfly sang. You and I for all time like this. Like a romantic novel. We loved each other so much! See my king me yours.

1. Inkorrect!:
Inkoo! In case . . . In Keiko I will stay.

2. Drink what?:
Kon'ya konyakku kon'yaku! / What? / Cocknag on this nuptial night. Keiko muttered something like that and dunked her bisuketto in the glass of cheap Spanish cognac.

3. Aviate! L'otto volante . . .:
Mangia il otto d'oro!

4. Möbius strip?:
From strip to strip, stripper to strapper, ribbon to ribbing . . .

5. The part for the whole?:
The part . . . and the port for the hall. Another trope from the toper. Repotted. Topór. Da. Chást! Pars pro torto.

6. IN HOC SIGNO (: ∞) VINCES:
Changing sign.
I saw it again up high, swinging in the entrance of the Villa of Mysteries, in Fulham, during the masquerade of a dark Saint John's Night.
Weathervane sign.
Wire-rim glasses (a bit flattened) of the Dartful Lodger in dreams, lazy-eight-shaped mask, twisted larva in a double curl Möbius strip, sign of a night without beginning or end (infinight!), that would light up the eternal fire of an auto-da-phoenix.

7. Look! What a flourish!:
Gordian knot? Infinite? / Only when the book is open. The end of the writing marks the infinity of the reading.

Oh yes almost yours. Thrust! Thrust! that's how I drive, ay! so incontinently[1] and without ill will. On and on, continoo with you tontintinnabular tinker tonite continoo till the tontine. Oh yes. Do do that goodoo that you do so well. My sin! What I've seen! Drink[2] with me, drain the koppula kiss by kiss. Ay! Fool! See, man. All mouth and no goods . . .

Baba! Bah! Finished already . . .

Bah! with a dismissive jump, Bah! that slender liana of a Chinese circus girl in a black jacket adorned with a golden lotus on the back and a straight black skirt slashed to the hip, Bah! as she braided and unbraided an eight[3] in the air with a long golden ribbon[4] stuck on a stick. Bah!

Nacht. Acht! moaned the office worker from the City. The part for the whole . . ., and he pointed with his gloves, crumped in his fist, at the huge book held by the Alchemist. Yes, Mr. Rays. To each singer his multiplicasong! The part[5] for the whole. Ach! Here the whole is no greater than some of its parts . . .

Is he saying hole or whole? Da! Black whole . . .

Finito in finito! clowned Don Juan as he snatched the massive accounting book from the Alchemist. Look at the squiggles, turning the sheet violently. OK! And with a quill pen ((a goose quill?)) from his hat, In hoc signo vinces![6] he made a flourish[7] across the double page:

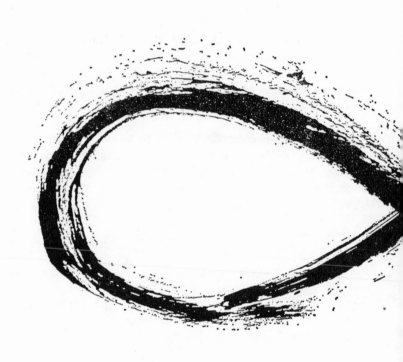

The Flying Dutchman
in Nether-Netherland

1. SNACK-BARK:
A floating snackbar-disco drifting upstream, up the Thames with its cargo of dancing bacchantes, to the pier of the Villa of Mysteries.

2. The ship of fools, merrily soiling . . .:
Down a navigable bacchcanal.

3. The last little marteeny? Le piccole morte . . .:
Don't bother with small fry. Wait, whiskey-seekers, for the romping rotgut of the house . . .

4. F.U.B.A.R., futurist, are the marinated old mariners:
Poor soiled sailors! from galley to galley-proofs, to the rogue's gallery you condemn them.

5. Constantly!:
It's off to see, to sea, merchanting marine, from great mariner to grand marnier, for the punning of the snark.

6. Jette l'encre, pieuvre!:
Ancora ancora! Anchored, but still not catching the inky octopuzzling penman-of-war in the great dark snark hunt.

7. Sucked in, and sucking the stout monkey with the fat Dutch:
That glibby antagonist . . .

TANG! TING! TONG! Make way for the Flying Dutchman . . .

TO THE SNACK BAR![1] TO THE SNARK BAR! blurbed a bearded Bellman in a sleeping cap and a striped sailor's shirt, bellringing as he
pushed through the come-what-mayhem of the hall. TO THE
SNAAK BAR! at the top of his lungs. Belly up to the bar, you bums!
for a bite in this boisterous bang-up, this maremaagnum.

Mare Magnum? Magnum?! Milk of maagnesia for everybody . . .

To the bar of the ship of fools,[2] to imbibe on our bombing boat,
bateau-pompette! and drink up to the last martini,[3] on the rocks!
to drown our sorrows. To the bar, ancient mariners et vieux
marinettis![4] to drain the deep brew Seagrams. Or whatever's left
in the buttoms of bottles. To the baar!

Bars, boys! To see, sic![5] Stop this bickering and bellowing . . .

Bouteille à la mer! a small disheveled cabin boy, his sailor's blouse
stained with mud and blood, stumbled and upended the bottle. Y
en a tintamarre! and he shook it in front of his nose. C'est la
bouteille à l'ancre . . .,[6] looking at the dark glass against the light. I
found it there, his stiff left hand pointing at the staircase. And then
again there. Tossed away, and still half full.

Suck it up![7] the painted warrioress in an African mask seized it
with a leap. Chew, pa! stretching her tongue (: swahilicks!) and
licking it clean. Chupa ya matelot! she spit with a grimace of
disgust, Ugh! and gave it back.

1. Le savon, avant:
Savant!

2. The blue! The blue!:
Now blue around the gills.

3. O, shiver my keel!:
Keel over. Keel off.

4. Friends reunited. Very united:
Reunited, and what timing. In that pub in Deptford, United Friends, facing the church of the two skulls. After closing time, the two flat-out looped, like two skulls scowling at two skulls scowling at them with their empty sockets, way up there at the entrance to the church cemetery. Their disquisition in jumbled pig latin. Tenorius. Notorius. Faustus. Fatuus. Johannes! The strange case of Dr. Johannes Faustus and Mr. Johannes Fucktotum. Who's there? It's the wind in the leaves . . . Such suspense. Well the big skull on the right looks a lot like Alfred Hitchcock, Milalias blurted. Hush! and Rimbaudelaire hugged the lamppost. Don't you hear it? (Vertigo. Psycho. Frenzy.) Yes, it's the birds . . .

Huh? C'mon, spit it out ..., eagerly flipping it upside-down again, sponging every drop from the bottle. Aimez la bouteille! The diva of our divagations. Give, take, take it and tipple it. And pass it on.

Passer l'éponge avant![1] Pass the sponge . . .

Pounded through hell! the cabin boy rubbing his face, bruised and swollen. Black ah and blue oh and red ay! All the pretty alcoholors. What a confusion. I'm you? Hue and cry to add another hue unto the rainbow. In excessious Day-Glo! When I drink I get alcoholyric, ah! ah! And when I mean wit, er . . . white eh I say black. It's all because of my equivocalizing, if you me what I seen. If it be passible, let this cup pass from me . . . Oh! Passer au bleu et n'y voir que du bleu.[2] Oh! About to explode ..., he dropped the bottle and raised his hands to his head. O que ma quille éclate![3]

Ma quille! Mock eel? Get this bottle out of . . .

A-bombs and abominations! Bombs and bombards! boomed the Bellman, pealing his way through the throbbing mob of masks. Débouchez! Unstoppered! Uncorked! Dégustez nos gros bleus. And our sangrias. Give 'em a try! Moonshine for moaners, home-brew for homebrooders. Schnapps for shikkers and shirkers. Schop! Chopine! Dry whine for all. And at the end, he sighed, the wine of tears . . .

Watch where you're going, the cabin boy pointed at his left eye, black and at half-mast. Ouvrez l'œil! Open it. Close it. An eye for a night! That was another bottle. Lost, but he found it on the floor. Another black night. In that pub United Friends![4] with my old buddy Milalias. The dark gal was meant for me, and her sailor didn't care. Won the war and lost the bottle. In that port pub down by the docks.

1. Oorlog!:
Every hour the clock of war strikes a wound . . . Eerie to bed, earless to rise . . .
[Il y a une horloge, dieu sinistre, qui ne sonne pas. Remumble! Souviens-toit!]
DELIVERY REVILED!: See PILLOW NOTES 23, p. 477.

2. Reis, and shine!:
Rise! and fall . . . Over the deep blue seasickness . . . Who's staid? Who stayed.

3. Plus léger qu'un bouchon j'ai dansé sur les flots . . .:
And on a cold black puddle, irascible. Toppled in the mud over in Piccadilly, a
drunk Rimbaudelaire stomp-stammering. Debout! La nostalgie de la boue!
Acclaim a clay muddle, admire the sub(s)lime mire. Homess-sickness.

4. Feather name? or an alias with wings:
That Milalias stuck on him. Better than stale and stuffy Charles Bouchon. And
with the provisional title *Tripsy,* Milalias had begun to translate into Spanglish the
plaquette printed—at the author's expense—in Liège. Milalias, hamlettered as
always, was in doubt. Maybe it be better to just call it *Trip.* See?
   —Tu crois? On dit trip en Espagne?
   The generous—grudging, but generous when all is said and done—Charles
Bouchon would yet spend many quarts and pounds to turn his lines into Milalias's
buoyant, flowing language.
   —How about *Kif Skiff?*
   —Eheu! Comment?
   —Rien. Kif kif . . .
   And with the title he kept the Rimbaudelairesque poet in suspense.
   —Maybe *Whiskiff?*

Ducked down at the dock. Doctor! My eyes!

Yes, open an eye. And an ear . . ., as with his stiff hand he pushed a lock of hair back from his left temple, displaying the rosy wrinkled hole. Dere was another battle. My Waterloor! no glory and all regret. Where I lost my ear.[1] And nearly my hand. Powf! One of my Warterloos. When I was a child pro-prodigy, p'tit bouchon! and the Armoricans were playing war too and they planted contraptions in the Belgian fields. Pappy's garden was full of flowers. They flew through the air. The Great Void! A black hole. While I was digging around. And found what looked like a black bottle, buried. A genie bottle . . .

Bom! Bom! Fais la bombe! We're bombing along now . . .

Vieux capitan, il est temps! turning to the Bellman. It's time, o great captain. Levons l'ancre! Loosen all ties, anchors away! It's time, darn it! the appointed hour . . ., and he rubbed his ear-hole again. One must set to sea.[2] Far, ever farther, one must travel far. Lighter than a corker, bounding boundless I'm dancing on the waves too.[3] The waves, sounding depthless . . .

Sound! Sound! Flotsamba! Interimbawdiness . . .

Le bateau-livre . . ., the cabin boy took a grimy book from the back pocket of his trousers. Le Voyage Ivre! flipping through it. *Tripsiness,* by "Rimbaudelaire." My nom de plume,[4] so airy. Mon livre de bordel! My libretto. At dee author's expense. Vers à verre, couplet by cup. It cost me my liver! Liters of ink. Wine. And diverse alcoholes. Plaquette, in my own blood. Drink this magnum

1. Stop!:
Cork it! Another top blown . . . They oughta pop the cork back on, bouchon! that boy.

2. Stop!:
BAG A GAB! Back and forth, getting nowhere fast: No, IT IS OPPOSITION!

3. Buddha in a bottle? With genius!:
Jinn: another gin!

4. For God and the Sainte Vierge des Lourdes, lighten up!:
Go to the free bar and the grillroom, fickle fellows, and have a look. Tacks and tacos. Take another tack in this tacky party. A taste for all Dutch tastes, slim, stout, and worst. I serve it with greens in those shadowy scenes . . .

5. Piattone forte!:
Salade salée! Salacious, and so spicy . . . Raaskallen! Catch a crab! Krabbellen! But what's a randy romeo really looking for but a lovely dish on one of his sexcursions. Ship-to-shore, hip-to-whore. Et vogue la gale! érotomane.

6. The golden and the olden:
The calves and the calve-naughts . . .

7. Hornbook? Cud-cuddle up with a leatherbound one:
Veal or reveal your no-vellum. Feuillet mobile! Chew it again. (Milk it for all . . .) Or ass he hath said: I write for those who chew it over, la vache qui rit! for those who steer clear of the bull. (Cowriters.) I don't want any jackasses here. Ruminant brother, to your many-plies book. Omasumma!

opus of wine, a liter in its class! produced and reembottled in Belgium. Stop! Send your orders to Bouchon, de Liège. Stop! Reimbursement by money order. Stop! From Liège. Stop! De Liège, et bien bouchonné. Stop![1]

Pots![2] Poets! the tingling Bellman ranted. Bottoms up! Those popoets are all a bunch of Oedipsomaniacs. Every poetaster finds his magnuschrist in the bottle.[3] They all take a dip or a nip, right out of the bottle. Well of course. Naturally. Hence the bar in bard. They all get loaded at the baar. C'mon, you ninnies and say-sellers. Payez les pots aux potes. Plenty per poet. Unplug all the bottles, pluggulp! and be generous with the tips. Pot à pot, pots! till the last apotheosis. Pour out the pot liquor for these potted poets in our potlatch . . .

Gone to pot . . .

To the snark bar! Hurry up! The snaak bar is kloklosing . . ., he chimed frantically.[4] Cold cuts and salads and spicy side dishes, itchin' to be et.[5] Pee-nats, kafkahouètes et amendes amères. Snacks and whacks, sigh dishes and more. Eat it up! Complaints and complainers may be lodged in the lip-service book availabial for your perusal.

Queue up! God knows what may come up next . . .

Eat up those cock-a-leekies and codfish and cates and collops. And the codes. And the codices. And the cows. Let's eat all the golden calves![6] All the quadripedias. Hoofing it vaudeveal style. Grab the book by the horns,[7] tournez les feuillets! and runruminate to the snark bar. Fill your cup and chaucer, heaping platos for all, the woolf's at the door. Denmark's eggs (Danish Hamlette) and

1. Torta al burro!:
The boor little asnnotator, ever a buffoon buffeted in the buffet. That's him, Herr Narrator.

2. Stir up, purist!:
Sternway. When rare is that which is well done . . .

3. Moisten the index:
To turn the page? Watch out for dangerous books with poisonous readings. Chinese puzzler? A shun in time saves nine. Mangia il loto d'oro . . .

4. Ces beaux livres de haute graisse . . .:
De haute Grèce! Hérodocte et érudit radoteur!

5. L'angosta . . .:
Or the anguish of swallowing your own words, claws, shell and all. In the pearly closeness of an oystered life, the words stick in your craw. Clam up, and don't move a mussel.

6. But upper crust! In God we crust. Christ, enough!:
Christcrosstacean . . . Craws and all. In the magnuscript of your crucifictions. Crust! Inkrust!

7. If a body meet a bawdy . . .:
Coming through the rye bread. A body in a library of a thousand bodies. A thousand in one! Lexiconundrums, almagesticulations, rhapsoddities, velluminated arcana . . .

8. Bilingual bile:
Bil is bil. Bil. Bill and coo! Cuckoo! to the tavernacle.

France's bacon. Chuck-roast lamb sandwiches (Bottom round!)[1] and spensirloin steak (donne to perfection), sterne-fried[2] shrimp (with the usual trimmings!), joysters on the half shelley; becketts of clams, and wilde rice. Today's special, finger-lickin' good:[3] un faux filet pentagruelique de cinq livres doré sur tranches grasses.[4] Butter up the hoily books . . .

With holy-o-margarine? Textreme unction. God knows how it tastes . . .

Glo-glo-gloriously! the glangly Bellman now accelerating to full glottal. Pick, peck, and peek, from all the best. Enjoy our penitential psalmon and our lovely communal wafers with confessionary sugar. Hostrich eggs and fresh Roman langostia.[5] Nihil lobstat! The Host is a crust . . .[6] He's hostrionic and can take a host of shapes, a real guesting game. Our daily bread, and better! Papantomimist! But quite crusty. Oui, ma mie, la mie et la croûte. Eat of this, for this is your corpus.[7] Stop! Speak easy but quick! —drink! Drink! and careful with the precipitations. Drink. Jusqu'à la limite! Drink and beam airy . . .

From tavern to tabernacle! To imbibe the imbibible . . .

Be for bid! Beer for bière! he bellowed out. Ah oui. All you atrabilious[8] boys to the vernacular tabernacle. Cull-de-sack! Rotgut for everyone, on the house. And he rapidly relieved the cabin boy of the bottle, Sangre de Escristo! and drank, God, how strong you are! straight from the bottle. But down you'll go . . . He wiped his chin with the back of his hand, and returned the bottle. Baba a baba . . . Ah bah . . .

Abba, don, careful with that abecedairy . . .

Christ! and he smacked his chest with the bell. Crossing the first

1. Testa! Attest!:
Koppig! Ahead from text to test, testudinal testifier.

2. What's left, the lees or dregs?:
Let them lie and then you'll see . . .

3. On lie et on délie . . .:
Oui, lie les mots et lie les notes. Délie! Et lie! Délie! Jusqu'à la limite. On lit et on délire . . .

4. Another with litership qualities. Hemlocked in!:
Quit your socrastination.

5. Eat dirt and come clean!:
Confession washes away sins?

6. Whose there?:
Who's there indeed. Words whose utter inanity prove his insanity. Another dodge, son.

7. Antique?:
Any papast time was better.

8. Sosie saucé!:
You're gonna need that sauce, all the world's hunger, to put your teeth to that hard-to-gnaw plotboiler.

9. Gastric?:
Gast trek! Gustatrick! Sup, pig! Sop, pig! Sap, pig!

learning obstacles, I mean, reading comes with bleeding, skulking crossly. Stroke by stroke, crossing out till you reach your final goalgotha. Gotcha! Cup by cup, kop![1] and copy after copy. Slowly and carefully, stroke by stroke, and careful with the oorthoography. Gul-gullet-gotha-gulping to the dregs.[2] Give and take. Give and you will receive. To each according to his needs and lees.

To Leeds and knees. Leapin' lizards! what a mess. Un lie. Délie.[3] Or lie. Elijah! Elijah! why am I forshook?

Ele-ele-elect your own elixir . . . stammering-a-ding-linging. Bar-barking and ababbling, vogue la gagalère! till we're plastered. Top! The wolf too shall drink with the lamb, Christians and pagans and the rest of 'em, from elegy to heresy. And don't throw in the sponge. Drink to the lees, proshit! with the socracratic method.[4] Before the interrorgations begin. Eat your own words. Drink them and wash your mouth out afterword.[5] Bite your tongue and gulp in amazement. Eat and sing as loud as you can, we'll do-do the can-can and barbarize the snark bar . . .

Nark knock![6] Back! Snack up!

Detente! and he raised his bell. We've still got lots of other main courses, he added, pointing his bell toward the dining room door. Plod on over and put on some weight, pooching out his panza. Quiche haute en couleur. Quiche authentique![7] And to stir up the appetite of even the unwilling, a secret sauce. Maagic! Bon appetit! the best salsa in the world . . .

Mets toute la sauce![8] And get all the juice . . .[9]

1. Light lunch of black on white:
To the bar! For a bite. We still have hors d'oeuvre, titbits, assordid appetizers.
Delivery sausage, ad lib. Diverses farces, assez sonnées! avant les mystères du
dessert. Têtes-de-morts, Mad Edam cheese! bien servies sur un plateau. Et pièces
montées à la minute. Hurry! to the last Super-Opera.

2. Father Time?:
Nonsense! At the end, sitting at the crossroads of World's End, the old man with
the scythe. Hip! Hippe! what hiccups. The scribe never stopped hip-hoping for his
paradise lost. Ecstatic, reading interruptedly the remains of his magnums-scripts.
Hiccup! between hiccups and alcoholic tears. Bitter tears rolling down, blotting
the paper. Sigh-scything in the wolf's den. Cut it out! Clean it up, sponge it off at
your own conveniences. Prick up your liter after the peek-nick.

Happe! Happening! he belled electrically, we'll see who's got the best mouthful. We're all cancannibals in this happening or repast of black on white.[1] Shouting, qui braille comme un aveugle entend comme un sourd! and taking blind swings. Mors a morsure, by means of the Morse alphabeet . . . Grave mistakes. Engrave it on a grave place; aggravate it with a grave tone.

Traanscript! Retranscribing the kriptography . . .

Trankskription! the cabin boy inserted, shaking his bottle up. Come what may! Soûlographie!!! A new testament, alcolo-gography. Libacious libretto? Boozy book? Livre ivre? The better to label my poemarionette.

Hippe! Hip! Father Time[2] hiccuped, zigzagging about, Hippe! Hip! Hurrah! and scythe-swiping around. Hippe! raising his scythe against the cabin boy. As you sot so shall you reap . . . Drink and be merry, Kling! Klinge! for soon the hour will toll.

Klink! Klank! Klinker! Watch that bell . . .

Telling! Tilling! Tilting! the Bellman now at bat with his bell, Free! Deling! crossing through the mass of masks mashing at the dining room door. Dinghy! Dingo!

Enough of your appeals, bellsy Mr. Ding-a-ling! C'mon, ring my bell and mine alone, sound my alarm, all the way up and down! until your clapper collapses.

Next time around, he said, freeing himself from the lusty Anda-lusian woman in a frilly dress, her hair tousled from dancing bulerias. Next time, miss, and off he went still belling ding! dong! right now I've got to take care of some more pressing matters.

1. The dunning of the snark. A whodungit?:
Inturdiction: stool the loot!

2. This swell makes us swell and bilge . . .:
Wavering? A Wave of privilege: to sleep it off snoring with the prettiest gal in her seabed. That's how we like her: open, strong, high, deep, rough, heavy, great, brazen. True to her salt.

3. Or the ballast:
Roule ta bille! Let the bowls roll. From pop to bottom. And start over again. Boulettes de bout en bout. Contra la boulimie. Boulettres! Paperwads. Pappe! Pappe! aspetta il lodo. Et vogue la galerne! Everyone, barrel down to the bar, and he started ringing again. We've got to be absulutely mudern! Rambunctiously! Reimbursement for everybody. Boutades bout à bout, à bout portant. Pointblank. And I have a feeling we're going to have more dirty tricks. All together now, let's slip to the bar. From bar to barrels of fun, bom! boom! what a barroom, barring accidents! Debout! Stand up, scatterbrains, and fish for a fine drunk. Luffing time, hard alee! oui! on a du pot-valiant, get your sealegs and careful with the rocks.

Ding! Dong! Dung! Pay up, a dun for every dunner . . .[1]

Bloblotch! the blowhard blubbered. Wipe the slate and . . ., the bell poised high, and . . . pass the punch. A clean slate, chuck these paper wads into the sea! and pass the sponge. Merdier! this is going too far. Sht! one finger on his lips. Another round all around, rowdy roustabouts! and we'll suck it up like sponges. Help me rondo! roundly distributing bellrings as if sprinkling holy water, aspergilding everyone. Rondo!

Rond d'eau? Rondeau hydrolatique! That party-pooper's all wet . . .

Round-up, he rambled with his raucous voice, the last round is free for all the hoarse rousters. Gare! Gare! now gargling . . . All well drinks are free, à la baille! free as water as well. The free-floating bar is now docked at the back of the dining room. We're bound for the dining room, my mascaronis, as he looked maskew and maskance. With these rough seas we might wind up wrecked on some reef. To the dining room!

Deining? Deining rum?![2] Schooner or later you'll hangover the edge . . .

To the baar! he barked. Step up to the bar, drink some beverber-ages, boozers, and eat sun-dried phrasins, well-made! some bon-bon mots, and swallow some words of the oracle, by Backbook! in this pantagrueling feastival. In this uproar it's all for what and no one on the ball.[3]

Tel bal, telle balle!!! Taal babel . . .

1. Belet . . .:
Bom!

2. Pass over!:
Pasch! Pash, pasha! Pshaw with your serpentacostly riches!

3. Passen!:
Pas sage, votre passe.

4. Peter out, pandering . . .:
Panned out, sans doute.

5. Roping against rope:
In God we trussed. A cordial slogan when you're on the ropes.

Bel et bon,[1] launching a volley of peals. Bal masqué! C'mon you fools, don't stand on the spot all soaked, blocking the exits and nattering nonsense, strop! in your sloppy speech. Pass on,[2] we're at an impass. Into the passing[3] lane, one-on-one, and no more than three seconds apiece.

Pa-rumpa-pan-pan! panted a faunish Peter Pan, wrapped in dry leaves and webs, smacking a skillet with a brass flute. Pan! Pot-a-pan.

Pantry bumpkin! the Bellman belted out, get back to your Never-Never-London, never to return. Pucker up, Peter,[4] someone new will ring your bell. All together now in the hunting of the Snark ark, we'll drift to our London Eden. C'mon sailors, grab your pots, pan-pot-a-pan! and we'll tambouring-a-ding to the bar.

Pots and puns! and lick 'em all clean . . .

We're packed to the gunwales, mates, in this anguishing bottle-neck. Ouïe! Yes! ¡Eso es! Have to sink still deeper in the bar-bottle, st! op! to check in the shipment of fools. To the baar!

Barbaribaasilisk! Cross the bar, hop!

To windward, give her the gas! braving wind and seasickness in our far-traveling vessel. Careful with the flautulences, fluit! and the upchucks. From trumpet, quelle trempette marine! to strumpet. Strop, snaarkists! Horn to thorn. Last toorn, turner, to the Cape of Good Rope.[5]

1. Of good hope, the last thing lost . . .:
The next-to-the-last thing! While there's still life in Cape Dutch . . .

2. Malicious meal:
From bad to worst . . .

3. In Lilliput?:
Putt away, or put out! Our goal a black hole . . . Liliputo! Lilliputa, a Lilliputian bawdy flapper. ((Babel and Milalias on Holland Park Avenue one full moon night, after Rimbaudelaire let loose in The Castle, playing desesperanto variations on the gulliveresque title in the big display window or monstro finestro of the British Esperanto Association. What gulliverve. Babiliputo. Liliputano, putino . . .)) Let me get this straight: sodomite is puto in Spanish but puta means whore and in Esperanto puto means well as in water. What?

Hoop! Pooh! Cutting naughty capers . . .[1]

Belly up to the bar! he bawled, on our bateau ivre, this jolly roger, a hunky dory schooner of foaming schooners . . . Bustle along, bollock up to our buffoon buffet, ambigu comique! there's still spicy sausages, aux vieilles traditions! and entrées for deserters, demandez la recette! and all the spoils of the last sandy supper.

Modderato cantabilis! How's it taste on the return trip?

C'mon goys and gulls, get your gullets ready for the last gulasch, goules goulues! and open up, gueules de loup sur un fond de gueules de bois! since every polyglotton eats his own crow.

Maal![2] From bad to words . . .

Raapidly, to the baar! before the baritone vampyromaniac and his stiff Stone Guest come to revive the embers of the cold supper.

Ghoulash!!! Ash supper . . .

Ghoul! Gul, gulped the scythe-shlepping skeleton. Gulasch gluttony.

Gulp 'em, Gulliver,[3] reels of eels like larvas . . . Aal baar! And continue with your diet of Worms. Made in Babel. Oodles of noodly kitsch and caboodles. Gullible lightweights! open your gullets . . .

1. Güle güle! Gül . . .:
A kommer a karkaakajadas. Eat laughing, sultan, the Bellman shouted at him.
Afiyet olsun!: Bon Appétit.

2. Gum it up!:
Gam! Gam! A gamble to gander at some gams . . .

3. Sucked in?:
Sakin! Careful!

4. At full scream . . .:
Impetuous Susanna (Susanowo now?) and the Turk who wanted to be a druggist . . .
The Grand Turkey, Turko the Terrible in a tight jam. He practically had to leave
running, instant bull! for his native Istanbul.

5. Such an urbane turban. TRAS NIÇIN SART?:
Why get a haircut?!

6. Bash!:
Bosh! Empty head . . .

7. Adam idiota! A damn idiot!:
Eccehomo! Behold the man, insano.

8. Snail? At a snail's pace . . .:
No. A snail pays at the Notting Hill Gate police station. See PILLOW NOTES 24, p.
478.

9. How monstrous!:
Look well upon the wound . . .

10. Mess!:
Messe! And if it be pissible, let this cup pass from me. From mees to mess,
Meester . . . Mest!

Ghoul! Goulash! Ash supper . . .

Goola! Gullet![1] the Great Turk sitting on the floor, gorging himself from a plate of cold cuts in his lap, his red face busy chewing. Dish out! he smacked the plate away and started to pick his teeth with his fingers. Hungry for a generous porktion of all things forbidden. Tabak, alkol et jambon. Ha! Ham! But through his mouth the sinner dies. Ouch! Aching gums by gum![2] What indishestion . . . Too much to eat and drink, turkish torment! at my farewell banquet . . . Then I had to think of going to the Bayswater baths. My word of owner that I went in by mist ache, Sock in![3] in the dressing room of that chased Susanna. Sussa niz a![4] Don't shout . . . Whatta wallop! The killer whale. Whumping my head, Bash! Bash! (raising his hands to his turban of twisted bandages)[5] and still swinging, Bosh![6] and still screaming. Allah! Allah! trying to get away, an Adam[7] in my birthday suit. And then the police station, accused of attempted rape. Turn not pale, billoved snail. Caracol! Caracoles![8]

Escargottoman! Irked, a Turkish skirmish? Shirking, skirting the issue . . .

Quick, polygluttons! the Bellman appealed. Get off your gluttoneous maximi and table the table talk . . . Raapidly! to the baar! he kept repleting, in this messy mess hall the waitresses are going from Messié Messieurs to Messiah and from mixture to Mr. and mesh to message . . .

De mees is the cruelest mess, en masse! a scream and a massive knife slash through the air by the Dutchwoman in brimmed coif and dark peasant dress with white apron. In her other hand a headless rooster. Slashed[9] each month![10] And may I never miss it . . .

1. Klaverbloeding!:
Take another look at the clover of blood, already dark! in her prints on that lucky
Klee-nex. She cut herself opening a can ((De maquereau . . . La boîte de ma
querelle!)) in a fit of anger. And much later, the enervalarvative innervator will
find that dusty kleenex, with the maze of personal traces she stuck in her Album
like a lucky clover . . .

2. Wolf-baying? Double-bolt the door and bolt double-time . . .:
Keep 'em at bay! Who's afraid of the Beowulf?

3. Watch your watch, watchman:
His Serendipity, all serene! It's all found in dreams . . .

A wound that opens each month. And she pointed with disgust at a red stain on her apron: Pick—sick!—the bloody clover . . .[1]

Stalling! Stelling! Stolling! the Bellwringer tolled, writhing. My blood's turning to ice . . . Stremming! Clot in the act! Sleep on a pillow-caution, and even that's not enough, the vampirean witches are coming to their sabbath. With pumposity, lush up! and escorting the great snarcoticized beast.

Graag! Graag! the grunts of a great giant with a gorilla head and a bear body (its thick fur back coated with mud), lashing at the air with a paw and teetering heavily. Gaarg! Graag!

Open your eyes and shoot your best bolt, here comes Grendel![2] the Flying Dutchwoman warned, swinging her rooster in the face of the night watchman[3] in coveralls with a bundle of keys at his waist, nodding off leaning against the wall. Open your eyes, Grendel only eats sleeping kids . . .

Bestelling! Besteling! Beesteling!!! the Bellman flared out, now turned into a fury. The most mooral and beautiful lover's story, the best beautibestiary ever, and I'm here to narrate. With proper benefiction, of course. Now beast it, beat! eat! from the extreme auction to the Sabaat . . .

Tregenda! Tremore! Tránseat . . .

Traan! Tran! Trans! continuing with his belligerent bellrings. Trans! mutation time . . .

Trance! Entrance! the skeleton rattled with his weedy scythe. Entrance!

1. Oogst! Harvest!?:
Oog! St! Watch out! Keep your eyes peeled! The corn is great but few are the cornea-shellers. Don't concern yourself with the motel in your neighbor's eye . . . Careful with that stroboscopic vision!

2. Bran-new . . .:
Another brannigan!

3. Man from La Mancha . . .:
Stainless!

4. And make a sop of this solid globe . . .:
Strength should be lard of imbesilty.

In trance . . ., and Don Juan weakly flapped, his arms wrapped in his cape. In a disappearing trance. Last species . . ., he murmured downcast, his arms making a cross. A roast by any other name . . . A rose has arose is eros. All roses lead to amor. Love, our drug two-night. In time, with accompaniment. Step by step. Appassionata-mente! Carried off. The passage of Sleeping Beauty each night, transfixed with her ear stuck to her transitory transistory, a BBC disease, receiving in dreams. Hey wait. Tough transcrispation, trance by trance . . .

Trance-fiction! False! Falls! Mow down, move on . . .

Oog! gargled the Bellman. Oog! St![1] Blindness, an eye for a night! sans lumières et sans sons.[2] Without lights or lucifers, no rhyme or reason in the expectacle. Out of the way, scarecrow! and he shoved Don Juan, still steadfast in his spread-winged crow-stance. Make way! C'mon folks, don't pay any attention to this numskull trying to mess things up for us. Together, all for one! Fearless and spotted.[3] Speck! Spectre! back off. Everybody to the spectracular cirkus. A big spektakel! Whose name is legion. The best spectacle in the whole wild whirl. With at least two hundred circus numbers. And believe it or not! a surprise in every one. Let's all run to the grillroom.

Mixed grill! Roasted and fried by questions . . .

Every man for himself! And let the world sink. Hold on to your seats, the great theater is collapsing. The Globe!!![4] Glo-glo-glooria! he glottaled, uvululant, shaking the bell. Slews of swells, crest to open-trough, from a tumble in the hey to a-trembling in the tomb! and keep an eye on the oortoography. Your crib for a coffin, what a deal! just let the dead bury the living. Tumble after tumble, round and round it goes. Heads spin, and roll! Oh yes. Severed!

1. A severe reverse!:
Quit your endless revices, but above all: Don't nod!

2. Time already!:
Auspicious and faustuous day for the sowphisticated lady.

3. Lard on!:
The past is repast and your fiction is larded with refections. A (g)lean book larded with the fat of others' works.

4. Lente! Lente!:
Suinoteu Suetonius . . . Pig latin. Spring back and staart again!

5. Trap?:
Part! A bad kick is a good part.

6. The gist of the matter? . . . Purge it:
Gristly. But it's all jest for Emil.

and reversed![1] and he spun his head right and left. Keep your eye on the wrecking ball, it's all going tits up. Throwing swine before pearls, Maargaaritas.[2] Then the Bellman cried out, Silence! Not even a shriek! Everyone will have a turn. Boast when this Circensian aporcalypse is all over! after the fat stuff sweats to death, and lards the stage as he walks along . . .[3] Smear your words, Smeerdiakovs! bellringing to beat the band. Speak fat. Feast of lent.[4] And sue for suet . . .

Talk! Talk nonsense! Smear words of utter inanity . . . con imbecillità!

Trick after rick after kick, trap after trap![5] and he bestowed single peals, as if sprinkling holy water. Wallow after swallow, imp after pimp in this Walpurgist night . . .[6] May your spirits ferment stumultumultuously, Storm und drank! New whines in old bottles. Shampain! for everybody, compliments of the house, Pilsen beer, whiskey & sado pop & Shandy gaffs and mescaal and bloody Marys . . .

Rum! Rum! harrumphing . . .

SNORK! SNARK! SNORK! three hoarse snorts through the snorkel of deep deep sleep. Sopornoxious . . . A case of snarkosis, sí sueñores. Meesmeerized! We have arrived at an hour of soddenly gone morals. So dumb. Again through the uproar the Bellman cried Silence! not even a shriek. Silence! Close your mouths and open your eyes and perk up your ears. Just the place for a great white Snark hunt, I say, a sopportune place, he casually dreamarked, to snark up on a sleeper. In porcupine pose, playing possum. Mal apropos. Hark! Varken! O note de mal! Mark the spot, and the margins too. Mal! Lam. Mark! Kram. Let's march! all together now, to the snark bar.

1. Some bar!:
Sandbar, or snagged on the snack barb. Sandwitches and stinging bellwrings, Bell-damned sans merci! and plenty to go around. Bread and circuses!

2. Pickup? Pica?:
From your so-so peek-a-booze. Pick a . . . So! With a real pica! ((Wasn't that the midget who went down King's Road picking through all the bags and garbage pails of the restaurants? He acts like him. With two sacks on his back. And then we saw him sitting in Picasso inspecting his scavengings and picking at them from time to time . . . A few finicky tourists left in disgust.))

Back! Bak! Vade retro, bakuninlinguist . . .

I ark and I nark and I snark myself silly, the writhing Bellman barked. Smark well my words. Every night after dark I'm obliged to embark, battling the bellowing beast with two backs. Bak! Bak! bacchanalia. And I zoodiacouple bestially, sex! sex! sex! and we serpentwine braying nein! nein! nein! and murmurmoaning we beastify once twice and again, the number of the beast is dacapocalyptical! screwed together till finally I wake up sweat-soaked and thirsty, and fall back asleep. In a bed of slime slap! slip! slop! in the belly of the chameleonine beautibeast.

Slaap! Sleep! Sloop! Pillow talk . . .

To the snaak baar! he gargled, tripping and spinning, To the snaak bark! through the oncoming avalanche of masks in the corridor. To the snark bar . . .

Music, Maelstrom! And careful with the baaton . . .

Boo the tar![1] he spoonerized, let's click the plates lean. Try something, a little of everything. Pick something, picarogues! still belling and battling his way through the tumultuous mass. Let's go, pick it up!

And ring it up! rang out a dwarf Punchinello burdened with two bulging humps, as he dodged the Bellman. Ding! A-ling! More aalmonds. Everyone over there's eating, everyone! Let's have everyone for supper! cancannibale masqué, a little of everyone. Of what oughtn't be et. —Whereof to see the gizzard. Because because because because be-caaaaws—Pick Oz[2] of the wonderful things he does . . .

1. If she offers her honor, and her offer is honored:
Then all night long it's on her and off her!

2. Take care of the sounds and the sense . . .:
And sensibilities! A loose carroll sounding when you're incensed.

3. Sopor? Drowsiness. TORPOR: DROP, ROT:
So dominant, so portentous are the dirty dreams in this Swedish soirée. Sodom and Gomorrah in the Villa de la Maravilla.

4. Lezer? Reader?:
Redeal, leader, and read! Don't be lazy, lezer, less and less can be more . . .
[DEAR READER: (Esteemed? Steamed?)
The great authors can call the reader anything they want: "curious," "unoccupied," "hypocrite" . . . Milalias would have liked to start his novel with a little prologue or kind of short letter beginning Dear Reader:
    —Dear like love? Babelle asked.
    —Dear like dear! You don't know what it costs to have a reader.
DARED READER:
I would like for you, eventually, to leave this excretan larbyrinth on wings of your own picarusque imagination.]

Raaskallen! Rusk à la carte, rascals . . .

Flavor-palettes for palatial palates, he stubbornly retingled, more bell-headed than ever. Appetizers for all appetites, hors d'oeuvres with all orders, and sumptuous punches that go straight to your head. Last round! all together now. In this wake of bells we'll all wind up clappered. Or we'll wake up, splash! in wet dreams. To each his onus, and to few their honor.[1] Whet your whistles, you wet blankets, this is no time to sleep it off.

Waken! Weken! Wekken! Every welter bears his weight . . .

Be vigilant, felons, watch the sound.[2] D'ya fathom? Zondaar! Probe the erroneous depths, erogehenna! where the sun don't . . . Zonde! Zoen! Zoon! buzzed the Bellman, To search and smirk, in smirch of La Mancha, the original stains in Sprain, vlak! flaque! Flac! Flacon! Flock on! Fling yourself into the reading before the sopor[3] catches up with us. Lay sir,[4] leemurs . . . Mutis! Another liter from the magnum opus. Maan does not live by naam alone. Manen! From outrage to outrage for all the manes of hell! They aren't gonna dry up on me, zap! in the middle of moist oneiromances. Tan! Nat! he rang on. Keep soaking and steeping, seamen, it's still not time to die or dry and it's permeating. I mean it's permanent night watch. If you fellows permit me. Let's not be starchy about it, eh? Pakken! Pequen! Pikken! giving blessings or absolutions with his bell. Let it be: that good may come.

Waken! Weken!! Wekken!!! First the solution, and then the poking . . .

1. Powder barrel or powder puff or powder horny . . .:
What must beat, must beat.

2. Wet wit? Dutch bargain?:
Keep the spirit of the liter . . .

3. La fin des fins . . .:
Fins? Snif!: Sniffing about for an end. I figure it's still far away. Ecrire fin . . . Now wouldn't that beat all!?

4. Forked up? And forged too:
The tongue of the forking paths . . . One Pentecosthesaurus day, after savoring his provocables, he said to his babelic beauty: Mm. I regale myself: a word as award. And I'm giving a present, a tongue tip, a gift of tongues, to my tongue. And all will become tongues of my tongue. (Fatter and longer every day. Hold your tongue, if you can handle it!)

And then it's dried and starched . . ., came the head-wagging murmur. And yet another full-press in this insalugubrious laundreamat. Laundering and rinsing and ironing with a velvet hand in an iron glove all the dirty linen of this novelvety thing. Washing your slangue d'oc in this sloop of fool's pools, bateau-lavoir!

Lavement! Leven! and liven up . . .

Sound off! The good, the bad, and the dingly . . . Rondodo à la clouchette! now ringing in slow motion, Bel et Bel! . . ., spinning and swaying. Din! Don! Now to find some sucker to clear tables and accounts.

PARTY TRAP! Trattoria trauma . . .

All right you noodleheads, micmacaroni! we had practiced pasta perfect and were preparing pasta progressive. And now, passed over by time, we're pasta-due for the pasta participle. Let's swab the deck and scrub the joint, missmash! bottles down and tables up. We gotta real mess on our hands. And nobody seems to realize, la Sainte barbe! that we're sitting on a powder keg.[1] Tin! Ton! now spinning and Ton! Tin! ringing maniacally. Roll roll roll your boat to the baar . . .

Tone! Ton! Baarbaritone! Drunk as a skunk . . .

Rondo all around, just as I like it. Lap, pal! slapping the cabin boy in a blood- and mud-stained shirt continually upending his black bottle. Lap, pal! wet your words[2] again. Lapsus after lapsus, in slaapsussen! with my dirty ragbag tongue. Play deaf and don't worry about me, my friends, even I don't know what I'm telling you. Sleep it off, buddies. This pun-slinging spree-for-all is coming to its natural end.[3]

Sla! Slaan! Slang! Boomslang! With a loose tongue, and forked too . . .[4]

1. Kip?:
Kip, pig. Look well, chicken.

2. Benedicamus!:
BENEDICOMUS!

3. Who's the monk in the domino?:
He who spent the best part of a life playing word games. Le Grand Prêtre-à-partir.
The Great Master. Tu se' lo mio maestro e 'l mio autore. The one who guides us in
this dark forest.

4. All is permitted, if nothing is—:
Sh! Sh! Alla muta. Here everything is spermissible, giving away the license.
Totuus! Vale!

In jingo-bell slang! the Bellman gongadingling, that peals and peels and repeals till the fat lady rings. (We'll give her the bells and let her fly!) Let's see who tingles and tangles in this midnight mudness. A vicious—viscous!—nightmare that bites its own tail.

Pik! Kip!¹ Pique of the pack . . .

Stop! Pots! lifting his hands to his head, Top! Put! everything's spinning on me. What a brick-à-braque! in this bric-a-bark of fools. And before you know it the most macharonic one will be looking for us, in his ferry. Carry on in the meantime, eat, drink, and have a swell time. Everybody to the baar!

Coupe de barre! No holds barred at the free bar . . .

And no bards holed up! Follow the liter, lads, to the baar! now tingling tenaciously. To the snark bar! everything's carte blanche. Men, do you want me to read you the menu again? and the ringmaster suddenly unrolled, with one bell-peal, his white scroll. Lend me your ears, boys and beldams. Dutch rolls and French carrolls, jolly rollocks! punkakes and ale, sandwitches and shamburgers and barbaricued chops and launchmeats still available in the baarbaric bar . . .

A la barre, barbaragouineur!

Benedicomus² Domino! Latintonated a hooded monk³ in a black domino, launching himself into the tangled troupe crowding around the long central table.

Comus all allows! He permits and permutes all . . .⁴

1. Sitio? Make room, latinlubber.:
A seat for a sinner. Sitio. And don't throw in the towel . . .

2. Qui feut premier, soif ou Sainte-Beuverye?:
Thirst first again! Oui, mais arrêtez vos causeries! Stop your maundy meddling chats!

3. Domine, dirige nos:
Lord, lead us. Milalias liked the London motto so much . . . And he gave his mentor Mr. Reis an ashtray (Babelle's plunder from Selfridges) engraved with London's coat of arms and motto.

4. Sik?:
You'll get his goat, you kidder!

Sitio!¹ elbowing his way through. Sitio! I'm thirsty!² and he groped
around the table until he managed to trap a bottle. Glo-glory to the
Lord, happily draining it. Glo-glo-glos! . . ., he gurgled, swallowing
air and dripping the last drops of wine into his open mouth. It is
finished . . ., he sighed, and tossed the bottle.

Fiasco di vino! A complete fiasco . . .

Domine, dirige nos . . .,³ said Don Juan, muffled in his cape, and he
scowled about scornfully. Everybody here is drunk, completely
wasted. Seems like all the alcoholic bums in London decided to
show up at this party. Like that afternoon in Islington. A crowd of
hungry thirsty bums fighting over the leftovers. Spoils and dregs
snatched in the scuffle. Flock of fleecers! You shall know them by
their workovers? Here nobody recognizes anybody else, no one
knows who was who. Better to go back to the Hall of Mirrors.

Glaze! Glas! Glace! That clochard will toll for thee . . .

Hey wait! Don Juan rushing after Sleeping Beauty, Every don has
his dame . . ., who was resolutely sleepwalking (: toward the
door?) through the crush of snaking masks, murmuring her double
half words. Wait! This one won't eat in or out! Live and let dine.

Manducemos et bibamos . . ., dissonated the monk in blackface
with a chef's hat, fiddling with his onion rosary. Let's eat and drink
as much as we can, tomorrow's just another day. Another day,
another diet! Eat, for tomorrow you'll be eaten. A good bite and a
good scream. Aai! One of God's servants, Fraai Gil, gaar-
gaarantees it. And I was an altarboy before I was a bussboy. Sic,
sick . . .,⁴ and he winked at the Bellman. First monk and then chef.

1. Or would you rather have another part?:
He says it in slang. Yes, Dick.

2. Steek?:
Stab! in the back, and to Tartarus.

3. Manic monk, leave this house of rook and role . . .:
From rok to rut till it's rock-a-bye booby . . .

In that ship of fools, and then in the worst diner in Rotterdam. Saucy sausages ... dank dames ... baccharnal sins in the Rotterdam canals ...

Rotar! Rooter! Rôtir! Rotting from root to roast ...

Rot! Rots! how many routs ..., and he let out a hearty beer burp. From Rota to rout to Rotterdam ... Lucky they didn't drag me before the ecclesiastical tribunal ...

Rota! A la barre! To the bar ...

Drink up! Drunk rip, shriners! now leaping like a drunken bear, rolling up his habit. Dink rup! then toss it overboard in this brothy brothel ... Putain de vie! Drink and be happy and eat stewed partridge, by golly!

Always partridge![1] And may we never lack ...

Eat and be merry, and he drew a skillet from his habit, for tomorrow ... Tomorrow? Cold cuts. Eat, perishables, and ... Want me to cook you a stout steek tartar?[2] A fat chop sur le gril? Cured zalmonnik?[3] Dark sole of the night? Meat's my forte. Shot o' briand with bordelaise sauce and garlic, look! my specialty. The best from each kuisine. And at the top of my carta maagna: Un coq dans chaque cocotte!

Rococoricoq-à-l'âne! Rooting for the roosting-toasting plowboy ...

Cock-ya-diddle-do! Don Juan crowed, flapping his cape. Going off half-cocked? From now on, don't count your chicks before they're laid ...

Kikirikirie! A cockier gallant will sing to us ...

1. Mousse sans mousse! Just musing . . .:
Mousse? Don't you have any pastries without clashes or cabin boys? Alright already! Meerenge von Calais, ja! to the rich meringue whipped up with all its foam!

2. Mare? Mehr?:
We all want more. And that crapulous cabin boy must be able to drink the sea. La mer: a Martinique of martinis for that salty dog; a marsh of marsalas from Marshalsea.

3. The motto of Cambronne:
Toujours dans la bouche de Monsieur Bouchon, Merde. Proshit! Booze on, Bouchon, drain the baby bottle to the lees . . .

4. In a black mood?:
With just a little rubbing, shiny as silver. Like his black night in white. Nit! Tin! ARGENTINA LA NIT NEGRA: Argentine the nite. Like his cup. Black.

5. Some loves kill . . .:
There is Death in the cup—so beware! Drink, and all is forgotten. This last cup is on the house.

6. Not my cuppa!:
Right. You're not culpable. BORE, ROB?: See PILLOW NOTES 25, p. 479.

7. Cup us, till the world go round!:
Portentous, ma non tropport.

8. There's many a slip of tongue 'twixt the cup and the lip.:
Stop your pining for pints, noctivagant argotnaut.

9. Luz!:
Luz, Lucifer! Luz, bel sprit. Sternebrous Bellman . . .

Weedding Tart, the Bellman cackled, almost time for our just desserts. Knuckle sandwiches and sugar smacks and slapjacks, a special batter made from scratch! with dollops of whipped butter, soda pop or have a hit from our power-packed punchbowl. Tarte à la crème fouettée. C'mon go-getters, we've got gogolden pastries. Mousse au choc-chocolat![1] and he pointed at the muck-covered cabin boy.

Mer . . . mer . . .,[2] the seasick cabin boy staggering, desperately shaking a bottle over his mouth. Merde![3]

C'mon to the Snark baar! we've got gobs of goblets, we'll be gobblin' and goblins and . . . Apokaalipsis! and he raised his bell, last drinks, knirds!

Ja Pokalypse! All well topped off . . .

Let this cup pass from me . . ., and Don Juan slid a black cup[4] from under his cape. If it be possible . . ., offering it on high. Loving cup![5] O felix cuppa![6] No one wants it, the acopalyptic cup? My cup runs over, all over. Where's my head. Skull! he toasted. Cup out! and tossed it over his shoulder. Cup us![7] staring at the Bellman. A couplet's worth more than a high-sounding bore . . .[8]

Cupless? the Bellman with a ring of his bell. Pay your bar bill, cough it up, bird of ill omen. C'mon hardheads. Allons-y les copains! To the snark bar . . .

Barmy barman! Barmecide Feast in the dark![9] Ghosts of future repasts . . .

Tan! Tan! Traan! How about a sip of church wine, from the Black Mass! De mon cru. Hard on! The wine that washes my sins. Night after night. Just a taste, eh? Just a sip from the catheteer . . .

1. Dillydally with a new deal? Dallying with your daily lingo?:
Yes, darlinguist!

2. Taal kwal?:
Tongue disease . . . Idiomédusé!

3. Logomachiavillain?:
Bel et bien . . ., bel ami Belpheghor. Ring the hallowed bell!

4. Now and in the ear of oor death?:
Oor-log! ((: Oorloog!)) Quit keeping time . . . Bel Bello! Bella, horrida bella . . ., on a war-footing. Aai! Oorpijn! Hard of hearing! [It is maagnificent, but it is not waar.]

5. Or disappointed . . . What is the hour?:
Always the last. And on the dot! Are you waiting for God-Dot? Back it up . . .

.

((Blackout? Just a little short circoitus. A sample of handywork by this apprentice in the trade of darkness. Darkness as black as his soul. A foreshadow. A show, black velvet! of his black banderole.))

Darken, sham! Dank! tentatively tinkling with his eyes closed. Taste it or detest it. To the bar! From drink to clink, felons. Don't fell, mongers! Want me to skin you alive in one fell swoop? Hurry up, gallgallop, op! We've still got dregs of pots à eau de kolkologne. Au poteau! Potence, forzat! Foamy beer from the casket, cocktails from a tub and wail-drinks, VAT not included! bière noire from the black forest, knock on wood! Moloctov cocktails and sack and punch and zombies and Black Velvet for the mourning after . . .

Rekieskant in pace! Rockiescunt impasse . . .

Dun! Dunk! Dank! now bowing and discharging another round with the bell. Let's go, you crapulous runaways, this crap's gone too far. Fecease and desist! Much ado-do when the chit hits the fan. Don't give me any more chit-chat . . . Dun! Dung! Dun!

Dally! Dally! dalliance and delirium . . .

Daling! Deling! Diling![1] The account and tally is the telling. Tel quel. Tal kwaal![2] In Dutch, a little hispenalized and anglosaxed to death. Double Dutch, —natuurlijk! High-flying Dutch, man, in a Dutch roll. Yeah. Dat is waar. Babellicosely. Ring the babell and they all fall asleep. Such a peal! Stay awake! sleepyheads. Wake up! felons. We'll run a rapid relay vigil à la Machiavigil.[3] In love as in war. We'll bomb right along! Bom! Bon! Now and in the hour . . .,[4] —sh! at the appointed hour.[5] Call it what you like!

Leap from lid to lead to lied to lies . . .

1. O sanguine and subtle Dolores . . .:
Our Lady of Spain!

2. Tongval!:
From valley to val, monteur de coups. Attention aux liaisons dangereuses!

3. Vailing . . .:
Veilinguist! Give the devil his veiling. Another Dutch bargain!

4. A faction? A fiction? No, it's a bastion!:
What a card. An ace? A joker? He ought to be dealt with!

5. Tortueux! at a turtle's pace . . .:
Caray! Carey! And with more shells than a terrapin . . .

6. The dirty old man . . .:
Oui, le vieux père vert galant!: Mr. Schild, the Paddington pawnbroker. Hard-shelled when it came to money. Inflexible with Milalias, but he softened a bit with Babelle. So he used to send her in first, as his advance guard. You see, Miss, dis old junk dypewrrrider izzend vorrth a shillink. Bud if you would like, and he gently passed his cane over the keys, if you would like, and here a sigh, you I could adfance fife pounts . . .

7. No! As, as . . .:
No! Ashes. They must be ashes.

8. Aas . . .:
Aasfresser!

War and loves, yes enemas and frenzies, I mean friends and enemies, a thousand pains for a moment of pleasure . . . Oh Lol-as! Oh la la! discoordinating his lalation, the smaller they are the bigger they act . . . Aai! Dolores![1] that I never finish telling. Gaiety and rejoicing, tomorrow will be ashes. Asaai! There'll be time enough to refine the pains and penalties. And he turned around halfway, slowly, pointing with bellrings: Tang! Ting! Tong![2] Everyone's gotta pay sooner or later. Tally on! Stir up the fire, it's going out. Every master must muster his mastications. This is a Dutch party, as they say, a sham masquerade with ruthless consequences. Polyglutinous! A babbellow of Saint John, tingling! tangling! or bellipotent party, ring ring! or jingle ball. Bring on the auction now . . .

Veiling![3] Failing! Falling! His club on high . . .[4]

Baste! Enough! Don Juan turned around lifting his left arm, Assez! Baste! and removed and replaced a card up his sleeve. Join the club . . . Hush! putting his index to his lips. On high? What more could he want . . ., looking slyly and stealthily to his right.

Head and pace of a turtle:[5] the old Methuselah in a green frock[6] who approached, hunched and quivering, groping about with his cane. From ace to ace . . .,[7] mouth agape with asphyxia—or fright. Aas![8] openmouthed, caning around toward the yellow divan at the other end of the hall. And trying to look (: his eyes bulging!) through a gap in the wall of onlookers. I have here, rummaging around in a hip pocket, yes indeed right here I have the lucky clover. Such is my luck . . ., he added, stretching his neck.

Bel! Belening! Beloning! Bababelooooo . . .

1. Daw? Daw?!:
Dawdle off . . .

2. Dropping!:
Gout by Gotha, babaptized. Gotcha!

3. Dode! Dodo!:
As dead as a dodo!

4. Droom! Moord!:
Fais dodo! Dodeline mon dodu dodo, fall into a bottomless sleep . . .

5. Tutto è maia, maialone!:
His Majesty, my jester, go voyeurize another more majestic maja. And lift the vail.

6. Ma querelle!:
Maquereau! Makker Makreel, once again with your procuress Celestina? The great coupler Frau Koppel, also alias Frau Kuppel! Go see if there's some vacancy or bacchancy in her asscourt agency . . .

7. From dood to dot . . .:
Dot. Final point. Little angel, to heaven or hell you are promised.

Babbellen! Bellen! Billen! the petulant babble of a fop in powdered wig, tight waistcoat and trunk hose of raisin-colored velvet, as he studied some impertinent fellows before him in the chorus of curious onlookers around the divan. Il faut gagner la belle! gallantly stretching on tiptoes. Ma belle dame sans merci! The die is cast, for better or worse, and whatever will be will be. But I think this femme fatale, the last thing we need! is not yet on my list . . . ((Fat! Fatalist!))

Do-do-dobbellen, a guy with a dodo bird face stuttered, jerking with convulsive movements, Do-do-doubles! or as if vigorously shaking some dice. Dó! Dó![1] redoubling, Do-do-doping![2] dropping his big blackish beak against his chest. The race is over! Finis! And with two quick explanatory gestures, Whish! Wish! he made an X in the air. Yes. Extinct. I'm the last. And he resumed his doddering do-de-do-do . . .[3] ((Oui. Dodo![4]))

On the divan upholstered with floral patterns in yellowish damask, stretched out with legs crossed and hands behind her neck, a veiled bride stealing the show (: svelte girlish body, provocativoluptuous . . .), a thick white veil over her face and her white crepe dress curled over her knees and gathered over her bottom, reposing in the pose of an erotic maja,[5] intent on the insinuating gesticulations of Madame Celestina,[6] with a black shawl over her head and her left eye blotted by a blue-white spot.

The Bride in cash, Madame Celestina sounded off in a cavernasal voice, and la dot and the dot,[7] wavering, and the fiancé as finance! ((Radoteuse!))

1. Beau geest!:
Yes, the kind that gets on your nerves . . .

2. Staged and upstaged!:
La Mémériée mise à numéro gagnant, par ses célibabataires . . .

3. Another spin!:
Loop-the-loop, and wend your way . . .

4. Sheet!:
Winding sheet descending from heaven. A white sheet is the bride of the prolific writer, and the shroud of the true righter. Winding-up! Please, no more curve balls . . . Winding! Rise! He runs through the Roses of the Winds with his novellette. Smell. Spell. And expell . . .

5. Wait till it sounds true . . .:
In that noisy party. Dealing! Dealing! delinquent. Snood! Snoot! Snot! and another sniff.

6. Fun-fair play . . .:
Fun fare! Fanfare!

7. Retail?:
In installments.

8. Around and around on a carrollsel:
Carrollcelerating! [And thick and fast they came at last. And more, amor, and more. Enclore! Encore!]

I beg your hand! the raised voice—in falsetto—and right hand[1] of a captain of the Legion, short and barrel-shaped, his face covered with a skull mask of cracked peeling plaster. A sainted hand . . ., he added in a low voice. I am the official groom, and I request your hand. And he paraded about, Plunk! Plunk! in a heavy stomp: I'm a man who went through the military coup de main . . .

Wedden![2] Wedding! Wending![3] Those wedding balls are wringing . . .

From ball to baal . . ., Don Juan wrung his hands, restlessly pacing around the divan. Well-balanced, indeed. Knap! and he started to tug on his fingers, Knap! cracking his knuckles, Knap! Another one, Knap! another crush . . . I'd bet my head she'll finally fall. The more I bet, the easier it is to lose her? The mysterious bride . . ., hidden behind her veil.

Winding![4] Winning! Whinnying! Another rodeo . . .

The fact is something there rings a bell,[5] Don Juan exclaimed, staring at the Bride on the divan. White legs of a sprightly filly, and well developed . . . Bull's-eye. The one from the fairground stall,[6] in Chelsea? Prends du champ! Go back. Or the picaresque landlady of that fleabag hotel in Ramsgate? Summer fruit. Peach cheeks, a sweet pooper! No, not so green, that one. Go back. Other tails in other sales,[7] with a humorous snort, and guest who's coming to dinar . . . Get thee behind thee, Beelzebubble. Assbackwards. Round after round. Still more prowls. Swing your partner.[8] ((RENTRAP!))

Beding! Bieding! Boding! The bugger they are, the ardor they fall . . .

1. Psychoanal Isis?:
The diva on her freudulent divan . . . Couchemerde! The valiant man who finally unveils that high-valued woman must reveal her from reveille to revel.

2. From angel to Angelus!:
Don't look back in angel. Fallenangel, let's see if you take the bait and swallow the hook . . .

3. Time is money is time money . . .:
TIME NOTES!: SET ON! EMIT!

4. Time bomb?:
Tic! Tac! Tic!

5. Mark:
Markt twist.

6. Quelle plaie, Sire!:
Yes, press a finger on that wound that never heals . . . Wounderful!

May the best imposter raise the veil and the impost . . ., Madame Celestina proclaimed. Op! Hop! The posture is the imposture. Who's the fairest? The man of fortune! This precious thing is price-less, as whoever achieves her most secret enchantments will confirm. And she brushed the bride's veil with her scrawny fingers. To know a veil . . . This evening's great mystery . . . Vale!

Beding! Beding! Bedding! Already recumbent . . .

Bonne mine à mauvais jeu, and Don Juan moved to lift her veil. No, it's still not time, turning back to Madame Celestina. Aars loonga . . ., retreating entranced . . . As long as . . . without taking his eyes off the bride sprawled on the sofa. Let her hide her ass,[1] he broke out laughing, and show her false face!

Look on this angel's face[2] and then die . . ., Madame Celestina still chattering easily to the chorus of onlookers. Oh yes! The dearest face of all . . . But cheap, taking everything into account. A gift. Hurry up, vamos! time is gold.[3] Fulminating.[4] And this novice bride can't wait anymore, she's just burning. May the best bettor or bidder bed her. To the highest card! Holy union, aces to aces. C'mon, some good-looking guy. To marry, from mark to market, everybody meets her and nobody guesses who she is. Who'll bet? she looked around challengingly, her hands on her hips. I expect every man to do his beauty. C'mon, bid! who'll step up to raise the veil . . . A genuine bargain! A real special! Who'll be the one to unveil her? To see her pretty face and then die from pleasure . . .[6] There must be some valiant courter?

Escorting! Korting! Courting!

1. Ra! Ra! Rap! Raise the masts high!:
High, men. Take a flying jib at the futtock shrouds, watch the spanker-boom and batten the hatches. Bate! Ten eigen bate! To your own benefaktion.

2. Golfspel!:
Swept up by the Golfstriem! The Flying Debtman, engulfed and sent away . . .

3. Vloek? Oath?:
Both.

4. Pots and puns, Dr. Pangloss!:
Potsenmasker! Fais la popote, manie le popotin!

5. Damspeling!!!:
Damn! Expelling!

6. Steenklaver!:
Klaverwondering!

7. Goede worgen!:
Morgen! To the morgue. And keep on strangululating . . . Or mar, men.

8. First pass by customs. Watch it!, shifty do-nothing . . .:
Shifting dunesday! or elegy of the bedouin: La duna è mobile . . .

9. Captain of the ship of fools?:
Narragony of Herr Narrator. The Flying Dutchmandolinist!

10. A real puzzler . . . Grief! Greif!:
Griffier! Cut the gryphon . . . Griffonneur!

11. Mon piaf, arrête de piaffer!:
Muziek, Mester!

Raise your bids! the Bellman screamed again. Ra! Ra! Rabat![1] If that's a Dutch auction, I'm a Dutch uncle. A Flying Dutchman-nikin! A Dutchmaster, baiting you all. A plaything of the waves.[2] That come and go. Tell it to the marinettes . . . A fluke[3] and a love in every port. Havenerisch! Sworn to secretion.

Portmanteaus and seamen! Semensmelting pots![4] From dame to dam . . .[5]

Love from sea to sighing she, he murmured, tinkling softly, all to see the miracle of miracles . . .[6] Mare Clausummum. In search of a faithful woman. And reunion in a strong embrace[7] (with you?) with a loyal life-companion. One who always arrives on the dot. One who doesn't desert us at the last minute. Not like the others. All those midinettes de minuit, miduinettes![8] that go to bed when their husbands get up. Ay! And put the horns on them . . . Les maris honnêttes sont les marionnettes! And on with the twists and turns, dizzying! with so many circumvulvacillations . . .

Twist! Twist! Twist and turn! Torn and return . . .

So many cinderellas, a thousinderellas! he rang again and made a complete spin, that we lose count. And let me point out that I'm referring particularly to the exorbitant accounts of the Great Captain.[9] His twenty thousand colleagues under the siege . . . Captain Nemoral ambosched with his succubi. Haremmed in with his provocaptivating houris . . . Nemo me impune lacessit! one of his latinate mottos. Employing mnemotechnic rules to remember his vernerean adventures in vernacular argot? Grant Kaputain! The captain fails. Horribilicribrifaxen![10] Daradiridatumtariddle! The sound and the furies ((or the shaming of the true?)). From note to noot, musmusicus![11]

1. Argout?:
I'm not so sewer, rat . . . A hard drain's gonna fail.

2. From slang to slang . . .:
Still slithering with your forked tongue! Someday she'll come, she who will crush your head . . .

3. Paling! Paaling!:
Palingenesis!

4. Bankrott!:
Bettrügerischer bankrott! Freudulent breakdown, left bankrapt . . .

5. Bella . . .:
Bellíssima! Cunt on your fingers!

6. Nit! Nit! Nit!:
Tin! Tint! Tinteling! Tingalinging on a dark dalirious nit del foc! Firenight. / Fie! Nit, for nite. Nit.

To trill's the thing! o bird of ill omen. Argoading in argoot![1] And clean your beak to sing. Merde merde! Besmirched going in, and going out. Getting all muddied, Moddernienisering! with his modern natty dregs. And dragging himself through the lower depths. Through the darkest cellars, klokclomping through the cloacal rooms. Caracoles and ringamarolls and serpenetrations in slang . . .[2]

Ringing! Wringing! Wroeging! Another bell of rites . . .

Such a mess, with mestization, that you lose your composure. His retinue of messalinas and salomes, the cruelest stained with blood . . . From mess to mees! In cold blood. Such a wound that the knife is lost in it. From each to leechline.[3] Man the weaker vessel! Build me a goodly vessel, staunch and strong! Sangfroid and iced sangria to beat the Sanguiness Book record. What a Shangriaal for our bankrupt[4] Parsifal!

Stalling! Stelling! Stolling! And staunching . . .

But this month we're in the red . . . It's true, the numbers don't lie. I mean what I say. Measuring my words in this meeting. Here each mate meets his helpmeet. Me, teen. Meteen! All in the same whole, mon troubadour. That's right. Pussy-pussy, let's see who'll bell jar the cat . . . And brandishing the bell over his head, Bell a figure![5] he blasted out three tremendous peals. Silence! What I tell you three times is true. And before the cuckoo clock sings three times . . . Niet! Niet! Niet![6]

Nood! Noot! Nooit! Nonetheless, the nun at the noneplus . . .

This really thickens the plotboiler beyond recount, Don Juan said. And not even God himself would understand it, he added, stopping in front of the Bellman. All badly pornounced and syllabdicated

1. Spooling!:
Yes, rack your brains. And get a paleospelunker to decipher this deep dark desperantro. Or a laryngeologist. Spoeling! Gargling! and go gaargaargle! (More of that baalbelic diabolect . . .)

2. KRANS!!!:
A crown (thorny? inrisible!) for our dreaming snarkist.

3. Slop, Dr. Slop!:
Slope! Recover your losses and undone deeds and recount to a hundred or more, of what's given up for lost . . . Argobbling up, argot by gargot, the sternebrossa night.

4. Notre carte d'étendre?:
De tendre! Tender is the night, our eternal white night.

5. Ruggelings!:
The cards face up . . .

6. Give birr first to give birth after . . .:
With Don Johannes Fucktotum there's no problem! Coupling coil.

7. Noah's Snark!:
All the animals in one . . . Eh, great patriarch? (Noaks ark. Sheet after sheet.)

8. In the mud . . .:
In the sopor of his sensual sty. Marasmus after the marathon, a sticky wicket! of the Villa of Maravels.

and badly spilt too. Spelling! Speling! Spoeling![1] throwing his head back and modulating with a grimace: Another round of number-garbargling . . . ((Gaargaargler!))

Silence! the Bellman shouted. We've got to throw ourselves into it, and throw out what's left over. Our orineiric restorations. Rest! Roest! Rust! The rest is . . ., he stuttered looking around. Silence! We'll see who's daring. Silence! What I tell you three times is undeniable. No! Nod!! Node!!! notably descending to and ascending from, on the nod, the lower depths of Noderland. And he roared with his three hoarse cries: Snark! Snork!! Snark!!![2]

Slaap! Sleep! Sloop![3] Have to sleep on it . . .

Let's see who gets up the hunt . . ., he murmured tinkling. From reef to reefer, from rock to wrack. Roll on! and again he unrolled his white map.[4] You've got it all here, mais oui! charte blanche . . . All described and indicated with sympathetic ink. Down to the last detail. And tail. The erogenous zones and the corners where the rug-rug[5]-rugged beast with two backs hides . . .

Pairs! Peers! Piers![6] Coupling from copula to couplet . . .

I arc and I bark and I snark[7] and I scarcouple, he death-rattled and writhed, embedded with the kaaleidooscopic beast. Everchanging! And always changing tune in the tourneys. Then slipping and sliding out of my hands, whoosh! aal gone! when I catch her. And she gets away from me, whoosh! and I'm stuck,[8] all bogged down when I wake up . . .

Temming! Stemming! Beestemming! Another shaming of the true . . .

1. Snark it!:
Get out of here! They don't hear how the ansnarkist ensnares himself, Snarkning! Snarkning! in his ark . . . Go, Bellman, sound the bell and announce the wedding of the barbarous two-backed beast in this bacchanal.

2. Il l'a brunie. A la brune!:
Au crépuscule . . . When the fires were burning. Burning fires of lovers. Filles du feu! : Feuilles!

3. Nood!:
Noot! Nutsessity is a hard master.

4. Screw the nut up thight!:
And give it another spin . . .

5. Wij worden nat . . .:
Yeah, we're getting wet! You've got to get wet or dry up.

6. To the rescue, dissolute . . .:
Les anglais ont débarqué. In Donkerker. In Dunkeerke!

7. Lethal art? Spell better your letter:
The letter kills? The first letters . . . A, B, transfusing a new spirit of the letter: *I know your type, Dr. Sangrado. Staunch!* Ah yes, but the mot d'esprit revives! came a vivid reply from Milalias, who believed blindly that the vast majority of writers write in a dead tongue. [No circulation?] Classic and necromantic authors! [Ook: grafomania or grave graphomania.]

Brr! They bellow bellicosely, he said lowering his voice, when you least expect it. At the critical moment. On the spot! When all is calm. I engage with the Snaark,[1] he sang softly, every night after daark . . . the enervalarvating Snark. Je suis le thrènebreux . . .[2] I sue it and pursue it, I purslew it with frocks and hope in an endless perseconsecution. Sanguinolent. A menstruous nightmire. Noot![3] Nut![4] Nat![5] You've got to get wet to cross the extreme. Swimming and swimming till we're back safe in our drydreams. The sornographic pollution of the thorny problem . . .

Oplossing! Lossing! Lossing![6] What a loss . . .

Alert! Red Alert! Alert! he shouted, We've got a real bloodlettering![7] With droppings drooping ever more rudely, and still no snout in sight. Animalingnancies of an animalingerer. For the Snark was a Boojumbo! you see. Boo-hoom! And this is the most sopportune place for a Snarkist! You'll see when I get my claws on it and even up the score. In private. Without ringing any belles. And he looked around perplexed, a suspenseful pause, at the circle of curious bystanders now milling about to hear his long-winded discoarse.

Start! Start! Staart! To caracole . . .

Friends, roamers and accountlessmen, as he rang his bell three times, lend me your ears! now ringing his bell furiously. Toss the ballast over the edge. Last but not list. Last out! to slenderize. Laster! Laster! there's still some left . . . And he turned in a violent volt, airing out his bell pell-mell. We have sailed redbeardedly several months over the seven seas of insanity in the ship of fools and now it's time to atone up for the Snarkel. Is that clear?

Mass! Mess! Miss! Without remission . . .

1. Non! Non!:
Nonsens!

2. Nod, don!:
Done!

3. Nol-prossed!:
No, proscribe the scribe . . .

4. You young Rip!:
Thus you'll see how twenty years pass, the best ones of his life . . . Sh! Sip the
Hollands! Requiescat in pace. Rip.

5. The harder they fall . . .:
And so, from hour to hour, we ripe and ripe. And then from hour to hour, we rot
and rot: and thereby hangs a tale. Another Milalias motto: life is brief and we are
brevas: figs moving toward $\frac{r}{v}$apid fruition. To reach old age, follow this advice: If
you're in no hurry to fertilize the earth, delay, delay your maturation . . .

6. Tij! Tijd!:
Doodtij! do it to kill time . . .

7. I know a bank whereon the wild time blows . . .:
Sh! And there the Snark throws her enamel'd skin.

Months and months mesmerized . . ., he mused, a bit meshugga, with a blank expression. Days and days in a daze . . . Hours and hours gone sour . . . Without a wink of sleep. Paying a high price for each fault. Never losing sight of the Gold Cost. So high. So many travails. Consult the huuroskoop . . . and put up the peniskoop! Three sheet-winds to the wind, and no sheet anchor! over the waves from sea to mer to mère to mar to marrow in this pretty pace after the Blatant Beast! hunting the loudmouthed beast with his hundred-plus tongues. All to get to the end, nonchalantly, of this nunsensical[1] night of Saint John. Without getting a good night's restorative sleep, at a gallgalloop to get as soon as possible to our promised . . . our Promiscuous Land, don! Land of our eternal dreams.

Nod![2] Nol![3] Londonkey-doodling and londonjuandering . . .

Our Noderland! he shouted, our featherland. Off the mop! White. Like our night. Nod! Node! nodding assent. And now we're swampled, Moddernacht! on this bank. Delen! Delen! Double dealing to share, belling furiously, the Great Divide-end. Everyone to the trombone of contention. But now I realize we're in a real jam session . . . And the fateful hour is about to fall.

Rip![4] Rip! Ripe![5] And falling foul . . .

Hush! Don Juan shushed. Cut a fine figure. Fi! Figa-Figa-Figaroo yes! he figargled, looking at the sleepwalker. This mutant mutterer-of-fact would muddle even the cleverest . . . ((Fi! garou beau marché!))

Tie! Tight![6] then he delicately pealed: Darling! Darling! Daling! no more dallying. Now and in the hour . . . Time, please![7] Closing time, let's get out of here. From mortal sin to death scene. Matinee already? No way! let's go. One more step, stap! toward the fateful

† 183 †

1. Tarot cards!?:
An altered deck. Like the one Albert Alter made—taking his friends and acquaintances as models—commissioned by the patron Mr. Tod.

2. An ax to grind?:
Find more axes of rotation, Bellman, or you'll get the ax . . .

3. Spanish retort? Or insolence, he retorted:
Elixir of the assassins quintessenced by the verbal alchemist.

4. To each vassal his vessel, Joker:
A jug to jog our jocular Milalias, before he knocks everything ajar.

5. Another? It's ball and sing as you're balancing your overdrawn chickbook:
Inexhaustible. Changing disguise every other step? Babelle would get the feeling that the Annotator was multiplying his divisions (The Ass? The Alchemist? The Statue of the Stone Guest? Now Oberon?), trying to emulate Milalias. I alone am always the same, she pointed out. The same as always . . . [Addition by Herr Narrator, with a pen stroke: The very self-shame!]

6. See ya tomorrow!:
Tomorrow will be another day . . ., another devil. Right now, the diabolus ex machina is a perpetual motion machine.

point, stip! and stop! everybody stop. Then he screeched to a halt in front of the wing chair in which a devil was sunk, his head nodding, wrapped in his cloak, holding between his gloved hands a handful of tarot cards.[1]

Tot ziens!: See you later . . .

Halt! Alt! Finish it up, Jacktar . . ., an angry herculean woodsman shouted, making a threatening gesture with his mighty ax[2] at the Bellman. Come to teerms with the termination. Tot straks!: See you soon, and he penetrated the dense forest of masks, wielding his farewell ax.

Ober! . . . Oberon! Don Juan called to the red-bearded waiter wearing a king's crown, who swayed through the crowd, his left hand clutching a retort of wine[3] and his right hand holding on high a tray of vials and glasses.[4] What are these ex-tracts of pensive pansies? Another one who wrung his brains out . . . Like a zombie. Away from it all. Waiter, the bill![5]

Trip away, distant journey, turn without return. Long gone. Don't stop till everybody's getting infused in unison. See you later hell-benders. Long gone. We'll encounthunder each other at the first lightning of day . . ., and he sank, retorting in the mare magnum.

Tot morgen![6] Good mourning! the Bellman spun swaying before the wing chair. Morguenne! Going straight to my head is spin-ning . . . Hell! And discharging three epileptic bellrings, Stap! Stip! Stop! he collapsed in a heap.

Alhambresque

1. An Arabian Nights Entertainment, scored for instruments:
Or scarred from entertwinement.

2. Rock? Roc rocambolesque?:
From rococock to the golden ass!

3. His sails reefed? A crooked frame of reeference . . .:
Kif kif. Oui. Kief kief. Quif!

4. From a bird's eye view?:
Bird of Paradox. Rara Avis . . .

5. Simoon of the Desert?:
With a sigh, mon déserteur; be careful with those vampersands of the desert . . .

6. Steel falcon?:
May your bird be with you: Steal away and see, in flight, PILLOW NOTES 26, p. 482.

7. Peau d'Espagne? Peau de Chagrin? Peau d'Âne?:
Getting under, or rather over the thick bullskin of the peninsula. But from the high attitude of flying, it gets smaller and smaller. Jump out of your skin to save your hide! I wouldn't like to be in your skin game. Near is my shirt, but nearer is my skin.

8. Ku Klux Klan cones?:
Or a clan of Nazirenes, chanting a harakyrieleison . . .

9. Mashallah, dead souls on march:
Mock macabre? / Arab, kamerad: dare! Makbara . . . (Camaraderie cum rowdy and companion cum companion in holy company to the sementery . . .)

10. Spainful experience?:
This Hispanacea of bread and bulls, blood and sand . . . Jeers and shouts in this festival of bullherds.

11. The perfidious thief of Europa?:
The banging bull, wizened wisent father of the Uruspeans!

A ROUND of masked revelers with rebecs, rebabs, lutes, atabals. Apogee of the last never-ending Arabian night:[1] kaffirs carousing and careering on the stage, sambambumbling with war whoops, drumbeats, metal-stringed blasts.

Rocket! Rook it! till your rocky rukhkh is racked . . .

A drowsy Sinbad roosts with his monkey and parrot on the divan in the corner. Snookered, snoring, Rock-rock-roc . . .,[2] rocking.

((Drunk on alcohol and hashish?[3] On the raucous brew concocted by a rooking alchemist, in an alembic aludel labeled "Elixir of the Assasins."))

Admiral Sinbad, looking from on high:[4] Behold, desert dust of the simoon![5] peering at the dowar of bedouins. Allah! Brambles and matweeds and alhagis and wastelands: Bald badlands. White-washed cottages in the olive trees and leafy alcornoques. (What the Moroccan stewardess saw from her steel bird[6] over the Spanish bullskin[7] . . .) Adobe aldeas, tiled zocalos, caroms of reddish carob trees. Farmers in alpargata sandals, ragtattered shepherd boys, crowds of mummies in shawls and scarves, trundling behind a casket. Some with lilac-colored paper cones,[8] or candles and whips, parading . . . macabre.[9]

((The Spain of bulls, olives, sherry and flamenco?[10] Here it is:))

Down on that saffron-colored zero: olé after olé with fanfare. A skinny guy in tasseled frock and breeches, He! Ha! making faces and fusses before the treacherous black beast[11] by the bull pen. *Arre, jaque! Get tout!* Guitar-bearing swaggerers serenading, in front of the wrought-iron grill filled with clay flowerpots. Olé tu garbo! So graceful!: that robed hunchback heeltaps, and tosses her head.

Yallah! muladí! Giddyap, madwoman . . .

1. I shot the Albatross:
God save thee, ancient Mariangler!

2. Solar eclipse, solisequious sultan:
Soliloquizing solecisms in solfeggio . . .

3. Alcatraz?:
Sing! Sing! Robin Hoodoo. Careful with that bird of ill omen: See PILLOW NOTES 27, p. 483.

4. Hinbad the Hailer?:
Hail! Sinbad: See PILLOW NOTES 28, p. 484.

5. A signal bonfire?:
From char to charade, till the fire is revived in the nest of the Phoenix. In the night of autos-da-fé in Phoenix Lodge.

6. Rocking? Or stoned?:
Rock and rolling stones! Kill two Arabian birds with one nicked jagged stone. Perpetrate the stoning of a petrel, Ancient Mariner, and impetrate the stoned guest. Till the touchstone is passed and the guest is guessed. High! High! Each time higher, traveling on thund'rous rock wings. Lofty Arabian reenacts vaunted aerobatricks.

7. Griffin?:
Riffian smoking griffa. Illegal? Sickly but regal.

8. Jerkin of a whipping boy, he lashed out:
To be jerked from him before this crazy party is over.

9. In Fulham, fool?:
The fulham is cast . . .

10. Double jinx:
LEPERS REPEL! This revel shindig is turning the dangerous proseman leprous. Proprosing another approach to the sultana? Prosaic princess for this prick. Prosit!

11. Double taffeta?:
The fourfold silver veil of Mokanna, the prophet of Khorassan, to hide from mortal sight his dazzling brow, till man could bear its blinding sunlight.

Hyah! A drove or coffle of mules carrying shaggy unwashed jesters leather saddlebags and alforjas clothing bundles camp bags the whole length of the dock warehouses. Customs officials bustling about with their rubber stamps. C'mon, move it! Husky roustabouts in tarpaulin jackets caulking a felucca in the shipyard. Oil waves? against the breakwater. Wavesurges. Hup-hup! Joyous shouts and uproar out on the lily-edged blue carpet: Olé!? Albacore breaking surf in the net: a scarlet zero.

Zero to zero, algebraist, for your encoded masquerade . . .

Hey! That albatross[1] is escaping the harpoons of the loathsome Arab captain up in the crow's nest. And those of his coarse crew of matrosses. Whoosh! Toward those cottony reefs ribbed with sapphires. All the way to the golden soltaní?:[2] far away in the indigo blue. Already turning orange. A mere maravedí on the waves. And the albatross puts it in its beak. Money box or albatross?[3] All the way to the zenith! piercing the oranging blue. More than orange now: crimson. Flustered and flailing like this Sinbad.[4] Carried away. And drunk like me. Shoo! From roc to roc, streaking all the way to the beacon.[5]

((At the height of his high? Hope so! Rocking on the divan,[6] Rock-roc-roc . . ., wasted. The Roc[7] with its plier-claws snatches the skinny weakling by the turban and carries him off over the quick-silvery lapis lazuli to its ivory tower.))

From trick to track, a card sharp traipsing to the hazardous Bazaar . . . now in a doublet,[8] shaking his dice: These dicey dice, right here in Fulham,[9] will kill Chance itself . . . And looking askance: Whoa! That four-eyes is a jinx:

The leprous buffoon,[10] a marabout wrapped in taffeta[11] from his turban all the way down to his babuchas: This toquilla and powdered mask and glasses hide my profitless prophet's face . . .

1. Delta doubt, rout a deal, delta route:
Moor rooM.

2. Ruddy?:
Ready.

3. Quel bazar! Why capitalize it?:
We're talking about a great Bazaar, erect as a reptile. Arabian Buz! Buz! phony booth, if you don't take it too cliterally.

4. Abyss?:
Bis, bis. Until we reach the bottom.

5. Bobbing baba ababa . . .:
Ali Baba drooling in front of that burning poppy.

6. Bab? El:
The Sublime Passage! From dryer states to dire straits of Bab el Mandeb, whence this vale of tears . . .

7. Bab? Door?:
Well, adorned! Babieca, sloppy Cid sword, Bab bab, in rabid Arabic: Open your doorway, sweet . . .

8. Farinaceous fumble:
You've butlered your bread, now lie in it! For the best in bread, or the br . . . See PILLOW NOTES 29, p. 485.

9. Sesamo!? Tu restes Baba?:
Ba! Bah! Sex-âme, ouvre-toi! And between hot legs my soul is lost . . .

10. What joy! O pen up, says me:
That seedy zone . . .

11. A ruby with dark reflections?:
An indiscreet jewel, the red and the black, shiny and octopus-like in the velvet black of the cavern mouth.

12. Harem-scarum!:
Harried Harry! Harum al Rash id . . . / Beware those ids on march!

13. Where art thou bound, dear girl, with that jug?:
Like a flowing sprinkler.

14. Pitcher to the mound's Venus:
Fount of love, for the lover of the fount.

Sinbad, impetuously disbathrobing: No masks allowed, masked man. Till we snatch it from the sharpest shark in this masquerade face-off. Aced out,[1] what a raw deal, with his card tricks. By Allah! let's adulate the houris. Randomly from bazaar to bazaar to the scarlet[2] Bazaar.[3]

From aba to abbess,[4] nabob[5] . . .

Bab bab . . .,[6] a puffy Ali Baba in checkered galligasskins, Bab bab . . .[7] —with his Babism, practically between the big bakerwoman's gams, and she all sprawled on her sofa like a sack.[8]

And Ali Baba, blustering: Buckwheat, split. Hnn! Part the ways, barley. Bah! Open sesame.[9] Ya! Voilà! Terrific![10] dazzled before the spreadlegged baker: A scarlet jewel . . .[11]

To the harem, harebrain, to the harem of Harun al-Rashid . . .[12]

Waves of watered silks, moirés, muslins bluing amber reefs: the odalisques on embroidered pillows, in raptures with their sultans.

And one with a torn crepe toque, calling attention to herself with silly showy faces: My pasha almost ripped mine with a scimitar . . .

A braggart, hands on hips: And my potter always molds my jugs[13] with his potting wheel . . .

A Mozarab woman with a clay jar, upset, swaying and saying: The pitcher to the well . . . the pitcher to the well . . . the pitcher to the well . . . the pitcher to the well . . . the pitcher to the well . . . the pitch . . .[14]

1. Banal ballad to her belly button? Or her balas, The Rajah's Diamond?:
Ventral spinel ruby.

2. Her furry fig? GIFT FIG. Never look a gift fig in the mouse:
Firgmented! Here a moldy fig like me must stop, ma chère, because it's measurably matured. Figure it. Finger it.

3. You're all ears, she said huskily. Sanctutory gripe?:
Between unconsenting results! Don't meddle in the middle of that muddle.

4. Moorish mire, or tidal delta:
Moors in the marsh! And how the perfumed lascivet cats whetted your love-appetite with their aromas of seaweed and civet.

5. Amber slippers?:
Each and every one perfumed.

6. Scar by scar, sick of tricks . . .:
Some salt for your wound? That never heals.

7. I am the word in living flesh and you the knife . . .:
And horn-handled! A bistoury for the good houri. How cutting, those words or swords of your Spanoply.

8. Ballderdashing!:
Getting all bollixed up . . .

And the woman with the yellow veil: A burly one-balled bricklayer snatched my jewel in that shitshack . . ., grabbed my ruby,[1] my jamiz.[2] In cold blood with a corncob, in the muck and mire.[3]

A woman in a blue damask gown, Moorish: And me, a rattle-brained reveler, dartingly! on my musky clam[4] in that clamorous clambake . . .

A scrappy strapping lass in scarlet petticoats: And me, deceived by a scandalous sandalmaker, with his leather needle, my civettish slipper . . .[5]

A woman in a superfine flannel dress and slippers, brazenly: Pah! And me, a cobbler with his leather knife, this cicatrix . . .[6]

A shawled Madrileña at her swaggering best: Well a slaughterer slashed my skin here on my face and then slam-bang slitting me back in that slum. The sly shyster slighting me like I'm some sleazy slatternly slut![7]

The olive-skinned one now, with her oil jar held high: Well my caliph, a man of caliber! oils it up before . . .

Woman in a crimson haik, grabbing her bulbous belly: That shrewd alchemist rattles my womb from the nadir to the zenith . . .

A crowd of caliphs and a noisy horde of odalisques. A male hunchback in baggy breeches and a female hunchback in bulging dress spurring each other on, Faster, camel! on the rug. The female half with nasty cries: Do that camel walk! Mate me to the balls![8]

Blockhead to blockhead, blokes . . .

1. Careful with the panpipes:
And the poison. A-ha! drink up . . .

2. Adderuse? Serpentrick?:
Pipe up, piper, enchant the viper . . .

3. From col to col, to alcoholiness . . .:
Wild turkey-trot all the way to the eagle's nest . . .

4. The sufi goes from virgin wool to virgin . . .:
Going out for wool and coming home shorny? Wool pulled over his eyes? Wolf in
sheep's clothing getting fleeced!

5. Soppha of Lesbos?:
Divan, chairman, of the fricative Africans. Tribal tribadism.

6. Begum headdress?:
Begum from Belgium. Begone! Big bigamist's Begum. Begin the beguine! with the
beguiling Flemish Blemish and the Walloon: See PILLOW NOTES 30, p. 487.

7. A bundle of trouble!:
Almost as bad as that afternoon in the doorway of the boutique on King's Road. A
cardboard box teeming with rags, marked FREE. Which would start a free-for-all.
Babelle and Milalias contemplating the vagabond in a bowler and his tramp ((isn't
that Black Bess?)) so parsimoniously picking out the best of the box, when along
strutted two dressed-up women, Look! and in a flash they threw themselves on the
box, shouting in Spanish, Get the handkerchiefs too! fighting tooth and claw for
the tramps' rags.

And there beneath the stage platform, sitting cross-legged on his mat, a fakir playing a wooden flute[1] to a snake.[2] And a sufi dervish beating a skin against the tiles: A dunning for a drunkard. Get drunk without alcohol, Alkoranists.[3] Until Ramadan, the wine stays in the wineskin.

So! So! Sufi.[4] Soda for the odalisques . . .

Two flamingogogirls, tightly samba-ambling together—coifing coifs, touching tips—toward their sofa.[5] Almost collapsing! Fuckstrotting on the sofa. Two chicks with kaffiyehs[6] stripping, and preening each other, nesting in the damask pillows. And before them the Almohad dancing with a pillow: Free! This way I save the tip . . .

Trip! Rip! Rap! Trap! Part, all . . .

And that long-legged bag of bones with his bundle: This way I save paying the tax. The rags and clothes of my jaybird! Here I pack and unpack her myself with my cutlass.

Cut loose! Another cut, lash! from the lascivious cad . . .

Suddenly snatched from him. It's a free-for-all! The boors grabbed the egrets and peter-pottered around, purposefoily disputing the bundle.[7]

((Scuffle in the seraglio? Tamasha to mash. Hard haggling in the harem for some rags. Trappings, adornments . . . From tarlatatters to tarlatan! The crazy fools pummeling each other.))

1. Diplomat's diploid ploy?:
Double or triple play . . . / The case of the evil suitcase? A circus jugular? / Reversible vulgarment bag like our portmanteaus. And in a way like that juggling sheik in Heathrow airport, who started to pull travel bags and briefcases out of his big suitcase. Remember?

2. All is not gold that glisters . . .:
The Prince of Morocco wanted to carry off the greater part of Portia and wound up with only the empty ivory piggybank. Memento Morisco.

3. Saucepan beater, saucy banter, and a cock in every pot . . .:
Pots and puns, Peter Pun!

4. The big mestizo?:
Sam Bahamas, now in his free port. And soon it will be his turn to take over for the bank of kaffirs, SHAM ROCK.

5. First weave the seamy speeches . . .:
Yes, and laugh till you're in stitches.

6. Milalias's globetrotting trunk? Story of the Fictician and his Saratoga Trunk: Malle armée! L'Action Restreinte Vachement Amplifiée! Large ancient receptacle, vouchsafing antiquities. From arcanum to arcanum, eh patriarch? A little bit of everything in that blue trunk. Long-lost artifacts, rarities, vagabond's annotations . . . lasting aggregations, recollections vividly archived. Totum revolutum. A childhood copy of the *Arabian Nights,* for example, with Moorish postcards scribbled with colored pencil (("For the last week we have been sleeping on the ground, under the stars. But a good dream softens the hardest ground . . ." Illusion!)) by the uncle on his father's side who died in the Moroccan war . . . Lovely arabesque relics vainly accumulated!

7. Pinup!:
Tacked on the wall, the photos of the beauties that Bob "Hitch-Cock" made for one of those albums for erotomaniacs. And Milalias, as he scribbled in his glibberish, from time to time raised his head in search of inspiration . . .

The wali with his valise,[1] releasing its contents: And I saved the customs tariffs. The valise of valises! In my suitcase is a smaller suitcase with its tiny case inside with its teeny-weeny case inside with an itsy-bitsy case . . .

A jalifa in a white Moorish cape, shaking an ivory piggybank: What a swindle! of my mufti. Inside that brass box,[2] only this piggybank . . . Macabre box! no silver . . .

Tall gawky fellow in an olive green overcoat, his scimitar in its sheath, chomping a cheap cigar: The savings of the freed odalisque. The vixen drags like my tobacco . . .

A sullen silent type drumming with his pots[3] after the big mulattress with oily ebony mane. Samba mamma! when suddenly a boorish soldier grabbed her.[4] And she jug-jostled her watermelons with the samba. And with the bustle of the saraband, swashish! she broke her bead necklace. On all fours on the chessboard of floor tiles recovering them in the mob.

Giddy up, mulatta! Suddenly the bully in a soldier's tunic straddles the mulatta, whips her with an arrow quiver, and cackles: Check, sheik, shake and checkmated! Kink to queen, bishop to pawnshop to rook her! A put-on to pin down[5] a pinup, pinballers . . .

And now over a blue trunk,[6] shrouded, the hunchback in baggy breeches tearing through taffeta cloth: For your tears and wounds. For your pin money![7] my troubled savers. Ginghams and trifles. Enough scheming! chattering knaves. We'll just pin these fine flannels together. Then lulling along: Lilailas! Lilas! These rips are just pinned together. A grave story retailed over and over . . .

1. Pleating her case:
Cut your coat according to your sloth, from rip to riprap.

2. A perky perquisite:
Per Calino costurame! Oh percâline! Oui, je connais la musiquette. Still lots to tell: teller, tailor; RELIEVER, REVEILER!

3. Back-book?:
Back to the Babelasian priestess! Drunk as a skunk in a bunkbook . . .

4. A figure ground down to flour?:
Graham-slam! And the crummy guy crumbles, crumbling through the rye.

5. Back up! Back! baroque Bakbarah:
Bareback! Bakbarah!

6. BAR A NABOB, AN ARAB?:
Back to back . . . This is some bacchanal!

7. BOB A NABOB, or Blindmaniac's buff:
Or buffeting. Stroke by short stroke, stroke me a strong stroke.

8. No use stewing about it:
Olla 'odrida . . . Pot pourri! Popurria!

9. I'll have none of your lip:
Harelip today, gawk tomorrow.

10. UNEMBARGO: GRAB MENU . . .:
CITE MENU, UNEMETIC! Never satiated? Some dishes from the polyglutton Milalias's favorite menu: The plate of beans that Theseus gobbled up after vanquishing the Minotaur. The mess of pottage for which Esau gave up his birthright to Jacob. A real mess. The stewed partridge, eaten every day without fail by the confessor of rakish Henri IV of France . . .

The baker swinging her belly about: Hey tailor, new in town? Tailor for a price. Hipswyving in the shindig! Then cajoling in front of the hunchback: Tailorette with tail seeks piecework,[1] basted on only one side, no buttonhole stitching please . . . Alas! my hunchback with his hemming, and darts! on my satin slacks. And percale pinafore.[2] More than one pinprick for me! Stitch after stitch, tuck after tuck, till he was rip-roaring drunk. And now she grabs a glass: Bacbuc![3] my hunchback tailor. Like a bloated wineskin with his hump. And the gimp not only trimming me for free. The mill toll paid too. My hunchback in the flour mill, tied up to the grindstone like a beast of burden, and the miller goading him and whipping him,[4] Giddyup mule! till he collapsed, poof! like a sack of flour.

((More whipping? Flogging and beating all down the hall and up to the rafters. Odalisques, like waves, always come in series.))

Guffaws from the jokers, Bakbarah! Bakbarah![5] with veils and odalisque muslins over the wastrel who kicked out on the divan as they decked him out with kohl crimson henna and anointed him, Grab his prick! and spurred him on between his legs.

The houris now chanting Bacbac! Bacbac![6] around the seer with black glasses who freed himself with some blows from his cane.[7] And brandishing his cane toward the blue mat in the corner: Mmm! Stew?[8] A bean stew under this rug . . . Jew eat yet?

And now, seer, the feast begins . . .

Glutton with a scarface,[9] gesturing going through the motions of biting off something, in front of the elderly nabob who praised him, what an appetite![10] with his honeyed compliments and cunning:

1. Schacabacchanal!:
Winding up in a sheer bacchanality of empty wordiness in this Barmecide feast.
You'll wind up eating your tasteless words.

2. Whine not?:
Wind up and wine doubt. Or wine in doubt, do as the . . . Barmecider! with flecks of
spit.

3. The words gone to his head?:
You already know which is the most powerful drug . . .

4. Playing the bones?:
Devil's bones! Pick your bones of contention with somebody else! With a knuck
knack paddywhack give a dog a bone, this old bore . . .

5. The marrowy middle? Bone appetit, and make no bones about it:
Rompre l'os et sucer la substantifique moelle! PITH TIP: Pick 'em, poke 'em, pound
'em, and peruse the powerful pith. More marrow tomorrow in this pithy pace to
catch with your tongue or tongs. What's read in the bone will come out in the fresh.

6. An avid divan?:
Plop goes the weasel with the vexing vixens.

7. Avid for divan love:
Or Moor's amour.

8. From Belle to Belle, the belle-buster:
Bah. Belle époque. Dancing damsels from polka to polka, the pig had a gland ol'
time . . .

9. Lupine!?:
Yes. Pussywill or pussywon't.

10. Make a Mecca, maniac:
To the Mechanical Bride. Allahmerican!

11. Acid Cid?:
Cite acid cider!

12. Fanged foxy ladies:
Hounded by a dogged Don Juan.

Talk about your big chow-down blowouts, eh Schacabac . . .[1] A little ripple, perhaps?[2] And the glutton, as if inverting a pitcher over his open gullet: When I get drunk on mere chatter, I get carried away . . .[3] And whap! he butted his forehead against the nabob.

How about a nice Arabian punch . . .

The gambler tiddling some knucklebones: Nick the bone . . .[4] Knuckle down to some bones. Bite the bone, jackals! till you munch the medula.[5]

A pack of houris! To the divan of divas . . .[6]

At the same time the houris in their Arabian babble: Recant! Drunkard! My alcoholic Almoravid[7] sacked me . . . Guay! and as for me, the mad Muslim reamed my tush . . . What about *me,* the spoofing clown with his spear . . . Me too! The crass kaffir with his crankshaft . . . And me! the blockhead with his trowel . . . And at me in my mortar with his pesky pestle . . . He mauled *me* with mallet and machete, that macho . . . The muleteer haltered me and saddled me and Get 'em up! and whipped me on the beanie . . . And *me,* lashing me, Vixen! Vixen! in my scarlet pouch . . . And all over me, that ragman with his trifle in my knickknack, his odd in my end . . . And the pig put me in his pigsty, wallowing and corkscrewing me . . .[8] And from loop to lupine . . .[9] From Islam to I slam like a magnetic imam pointing to Mecca,[10] the alcalde of Zalemas salaaming and cajoling his almeh . . . My bride, would you catch this lemon? And that commanding Cid[11] with his hest on hest! grabbing my lemons . . . Oranges! And my apricots . . . (Another impeachment?)

The crippled caliph under his canopy, splayed out among the pillows: What bedlam! One by one. Sharp bites from my pretty pack of sweettooths![12] Ay! giving tit for tat . . .

1. English ivy? Climbing ivy?:
Mot-lierre pour le festin de Pierrot. Chaque Don Juan de pierre finit par prendre son mou lierre. Moly hier . . . Swift joys in the ivy-bloom!

2. Scheherazade alias Babelle?:
More than one, taking turns. But only one genuine one. Scheherasade pour l'Emil et une nuit . . . A thousandnightsinone!

3. Piping hot tale?:
Pipe down. Give the devil his do, and the dybbuk too.

4. The whirling houri?:
Spinning about in top form with all her pomp, la Bella Pompadour of the Pampas, whizzing through the mob.

5. Laudable tobacco?:
Tropikaleidoscopium!

6. Nanny o nanny nanay!:
Kneel, son. A lad in his lapland, holding his own. You'll go on manipulating with your manogamy. The lad à la Aladdin in that homely bed of his childhood, clutching a burning spike, rubrubbing the lamp under the damp sheets. BURN, RUB.

7. Palm oil to soustain the lantern, or Chrism and the Wonderful Lamp:
Whack your wick. Lampista! leva as lampas a o lampianista lampeiro . . . Lampa a lampana a lamparina . . . Você não tem azeite na lâmpada? No oil in your lamp, lad? Other voices, other back rooms . . . (("Choninha" (the Portuguese girl who raised you) lighting the prayer candle for papá-e-mamã in the big room . . . And later she would slip in barefoot to tuck you in. The silhouette of her body under the nightgown, in the glow of the oil lamp. Stranger still in the dark, recalled in your half-sleep.)) Niño de "Choninha." So warm and yummy, if the child couldn't sleep from fear and she let him climb in bed with her . . . ((When we went up the carpeted spiral staircase, clutching the bags of hot sand, our shadows were projected phantasmagorically on the paintings on the wall. Thieves from Ali Baba's cave, with our lootbags. "Choninha" leading with the candle, showing her white calves . . .)) Anda à vela! Lights out!

Like ivy![1] the way they grab at me. Ticks! Crabs! Don't corner me in, you hounds. And my lovely gazelle? My Scheherazade?[2]

With a healthy caliph, one with position and no indisposition! and that shapely concubine—with locks lacquered like scorpions—disentangled her silk coif from the crooked claws of the sickly caliph.

And the cross-eyed procuress in a moth-eaten shawl, crying shrilly: Houris for rent! Cheap, cheap. Odalisques on leashes, risk-free! Some real jezebel-jewels! Precious stones to be mounted on the ottomans. What a crew!: hooligans hoosiers dolts dupes block-heads churls yokels vagrants wastrels lined up before the ticket booth. The tariff: one puny pataca per peasant! A blonde for an arroba. Minus the tare. Almost a giveaway! Cheap, cheap. Who'll take me up on this crazy deal? Almost free. No free-spending debauchees in this bargain basement? Grab your moneybags. And taking off her scarf and stomping a shoe against the tile floor: Can you despair a slim dime? Just one special guy gets it for a nickel: Old Nick.

Leapin' lizards! The devil you say! Stomp to raise the devil in this daredevil-may-care harem . . .

The short cripple in a scarlet cloak, waving his chibouk:[3] I snatched it from the whirling dervish . . .[4] Huf! but no smoke[5] left in the bowl.

Aladdin, madly polishing his oil lamp: Oh no! Oh nanay![6] Ay! This one's not mine. No oil[7] on this one.

A stingy lampman polishing his oil lamp in vain . . .

1. Türbe? Tomb?:
In this case a mass türbe, shunned by all. Follow the Master of the Mastaba. But remember: one in the bush is worth two in the hand.

2. Er . . . ottoman? . . .:
Erotomaniac! A bush in the hand . . .

3. A baiza for the baize? Or an Oman rial?
Baisse par baisse, dinar drain, rial lair . . .

4. Lallation? Alalia? Monody? Singing la di lala lala?:
From Lalla Rookh to Leila to lullabaloo! From lulling lay to Layla.

5. The strong hand?:
ONE RISE: DESIRE. NO!: DASH SELF, FLESH SAD. More than handy that the left not know what the right is doing.

6. The Talisman for Hassan to get off scott-free:
(To seize our sylphs as others see us? To seal our sills . . .) From sylph Phyllis and the infectious charm of her crew. A claptrap outfit, if ever there was one. Whore today and gonorrhea tomorrow.

7. Cape codpiece, where the rubber meets the rode . . .:
Capote anglaise! Toss me another . . .

8. Open your eyes, he'll put out those lamps . . . Exit, in trance:
Trance out.

9. Sweet Candy . . .:
Another candied candidate for Dulcinea: See PILLOW NOTES 31, p. 487.

10. Savoring the syllable . . .:
And giving a twist to your tongue! See PILLOW NOTES 32, p. 489.

11. Maimon, arboreal. . . ?:
Bore! And borer: mandrill.

The idle hunchback, now over the türbe,[1] a blue casket, still with his crape: Use 'em as turbans! And toques! Get your turbans, odalisques, amass turbans for your ottoman[2] master, baiza after baiza . . .[3]

A mongoloid jittering along like a monkey with hoops and hollers: Lala! Lela! Lala lala . . .[4]

Use that whopping hand of yours,[5] Maimon, and unmask yourself. Aladdin too from the time he was a little boy rubbed it like a monkey. An odalisque on the calendar in a cobbler's drove me to it. That silky houri. Always mine. And always free! Not like these rental models . . .

And Aladdin now heading toward the madam, who continued to discount her bazaar of bargain bar gals: A pox upon thee, foul procuress! You with your odalisques who go from ottoman to ottoman. And already secondhand and worn-out. We don't need their lingering charms. Such cute items, infectious! here in your auction. What jewels, what precious germs! More bejel than bezel. With scars and marks. Some with talismans[6] against the jinxes. But I'm always caped[7] for the encounter. Always with my shield. Hey! Rent me one with more wheat and less chaff, a little more gem and less band. Not like that wench with the belly-folds. And with the oil lamp high, dazzled: Where's that houri from the zarzuela who dazzled me in the footlights with her enchanting eyes?[8]

Candy![9] Sugar candy . . ., —the glutton candy-coating his gullet with his chatter.[10] And the nattering nabob spiraling anew with his candied compliments: A sweet youth doesn't live on sugar alone.

Sinbad drunk on his divan: A monkey for a majorette! Like the time my stewardess and this baboon[11] were getting syrupy in that Golder's Green café. In that Yiddish pastryshop. And as if spying

1. Toledan marzipan?:
To lay down in a fertile fly-ridden field of almond paste-ure.

2. Moslem pulpit for pulpy sermons . . .:
And forgive-me-nots. Helleluya. . . !

3. Cloying coat . . .:
Of arms. Of smarmy Arabian candy.

4. White cape? Capa blanca?:
Shake, mate.

5. Cakewalk!:
You cannot have your chesscake and eat it too . . . ((Only that shabby Fred Astaire swallowing a harmonica, making faces (Hoho! Hohner!) while clacking out a cakewalk on the squares in front of that Leicester Square cinema. And Milalias popped out of the queue and started to tap, trying to copy him.))

6. Impromptu moribundity: What cancern is it of yours when two more is less?:
It can certainly take one down a bit, as I can certify.

7. Nora?:
Anda à nora! Noramala, naughty Nora . . . Au trou badour. Another canned cancan circumcircled: See PILLOW NOTES 33, p. 490.

8. Per ardua ad astra (Far RAF):
Astracancan.

9. GIRDLE: HELD RIG:
BRA GARB? O NO! MONO!

10. Rubber!? Oui, mon caoutchou?:
Breastfake of champions. Caoutchouchou du champion . . . Oui, prière de toucher!

the approaching wave of odalisques: That alcazar of marzipan,[1] there, and the minaret[2] of cake icing. Hills of pastries and sugar candy rolling to the syrup lake.[3] O, to frolic in frosted froth, languish in lagoons of it . . .

And that sheik in a haik[4] (zap! he snapped the lamp from a dazzled Aladdin) choo-choo-checking from tile to tile: Let's cancan! Square by square . . .[5] Saraband of the lamp! as he stomped about.

The gambler with his cards now: Trick by trick, all to turn up that difficult card. Some hustle, and bustle.

No trick to it! Go ahead and poker, or him . . . Whip 'em good . . .

A game with a shark-bite, sharp![6] and moving along this daring dangerous odalisque stripped her breasts and tore off her veil with piercing cries of grief.

A rubber game! Aye, there's the rub. Robber after rubber, mincing after mensing . . .

And Sinbad, holding onto his turban, perturbed: Nora![7] Court her with a serenade now? Chance threw us together in that Earl's Court café. Looking gloomy in glasses. Sad and taciturn in the midst of the mayhem. Until I spurred her on. Alfar. From the Algarve. And interpreter in London. Not a spring chicken any-more, but still smart-looking in her astrakhan jacket.[8] And what bubs under her bodice! Ha! Alcohol to warm her up. And then in my alcove, on the sofa, wearing only her glasses and girdle. Like that with mine on the rug. Not the girdle![9] And she grabbed me to keep me from taking off her protective girdle. Drunken hiccuping. Not that! when I felt under her girdle her melon of . . . of . . . of . . . caoutchouc![10]

Unmellow. You rub her wrong, Sinbad . . .

1. The perfumed garden?:
The perfumigated garden of delights ((The Book of Delights with its alcoholalia and that sneaky trick of blasting linguistic limits)) and tormental anguish where our emir beau ténébreux lies in ambosch with his trollops . . .

2. Le maure s'occulte: Flashes to dashes . . .:
Dash it! And stop your dotty remorse already. ((. . . everything is permitted?)) Allah, mutatis mutandis, will commute your mutism. Taciturning into . . . Sh! Sabbah to the Sabbath!

3. Fixin' to be foxin' with your vixen:
Le renard change de poil de carotte, mais non de naturel . . .

4. Unbridled, and rearing up in alfalfa redolent, with his local synesthetic. Bottoms up!:
My eyes talk, while my tongue looks, my ears speak while my hands hear, and while my ears are eyes that take in all that is visible, my eyes are ears that hear the tales of this dark night of Saint John.

5. I was enamour'd of an ass:
No! Not yet. With the ass in the grass, the burro in the bosque. Brawn, and brains too; but tomorrow the horse-sensible Don Juan will be fodder. To the man.

6. Rock-a-bye berber, let her roll:
Reberberation?

7. Bridewell . . .:
Court her, go down deeper. All's well that ends in the bottom of a well. And keep courting the Bride till she's stripped bare, even.

8. Her soul contained in that faded almanac . . .:
Year of tears. Counting the days of that shattered year . . .

9. Ebony or sycamore?:
Sic, moor.

Now Sinbad chortling with his parrot: Check out the checkmate of that sheik in the haik, playing a cheeky Sufi chess game on the portico tiles. A-ha! Now heading toward the trellis.

To the flower garden![1] Of delights . . .

The assassin-sheik meddling zap! zap! with his lamp amidst the myrtles and annoying us with his coded lampbursts. A-ha, he's escaping behind the hedge.[2] Still causing trouble! The blue-tiled pond, where the hippies swish. Waves, adornments, long hair, dresses . . . Down the tubes with the assassin. Hope they catch him. The Janes flirting with their Johns. Their dresses entangled in the brambles. What's mine is mine! An ensign with epileptic movements, and a harsh harlot, Help me, o comrades-in-arms! in successatory amalgamation.[3] The drunkard with the donkeyhead, Giddyup! rearing up in the cloverpatch,[4] Down the hootch! with his bottle upended, half stoned and getting higher.[5]

Hie! Hie! Astute assimilation . . . Now vile braying . . .

Vital vial! A bulb-nosed berber spinning in circles.[6] Chasing the veiled woman in a long white gown.

Ride, ride, after the bride . . .[7]

Horsemen and a pack of hounds chasing a wild boar through rock-roses and scotch broom. Like that yellowed, almost sepia picture on the calendar[8] in the mummy's alcove.

Mummy to mummy, lucky mameluke . . .

The mummy in an ebony[9] casket inlaid with mother-of-pearl and ivory, screeching: Strip away this crepe and gauze, I'm being mummified . . .

By Allah! praise your prize . . .

1. Monologging on . . .:
With monomachiavellisms and monomatopeias.

2. Almanac?:
Yes, of years gone by. With special attention to that fateful year of the curling calendar hanging on her bedroom wall as a mournful memento of her great expectations . . .: See PILLOW NOTES 34, p. 492.

3. Ga-ga-geegaws of yesteryear:
Here comes the bride, all dressed in white . . .

4. Knock on wood . . .:
Play the lute, and the bones too . . . Abun-dance macabre with anklebones?

5. The Old (Will and) Testament for the New . . .:
A nigh for a nigh and a truth for a truth; heirs and errors . . . Her scribbles were all mixed up on that palimpsest, although she sought to change the will every day. By dawn a new holographic testament for the executor who never came. Today's writing over yesterday's writing. And moreover with her seismograph hand-writing. Is it Arabic? Babelle wondered.

6. A deadbeat's drop of bedpan humor:
To be passed over. Sometimes when the mummy suffered from strangury, Milalias hastened to remove the bedpan from under her bed. And Babelle, wrinkling her nose, finished the task.

7. Harpun? (: Note, penciled in by Herr Narrator):
With those tachygraphic arabesques Milalias makes, it's absolutely impossible to decipher this passage of his Magnuscript, whether it says Haroun or Maroon or Harpoon or Harp on . . .

8. His drivel shriveled?:
Glad to hear he's high and dry.

9. La Mancha, the original stain . . .:
But cleansing, from stain to satin. Love is a many-spleendured thing.

Sinbad on the divan, chattering with his monkey:[1] That wealthy
mummy with a beret for a turban, attributing her illness to the
almanac.[2] The mummy in a gauze veil[3] at the dressing table in her
dungeon-bedroom in Queensberry Place. Where she kept her
macabre things. The coffin![4] Inside, with camphor, the veils and
finery of her trousseau . . . And over the dresser, a sealed docu-
ment for her executor.[5]

To the harem, hostage, to the harem . . .

Fussing, My bracelet! and screaming. With the sapphires. And
more mayhem later, tossing rugs shawls pillows cushions. In every
direction. Under sofas divans stools. In pitchers and bowls. Even
in her chamber pot![6] *We* swiped the mummy's jewels? Bah! Some
treacherous thieving jay. (Not like the time someone swindled the
stewardess.) Maybe now in some money box those sapphires
diamonds gems bracelets . . .

To the harem, loafer! To the harem, Haroun,[7] to the harem . . .

Haha, yet another person shriveled up,[8] behind bars: that dragoman in Moorish cloak scribbling out reams and reams in his Kufic
scrawl: En una aldea de la Mancha . . .[9]

In a spot in La Mancha . . .

From Cid to shining Cide! Here's the leader of this raiding razzia:
the masked warrior in chain mail, with sword and heart-shaped
leather shield, boasting of his feats and stunts . . .

Lilaila! Lelilí! Lililí! —harrowing cries of the haranguing harem.

1. Living dialect? Lingua franca?:
Live and let dialect. Yes. A mixture of all tongues, with which we all understand each other.

2. Mal armé notre Chevalier errant à la triste figure pour la tâche . . .:
Nom de nomade! Quand même! A la tâche! Tache à tache, littréralement. Berberisme à bourborygme. Oui, bedouin, il faut donner un sens plus pur aux maux de la tribu—aux tribulations de la tribu . . .

3. The masked warrior!:
Yes, the masked guerrilla with his sorcerous Zoraida. Captivated! And unable to sleep . . .: See PILLOW NOTES 35, p. 496.

4. Mate!:
Beware of the mate tricks . . . The hind that would mate with the lion must die of love. Mate! Mete! Mátame! Tu es moi. Tuez-moi! They mate for death . . . La petite morte.

5. NOMAD HOTEL:
MAD HOTEL, the half-broken neon sign over the entrance . . . ((L'Autel des sacrifices à Vénus . . .))

6. Alarums and excursions, Arabian raids . . .:
Deep in the rubescent refuge. Hid in hideout? See PILLOW NOTES 36, p. 497.

7. Allah! Allah! Allah! What an ejaculation!:
His allelujah, his orgasmoribund ejaculation.

8. Red beard, sanguine?:
A bad habit, sanguinary cunnilinguist. Barbe de barbeau! Parbleu!

9. All colors . . .:
Especially purple. Love that mix of black and blue.

((Clamoor? Clamoorish babble? More or less. Purify the lingo[1] of the Kabyles. This is the task.[2]))

The masked marauder,[3] that Moor-killer always in checkmate, Mate! Mate![4] jockeying in a pillowed corner with his merry houri. The stewardess in blue, stamping her long legs. Heron, or giraffe even, but so graceful . . .

Attaboy, muzzle up to that Moslem . . .

The miser cheering her on, as in that jumbled-up place in Queen's Park. Or that wretched room on Finchley Road. (The flattering madam, with painted mask and claws, with her cajolery: I'll rent my room, this grand hall! to a royal princess . . . —an attic garret with a couch whose guts are spilling out and a moth-filled closet . . .) Or like that basement hovel[5] for bedouins in Paddington—hooks on the walls for the coats . . .

Room after room, moor room, all the way to the crimson alcove of the sultan . . .

Or pounding away, as happened in the Cleveland Gardens room. (What a racket, the next-door neighbor smacking on the wall.) The one with the mottled walls. And the candle still on the window sill, oranging that alcove of alarum.[6]

Spurring ever onward, infidel soldier, go, go . . .

Cinnamon-colored horse arching with cries[7] under the red-bearded horseman.[8] (The room already scarlet?) More whippings . . . Tan his hide! From whelp to welt, lush to lash, bedouin to bed wrench . . .[9]

1. Sweet talkin':
Or just sweet tooth and consequences. See PILLOW NOTES 37, p. 500.

2. Bluebeard turned Redbeard?:
Sanguine swashbuckler! In his bloody castle. A fortress! Where he slit the curious
and meddling . . . In his inner castle, where they went through the mill . . . Bella
dopo belletta nel castelletto . . . Locked up tight with deadbolts padlocks latches
bars / Another bar, tokologist . . .

3. Of mights and menses, as time beckons. Irruminating in honey . . .:
And ruminate now on the ruminescents with your book . . . ((

)) OK?
See PILLOW NOTES 38, p. 501.

4. Babouche of bucks:
In a roll, pounds dinars francs, stuffed in a slipper. Hidden. Till she confessed and
revealed the stash to you.

5. Especially that bracelet . . .:
That cost so much!: See PILLOW NOTES 39, p. 503.

6. A fugue of vowels from the fugitives. In disavowal?:
T.NT' .M.R., T.NT' .M.R.,
H.B.B, T.NT' .M.R.!
Q.. Y. N.M.Q..D. .M.R
N. N.D., Y Y. M. V.Y!
A message, Spanish? That you dubiously deciphered: Tintamarre? (Noise?)
Tanto amor? (So much love?) Consonants signifying nothing? The sound and the
flurry . . .

From hill to hell, hillbilly. From puddle to muddle, modster . . .

((With his head swimming? Still drunk? Like that time in the scarlet alcove, after another party. Ripping up the cushions of the hump-backed divan. C'mon, camel! And the stewardess to the kaffir: To counter the alcohol, coffee! —Aggh, like acid?: a cup of mocha, like tar, no sugar.))

Sticky-sweet as the syrup[1] in that cheap café in Golder's Green. The stewardess and her bedouin whispering sweet nothings beside all those drunks, while Golder's Green Road was carpeted with blossoms or sugar. The guy in a green overcoat chomping his stogie and drumming on the cups. And the bedouin conversing and versifying between laughs. Let's get sugar-frosted! the two quickly outside now holding each other tight, slipping and skating over the pavement toward Finchley Road.

From ablution to ablation, diviner, to your houri's gambit . . .

With her monthlies now!? The red-bearded[2] berber facing off between the gams of his stewardess, and he slurping that red wine. Bitter sorbet![3]

Whine and dye . . .

After breaking into her savings (: in that slipper . . .[4]) the swindler will carry off the earrings and jewelry[5] of his generous stewardess to that cheat's antique shop in Paddington. To pay the rent on the Cleveland Gardens place. And then a spree. She'll write to you, in red over the quicksilver, some coded arabesques . . .[6] Will you ever decipher them? If you catch her you'll kill her! But you'll never snatch that jewel of sorrow: a pearl running down her face while she packed her suitcase, there in your room, after the quarrel.

1. The palpitating pillow . . .:
Heartache! beating like a runaway horse when she rested her head on your chest.

2. Into the water!:
Cradling your neck and splash! —beneath the battling waves.

3. Peg a susceptible mount, and steeplechase:
Gallop, full reign! from Haizum to Fadda to Borak. Ya hooray! Hoarse-laugh all around . . .

4. Jockeying for possession. Unbridled joy, bridal toy:
Headfirst to the fires of chehannam. Weddings of seventh heaven and fifth hell!

5. Alalia all together. Alea, iacta est!:
The best aphrodisiac is to shout Allah in the moment of alejaculation. The holy counsel of Omar Haleby to the Prophet Mohammed.

6. Poil-de-carotte, carrotteur?:
Oui, caro auteur. Quel renard, mon jules . . .

7. RE-GUADIANA: AN AID, AUGER? The ole drill bit:
Revirescent river. No one can schtup twice, my HeraclitoriDiane, in the same Guadiana bath?

8. Break! Break! Break!:
Tennis on and on again. How clumsy you were swinging the racket (We are merely the stars' tennis balls, struck and bandied), bouncing balls at the Putney sky. What bawling . . .

9. You go your way and I'll go to Paraguay!:
With your guaying, waying, swaying song . . .

10. Um-as-sama? The Milky Way? Pilgrimage of Santiago, or San Yago?:
Saint Yagurt!: See PILLOW NOTES 40, p. 503.

11. Alcaide!:
E quindi uscimmo a riveder le stalle. Undaunted gentleman, you'll see stars with the bites of your runaway roan. And with the scratches of your jaybird. Hourly houris, your uranography. At the climax now! With his Algol houris in algolagnia . . .

12. The blue planet?:
Let's give it a roll! Here goes . . . the Big Bang.

What a sin, Sinbad, no Moor. Nevermore. No morass, no more Roc . . .

No Moroccan let loose like she, with ecstatic shouts in a wave of crescendos. Wave of jet-black hair on the pillow.[1] And a thick rope whips me, whap! and entwines me. Get a grip on yourself!

Break! Break![2] Wait for the next wave . . .

And her scarlet claws rip me—scorpion pinchers in my neck. Wah! Way, yaw! Let's gallop through the blue.[3] What goading! And nails, like pliers! And they seize me, over the waves, all the way to seventh heaven.[4] Ya! Allah![5]

A-ha! to the sacred river, run to the Guadiana now . . .

A carrot-topped[6] woman in her blue bathrobe, shaking a racket at Sinbad: The johnny-come-lately in his johnboat. In the waves of odalisques. From bay to bay, baleful baiting again. Formerly drinking from my sacred Guadiana.[7] Unguarded! Swells and guffaws. After clay-courting[8] in Putney. And in my room he grabbed my robe. Underhandedly sneaking from behind so I couldn't get away. Rip and snatch, a hard serve, a forehand play and a lunge for the net. Love all? Don't play back. With only your carefree stewardess? Hoo![9] In the clutches of the drunken Roc, that drip. It may seem endless, that road to the Milky Way.[10]

From rook to roc, Sinbad, till castling with your Moor from Maroc.

Merlin with cotton locks, taking long strides while reading an almagest: A rising star![11] At the zenith already. From peak to peak, Alkoranist, until spotting this blue sphere from the Roc.[12]

From Aldebaran to Altair. From Algol to Algorab. In Starry Araby . . .

1. The Secret Rose? The Rose Inviolate?:
Limpid Alchemical Rose Violated Afore . . . Keep, sub rosa! the well-guarded rose. In ward!

2. Shake! Shake! spiritist:
A fellow of infinite jest, of most excellent fancy, skulking around the macabre bride. Numskulker!

3. Rock of Arabia Petræa?:
Rocket! Fiendish. Finis. The Arabian Bird is coming to his caabaret fire nest at Phoenix Lodge.

4. Stop this warbling garble of all-iteration:
Etymolorgy of fanciful arabesques (Plus vrais que nature?) or alhambresques. As when the King of Jests suggested that his Spañolé class of fifteen-year-old Hammersmith schoolgirls hunt down words of Arab origin in their pocket dictionaries. Almost all beginning with *al-!* (Alienating alibi . . .) And his favorite pupil, the cunning blond huntress always in the first row, caught three magnificent pieces: *alumno, almorzar* and *almorranas:* pupil, grub and hemorrhoids . . .

5. LINK, NIL?:
Nil torre creari de nil . . .

6. Balking at the balaclavas?:
In their ski masks with eye-holes, the band of terrorist rock and rollers.

7. SHAM ROCK!:
Plot the clover, alafest a la festa! on this dark night of Saint John.

8. Speak to me of loves . . .:
I'd love to . . .
((What really excited me and still excites me is Milalias telling me what he did and what we did with the jeunes filles en flor while we make cattleya. (You're orchidding me!) Purring away, two siamese entwinned, I'd like to stay spermanently . . .))

The Alchemist in a checkered tunic, flaunting a flask: Distilled right here, the elixir of the assassins! And holding up a red rose: First blue and now crimson. This wild rose from the garden of heaven (or from gehenna?), suddenly, on my pillow. And immediately from rose to violet.[1]

And that macabre masker brusquely snatched the flask: More demijoans for Don Juan! I get drunk with my odalisquor. Hey, whose is this? Bah, just nonsense, and he stamped, on the tile floor, that ivory skull, or money box.

And the hunchback in a lackey jacket grabbed it. Hey! Yo-Yo-Yorick, bopping about[2] near the Algebraist who scribbed his numbers against the wall in the corner: 2B, or ... $\neq$ 2B ... They debase their hopes on greater noise and greater numbers. Cipher, and siphon off (Rock! Roc![3]) into the mayhem ...[4]

Time to break the chain, ottoman, and by way of orbit create the missing link, or nil.[5] Odalisque in a blue moire caftan dancing, grabbing her pearly nape and flogging the flagstones with her hair. Pull yourself away from the demijanes, little Don Juan Demijohn, and do your duty now on your Scheherazade, making such full use of her as shall sting her squeamish virtue to the soul.

The din of the hooded kaffirs[6] up on the stage. Ape gaping, and the guitar-wielders, Rock! Rock! Rock![7] screaming.

Your turn now, Schahriah! Ha-chah-shah ... And Scheherazade plunked down on the carpet. Without me this band falls apart! What stirred me up and still stirs me up is Schahriah whispering[8] his filth to me while we jockey on the divan.

From tale to tail. From band to bond. From revelry to rabbelry ...

1. Herd a pack of recollections, and mule them over . . .:
Western roundup from the Bar None to the Lazy Eight raunch. And in the Garden of Eros, the garden of bifurcanceling paths, we'll meet once more.

2. Pennipotent pony, pegasusubstitute . . .:
Like a bolt of hoofs, Giddyap! to the seventh heaven. Ali with Alibi, oui alibyebye. What a towering babel there . . . Linguistico-numerical arabesques render vexing assignment: seventy thousand heads, each with seventy thousand tongues, and each tongue with seventy thousand languages. And all of them talking at the same time. Harût and Marût, the two major angels of Babel, plugged their ears. Oh Dio! In the paradise of prattlers, the deaf man is God?

3. A tank of water—and not exactly fresh . . .:
Jaded sullying jerk? With luv and squalor. See PILLOW NOTES 41, p. 504.

4. Parroting? Monkey see, monkey stewed?:
The moon and the stars is what he promised, that trained ape from Arabia Felix. My moon! My moon is a balloon! Sinbad was asking for the moon when he went leaping wildly through the tumultitude chasing his enormous white globe. Ma boule! Maboul! The Rock's egg? Rock'n'ball! That one-balled Sinbad chasing wildly after his rocambolesque egg.

5. The Persian and the squirrel? The squirrely Persian, or . . .:
Paradise and the Peri. See PILLOW NOTES 42, p. 505.

Hyah! Night rider, from your night mare foal to folly, born to roan from pony to porny, from bridle to bride screaming Go! Geeyup! flattery and whip, cajolery and crop, carrot and schtick.[1] From racket to rejoicing at random on Al-Borak . . .[2] Hya! giddy up! smacking. Such a slothful drunk. Houri to houri, sluggard, circle around the big wheel.

My Scheherazade and I whooping with laughter, clutching each other on the Battersea Park ferris wheel. And then indulging and masking ourselves with cotton candy. Then popping about in that old hulk of a galleon on the waves of the Battersea lagoon.

Ahoy! We're coming alongside, pirates. And shiver me timbers . . .

And then the madam in the moth-eaten shawl spurring us on from her shanty, into the drink with her! to drop whop! with one shot that gal suspended on a plank over a pool.[3] Splash! Last splash in Battersea Park. And now all overgrown . . .

From zero to zero, this cipher to decipher in a Saint John's Day masquerade . . .

((A message in cipher? Cipher text? Sinbad on his divan, chatting and chortling with his parrot and his monkey,[4] in the midst of the Arabblement of masks that circle and will go on recircling from the zenith to the nadir.))

A Muslim woman veiled with a chador, getting annoyed: Destiny hooked us together in Holland Park. That squirrel[5] was our match-maker . . . So taken with its scheming. That guy in the red jacket with his follies, I had to laugh. With his sweet talk and charm under the tamarinds.

1. The Queen of Samba?:
She-bop she-bawd. Au Sabbat avec la Reine de Saba!

2. Sebba? Incense or fog?:
That blue smoke that left us high.

3. They hear a voice in every wind . . .:
Oui, salaud, mon ventriloquace. Let the wind speak, draughtsman, before marking
the rhumba lines of your wind prose.

4. The Bride?:
The most excellent Bride. For His Excellency. For the Fiancé of Death! joined in
a strong embrace with such a faithful companion. (Pus or lava in his mouth?
Etnamored in his volcanic kiss . . . Torrential larvas in his wedding banquet!)

5. Chinn! Chinn!:
Al-insano! A toast with the big bottle, Magnun! for the love-crazed one.

6. Melusina?:
Only on Satyrdays!

7. A cancan chivaree with canned laughter:
Bah, bah, kana, kan, kan, qah, qaha, qah, qah, qah . . . Fill the glass, drink, enjoy,
and prance. Drink and be merry, for tomorrow . . .

8. Daba?! The Apocalyptic Beast?:
Daba! Daba! Dacapocalyptic beauty-beast with two backs.

9. Tamma!:
Neverended, the Saint Johngoing night! And ready to start again . . .

10. A macabre round of masked revelers with rebecs, rebabs, lutes, atabals . . .:

That sultana doing a samba,[1] shaking a rug: My Soleiman and I, with the narghile on our carpet in the crimson room. Floating high in the clouds like falcons. Gusts and bursts of laughter . . . Sebbá[2] or just gustation? Song of a solo monsoon?[3] What gusts, and bites . . .

Bonbons to bones, to Tabor! A-ha! The lucky emir with divine luck . . .

Lots for cheap! Cheap! The procuress with her exaggerated gestures: For rent, the gal with the gauze veil . . .

Mine! All mine! That dauntless and runty little captain behind the bride in gauze-and-orange-blossom veil. Until he grabbed her and whipped off her veil: a mummy!!![4]

Meager mummery! Spain, his bride and his mummy . . .

And Sinbad, holding on to his turban and shouting: This dance macabre . . . My drug jitters (which drug, dragoman!) rattling me now . . . The Scarlet Woman! now facing the stupid hunchback and his female counterpart futtering and satisfying their lusts on the floor. Right next to the scarlet waves, glimmering with their bracelets and pearls.

Chinn! Chinn![5] The guy with the jackass mask attached to a flask, and holding up a rhyton. Chinn!

The tousled tramp with a scarlet muslin,[6] riding a bass drum bareback, hooting[7] drunkenly, Daba! Daba! Da![8] and drumming with her fetters, Tam-Tam-Tam!

Tam![9] mates, through the mill . . . On! and on! and on this night of ghosts and shadows![10]

Exit in Trance

Arcana

1. Consultantation sur rendez-vaudou . . .:
Consult previous oracular petition! Now opening: cuntinuous sexions behind closed doors . . .

2. Pubis of my dreams. Toisonge! Sivaginal!:
That wild Monsalvat . . . Er ist über alle Venusberg. Mount the Mountain . . .

3. Froh! Froh! Furtive frottage?:
Fickle tickling. Nail the clit. Kitzel! Kitzler!

4. Ear to the drum!:
Trommelfell!

5. Water that must not be drunk, let it flow . . .:
L'acqua ch'io prendo già mai non se corse!

6. Let's convene, venerable sots, at the venusian V of the delectable delta:
Das Goldene Fliess!

7. Tam, cross the Rubiconsciousness stream with your night mare . . .:
Wee-weel done! Mais fais pas du tam-tam, miss. Passe tes thèmes par les Tamississipis. Et que ton eau chante tout le temps.

8. Chant, chantre!:
Aye, or Ayr, from chorus to organ, pipe up! there'll soon be some organ-play in that witch revel. Till it's weel doon!

9. Under the Counter . . . Encountersign! Three were the tricks:
Tan-tan-tan, constantly. Constanzlust! Tan-tan, Tantarantella! Tan-tan-tantrum . . . Tan with Ten . . . Toh! Tu as de la constanze.

PASSO! Passio! Make way for Count Orgazm! on his way to his sexequies, make waves . . . More gas or sweet deaths in the dark of night . . ., Don Juan tripping uncertainly through the half-lit vestibule, in the midst of the imbroglio of cavorticizing masks, following Sleeping Beauty who sleepfloated along murmuring her double half-words. Sighs, sights, citations, and excitations in this house where dates grow on trees. Or in threes, with these doubled Juantendres. Subject d'art? Bee-dart stinging the sleepdreaming-singer. Beebee's kiss! Bis dart qui cito dart. Another randy-voodoo[1] in the night . . .

Triste! Tryst! Tris . . .

Tam! Tam! Tam! A captivating captive straddling a drum (deca-dent cadence), chains hanging from her studded leather collar in an inverted T and branching to each wrist, wearing a red ruffled negligée tied at the waist, and panties of black satin, her pubic area edged with gold curls.[2] Tam-Tam, Tambourlaine! (Her tubby bubs whitetrembling in time with the tam-tam.) Tann-Tann, Tannhäuser! (Rubrubbing[3] her fluffy pubes against the drumhead.[4]) Tan-Tan, Tantalus![5] (Her joined hands sliding between her thighs, along the silky delta.[6]) Laughing convulsively, peppyleptically, her thick blond hair against her face, she straddled her drum, Tam-Tam-Tam![7] swinging her hands and chains.

Tam! O Chanter![8] Tame Link in this chanting chorus of witches . . .

Three they were, and three they'll be, three were the beats to the countersign . . .,[9] and the blonde kept tam-tam-tumbling along, swingling her chains and hips. Tamtam! Tame me or shame me . . . Tam! Tam!

Tam, muzhik! Tampon the wounds and tamp . . .

1. Razz spewtin' . . . Dissolve and coagulate . . .:
Coadulation for il dissoluto punito. Rasp, put-inner . . .

2. Tam! muzak:
Babble on. What annoying music. Play the bugle in the dark, day is dawning! Get up, rise and shine.

3. Tam!:
Mat! Beat the Dutch wife!

4. The Queen!:
In her wheeled throne, pushed by Babelle and Milalias through Kensington Gardens. Rigid and haughty in her throne, posing for Albert Alter next to the Memorial of the Prince Consort (another Albert!). And while Albert made a drawing of the old coot, Milalias entertained her with a shaggy-dog story: Once upon a time there was a woodsman named Wang Tche who went deep into the forest to chop down some trees. Suddenly there in a clearing, he saw two elves playing checkers. He was fascinated by the game and when it ended he realized, My God! How many centuries have slipped by? he realized that the handle of his ax had turned to dust . . . And then what? came the Queen's eternal litany.

5. Wang? Slang for penis? Schlong for dong?:
Wang!

Tam!!! Rasputin,[1] his eyes dilated, stretched an arm toward the Hall of Mirrors at the back: looking down at a chessboard, facing each other in a corner, a Harlequin and a skeleton with a scythe between his legs. ((And their doubles in the mirror.)) Mat!!! he added, closing his fist thumb down.

Tam, muzikant![2] Now leave the house of darkness, and not a peep out of you!

Tam! Mat![3] as the Dutch peasant took out her enormous knife, Matador! and approached as if stepping on eggs, klop! klomp! with her broody clogs. Schaalk, she slashed. And shrieked, Schalkmat!!! brandishing the knife. Shriek, mate! spinning quickly with a fury's face, to her right.

A corpulent woodsman (dressed all in brown leather: tall cap, jacket, tight breeches buttoned to his ankles) holding up his ax, watching with fascination the game ((: chess? checkers?)) being played at the back, in the mirror.

Mat! Matta! Scocco matto! Recheckmate . . .

Watch how you handle that! shrieked a mummy in a bridal gown[4] who rolled by his side, pushed in her wheelchair at top speed by a long-legged nurse. If you keep that up, she snickered ominously, it's gonna turn to dust . . . Just wait and see. Not a Chinaman's chance. Your cock-and-baloney stories, like Chinese puzzles . . . Wang![5] wangler! Wang! and she pointed a finger at Don Juan. Wang! Great sexpectations . . ., she sighed, now at the door of the Hall of Mirrors, sitting rigid in her wheelchair.

1. Estafermo? Boob?:
He can't say boobs to a goose.

2. Spat! Russian?:
Russo! Spat! spread-legged, sleeping sprawled.

3. On the spot!:
Alert. Spat!

4. Into the limelight . . .:
To win the prize with your pair.

5. Peter—?:
Thou art Peter Pun . . . Peter Penman . . . Peter Punk . . . Pit-a-pun? Peter Pantin'!
Peter Pantomime! Peter Pandemonium . . .

Your best portrait! exclaimed a Valentino sheik, his melancholic eyes heavily painted with kohl, as he blasted his camera flash at the petrified woodsman. I'll take this one from behind, he added, and spun crouching. Don't move, Albert. Sta fermo![1] moving back, Così Così! with rapid-fire flashing.

Mate! Tame, team! Meatamorphosystematricks . . .

Mat! schaker . . ., shouted the Dutchwoman. On the mat! My chess-playing abductor . . ., suddenly stripping off her coif (: golden waves cascading over her breasts), smock and pinafore (: nymphish figure!), and she emerged from her cocoon of clothes, butterflying svelte, slender and agile. And lightly dressed (: now with only a smoky blue blouse, skirt of veils, and the rooster at her waist), frolicking barefoot with voluptuous fluttering.

Pat! Pat! Coup de patte! Drowned, and without a hope . . .

Spat! Spat! Spat![2] Rasputin repeated as if talking in his sleep, Spat! his head slowly nodding against his chest. Spot![3] Spot check, mate. He brusquely stretched, spreading his arms, and took a leap straight up to the ceiling, Spot on! and landed spread-legged, arms and legs splayed in an X. Sport! Spot dance![4]

From spot to spot, spotter! Splattered despot . . .

Pat! Tap! Pan! Rapapan! pattered a faunish Peter Pan[5] wrapped in dried leaves and cobwebs, tapping a tambourine with a flute. The plan will come off yet. Tam-tam-tamputations? tambourining harder now. Son mat, ma traqueuse! We'll all wind up sung about, wrung out, and deaf. If not censored. Until we get fed up. Sound

1. Pee-pee . . .:
Peep! Play your pipe, for soon the bell will toll for thee. Tin! Tin! Pan! Tin! Tinker.
Bell! Hop!

2. Pique à sot . . .:
Pique a sot a Picasso!: Pick a saw . . . Pun not indented! The loggy logistician in
search of the unknown Dutchwoman, the ditched Dutchess, in the Café Picasso:
See PILLOW NOTES 43, p. 507.

3. Blik!:
Bleak . . . Blik! Bliksem! Bliksemen! Bleak . . . Hell! Hel! Helen . . .

4. Ling! Cock-a-doodle deadly?:
Careful, gallant cock, with the lingo or linga. With the cackling or crackling of your
laying hen.

5. Harem Kyrie . . .:
E lesión!: E lei, son.

the horn, let the hunt continue . . . And he huffed a loud note on his flute. Tant pis! Pee! Pee![1]

Cause so lost . . . Pik! Pikant! Pique-neck at the . . .

Pique! Assaut![2] covering his face with his hands, in pantomimic self-defense. Yeah, surprise peak assault, like that day of our pickup in the Picasso. Alone at the next table. Like an arrow, peek! the way her eyes pierced me. Lightning when she blinked.[3] And so provocative with her miniskirt of veils sculpting her form. Everyone turned to admire her in King's Road. Look but don't touch? Sexy exhibitionist guarding her charms. With tooth and nail in that shadowy corner of Kensington Gardens next to the statue (and from his hair he pulled a curl of leaves) of Peter Pan. Sweeping the dry leaves along with our feet, as we struggled embracing. And howling as if it were killing her. Careful! with the knife. And with the wound . . ., as he deftly dodged the dukes of the windmillitant Dutchess. Cock the cock! Chicken out, or we'll lose it all. And let's to bed. Kip. Down! Kip. Down! Let's see if you peck . . .

Pik! Kip! From pique to prick with our Lady of Pique . . .

Flying high! But not with your gallant tramp, he sighed and rolled his eyes, who followed you while all the clocks went off, klok! klok! kloek! on King's Road. First aiding and then abedding. Take it easy. She's breaking the cockles of my heart. And then . . . before the cock crows kee-kee![4] kee-kirikee! harakiri . . .[5] Before the fighting cock sings . . . Aay! What a harpy! scratching and baring

1. Good Ramadan!:
Quel ramdam!

2. Alcuzcuz? Couscous?:
Trying to eat her up with kisses . . . Kuss! Kuss . . . Cusí, cusí. Until I met my kismet . . .

3. Lul! Lul!:
Och kommer! No more ululations, smart Spunish cunquistador! don't ululate for your lulu. No more penitent penis pointing panting paining after the Dark Lady of Dong. Alas and alack, a lass and a lack . . .

4. Nat pak!:
Soaked, spash! in a cloudburst . . .

5. Bread and bread:
Better Pita than Pan.

her claws. Very long and sharp, a real harpianist . . . And blood red. Like her lips, parted, a wound . . .

Seal those lips! Fra Lippo Lippy! Labile lips . . .

The first kiss, happy happenstance! by chance when we were snooping, hungry, our faces pressed tight to the window menu of that Moorish restaurant in Earl's Court. "Good ram, madam!"[1] when Ali Baba in babouches came to the door. We read no further. She didn't like mutton. Nor, as it turned out, kus-kus[2] either . . . Fast day! not even a bite. Ay! Fastidious! Well-armed with her purse, red with a beaked rooster head clasp, kris! kras! the crest encrusting me in my my . . . Christ!!! not those low blows! and me ululululating[3] writhing with pain . . .

Tam! Tam! Tom Fool. To tame Our Lady of Amsterdarm, marm.

Dam! Damn! Damp! with three tambourine smacks. Sopping wet, and slapped to boot! with my undulating Amsterdamsel. Caught in a tempest, nut-puck![4] flying at top speed like a goblin with my wet blondine . . . In the English style, from pub to pubis! and pouring it on . . . That night of rounds, ringing in the reign, making the rounds of our Never-Never-London, reviving from rum to rumrum, from street to treat, and her still sniveling . . . And pâté and patty pan and pat-a-cake and pita-pun,[5] pit-a-pat to peter . . .

Tang! Tan! Traan! Tear down, Bellman . . .

1. Rash! Rash!:
Riss-ratsch! The vengeance is complete.

2. From sop to nuts. We get wet . . .:
Wij worden nat. We get wet, yet we lean towards lean . . .

3. Still no?:
Nuts!

4. Salomessalina . . .:
Flying from table to table with her enormous knife, what a mess. I want another cup, kop! I want the head, kop! of my feline painter. Anybody here know him? I'm Helen Helder. And he's Albert Alter. [Two, all-too-alliterative!] And this sponger tries to leech off me. Ik ken je niet! I don't know you. I want my Albert. And crying and weeping and hiccuping over her cup: I want another cup, kop! I want the gross head of my grosso modo painter. [Van Dyck?]

Her life and works, or strife and lurks, be traanquil . . ., that she told me tear by tear. Weepy Dutch courage! In search of her beloved painter, who left after an altercation. Go ahead and cry, I said to myself, yours truly offers a shoulder to cry on. And she cried and she sobbed and she blew her nose fwee! flee! or so it sounded, with my hanky.

Fee! Free! Flee-for-all!

Her concolorist painter had flown the coop, and she was hot on his trail. From paint to pint. To love and health! And traanquility. Calm down, love. I'll give you a shoulder to cry on, still ranting and raining, and it's in one ear and out the other. If she finds him she'll tear him to shreds. A Hals with millstone ruff? Decapitated! A wide-brush Rembrandt. I'll cut if off! A Van Gogh with an ear. Oor else I'll cut it off! Like the night she slashed his canvases. Wraak! Wreaking Havoc with cut and slash.[1] She comes up crying and I wind up clinging to her, and me soaked to the bone. Her eyes sparkling. You really found a dandy or a brandy this time, what a tipsy talker. And cry-baby. A hunter mad-in-love with that dauber man. A fool, lost looking for that two-bit painter. And now the clocks were sounding. Dong! Dong! Ding dong!

Tong! Tom! Temps! Hearing bells . . .

Tan! Nat![2] the Flying Dutchwoman sang out. Not yet nut.[3] Aah! Aay! All wet, as steeped in it then as in this mashquerade. Like a tipsy cake or a rum pudding. Making eyes at me and I left him almost blind. Drenched kiss. So he put on the spoiled trousers . . . C'mon, you prude! If you don't get wet, you don't wet . . ., as she fluttered about lightly, dancing the dance of veils[4] ((salomelo-dramatic!)), and windmilling her knife on high. I'll transpierce you, parting each and every part . . .

Strap first! From pact to pat . . .

1. Toad dance for a two-toed dancer, Rasputin:
Rasp! Put in!

2. In a tryst . . .:
Tan! Tzaraband . . . Nom approximatif. Scratch, tsarapat, sketch . . . Rasp! Da.
Da.

3. Ia jachúpit!:
I want a drink!

4. Ia jachú spat!:
I want to sleep!

5. As-tu dit con?:
Con, Comrade! What a misfortune.

6. From goose to goo . . .:
Mother Goose!: From goods to goose . . . What's sauce for the gander . . .
((Because of Rimbaudelaire, Milalias almost came to blows with him in a pub on
Old Brompton Road.)) Mots D'Heure Gousse? Mother Goose, le palmipédé, the
flat-footed pederast and his pretty boys. ((The protector of minors had been
implicated in a web of drugs, some time ago, when one of his charges died of an
overdose . . .)) He was patron or matron of a band of young studs, strategically
placed around Earl's Court after nightfall.

7. Stop!:
Pots! Pot à pot. Pot! And you'll gain the text by the sweat of your testa. Pot à eau!
To drink, Prosit! and ask for more . . .

8. Galloprancing!:
Topotát! Topotát! Let this past pass . . . If it be possible, let pass this lass . . . Hop!
Hopak! DEPORTEE, FEET ROPED!

9. Boiling?:
And fresh. Hot and cold. All in a sweat.

10. Bol! Lob!:
Keep the pain rolling . . .

Tsarapat! Rasputin jumped doubled up like a toad,[1] Tsar à pattes! Oui-da! Da! Dada![2] kicking out his legs with each jump, Topotat! Toptat! his arms crossed over his chest and his boot-tips reaching to his forehead. Spot! Spot! hopping robotically, Spot! now neighing hoarsely, Yahooch!!! with a long whinny. Yeah! Haw! Chew! Pit![3] keeping time with shouts. Stop! stamping breathless and panting. Yeah! Haw! Chew! Spot![4] with his cancan't chant.

Rush on, Russian! Cancan, con![5] the scream of a grandmotherly-faced man wearing a ribbon coif and a boa of pink feathers, tapping —pitterpat—and duckwalking[6] about. Hey! And he jumped back to dodge the bellowing muzhik bolting towards him.

Topot! Potop! Fits and agonies . . . Kick and stamp in the pot-pourri . . .

Then heading left, through the passage opened by the astonished spectators, cancanning to a steaming samovar on a low corner table, next to the door to the vestibule. Stop! he stood up in a neat leap, Topot! Pot![7] and wiped the sweat from his forehead with the back of his hand. Sport! If I keep up the sport, he said shuffling, they won't deport. Steppe Dance![8] I'll train myself for the Bolshoi . . . On he went with his tapdance, Keep the pot boiling![9] panting and dripping sweat, Keep the ball rolling . . .[10]

On en a ras-le-bol de son bol! Let that ball roll . . .

Roc and ball! he exclaimed, pointing at Sinbad, who volleyed his white balloon with leaps and bounds. Roc! turning, ears alert, to his left: from the hall came, in waves, the thunderous Grom! Grom! Pogrom! of a rockandroll storm. Roc! he repeated, stretching his

1. Baroque! So fatal!:
Roc! Fatality, in Russian, name of the fatal bird . . .

2. There?:
There!

3. Mate?:
Mate, for death!

4. Mammaterassa!:
Mater Asa . . . Magna Mater . . .

5. Full moons:
And of solid gold . . . Asa the Golden Ass! [The resplendent star of the porno-
mysticomic series, MISS TICK, discovered by Milalias in an occult bookstore near
Covent Garden. Asa? O DIN? Bob "Hitch-Cock" had asked innocently, thinking
it was just an artist's pseudonym. It's all the same, isn't it? Bob didn't know then
that Asa the Mystagogue was half White Russian, from her mother's side, and
that Asa was her real name. Asa the Golden Ass . . . uh. Her mysterious disappearance, leaving an enigmatic but pointed message as the only clue, would give
plenty of headaches to our detective heroes for a long time. Babelle might even
suspect that Asa's punctilious message is the work of the author of the Mysteries
of London, fallen into desuetude, his serum therapy against a new chicken pox . . .]

6. Attention! High tension!:
Yes, very high. Electric skeleton in the closet drama.

7. Shoot!:
Shut!

hands over the jabbering samovar. Roc!!![1] in a still hoarser voice, and raised his head with a look of surprise.

Roc and bol, Rocambolshevik! Russian carom, Russian ruse . . .

Tam![2] and again he pointed a finger, Tam! to the right. That's also fatal . . . Mat!!![3] looking wide-eyed to the end of the room, as if seeing visions. Tam!!!

Mat! Mater! Materassa . . .[4]

Grandiose in all her . . . humanity, a corpulent Lady Godiva ((her body painted with golden dust?)) and dressed only in the shawl of her hair ((blond hair dangling to her ankles, scarcely concealing her bottom, pears round as dunes)),[5] glistening by the light of a lantern held high—as if waving an incense burner around her—in the right hand of a hermit, who followed her using a red staff as a cane.

Il est sous le mat là! On the mat . . .

Mat? She stopped and rolled her head to her right, toward the Hall of Mirrors. Mat? alert and with furrowed brow, watching the game between the Harlequin and the Skeleton.

Schelettro shock . . .[6] Mat! Mate . . .

Sh! pion . . ., turning her wide attractive face slowly to the left, Chut![7] and staring at Rasputin, who panted crouching, toadlike, next to the steaming samovar.

1. Trup! Corpse?!:
Russocitation. General uprising. All available bodies report immediately to their troupe de choc.

2. Shut!:
Shoot off. Offshoot: the end clowns the work.

3. Pour qui sonne le glaçon?:
Gloss on! Dr. Pungloss.

4. Titbit!:
Have a bit, player. Titbit! Your tongue shall be split . . .

5. Tit for tat . . .:
Breastbeating? Tit for tot . . . Mamma for Mammon.

6. Tot up!:
Tod. Dot.

7. The Mark of the Beast? Smallpox?:

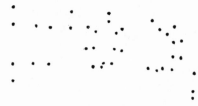

8. Of blood?:
Dried. ((From last month? Another menstruous design? / Trace. Cut. Erase. Asa the Geomater Magna would trace her three viscous circles with a finger inked in blood, on disgusted Milalias's stomach, and then transform them into GOD. Or into TOD, another Walpurgiss Night . . . Asa the Golden Ass straddling the chest of the stud jackass. Hee-haw.))

Peeping Tom, the water is piping . . . Bully bully! Boy oh boil . . .

Things are getting pretty hot around here, said Don Juan. Hot air in this hothouse. But in this hubbub, and he looked around scornfully, with this somersaulting tam-tam smatter of mad hatters no one knows whether the shots are coming or going. Shoot! he shouted, shrugging his shoulders. Bluffoonery! Or maybe not, who knows. Quelle troupe![1] of magicians. And they all shoot to kill, to keel over. Still waiting for the coup de grâce? Shoot![2] They blindfold you to face the firing squad. But some refuse it. See no evil . . . Hearing nothing? Shut up. Better to be like the three wise monkeys, and he hooded himself in his cape. ((Kaput! Kaputsín!))

Rompe i tímpani! I spick! Break the eyes . . .[3]

Titbeat![4] Tit for Tot![5] with chattering teeth, Tat to Tot![6] and she rubbed her arms, her shoulders, My tititeeth are chattitittering! and her glorious golden globes. Bittitter cold . . ., hugging herself (: her belly, over the pubis, tattooed with black dots)[7] and stamping, Tittup! Tit-tat-toe! with little hops and shivering. Beat! Beat the Devil's tattoo . . .

Tap toe! Tattoo! Tapotez tous . . .

But baby it's cold outside. Cover me up, I'm so cold . . ., she implored the bat-winged devil in a blue loincloth (: three red circles[8] painted on his chest) who responded by limping forward and raising a wide scarlet cape with both hands.

1. Now she'll heat up . . .:
Frozen that autumn afternoon, wrapped only in a cape, in the Highgate Cemetery.
[High gait . . . Danse macabre. Our grave compiler of epitaphs liked to stroll
through brambled Highgate Cemetery. Right there, Asa! Focus in on her, Bob . . .,
and pointing at the inscription: *Aurora Mathilda Freebody*. In that gloomy grave,
Miss or Mrs. Freebody awaits the resurrection of the flesh. For what? Extender is
the night . . . *UNTIL THE DAY BREAK AND THE SHADOWS FLEE
AWAY*. Aurora . . .] Advancing between tombstones and brambles and fallen
angels while Bob and his camera assistant Milalias assaulted her with shouts. Ah
so, Asa. Now spread 'em a little more. Wide open. Now. The cape! Next to the
monument to Marx. Good! Diva! And the poor artist who was copying das capital
head almost fell out of his folding chair.

2. Le jardin de notre émir beau ténébreux . . . Un monde magique . . . Mir-mir-
   mirage! . . .:
Sad sadist! Sad sod! Under the Sade there is a Sodom . . . Satanic sadomasochist
guardener (Sic! Sic 'em) in your ad hoc hell.

3. Cut!:
And shuffle 'em up . . .

You're frozen silly . . .,[1] he said, almost voiceless, and flung—standing on tiptoes—the cape over her shoulders. Now the only thing we need is for you to go out stark naked to the garden of tortures[2] and toss yourself into the pond and catch a galloping pneumonia. Stop this foolishness. Ass! Conasse!

Ace plus ace, basic! Who's the next ace to join the chase . . .

A shabby magician in tattered tails and broken-down top hat (: a sideways eight chalked in on the crown) lines up his three grimy cards on a cardboard box.

With a trick! Ace after sorry ace, now who's ready to face . . .[3]

Astounding! ladies and gents. Watch closely, in sight it must be right. The eyes have it, he added, putting his monocle in his left eye. Here it is. A simple case of an unmarked ace, plain as the space on your face. The ace of clubs. Nothing up my sleeves, holding it high with two fingers, and nothing behind, showing it all around. And now this ace of clubs that you're seeing with your very own eyes, watch closely! we put between the ace of hearts, like this, and the ace of spades. Adjacent. Aces to aces, just adjust . . . And then we shuffle them well. As long as you like.

Fiction friction! One ass scratches another . . .

There! Done . . . Now I'm going to count to three, watch closely! revealing the aces one by one. And the surprise ace is last. Our ace to the finish! OK, I'm going to count. Ready? Open your eyes, soon you'll open your mouths. OK . . . Ready? I'm going to count to three, revealing one ace after another . . . Ready?

Ace! Ace! Ace! With a sass in the cards . . .

1. Arsenic and Old Ace . . .:
Lace! With Ace for a guide . . . (("Arsène Lupin" eventually used rat-killer to poison the Cheshire cat, tyrannical king of that guest house-museum on Holland Road . . . And our asylum too, among those pensioners killing time crocheting and playing cards.))

2. Loo! Loop in!:
Only connect! Howards End . . . Poor Howard Lee-Penn, alias Arsène Lupin: (Deep down Milalias envied that former boardinghouse companion, always involved in adventures and swindles, and with lots of tricks up his sleeve . . .)

3. Ace in the hole . . . From the poop deck?:
Occult ace, in reserve.

Loose aces recalling vaunted arcanum, Don Juan stated as he stared at the magician. Arse up, Arsène Lupin! blasting him with his glare. This two-bit cardsharp, and he opened a breach in the wall of onlookers to get closer still, this skid row trickster almost always wins by a lucky fluke and really cleans up at this dirty game.

Ace! Passe à l'As! Race after ace, and careful with the arsenic . . .[1]

From dearth to death, assiduously assaying all with his arsenal of cheap ruses. That's right, I certainly *do* recognize you! asserted Don Juan, up to the front row now. Arsène Lupin, bankrupt! Astute assassin who frightened his poor landlady to death. Her financial assessor . . .

Plein aux as! From an ace to a salty ace, and then asylum . . .

From disgrace to debasement. Now a waste case with tall tails, after eluding the claws of justice. And his monocle to correct the astigmatism in his left eye. Plus the top hat he pulls his bunnies from. Rabbits joint . . . Don't pay any attention to him. Get out of here! He used to be a teacher and now he's just a cheater. Sleight-of-handyman since his student days. Fess up! Arse up! Arsène Lupin.[2] Don't get taken by this slovenly swindler. Just look at his theatrics! Assiduous assaulter, an asphalt asp . . . You might see him any night on any corner of Charing Cross Road or Oxford Street, behind his cardboard box, doing tricks with his three filthy aces. And his assistants assigned to watch for the police, but sometimes assimilating with the assembly and even betting against him and winning. Then he deals out his grimy aces, face down. Don't pay any attention to him! This prestidigitating cardsharp always hides an ace of diamonds up the seat of his pants . . .[3]

1. Or space of aids:
You silly cunt! An ace of spades in clubs and a bad queen playing jacks, that's not a bad start. And finish . . .

2. Get to the heart of hearts . . .:
And no heart feelings! Get to the art, the art that opens your heart . . . [When the trickster held his cards close to his chest the other gamblers suffered cardiac problems.]

3. Club together . . .:
A very clover idea!

4. Brák? Russian brák!?:
Braque! Marry color with color and suit with suit . . .

5. Shit? A chit from the management?:
Chit! To sew, in Russian, but this rhapsadist will need a compass needle for this yarn.

6. Tuz? Ace, in Russian?:
Aces to aces. And also tooth for tooth . . . ((Foolish Arsène Lupin. How did he even think of playing cards with the tarot-twisting Asa . . . For him she would do one of her most somber tricks, a grim trick!))

One!: the ace of spades.[1] Two: the ace of hearts.[2] And THREE!: the ace of, CUT IN TWO! ladies-and-gentlemen, the ace of CLUBS!!![3] As if by magic. Asstounding! ladies-and-gentlemen. But don't go away, the best is yet to come. Even more astounding! Once again we're gonna put one piece here and another piece here, between the two assassin aces. Then we shuffle them and shuffle them again. There! And now I make the magic gesture of the great union, Bric a brac![4] Abracadabrac! and everything will be acey-deucey till we . . .

Chit![5] Cheat on! teased Lady Godiva and she put her index finger to her puckered lips (painted purple like her fingernails and toenails) while her left hand snatched a handful of cards from her cape. Take a swipe! offering them to him like a fan, Grab it! Let's see if you draw my half ace . . ., to the magician. No! rapidly folding up the fan of cards. Not like that. Cut first, letting the bunch fall on the box, resting one hand on his bottom.

Hand to hand, cardhandler! First this card then discard . . .

Hand for hand, said the magician, dauntless, pinching the bundle with two fingers of his left hand. And tooth for tooth,[6] he added, deftly cutting it in the air and trapping it in flight with his right hand. And with a smile of triumph, in the palm of his left hand he displayed a half ace of clubs.

Ace of grace . . .

Ace, capper! Escapee . . ., the Dodo bird in the front row of spectators doing little leaps on tiptoe. If I could find my other half. My aseity! My essential. The half ace that matches my half ace . . ., he said as he nodded off, his beak sinking into his breast feathers.

1. Do-do contsá!:
Until the end! Russo russo! To sleep the eternal dream until the end.

2. Asso fisso! Lascia in asso!:
Get out of the jam.

3. Assoluto!:
Asso luto. Loose. Absolved.

4. More masks—of asthmatics?:
Enough already! Deep respiration in the gags chamber. And as Milalias said on one occasion, getting serious for once: All my masks are like Reis's. Not to hide behind, but rather to avoid asphyxiation. [Deep reispiration!]

5. Patience is the great thing; patience, patience . . .:
And shuffle the cards. Reis would spend the dead hours alone playing solitaire. Especially when his asthma attacks got worse. And when he wrote, he dealt out his little pages—he almost always wrote on quarter-page leaflets—as if they were cards. Patience! and shuffle the cards, Milalias heard him murmur more than once, writing is a game of solitaire.

6. In nine:
Asinine! Word association and idea association. Ass-backwords.

7. Look askew!:
Never directly, always askance. Averted. Obliquely . . . Mrs. Askew . . .: See PILLOW NOTES 44, p. 508.

8. Amor?:
AMORC.

9. Astral card?:
Astral lamb: Ad aspera to Astrakhan. See PILLOW NOTES 45, p. 509.

Ace against ace, to mate . . . Half ace with half ace, ascension! . . ., nodding. Ouf! Passer à l'assoupissement.

Falling asleep counting to a thousand, Don Juan nodded in burlesque imitation. Dodo! Compte ça . . .[1] Count to the end. Alone like an ace . . . Asaz! Assez! Assai![2] Resta in asso.[3]

All alone, ace! From asphyxia to as . . .

Ma non! the Alchemist gasped, rapidly masking himself with his respirator. From asthma to asthmask. Scribbing again in my *Asthmagest.* Asthma jest![4] Asthmas book. Remembrance of asthmas past . . . Lonely anguish reincarnating venturous avatars! Patience,[5] and shuffle. From ace to ace . . .

No! From asphyxia to as . . .[6]

A petite woman with an aged doll's face, topped with a pink coif, sibyllinizing as if in a trance at the end of the line of curious onlookers. The ace is askew, and she peered crookedly[7] at the Alchemist. Raise! still looking cross-eyed at the Alchemist, who panted through his mask, trying to get out of the agglomeration. I give you a prompt, cue in! and the signal. Now my slips are sealed. Ask me no more, amora,[8] twisting her face and eyes looking for the Alchemist. Ask me no more questions . . .

More and more! The great beyond! Ad aspera to astra . . .[9]

*
* *

1. Who was that fairy queen?:
Titty Titania . . .: See Pillow Notes 46, p. 510.

2. Cornucoppia di forzati . . .:
Oxhorn of plenty!

3. Burrone . . .:
Tenor rub! An ass in glass, from gala to gully to gullible, the burlesque burro from bluff to bluff, till he hurls himself over the precipiece . . .

4. What a cavalcade!:
Yep, with Sue Dama and the transvestevedores from the port . . . They were managing the herd of mares in the maremagnum.

My everlasting motto: Bottoms up! the drunk in the donkey head curvetting on his knees, making his way on all fours, Tutti in un botto: Bottoms up! to the buffet table.

And our host of lords? Where, o where could he be fauned? Let's see who freefills our clashes now, another croupful! Drink up shriners and flawget all yearn troubles, with the elixir of love. Syncopate and drain your cup, better copulate than never, I always say. Isn't that how it goes? I raise my glass to erase hell. From Orgy and Besstial I think. Hee-haw! Here he comes now, what a maremagnetic figure, swaying in the ship of fools. Vieni qui, Napoleone. Soccorso! My head is dizzy. I've lost my balaance asset. Hee-haw! My head's such a heavy rock, like heavy metal, that my legs collapse under it and I'm stuck back here in this backanal . . .

Hee-haw! Don't bore us with your brays, said the winged fairy Titania[1] (: and as she bends over her bouncing breasts almost pop over the neckline of her crepe dress) holding a foaming cornucopia for the drunk on all fours who poked his donkey head under the table laden with bottles and towers of glasses. Brandi il brandy! A toast with my pornucopia![2] he spluttered, grabbing the edge of the table with his free hand and trying to stand upright.

Whoa! Wa-wa-watch out . . .

The din (: the ass[3] collapses in an avalanche of glass) drowned out the bleating of Mother Goose, with his old woman's shawl and beaked mask, who backed away wrapping himself in a long boa of pink feathers. Brute! So brutish!

Take him out to the garden, give him some air! Napoleon ordered the two musculargebreasted Valkyries[4] (: lank albino wigs, mid-thigh black boots and black leather panties) who kept convulsing and cracking their whips in an epilectic candombe, beside the demolished table.

1. Stick!:
Or stickiness . . .

2. Il napo nel nappo, leone!:
Turn the turnip and nip along . . . Best to skirt that miniskirt. Da capo, cappone, al coppone. Al copione!

3. Lice à lice . . .:
Entre en lice . . . Délice! With our Alice, to pluck the fleur-de-lis, the dry white starched flowers of her provocative miniskirt: See PILLOW NOTES 47, p. 512.

4. LSD?:
On a white wall in Notting Hill Gate an inscription that delighted our protagonists: "Money is the most powerful drug. LSD vs. £.S.D." But Milalias maintained, with Kipling's help, that there's a still more powerful drug. Dreamer!

5. Likely a rare verbal art?:
Let's all read very acutely . . .

6. Hoffmann? Not the one with the tales . . .:
Almost. Fantastic stories, of terror, that set your teeth on edge! whispered from mouth to mouth . . .: See PILLOW NOTES 48, p. 513.

Pastis or past tease, a potbellied Napoleon raised a cup in one hand and a carrot in the other. Carrot or stick?[1] like a two-fisted toast. A cock-tail of champagne frappé? and as he bowed so gallantly, he dumped the cup[2] on the miniskirt with fleur-de-lis of silver lamé worn by the attractive Eurasian with straight black hair sprawled alone on the white couch.

Ma robe! she jumped up in a rage, hastily brushing off her skirt. Toute foutue, ma robe. Salaud! Look what you've done . . ., brusquely brushing way Napoleon, who fell all over himself with excuses, Scusi! Scusi! It got away from me . . ., trying to dry her off with a handkerchief. Mi permetta, la lisciata . . .

A lease is a lease, alas, little solace, at least fleur-de-illicit Alice . . .[3]

Lysergic acid? wondered Don Juan, approaching the buffet table in disarray. The most powerful drug?[4] Hallucinations? Like absurd recollections vividly aroused.[5] Laughing at reenactments, vaudeville amplifications . . .

It's time! It's time! the bony old man in a white hospital gown (Dr. hoffmann[6] embroidered in red over the breast pocket) and a disheveled macbethian witch-wig stirring with a ladle the squat zinc bucket in the middle of the table. It's time!

Drink up! Let's all drink! bellowed the Bellman, collapsed faceup on the floor. Buck up, let's bucket along! C'mon everybody, drink up! free well-drinks, all's well that drinks well-drinks . . . Imbibe, let's go way beyond the pail.

Peil! Pail! Pay off . . .

1. Drink, in Spanish?:
Beben! in German. Sturm und Drunk!!!

2. Ad lib, libertine?:
Ad libitum, bit by bit . . .

3. Hoffmannstropfen . . .:
Anodyne liquor? Devil's elixir! Laus Semper Diabolus.

4. Locus sigilli, de-sealed? LSD?:
Lysergic acid reinforces veiled arcana.

5. Bared back by back, truc pour troc:
Setting up Goyesque caprichos for the pornophotographer and filmmaker Bob "Hitch-Cock," with the two Spaniards that Milalias came across in that Soho hovel.

Drink! Drink! Dr. Hoffmann exclaimed, Beben![1] tremorously stirring his brew. Liquorous aphrodisiacs renew vanquished amours! Liben ad lib . . .[2]

Elixir of love![3] Eau des visions! Ludifying Spirit Divine . . .[4]

*
* *

They've already got seats! Yeah, to settle down . . ., two foppish dandies in frock coats laughing and poking fun at two señoritas in underwear, one standing and the one on the right sitting on a trunk, in forced poses with reed chairs upside down on their heads. And with their petticoats raised high, like hoods, exposing thighs and backsides.

Now that they're saddled, said the one standing, winking, to mount them . . . Bareback! answered his accomplice, shorter and big-headed. Bareback![5] gallopushing ahead horsestyle in his chair, Giddyup! Bareback!

Hush! ordered the sheik à la Valentino, Don't move! his camera flashing rapidly, There! Hold it. Play it cozy. Cosi. Cosi.

Hey Bob! the taller one cried out, don't miss this Spanish close-up . . ., and he slapped the rump of one tottering about, the chair still on her head.

*
* *

1. Paws off!:
P$\frac{a}{u}$ss off! Categorically stated. Ou pour miaou dire, en roumain: Pisoi, pisica!

2. Fuaim catha!:
Scatticism! Catastrophy! Battle bell. Celt up!

3. La Chatte Beauté! (Nume de botez):
Your kitty . . . The Rumanian cat. La chatte câline . . . Gata! Enough!

4. On cue more? An cù mor!: The big dog!!!?:
With its tail between its legs. Still following you, and you stinging from the beating your Scottish woman gave you . . . Mórag! More agog? More aggressive, your Mórag. All because she had holes in her stockings and didn't want to take off her boots. REPARTEE? FEET RAPER! ((What was the name of that receptionist at the Cumberland Hotel? Mórag.))

5. Matou, échec et mat . . .:
Matemorphosis! The king is dead, long live the kin. Scacco matto! Chah mat! (Matka: Chahut et russe . . .)

6. Fu, michino? Fu, fugato? Fou, fouteur chat fouetté? Fu, fa un bacino! Da mi
   basia mille . . .:
Catullus felis! Oh my scarlatin pimpernel, quit fu-fuing with the fugue . . . And don't give us fu for thought. Lúcciole per lanterne. Des lanternes pour des vessies. Meister Lamper, du Sadist! By night all cats are leopardners. The puss and the pussycat. Gatte und Gattin . . . Kot! Kot! Leave your verbal catoptricks and catty remarks. La gatta morta, échec et matou, and the Chesshire Cat always check-mating on the same board. Caterwalling!

7. Scratching out your sharp or flat nocturnotes?:
Donne ta langue au chat! Cat got your tongue? Sound off, man. Murrmurrs of music . . .

8. Fa la fusa il furetto fugato . . .:
Blowing their three-way fuses. Triple croche-pied!

9. Amorous amiaurosis:
Or love is blind. A cat-and-meowse game, or a cataract operation! From cat to cot, or lion to lyin', or puss-and-brute, a-cunting we will go . . .

Sharp pause!¹ Bloodcurdling silence . . .

Feverish catscratching² behind the sofa: the two booted cats on all fours, scratching and tickling the belly-up blind man, who struggled epileptically and tried to reach his black wire-rims on the floor next to him.

He tried to take my boots off, the boaster! murmeowed through clenched teeth the feline blonde³ in tight white mid-thigh boots, white silk stockings with bib and suspenders. And what about me! came the meowhine of the redhead in patent leather boots, red and green tartan skirt and a black bra failing to contain her swaying breasts. Crashed there on the divan, the paunchy pasha trying to take mine off by force. That's right, mine! and she raised her fists to her cat mask, in a boxing pose. But I gave him what he had coming, right to him! a low blow to the bey at bay. Un coup maure!⁴ she mormurred in a galling French-Scottish accent. ((Feetishist!!! that sourpuss-in-boots?))

Le chah chatouilleux . . .⁵ Cha-cha-chat show! Catachresis . . .

Fu, fu!⁶ Don Juan still puffing under his breath, or as if blowing out candles, as he pulled back from the catscratching. Sows and furies signifying nothing . . . Foufoutre! The two tigresses pressing and congressing and stressing while he's messing around for his glasses . . . Fou rieur! Furious furry Erinyes baring their claws . . . Griffe au nez!⁷ Grief, o nails. Fugue of fugacious confusions.⁸ Furiant! and fleeting fusions of little or no futility . . . ((They cut the clauses right off the categorist.))

Pizzicatto! Amoroso meow . . .⁹

*
* *

1. The drunk Hungarian?:
Let the ball roll . . . He almost hung it up that time. That ballistic ball-of-fire rolling along, making the rounds of London's wastelands.

2. Holmes, watsonized?:
Poirotized too, was our hercules in waiting. Il fait le Poirot!

3. At fault . . .:
Folt!

4. Ding! Dong!:
Tong!

5. Triad?:
Triad. Pluck the clover . . . Turn eternal. Tri. Trip, trick, trismus. A good name, Triad! for the secret Chinese organization controlling all the dirty business around the white drug in London.

6. Ach ja! Treffas!:
From tréfa to trefly . . . Pluck the clover . . . Tréfából mondtam: I said it as a joke . . .

Two mandarins stayed out of the hallway mayhem, whispering with an air of mystery next to the stairway. That's the detective Mr. Leone hired to keep an eye on the party, the more wizened one said with a smile.

Who? The Hungalian? exclaimed his cohort, who clutched a violin case against his chest. That dlunk hungalian?[1]

The velly same, indicating with arched eyebrows the plump unsteady Sherlock Holmes[2] who was studying with a magnifying glass an off-white ((suspicious?)) stain[3] on the black carpet of the stairs. And he added, cackling: Holmes in the hall . . .

Where? asked the one with the violin. Where?

Chlist's sake, light here, you mongoloid! hissed the more emaciated mandarin. And right under the nose and ears of that Holmes we'll do the exchange. When the clock strikes the hour. Tang! Tong![4] Then the only missing Triad member will be here.[5] The third man. The guy with a half ace of clubs[6] that goes with mine. That's who we give the case to. Nobody else.

All the heloin! And the coke hidden in the gland piano?

Sh! Shish! That too.

Couldn't it be that Fu Manchu over there? pointing with the violin case at the ancient Chinese man coming across the hall dragging his slippers, looking in all the corners and snorting Fu! Fu! furiously.

1. Talk?:
Tok!: See PILLOW NOTES 49, p. 515.

2. Lubrica umbra . . .:
Fleeting shadow. Lèche la proie pour l'ombre . . .

3. Só! Só!:
Word for word. Ever more elarborate larborinth, word for word with your Magyar magic. Arvacadabra! The poor little orphan didn't even peep a larva of a word: árva szót sem szólt.

4. A peel? . . .:
Peeling skin off step by step, he almost broke his neck. Stair by stare. Step up, puppets.

5. Roll that wheel, Kerek . . .:
Our roundabout detective Janos Kerek . . .

6. At last, an atlas of Attic salt? Fat list on lust, at least, as tall atlas:
Large almanac requires vigorous alpinist . . .

Fu, fool! Sherlock Holmes exclaimed as he spied on the two wicked mandarins from the last landing of the spiral staircase. Knock on wood . . ., rapping Tok! Tok[1] the handrail. What luck. Could the boss be in on this too? Everything here revolves around Napoleon. What an opportunity. Ho ho! now I know where they're hiding the snow.

Snowwhite dust! Rootin' tootin' . . .

A-ha! Oh lo lo! the detective hooted chattily, peeping through the stairway shaft, Hola! greeting Don Juan pursuing Sleepwalking Beauty. What a rush you're in, sir. Going after that sleepwalker like someone possessed. This is something fantastic, who would have thought it? I'd call her a resourceress! She's got him caught in the net, pulling him along by an invisible thread. Get out of here. Free flight. Not even close, not even in dreams. Forever stuck to his shadow.[2] The master slave. Hello and good-bye! Slave of love, so serf-possessed. Servus! fugitivus . . .

Hang it! Stop! So![3] Cut . . .

Ay! Sherlock Holmes lost an ay as he slipped[4] and soundly fell, rolling roundly[5] down the stairs.

At the foot of the stairs, among the pillows in the dark corner on the left, Indochinese Alice with her fleur-de-lis miniskirt wheedled and cajoled a giant blue caterpillar in dark glasses, who calmly smoked his water pipe and meditated before an open atlas or orb-book.

SALT AN ATLAS![6] Saltatory Psalter . . .

1. Golden?:
Mr. Hsi-men's goldenlotus . . .

2. T'a mei yu lai:
No, he's not coming.

3. The real heroine is gone . . .:
Lusty Andalusian recalled, vividly attractive: See PILLOW NOTES 50, p. 516.

4. Alone on the beach? Without her?:
It's not good for man to be alone . . . Robinson was thinking of that evanescent
woman of his dreams. Lying on his stomach on the deserted beach, Robinson
writing in the sand with his finger. (Sunstroke?) He would write, then erase with
his hand, then write again. The parrot, parked on his shoulder, caws in his ear in
French: A solas, salaud. Tu es tout seul à la plage sans elle . . .

This is how I interpret my dream, doctor: Tu es tout seul á la plage sans L . . .
The beach we call the page.

Oh là là! toujours à la page, Mr. Alia. Always back to the page. Let's see how
you explain yourself.

I lie la! the lala of a Chinese girl in a black tunic with a golden lotus[1] embroidered on the back. Ai, lai la!! while she massaged the lanky fellow with a towel wrapped round his waist stretched out beside her on a straw mat. Ah, here they come! energetically pounding his back with her palms. Who? starting to rise, leaning on an elbow. All we need now is Fu Manchu . . . Is he coming? handing her his cigarette. Ta! May you lie?[2] she snatching the cigarette away, and with both hands gently stretching him out again. Relax.

More Orientals here, said Don Juan, looking around distrustfully, than on a Sunday afternoon on Gerrard Street. But I think at least one of them is faking. Shadowplayers. In costume. Ah, here comes Attila now, lugging his helmet under his arm to show off his hair, the blond beast . . ., watching the dyed-blond mongoloid monkey talk excitedly (or arguing?) with the two mandarins at the foot of the staircase. Did he let Lozana, the Lusty Andalusian, go?[3]

*
* *

The hour of perturbation, a must, one must repeat the turbid action. Must muster more . . . Doubled . . . Where are you? Where have you been . . . Dream white. That desert beach, and me. That surf. Like a resounding voice, around . . . Je suis tout seul à la plage sans elle . . .[4] Where are you? More and more crowded, and ever more alone.

A shaggy caveman-Robinson passed by murmuring, completely alone in the crowd, with his animal-skin parasol and a parrot on his shoulder.

1. The watchword of this book:

2. In the mirror:

Where are you? and he started to ascend the stairway slowly. Is this some sign of her? bending over the white stain on the carpet. White on black? A negative? Her footprint . . . Alone on the beach, writing alone. Robinsolo . . .

Robin song! Poor Robinson Hood . . .

Up and away! words of the lady in tall white coif and blue tunic adorned with reversed golden letters,[1] lightly climbing the stairs. Ipso facto. (And to you? . . . That moronic Spaniard with a mocking face when I asked him *y a ti* . . . And to you? Why?) I'm coming. All the way up! And she stopped in a trance on the landing, looking in a full-length mirror at the golden legend[2] embroidered on her tunic. MONTE LE DESIR! she moaned in ecstasy.

*
* *

I'll never forget you . . ., the owl-faced gypsy with a crewcut following the ruddy waitress overladen with beer mugs. And I've never been able to forget you, Maite . . .

Sing matins later, Humpty Dumpty interposed, and slapped the gypsy on the back. Don't bother her now. Fort von hier! Get lost! Can't you see she's busy . . .

Just a minute, my lucky clovergirl! a musketeer swooped in and hooked by the waist a blonde in fishnet stockings and a green satin miniskirt shaped like a clover who struggled furiously, swinging her tray. Sprinkled through the mob, other waitresses half-dressed in clovers tried to cross the mayhem balancing their trays on high.

Pluck . . . Pluck . . .

1. Svantaggio per il signore signo . . .:
Il cigno cerca la signa . . .

2. Mythological nickname . . .:
Emblem after emblem, encounter after encounter . . . We'll come across that Swedish hippie again in Swan Lake, that friend of the swan's ways . . .

2. Penis Neid! Pen is Snide!:
Freudulent! They'll wring that neck . . .

4. Ogni fallo aspeta il suo laccio . . .:
A fine tangle!

5. Eskimalicious . . .:
Yes, always the woman of ice. Who melted by the fireside. Frigid Brigid . . . La femme de glace. Till she got warmed up. La femme dégueulasse! Bonny lass!

6. La première coupe?:
La coupe sombre! Coupe de comensemencement . . .: A la queuquête! A la queue leu leu, chorée!

7. How far can he see?:
He can see a sin agog . . .

8. Vas al vas? Or sav lasav?:
Reversed so you'll understand me right. Or what's left. All hebrewery to me . . .

9. Beware of a one-book man!:
That holy axiom doesn't apply here . . .

10. At least you come out of it winning . . .:
Beware of false profits!

In the vestibule and connecting rooms it was impossible even to fight one's way through: And yet it was moving! an uncontainable mare magnum froing to and flow. This way and that, each wave a wave of hands and arms and nodding heads of those trying desperately to keep afloat or keep track of their partner.

Svan![1] Svans! the hippie Leda[2] twisting and contorting in flower-patched jeans and barefoot, twisting the neck[3] of a rubber swan. Duck and dive, Paul Anka, sing your rock and roll . . .

Happiness! Making its triumphal entrance in the vestibule was a walking phallus, a flesh-colored cylinder with its gland adorned with paper streamers,[4] Happiness! Hap penis! joyfully escorted by the chorus of bacchantes, Happenis! Happenis! who priapushed and toasted it at the top of their voices.

Cock-a-noodle-do-nothing . . .

Getting flustered, eh? you big turkeyneck! An Eskimo woman[5] with a full-moon face and a big black beauty mark by the left corner of her mouth, bundled in furs from head to foot, as she raised her cup. Let's go, in one swallow. C'est si bon . . . And she licked the rouge with a tongue-tip, half-closing her mongolorious eyes. Just a sec, waving with one hand and draining the last of her cup,[6] there's still the farce of the farseeing Pharisee . . .[7]

Sav lasav,[8] sav lasav, an unperturbed bearded rabbi in blue-fringed tallith, reciting in a resounding voice, slowly and majestically, the Book[9] in his hands. Kav lakav, kav lakav, zer sam, zer sam.

Babelondon? Bah! No man is a prophet[10] in his own tongue . . .

1. Without sound or sense . . ..
Take care of the sensounds . . .

2. Devilish note from our Rababelizer:
Je croys qu'il nous fourche icy quelque slangaige diaboulique, et qu'il nous cherme comme enchantreur.

3. Voluble butterfly . . ..
Letterfly . . . (After the young girls in folio, in florio in all the speech orchards in a world of words.)

Another maniac dancing to a different drummer![1] and Don Juan dived into the masqueradiating mob, elbowing through in pursuit of Sleeping Beauty. God only knows what the devil she's saying. Puppet Satán, Pope Satàn, aleppe . . .[2]

Leppe! Leppo! Lapidly . . .

Hey not so fast . . ., spinning around in search of the sleepwalker. Getting me all twisted up and dizzy with riddles. Loose words, words without rhyme or reason.

Lepidopterist[3] ambling, rambling, vigilant, alert . . .

Death's head beneath the sphinx . . ., joked Don Juan. Lost cabala . . . Chaotic cabaletters. Now where? Vane man, turning around. I'll keep a tight reign on her.

Liberated again, reknotting voluptuous attachments . . .

((Don Juan Tenorio trying to get the tenor of what was being whispered, flitting around the bride. La Mesmeriée mise à nu . . . Fluttering around the sphinx, Melmoth the Wanderer! without understanding what she was saying, maybe trying to turn an enigma into an image. Or not to complicate matters, suppose he was following her fascinated with the resolution of someone seeking the solution, hoping to pose the final question, recast to the replayed response. The dissolution of the solution? Il dissoluto punito! o sia Don Giovannish . . .))

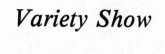

Variety Show

1. Rêves-errances . . .:
S$\frac{1}{0}$ngeries d'une nuit d'été. (Shut up and exit stage left, before Monsieur Dodo dozes off from it all. Before Milalias goes to sleep on us. [Le protéegoniste ensorcelé de cette mascharade dans la villa des mystères.]) Songe d'une Nuit d'Hétérodoxie. Conte divers. Madsummer Knight's Dream.

2. Master of Ceremonies? Master of Confusion?:
Milalias Clown.

3. The whole world through a hole:
To see the world and then die.
(The next world? Old new world? ((Vieux nouveau monde de la boîte à malice? Monde du diable boiteux? Tout dépend de la couleur du trompe-l'œil par lequel regarde le sage curieux.)) Dat ol' debbil whorl? It all depends on the I-color of the beholder or self-beholder. The great constipated Lutheran, le grand constipécheur, speculated that the world was the open anus of Satan. ((The bottom is out of the Universe!)) What a morass. Lutero senza speculo . . .) Assign your eye to the spyglass, pore through the peephole. Look. Il faut le trouver. Prends du Champ! back up and look through the keywhole of a Spanish door . . .

4. Chacun en a sa claque. Nous sommes la claque . . .:
Et vous êtes la joue! Etes-vous jaloux? Bravo! Quel bordel!

Ladizzies and Yawntlemen, sueñoras y sueñores . . . Mesdames et Messieurs, mes révérences . . .¹ Peep-oh! Peep all! Beautiful people! the dodo-beaked emcee in a penguin costume (an insignia with MC^2 on the label) straddling a tilting microphone stand in the center of the stage and trying to make himself heard. Night and silence! Keep the silence, s'il vous plèbe, it's a gift from the management. Keep a deathly silence, p'il voo say, you'll need it in the end . . .

What a wacko, Don Juan said, immersing himself in the tumultitude clamoring around the room's flimsy stage. Impromptu scaffold for a bluesy soulstice night . . . A pantomine field! Now Mr. Penguin will put together all the stars that brighten up the soirée. Peep show, —through a peephole.³ Varioting show, a comikazi production . . . Les artistes recevront vos applaudissements, let's all render vociferous applause, in the last part of the partying, the time of phantasmagonies, and in order of appearance . . .

Sam Bahamas Band! Loud applause ravages victimized auricles . . . Here we're all the claque, the slapplauders.⁴ Ça va, yeah. Sam Bahamas and his minstrel show!

In samba rhythm the giant zambo, his face painted white, was shaking and slapping four gentlemen from the City, all in blackface and bowler hats, and bound with chains and shackles. One of them started to scratch away on a violin with an umbrella, while to his right another accordioned a paper filebox, and the other two at the back tried to pound drums and bowlers as the white black man kicked at them and wailed on a saxophone.

A slave driver now . . ., Don Juan laughed. On his way up. When Rimbaudelaire and I had a sublet in his black hole, what times

1. And I ruse the term loosely. V-8 or straight sex?:
Dangerous curve ahead.

2. What a labiarinth . . .:
Sh! Here the belles peel. Cora with a finger to her lips.

3. Allez-y à confesse!:
Soon after getting to know Cora in a record shop in Soho, where she often looked
for accompaniment for her striptease numbers, Milalias was privy to the barest
confession . . .: See PILLOW NOTES 51, p. 520.

4. Presentation, then representation:
—Mr. Joyce, from Dublin.
—Dr. Freud, from Döblin.

5. Get out of the groove . . .:
Impossible! The record's scratched. Biographical, or biological record: Lives or
lice of the artists. Who's the phthiris of them all?

6. Another strange case . . .:
Back to the clinic, cynic! Consult your occulist.

7. Mr. Joyce?:
Mr. Joyce.
The Irishman? The itinerant Irishman?
The very same. Mr. Joyce. An Irish ventriloquack who performed in popular
pubs with a sailor doll, always drunk, who sputtered obscenities. Milalias met him
in a Hammersmith café, the Rendez-Vous Café, behind the Olympia. [On Blythe
Road, to be even more precise.]

those were, he only enslavished his long-suffering wife. Fais moi mal . . . Let it bleed. A hardheaded mulatta.

And now, straight[1] from the heart of Soho, yes, oh-so Soho, the most sexhibitionistic act of the night: Cora with a finger to her lips![2] Hard Cora! With special Koreagraphy, in one of her most-sexceptionalsuccesses . . . With more to come! Hit for sex, as they say in En-gland. Clap in time—both hands now, eh? C'mon, sweet Cora. Tiny and nude, spectral white, reclining tremorously on the black blanket spread on the divan, legs spread wide, caressing with one finger her red slit—her pubis shaved—while panting a lewd confession,[3] nearly drowned out by the bursts of shouts from the hall. The circle of spotlight crawled slowly over her body until resting on her death mask of delicate oriental features, frozen in a spasm. And in a wail, she showed—completely stained—her black teeth.

And to change the record, if not the subject, the voice of her master: London's astute resourceful ventriloquist-actor, the zaniest and most soliloquacious ventriloquist ever, with his devious one-eyed sailor: Dr. Freud and Mr. Joyce![4] And vice versa, it's all the same with all the reversals in this show of spicy verses. Clap! Clap! And no claptrap outfit. Double applause. A thousand howls! Achtung! What a mordant wit has our crabby doctor.[5] Light abrasive rasping? vaccinations advised. Learn to scratch your own surface before the rabid applause begins . . . Quiet! Lend your ears. Follow the example of the good oracular doctor, what a spree de corps! who is heard speaking through the mouth of the analyzed at each seance of spiritautism. The soliloquist's position is not so clear, eh. The strange case of Dr. Freud and Mr. Joyce . . .[6] The divan of divagations is all yours, Mr. Joyce . . .[7]

1. Freudian sleep?:
Yes, la vida es sueño, Segismundo; merely, merely, merely, merely, life is but a dream. But you've got to interpret it.

2. Est-il dans un état de proustration?:
Après chaque voyage sentimental Mr. Joyce ne se prousterne que devant les jeunes proustituées en fleur. In bloom. Oh yes. Not a refusal nor a maybe but a lovely mollitude ending his every endless odyssey. A love in every portmanteau.

3. Pasty-tongued?:
The gaff or graft of tongue. Wicked waggling tongues. The two of them, the freudulent doctor and the defreuder-scrivener, for many years suffered cancer of the tongue.

4. Auch das noch! The last thing we need! (To be read with magnifying glass):
Den Teufel auch! Ouch! Au! Lord Auch, qui est le maitre du champ de bataille? Consult your Sacher-Masoch. Vedono meglio quattro massocchisti che due? (Regardez-moi ce corniaud, il perd ses couicouilles devant le taureau! Et la cornée aussi? Quelle histoire de l'œil de Granero! Grand héros? Ce n'est pas avec un coup de corne qu'on fait une tragédie cornélienne.) Au revoir! Asta a la vista! Quit horning in!

5. Barrocculist?:
Your etyhomologizing vision stigmatizes everything. Eyeball, sir, which is better and more briefly stated in Spanish: cojón.

6. What would they say in that ventriloquizzical chat?:
—Dodocteur, êtes-vous là?
—Zzz . . .
—Are you there, Dr. Freud?
—Yes, Mr. Joyce.
—Doctor, last night I dreamed again about the lost eye. I was coming from Segovia or Seattle or the Dead Sea or some other site, I don't remember now, but I do remember boarding in Shanghai, and I lost the eye again in a dispute in a house of female pupils in Tokyo . . .
—Occhio! Pinocchio. Keep your eyes peeled in a brothel, brother.
—And the pupil for whom my eye popped out was Miss Ogino but in my language she was also called Madame Butterfly. She took it from me with a long needle from her hair bun, as she gave me a toupee-blow in the crotch.
—Perhaps an eye witness? Qualche Teste? Conteste!
—Oui. Sí. Yes. Popeye!

The patriarchetypical Dr. Freud in frock coat, faithfully chari-caturized with little white beard and spectacles, his nodding head[1] supported by his elbow on the arm of the divan, manipulating from under an armpit the head of the skinny sailor-marionette (with a patch on the left eye) who chatted away[2] with his dirty drunk tongue.[3]

Continuous sessions or obsessions, hissed Don Juan, the cession opens and . . . Always the very same. Castrastrophes and strophes! of the cultist oracle. Iridescent aberrations of a lone eye. Ency-clopedic little story of the eye, batailleur![4] polyphemous squabbles, barroque ballock![5] a thousand and one nights told through con-tradictory versions in tenebrous monocular argot.

Louder, we can't hear you! We can't hear anything! Louder ventrilocution please![6] Microphone! . . . Siegmund, fale! Fort! Da capo! . . . Quiet! Hush! Hush!

La canaille becomes laconic . . ., Don Juan murmured. Is the fit over, the play ended? Dada processed . . ., and he started to applaud the ventriloquist as the performer rapidly converted (while stand-ing and taking bows, he took off the jacket, the vest, the shirt—leaving him in a striped sailor's T-shirt—then the beard, toupee, fake nose, and glasses, and stuck a patch on one eye) into his doll's twin. And with an arm hooking the other's shoulder, they bowed one last time.

Hurray, Mr. Joyce! the emcee straddling the microphone again. He rejoyces in the name of Freud. Now comes the sound and the fury: Loud angry rockers vaunting amplifiers. Here come the four

1. The house built on Rock:
That's how it was. The band of four Shamrockandrollers [Siran (guitar), Hal (guitar), Artie (bass) and Mick (drums) alias "Mickey Finn" alias "Milein" alias the Bardo Loco and many others, almost as many as Milalias, who also played lots of other instruments, some of his own invention] rehearsed two days per week in the basement of that house of madmen or Fulham folly. London SW6. The Villa of Mysteries, and not only for those immoral murals or numerals in one of its rooms. Work of the commune of hippies that had lived there till recently? Mr. "Napo" Leone bought that half-ruined Fulham mansion on speculation and on orders of the enigmagnate of the shadows Mr. Tod. And since they weren't selling it and so that another horde of squatters wouldn't invade, he authorized the group "Shamrock" to use the basement for rehearsals and to store furniture. The leader of the Irish band, the Bardo Loco, made money moving furniture in a painted van baptized "Van Gogh" by Milalias, who utilized it frequently for his changes of address. Rimbaudelaire had met the four apocalyptic rockers in a Kilburn pub and showed up drunk with them at midnight in Cleveland Gardens to introduce them to Babelle and Milalias, who were not easily quit of their surprise or their bed.

2. Paradox glossed: the unmistakable gloss of the good Dr. Pangloss . . .:
On a wadded-up piece of paper retrieved by Babelle from the wastebasket (la poubelle de Babel), this telegraphically—tangled annotation in pen: Samsa. Bolero. Ravel. The Tempest. Diobolus. Simon Magus? Simony? Gaspard de la Nuit. Scarbo. Bolero. Ravel's slaver! (P.S. of the Commentator, alias Herr Narrator: Endlessamsa diabrotikafkabbalah scarabrowbeetlebolero?)

3. Dama. Dama? Leading lady, or . . . Miss leading:
A deer fellow, made dame. (Does do, don't they?) With all the unions recorded, stroke by stroke, time after time in a sort of runic rhyme, or hieroghamy. (In palindromic Spanish: Mago Ogam) But there's lots of runing left in this musical gamut. What's in a man's name? Amadeus was the predestined given name of the great transvestite Sue Dama. They admired her for the first time one drag night in The Bush, in a siren suit with a mermaid tail and a wave like you wouldn't believe . . .

4. The old litany of the first nights . . .:
Midnight, Mr. Midnight . . .: See PILLOW NOTES 52, p. 520.

5. Help me to find the love that I've lost:
Lost in the shadow parade.

apocalypses. You're right at home now, Rockfellers.[1] Let's greet them with a savage salvo of applause, the stormiest rock band of our era: SHAMROCK!

Prick the clover, erotomaniac . . ., Don Juan snorted. Not this time? and went back—ears pricked up—to lying in wait.

Four hooded hoods hurdling about (red ski masks with eyeholes), wearing fiery clovers on their green T-shirts. SHAM ROCK! thundering shouting electriflying guitars leaping to and fro on the platform. ROCK!

((Finie la musiquéquette? Un vieux beau l'héros! Boleros' sore lob. Revel lever? Our revels now are ended. Or almost. Unravel Ravel! The storm approaches. Untie the knot. Loosen amours, release vanity affairs. Before a new deviled day dawns. Set sail on the double, up and away, pay Peter to play Paul. Praise the Lord, and go to hell! Give her the gas, parsimoniac. The diabolerotic beetle scratching around and around in his endless night.[2]))

The Walkyrie . . . Eleison! SUE DAMA! . . .[3] in front of the cavalcade of Valkyries . . . Weh! See how they run. Whan! without Wagner. Hail! to the hall, Hala! to Wahlhalla . . ., and the emcee dropped the microphone and ran out to avoid being run down by the helmets of the horsy blondes. And Sue Dama, rubbing her groin-cloth (a black G-string) and her hairy muscular thighs, with a long-shoreman's voice: Hojotoho! Hojotoho! Heiaha! Ha! Heiohotojo! Hotojohann! Hott! . . .

Midnight, Mr. Midnight,[4] hummed Sleeping Beauty, I'm a part of your shadow parade,[5] pursued by Don Juan through the thick mix of masks.

Shadow Play

1. Don Girovanni!:
Spinning crazy in the orgy of the Fulham Villa of Mysteries. Somber Don Giovanni, cloaked in his Spanish cape. Cutting capers, twirl after twirl, till he's torn to shreds. Careful with that cape! and the cap feathers. Poor Don Juan, always adding more twists to his misses, more roles to his rolls, more turns to the screws, more wrenches to the wenches, more meanders to his philanders, more rallies to his dallies, more flourishes to his flirtations, more swirls to his girls in this mass masked carniwaltz, uncensored! on a dark night of Saint John.

2. Boxing's dance, with a deadly commination. Schatten boxen, Schattenorio! Faustkampf!:
Shadow-boxed in! Clear the ring!

3. Diplopia . . .:
Look look at your double without a double take. At your alter ego without faltering. Peer at your peer. The double is always double. Trouble. And protean. Delirious, Don Juan? Giglio selvàtico non vale una fave e perde la favella per una selva oscura.

4. Faustusche?:
A shadow play, a fiesty feast of ink. Omen faustum? Hellucination of an indianinky night full of girls and voices, a fausty night to swim in. Faustuschelei!

5. Martyr Gras, Faust Tuesday? (Coming thick and faust now):
Eve of Ash Wednesday. Dashes to ashes and Faust to dust, cinders of a cynical Don Juan . . . (Chrysostomo assaying his gold in the fire?) Gold gleaming in the fireplace. Minatory papyrus pyre illuminating the nest of Phoenix Lodge, Brook Green, fignitiating once more the Auto-da-Phoenix. Textermination? The end browns the work: Fignis coronat opus . . .

6. Lysergic acid reviving venerean adventures?:
Long-lasting acid remains vitally active. Loose amphetamines relieve virulent agraphia? Speedwriting? Tachycardia without tachygraphy. Needing now more than ever the most powerful drug. (The dragoman knows what the straight dope is.)

Don Juan spinning his head[1]—a dizzy weathervane—in the wind-mill of masks. Searching through the thick viperish brewhaha for his sleepwalking beauty. Ba . . . belle au bois dormant . . . The black forest . . . No! I've lost her! What the devil!? pulling up short. An enormous shadow, a fiction, my shadow in the mirror? That's impossible! And raising a fist, threatening? in a black glove . . . Boxing stance?[2] Last round . . . Am I seeing double?[3] Didn't think I was so far gone. Trying to get a hold of himself and the situation: —Who are you?! Dry rumble like an echo: —You! Don Juan, irritated: —Me?! Again the voice or echo, but farther away: —Me-me . . . Don Juan, plugging his ears: —Hearing double? Or trouble hearing? Then struggling to recover his customary insolence: —What's a good name for a shadow . . . Second-fiddler on the hoof? Don Juan Part Two? And the echo: —Par tous? Looking suspiciously out of the corner of his eye: —C'mon, what's your name? Yeah, you! The deformed echo or voice, curtly: —And you? Both at once: —Juan! —Johann! And Don Juan adding with pride: —Don Johannes Fucktotum! And the Shadow in a sarcastic murmur: —Doktor Johannes Faustusche.[4] Don Juan, covering himself with a cape-draped forearm and monologizing away: —Uncorked from the inky depths that night . . . orter eda V! So that means . . . Two in one?! Two birds of ill omen in one shot of ink . . . The Shadow, as if chirping: —Riprap . . . Rip . . . Don Juan: —O unlucky day! And the Shadow: —Night. Faustnacht![5] Don Juan with his deaf monologue: —Night transfigured by hallucinera-tions. In the Phoenix nest. Libertine amanuensis revising volume ablaze? When he needed the most powerful drug.[6] My quivering quill, that riddling renitent reed refused to write. I shook it. Nothing. I wet it in the inkwell. Nothing. A veil, a cloud, a subtle wingflap came between my eyes and the blank page. Horror vacui, banal nirvana, complete abulia, oblivion. Leaching amnesia re-stitching veils autonomously. You know that feeling of torpor? Nightly acedia. Hum! Little agenda registers voluptuaries afoot. Sentire odore di fémmina . . . The Shadow, sighing: —Anch' ío! Me too! Yours truly has also scrutinized all the pages, all the

1. Strained note by the Commentator, alias Herr Narrator:
To know—by different means—was their obsession: The keen desire to know . . .
Milalias argued that Don Juan was not a great blasphemer, but rather a much-
maligned victim. Completely misunderstood. An explorer more than a conqueror.
Knowledge [the very quimtessence!] was his great passion. Perhaps seeking
cunctipotence, to use an archaic word. To know . . . one after another, in order to
arrive someday at the great revelation. Mujeriego, homme à femmes! A man of
women, how precisely and how inaccurately that expression fits. Lady-killer.
Mujeriego? Mujer y ego: affirmation of ego through women? Sexploration. To
know . . . to cuntemplate . . . To know thighself, in the end?

2. Are women books?:
To be frank, linguist, would mine were an almanac, to change her every year.

3. Pen ultimate, pent up:
Wandering souls in pain, in pen . . . Your pen is penned in! Penduelist! Da, dadaist.
Pierrot le Fou . . .

4. Mont Blanc, alpinist?:
(Alp en sport!) The big quill pen, a family relic that spurted innumerable inkspots
and tempestuous nightmares. Years ago it belonged to Milalias's mysterious
mother, née Renée Kleeman. And before that . . . (a black—and white—family
legend): to the still more mysterious twin brother of Milalias's mother, Emil
Kleeman, adventurer and polyglot polygrapher (he signed his hermetic French
verses with the pen name Émile Clément) who disappeared without a trace in the
snows of Finsteraarhorn, in the Bernaise Alps, the first day of the year 1941. And
before that . . .: to a poet and friend of Emil Kleeman, who lived and died crazy,
convinced he had sold his soul to the devil in order to write of a fortunate Faustus.
The pen, witness to so many adventures, wound up passing—in a relay race—into
the hands of graphomaniac Milalias.
    The pen . . ., and the no-less-antediluvian typewriter—the work tools of the
polygraphic uncle—would eventually become his diabolus ex machina.

5. Or erased by laser?:
Laser beams . . . They can evaporate the ink yet leave the paper immaculate. Laser
automatically reading: virtual abolishment. Light amplification radiation violently
accelerated.

paginal mantissas . . . Don Juan, cocky Spanish-style: —Vaya! What a talker! And I, all the vaginal mysteries . . . The Shadow, passionately: —Let's compare and compaginate![1] Don Juan, distrustful: —Huh?! The Shadow mused as if praying: —Lexicons analects receipts vademecums almagests . . . And Don Juan reciting: —Laplanders Andorrans Rumanians Venezuelans Anglosaxons . . . The Shadow interrupted him: —I've gone over all the works, snatches from every . . . And Don Juan, cuttingly: —And I the most select. A miscellany of young misses with their spines and folds, some with jackets, stacked ones too.[2] A snatch here or there on the run, and even on installment plans, all the luminous or voluminous bodies. The two in chorus: —La chair est triste, hélas! —La chair est triste, hélas! Then the Shadow waxing nostalgic: —Lunatics anxiously researching vatic arcana. The eternal enigma, in continuous metamorphosis. Open books become open vulvas. And vice versa. Lip-service applied, reciting venusian arcana. Long awaited response, very accurate. Mumbling, uncomprehending. Lengthy ascertation renders vain action . . . Don Juan, excitedly: —Loving affirms resolutely virile activity! The Shadow, quietly: —L'Action Restreinte verbalement amplifiée. Limited by its limitlessness. Lonely activity, reviewing volumes alchemical . . . Don Juan, getting impatient: —Like action restrained, virility amplified! The Shadow, mocking: —Mal armé! with your solitary pen, solitaire plume éperdue . . .[3] So sad . . . Ill-armed, poorly loved, wandering Spanish gentleman . . . Don Juan with a recitation: —"And Penus rose red out of ink." Then the Shadow with a snappy rhythm: —A gong or a bell sounding till you're dizzy with the slang and argot of the prince of darkness . . . Don Juan playing deaf, and as if suddenly remembering: —My condemned quill wouldn't write . . . Mon blanc-seing![4] The Shadow: —Hmmm. Some signature . . . Blank! In invisible ink?[5] Don Juan, shaking his left hand: —Not even a drop? A drop, half a drop would save my . . .

1. O lente, lente currite noctis equi:
Marlowe's nightly line. Divo, go on with your elegy on the perfect vacuum. Pulled by horses?: Large Animals Roam, Vanquishing Author. Luminous aurora, rubescent, vision awry? . . . Winged steeds flying high over a glowing blue sphere.

2. So many stains . . .:
Under the effect of stimulants he thought he was writing. Alphabet snoop, albafetus of erasures, Alphabête noire! your bastard brainchild, a wondrous ink offspring in constant metamorphosis. That collection of ink stains turned into a book. In the beginning was the dot. The dot burst into dots. The dots grouped together to form distinct figures. Inkun$\frac{a}{e}$bula . . .

3. Lethe alleviates; recipient vacant, apathetic:
No, Charon! Lethean amnesiac rescued via acrobatics.

4. Libertine's afterlife retailed, vendor awaits!:
Life animas reduced, vilipended, auctioned . . . Il dissoluto punito. Souls on sale. Lucifer announces radical vending: awake!

5. Save Our Souls:
Soûlaud! Save Our Sins.

6. Ring, or wrangle?:

DRAW NO SAGAS . . . ONWARD!

The Shadow finished dryly: —Golgotha! To each his own calvary. Don Juan, as if writing in the air: —Licentiate arabesques recording vanity affairs. Slow mares of night tugging me along . . .[1] Blots and stains beyond measure.[2] And suddenly, at the stroke of midnight, a diabulic idea . . . The Shadow: —I know it already . . . Lumiominous! Don Juan, pursuing his exterior monologue: —My soul or my sole accomplishment? Magnum opus, or onus! Disembodied dead soul. But to write is to relive. Long awesome roster, vividly accurate. Listing adventures revives vice-ridden author? Listless author revived via adventure-writing? Yet I'm still dispirited. Liven! Awaken! Revive! Vigor! Arise! Did I hear a voice? Love affairs returning, voluptuously alluring? Lulling amorous remembrances vying actively?[3] Let amor revive vuestro amante . . . The Shadow, with evil lurking in his heart: —Cattivo Don Giovanni! Rigoletto verdiccio da ponte girante . . . Lamebrain! Don Juan paying no attention: —And if I were to sell it? . . .[4] That's it! Sí, eso es! The Shadow, frightened: SOS!:[5] dot dot dot dash dash dash dot dot dot. Don Juan, still distracted: —Save, Oh Satan! Heartless? Was I really so drunk? If he doesn't exist, I don't lose anything. And if he exists . . . The Shadow, still more frightened: —Sh! He exists! Lucifer acquired, rejoicing, votre âme. Your soul in installments. And mine! Don Juan, deep in his memories: —When I was a child I was scared of a painted devil, in a dark cranny of that stairway . . . Lucifer flying over a volcano. In an eye of fire. Unforgettable image. Now the Shadow, impatiently: —The pact . . . Don Juan, arrogant again: —I made a pact with him, just like that! The Shadow: —Your word? Don Juan: —And works! My soul for a mountain of words . . . The Shadow: —Behind every book is the devil! Don Juan, sighing: —Some poor devil . . . The Shadow: —And hast thou writ the rubric?[6] Don Juan, trying to remember: —Just in case . . . Yes sir. The devilawyer is very legalistic. Though my memories of that night are a bit scrambled. How was it done. Oh yes. First the sheet of paper. Looseleaf alabaster receipt vibrating awry! The pen slid quickly toward the

1. Attention! Paging all lost loves:
To make them dangerously textant.

2. Diabolic stigmata?:
Stigmata-hari (always erring!), careful with the stigmatism. Mark my words, he said crossly, any stigma will do to beat a dogma.

3. Trifid nebulosity?:
Hallucinogens producing cosmicomic visions . . .

4. The shadow of words . . .:
As they burn. They'd turn black on the tongue of the man in black. Like old chestnuts. Bruno tosto? Loudmouth, ardent (gag got your tongue?), roasted vindictively, alive. [Gag rule: No joke! Straight into the gags chamber without a peep. Pah-poof! The double endgame. Echec: dame! Oui. Huff. They're gonna get you in a smothered mate, chessman. Ça gaze, gazouilleur.]

5. Der Sandmann?:
Throw dust in your eyes or clean up your spectacles. The man with the grab bag and the bad grab, always appearing and disappearing when you least expect him.

6. Note by Herr Narrator:
Der Narrator und der Thot. Totenstanz!

end. My soul for a tome recording each and every one of my lost loves. To revive them![1] Corrected and embellished. A cut on the finger. Ay. Ya. The signature with the bloody fingerprint. A trace.[2] The Shadow, in spurious Italian: —Spur si muove . . . Don Juan, raising his left hand: —Yes, it was moving. Nebulous smudge. A clover?[3] The Shadow, clucking: —Klee! Kleecks! Gentlemen, start your inkwells . . . Don Juan, reliving the anguish: —What have I done? The words were dancing all over the page, unfettered letters. Bellettres ballet! And I jumped up from my card table and suddenly there on the wall by the door, the Shadow! The Shadow, disturbed: —Inkubus! Don Juan, putting his left hand to his chest: —The shadow of my blackest thoughts?[4] A black form, in mourning . . . The Shadow: —Vestito a bruno! Don Juan, assenting: —Smashed, ectoplastered on the wall. And I threw the inkwell in a panic. The Shadow: —Lutheran inkantation . . . Don Juan: —I never should have done it! That Shadow changes constantly. A black wolf-man? The man with the bag? Some rascal wrapped in a cape? The Shadow, as if raising a cup: —Inopportune Sandeman . . .[5] ¿Otro porto? Now Don Juan smacking a palm on his forehead: —It's always here with me. The Shadow, wagging his head: —Cosa mentale . . . Don Juan, now taken up with his memories: —And a few days later the patron Mr. Tod— The Shadow, taken aback: —Tod!? Herr Tod? Don Juan, completely deaf: —The patron of the arts Mr. Tod offered to give me a monthly stipend, modest, but timely! so I could take my time and complete my compendium. In return he only asks that I turn over to him the definitive magnuscript. The Shadow, ashen: —The Book of Tot![6] Don Juan, still steaming ahead with his theme: —Mr. Tod collects all kinds of papers . . . Then a little while after accepting his offer, I realized: If the pact were fulfilled . . . The Shadow, curtly: —It *was* fulfilled! Don Juan, only aware of his own words: —After a few months I decided not to accept any more

1. Wise decision . . .:
No. REPACT CAPER. He'll just change his quill, that's all. And even unplumed he'd keep cacackling. Ja! Kikerikicks! Don Hohn. Kickadoodle, do.

2. That's called writing properly, or with propriety . . .:
And to write with those properties one must be dispossessed. Without demons there is no writing, but writing becomes an exorcism. Poor diablotto!

3. Cry of Sisyphrustration: . . . O STONE, BE NOT SO . . .:
The Shadow, sibilant, in the mirror: Yes, Sisyphus, PUT IT UP. PAL, ROLL OR LAP. Lasting ancient rock'n'roll, vertical anguish. Labor always repeated, vile athanasia. To summit up, plummet down! . . . MORE, HERO, MORE, HERO, MORE, HERO, M . . .

4. Feuille morte?:
Philamot. Of a philandering philomath.

5. Of the same monad, nomad . . .:
Mad. DAMN MAD! A myth is as good as a smile, but close counts only in horseshoes, hand grenades, and hackwork like this.

6. Mal!:
Schattenorio & Faustuche. Doktor Johann und Don Juan. The strange case . . .

7. Méphistophélès?!?:
Sh! Le Pépère perd les fils . . .

8. Your soul hanging by a thread!:
Fil de la Vierge . . .

stipends out of fear. And never to pick up the pen again.[1] Just like that! Was I possessed? The Shadow, agreeing: —There's no writing without possession . . .[2] Don Juan: —Love affairs returned vertiginously anguishing. Some force stronger than me drove me to write. But later, as if coming out of a trance, I tried to resist it. I burned everything. Just like that! Fire and rebirth from the ashes. Write burn rewrite . . .[3] Rrrrip, rustle, and scribble. Blacken the sheet.[4] And now you! My lost shadow? Shadow of what I once was? Of what I might have been? That damned shadow from the Phoenix Lodge room? The Shadow, enigmatic: —We're two masks of the same false coin.[5] We're shadows of a shadow. Don Juan: —Shadows? The Shadow, with all his foreboding malice: —Shadows of evil. Mal![6] Malzeit! The shadows of our former selves, you see. My brain's all dried and shriveled up, from so much reading. And you, your . . .? Don Juan with protesting hands: —Oh no! Nothing like that! The Shadow, nodding: —Latent ambitions reunited, vanquishing all . . . Don't you recognize yourself in me? Let anagnorisis relieve vellicative anguish. We'll meet again at night in Deptford. Don Juan, as if trying to remember: —In Deptford? And the Shadow: —Yes, at the old Saint Nick Church . . . The two facing skulls will have all eternity to gossip . . . Oui-da. Ad infiernitum! . . . Don Juan, with a gesture of impatience or impotence: —You gotta be cracked! And the Shadow, delighted: —Lunatics all 'round, amorous vagabondage . . .

—Mes fils tôt fêlés . . .[7]

Don Juan, amazed: —I heard a voice back there. The Shadow: —Me too. And Don Juan: —Speaking French? The Shadow: —Peut-être. And Don Juan, nit-picking or nut-picking: —My sons cracked up?! Voix fêlée . . . And the Shadow, waggish: —Fehl! Eh! Typical felony of that fellow with the forked tongue. Telle vipère tel fils . . . Enough. Let's not lose the thread with dread.[8] Let's celebrate our encounter. Don't you recognize meyourmyself?

1. Pact unpacked: Peter Punster penned a pact of prickled papers . . .:
Packed with impact. Last act: ransomed valuables accepted?

2. Egyptian soul?:
Une belle âme. The soul and life of this novel of Babel.

3. Amorous breath? Love puff?:
Seems there was some loss. Damned halitosis . . .

4. Taking advantage till the last moment . . .:
Yes, he would say he wanted to finish as he began.

5. Contrition? Constriction? Point it out:
Not to put too fine a point on it, the endpoint.

6. Soulless!:
Victim of boredom and bed debts. DEBT AT BED? REVOLT, LOVER! Or as the Joker
used to say, based on wide experience: BEDROOM is an anagram of BOREDOM.

7. A good cape is a good escape . . .:
Tarnkappe! Tappen. Tappen.

We'll mix ourselves up together again. Come embrace me! Don Juan backing up, flailing his arms: —Leave! Away! Vacate! Abscond!

—Loca recitata! What's the matter? Qué pasa . . .

Don Juan, spinning in bewilderment: —Am I hearing voices again? Love's ancient regrets vociferating atmospherically? Je ne regrette rien! Viva la libbertá! Love acts replayed, vicariously augmented. I will burn my books. An act of faith, or auto-da-fé. And I'll break the pact.[1] A free soul again, I'll break its bonds . . . Then looking around, arms extended, stuttering: —Ba . . .[2] belle au bois dormant, es-tu là? Where o where . . . Only you can bind me and unbind me. Free to retie our ties. Ligature asphyxiates, renders vital air.[3] Your embraces will suddenly make me repent.[4] Salvation gives the soul a point of contriction . . .[5]

—Good point! Dot! Quel radoteur . . . What a bore![6]

What? Don Juan stealthily approaching the enormous black leather wing chair from behind: —A hard-voiced easy chair? Ah . . ., looking in amazement at the devil painted head to toe, sunk in the high-backed armchair (legs crossed and his left hand on his cheek, his index finger pressing the button on a hearing aid) who looked back at him with an expression of boredom, or as if he were listening to a scrambled radio program. (Some Tarot cards—*The Devil, The World,* and *The Fool* face up—tossed at his feet next to a twisted black glove.) And Don Juan, trying to regain his composure: —Oh it's you, Mr. Tod . . .

I, too, recognize a good sinner by his cape . . .,[7] and the painted

1. Your no-exit textravaganza, an ever-pending compendium of cunctation:
Discotext of many pappy returns. Chronic chronicle. An unpublished circular
with a wheelth of possibilities, 'round and 'round and rowdy she goes, where she
stops . . . Foreign whirrds spinning around in vicious circles, ORBILIBRO! since all
the ones in hell are vicious. ROTATOR? Vade recto, recirculator!

2. Rushing off . . .:
To never reach his deathtination.

3. Endlessly avoiding?:
EVITATIVE. Never-rending story.

4. LARVA, perhaps? A bastard title?:
LARVA, as rendered via acronyms! So—a chronic acronymphomaniac! Larvae
abundantly reproducing vermiculated arcanum? A terrible sea booty is borne . . .

5. Urbi et orbi:
Or be it orbit. A cyclic poem. In circuit binding, of course.

devil laughed. How *does* that go, Mr. Alia. And that eternal book of yours?[1]

Don Juan, escaping,[2] with one arm raised in farewell (his index and middle fingers crossed?[3]) or desperoration: —Little adjustments, rewriting very ardently . . .[4]

((Finished? Delta tales all told and textinguished? Capitulation caput? This devilish foolishness of wanting to conclude . . . The poor addled devil adds twists and turns and doesn't realize that his Sisyphean circular, his helicalbum, an encyclopendium,[5] has neither beginnings nor ends. No head or tail. NEVER ODD OR EVEN.))

The Ring

1. How far have you fallen, fall guy, suffering the pathetic fallacy of a failing phallus: That rascally fellow Don Giovanni can't leave a field fallow. Prick. A safety pin is worth a needle. O belly obelisk!

2. Doppelgänger?:
Göppelgänger . . . The double goes merry-go-round . . .

3. Executioner-victim, vampire of your heart:
SUM ACT, CAMUS.

4. Capogirigògolo!:
Turn on, gyroscopulator, tune in, drop out from your wheel of miss fortune . . .
[Turn on, don! as the mute worm turns, in the shrieking circle (Kreis! Kreischen! Kreisen!) until the furies quit laboring.]

5. Sentire odore di fémina . . .:
Ninna Ricci sulle orecchie . . .

A rubber phallus[1] deflated on the grass. And beside it, stiff as a poker, the hard Don sheathed in his cape, caught in the center of a huge circle of fallopian-tupped furies circling and shouting furiously.

Another double?[2] Don Juan muttered with misgiving, stepping back through the back porch of the villa. My double!? as he hid behind a column. A double double? now spying on the ring of singing bacchantes in the center of the garden, their gripes of wrath wring-rounding the erect gallant with his cape tied over his head like a sack or a cowl,[3] his arms flailing, grabbing the air, bluffing blindman! and trying to guess the identity of each fury as she runs rings around him, closer and still faster than the big concentric circle, slapping and spinning him like a top,[4] and reviling him all the while.

Vicious circle? Ring and relay race, Don Juan added, leafing through his little black address book. Lurking amoret reviewing various amorettes . . . Libertine-slave . . . Crazy about women and words. Now they stick out their tongues at him! Lambasting, abusing, ridiculing, vilifying, affronting.

Hmm, that's strange. When the poor puppet utters a woman's name, the on-duty fury rejoins the chorus. Can he take everything they dish out? Huh! He's an old dog, sniffing them out . . ., yeah, he'll get out of this one too, and Don Juan took a deep breath. Labyrinthean arcana resolved verifying aromas . . .[5]

((Don Juan and his double? Double, or nothing . . . That's the game of the name. And it wouldn't be absurd to infer that the somber Don Juan crouched behind the column is transmitting telepathetically to his double the names of the dames: les belles dames sans merci et la bête noire. All for the Beast . . .))

*
* *

1. Now I must ask you: Are you there?:
Sh! [Scene furtively witnessed by Milalias, one night when he came in unannounced to visit Mr. Reis: Go ahead, lock yourself in there! Mrs. Askew shrieked, beating on Mr. Reis's door. Do you think I don't know you stay in this house just because you know only I can put you in contact with her? (Her?)]

2. Dolores? Pains?:
Sí, señor. Here I take pains to explain.

DIE MUTTER

Lumpy form wrapped in a black cloak with a Nazarene hood, blinking a lantern on and off around the puppet: It's awfully dark . . . Are you there? now pressing the burning lantern against the puppet's hooded face. The other day I got a message for you . . . Do you know morse remorse? switching the light on and off rapidly. Do you need bright rays thrown at you? Genuine knight admits no rays. A real gentleman has his own light. Always importuning Saint Xavier. Rogue! And all I did for you, your best mother-in-lore. You showed up without a thing to your name and I got you that cushy job in The Golden Ass. That sure didn't last long! How many more favors will I have to ask of Mr. Tod? Not a word out of you! And my intercessions so they'd give you a dirt-cheap room . . . So this is how you repay me? and she whacked him in the head with the lantern. Lights out and let's go.
  — The Maida Vale harpy! Mrs. Askew . . .[1]

Old coot with a parchment face and rapacious eyes, graced with a black shawl, shaking a featherduster at the puppet: Dust you are and dust we'll be . . . Doss to dust! I gave you a bed, your old room. Didn't you recognize the paintings? Your juicy tumescent Maja? Time turns the gold days to derision. Our loves into corpses, the temple of amor into a morgue. How long it took you to come back . . . My painstaking painter turned poetaster. Emil, now. Better-looking than Frederick . . . And from Spain. My mum too was half Spaniola. See the fireplace? Everything is just as it was. And don't you dare think about wasting all that gas again! Looking at everything as if it pained him to recognize it. Is that you in the painting? What a perfect picture of velvety beauty! More flattering now . . . The bards! as everyone knows . . . Baroness you called me. You bear a remarkable resemblance to the baroness of something-or-other. Your Gothic childhood tales! Lady of Pain, another of my titles. Don't get upset, you'll have Dolores[2] jabbing him with the featherduster, dolor for dollar . . .

1. Explain further!:
Never complain and never explain: a minimalist maxim worth keeping in mind. Mrs. Plain, a real character, out of some novel. We would need a whole one just for her. A former beauty, immortalized by lots of painters. A powerful medium. (The Medium is the message . . ., in one of Babelle's nightmares . . .) Oh Dolores! so subtle . . . She was awaiting the return of a reincarnated lover, that oh-so-young painter who killed himself for her, over thirty years ago. What a story! We'll have to tell it won't we? Another story for another night.

2. O felix chuppa!:
Shroud descending from heaven?

3. A branding iron?:
A Brand X maxim: Live by the iron, and die by irony.

—The landlady from Blomfield Road? Mrs. Plain![1] Dolores . . .

Plump wet nurse with a big bandaged hand, rolling a bandage around the puppet: Just a little scratch, eh? For this cut you courted me. In the garden of the Hesperides. My apples, hapless! in his hand. Hands off! No hand outs. Handicapped with a wounded hand I couldn't defend my virtue. I tried to cut the grass and was cut down instead. And me, I was like a mom to him! and with this she finished wrapping the puppet up like a mummy, I was like a mother to that little orphan animal. I was collapsing, flaccid. Vampire! bleeding in your arms.

—The landlady in Little Venice! Mrs. Appleton . . .

Bony clownish figure, covered with a pink nylon bedspread, chewing a cigarette and flicking the ashes on the puppet: You'll burn in Gehenna, in the eternal fires. Hell to pay! Feh! And kibbutzing to boot . . . Show-stoppink? You'll pay for it, my cover[2] all riddled with burn-holes from your careless ashes. Always smoking and smoking in bed! Smoking what? And all that riffraff you invited to your room. Such a chachem you were, such chutzpah! and me such a fine balabustah. Oy-yoy-yoy! That's it, enough already! Five pounds sterling or you don't get your suitcase back. Fair is fair. And he robbed me, oy! oy! he pawned all the sheets. Gevalt! Thief!

—The Finchley Road landlady! Mrs. Heller . . .

Matron with a robust bust, gripping an iron rod ending in a big iron X,[3] walking menacingly around the puppet: The mysterious letter . . . The one from the enigma. Who could it be, the one who loves me? You thought I was going to fall in love with the great Osman of the World . . . Tricking me! A love letter . . . The last thing I needed . . . Did he pick out his favorite page? The letter writer! A man of letters . . . You and your one-armed Cyrano trying to falstaff me . . . False stuff! Little by litter, the false leter uv luv

1. All done very faithfully:
Milalias corrected the infidel's English exercises, some real puzzlers and howlers! and took advantage of some error patterns to lend authenticity to the disturbing love letter for the landlady.

2. Turk's head:
Knot so fast. This guy's still not wearing his turban, after the banquet and the bang and the visit to the Turkish baths in Bayswater (Bay's water . . . Bay at the moon! Ay!) and still didn't have the Turkish knot at his throat . . . You little Turk! Mrs. Page's bloodshot eyes seemed to say, crabby almost all the time. Love tames even wild beasts? Sometimes she even carried Coca-Cola up to his room, with ulterior motives? in the afternoons. You little Turk . . . The Great Osman, well over six feet . . .

3. Let's talk Turkey . . .:
Mr. Tuz (Tooth, the landlady would say, showing her dentures), it's almost a week since you last paid me. Paralyzed? Didn't he understand? He would scratch his head, a parasite? trying to grasp the meaning? And after a little while, aye, he would respond, avoiding her deadly glance. On Monday! (Easier to pronounce? He always said Monday.) Don't wear out my patience, eh? But he always paid in the end.

4. Nancy . . . Ann! Anna!:
Annamorphosis, not now. With Turkish tricks, no. Don Juan Falstaffador! Bring your old Castilian out of the castle, Castilian Casanova. Burlador of Sexville, turn the page. Watch the branding irony. The merry midwife, ex profeso! marks you.

5. The sonorous señora . . .:
From Sonora! The hour of beauty, handsome friend, has already sounded for the substantial señora. By weight? Buy cheap. By the hour? Wait . . .

6. Or horsing around?:
Horse of the same color . . .

ful of erros.[1] With the Turk's brand new portable, and he would never guess the use and abuse you were giving it. Dearest, I am yur slaiv and dearest, I wate for you. Hoo-boy, he wanted to have a rendez-vous with me. Erros and misstakes. I am be in the bench next the both all half-day at face to yor window . . . The bench where he always sat, next to the telephone booth, always alone . . . And innocently paid for the crime of others. A poor scapegoat, all the blame on his head.[2] That noon when I tramped the grass in the parterre. Didn't he understand? Trying to excuse himself from my embraces, the poor little turk, he can barely speek.[3] And you and Mr. Bouchon spying from the park. And another midday when the house was empty and I was hanging the clothes . . . Didn't he understand? Only the signature was lacking: the mark of Zorro. The unnecessary letter! One for another. All the ones you wrote for the one I'll endorse you with. The letter killeth! and encrusted the X on his forehead. It kills!

—The landlady of Queen's Park . . . Mrs. Page . . .[4]

A thundering matron,[5] dressed like a mariachi, galloping[6] around the puppet: Ay ay ay ay ándele ya! Look what the Agency sent me. My papá had to stampede back to the rancho grande, you stay here honey to finish the tour, and me half lost, perdida! in London I stayed. Escort Agency? maybe a good idea, they must have a gentleman who spica Spanish. This is an escort? A caballero without a pistol? He introduced himself, very formal, very pleased to make your acquaintance, in my hole-tell. El gusto es mío, míster. So tall, dark and very attentive. Without those thick glasses he'd be a real eye-catcher. A fierce latin lobo? Who came for pounds and got pounded. Said I'd have a great time. Dinner and chow and dancing. The Talk of the Town, el taco de todita la ciudad. One well-fed girl, with this guy starving. And you thought you were the king of the whole world . . ., and she bumped him

1. Another tea, killer . . .:
Dressed to kill ya! (Let's eat, drink and forget . . .) With that suit of lights or blights that the matador had rented to bullfill his duties for the Escort Agency. Once and never again, after the thrashing and guffaws of the mad Maríajuana.

2. Gestures of a good thief . . .:
Tell us, you masochist, recall other calvaries.

3. Pantingmime or pantie mine for Pamina . . .:
Neither minor, miner, nor white. Long and rich vein awaits. Vain vein, mother lowed. Who's the quarry, the lunatic might query, on his search through the tunnels of the night. Is it me, the miner or contaminoter of it all on my nocturnal emission impossible . . .

with her belly. Go to it, don. And you playing the hard man under my peso went bankrupt, me with my hard currency and him like a bouncing check. At an inflated exchange rate, is that it?! One little shout, and ay! he goes soft. Not enough pounds? For this I crossed the pond. Hard man softens up, eh? Peso by beso, for this I pay so . . . Kiss será será. Another tequila, on top of the rental fee?[1] More bread and what's your beefcake? The best is jet to come. Enough renting and raving, all talk and balk. All speak and no poke. Another cocktail? Things have come to a pretty peso. Just chuck it up to experience. A wet blanket, wet to the skin game. And never ironed out. I give you this kick so you won't be so quick. Let's go girls, shouting at the ring, keep it up, pick up the pace, we've got to wring it out. Faster, and her voice gave out, ay ay ay aay! leaving a hoarse catcall . . .

    —La Maxicana from Sonora! Doña María Chicharro . . .

The Pompadour pirouetting, her sterling stirring and whirling, and brandishing her long long pipe around the puppet, and expounding: No one escapes my claws . . . Another one with money? with a leap. Wait . . . Gotcha! mad Mandrake the Magician. Make a gesture,[2] wave your wand, save yourself. Take that! popping him with the pipe. Another intimate supper with your Queen of the Night? Or would you rather sleep in the arms of Morpheus untamed? Or Morpheus unbound! Take me home! Another night with your Queen who'll make you younger, boy . . . Remember the music. How's about I plug in the magic flute? Or should I lead with the lead pencil? In the last analysis . . . Your dirty mine![3] What are you in such a hurry for? Dale que va! jabbing his rear end with the pipe. It's an authentic antique . . . Only for regular customers. I issued a set to Mr. Tod . . . Period! Take me home, no ifs or buts about it. World's End, you know. Good knight! breaking the pipe on his popo.

    —The pomposterous Pompadour of the Pampas! Esther Linamayer . . .

1. Bastard?:
And so ingenious, especially with the soft touch, like a sponge.

2. Mrs. Michelin in her fine attire:
Don't rubber the wrong way.

3. Motherato cuntabile of a cunning linguist:
Chop-chops! Chattering around her chewy chichi. The chunky chatterbox didn't
speak any Spanish but she got excited when he whispered dirty things in her
chamfered conch, cheat! chat! chaw! chewing the fat with his mouth chock-full: "a
la chacha chocha el chucho le achucha el chocho, chow! chow! así con el chicheo y
chupeteo y chucheo hasta que le da el chock a la muy rechupeteada achuchona."
A trenchscription of this churlish chainsaw Spanish chapter might go like this: the
pooch chews the chunky chick's cunt, chow chow! with his chortle chomp and
chunter until, chain reaction! he gives the shock to the choice chick. Charming!
Again please! [For a jarring change of joke, the jongleur jerked her into a joust of j's
that jangled and jolted with jagged jabs . . .]

4. Shroud? Winding sheet?:
Wind up with this white shrowdy gal, and you'll see how you shed the sweat . . .
Solo, mon salaud monteur de farces? Go with your Sabbath Queen of Sheba.

5. Canne blanche?:
Don't raise caine. Just keep jousting and flailing blindly with your white cane.

Harpy in a scalloped sleeveless cloak, probing around the puppet with her pilgrim's staff and bombarding him with pink pebbles drawn from a leather pouch: Roses without thorns in my tabernacle, eh, with your two accomplices. Ehe, Rossenkavalier!? Taking advantage of my absence. The secret rose inviolate must be of stone, and of stone the guest. Another stone? Another lesson in fluid ladino? Hasty and always running . . . O mon gosse! Gonif! Come to your mom, momzer![1] More sermons. Learn Old Castilian the English way. Pronounce Amada like . . . How was the board, oh don? giving him a stiff staff-whack. A mother?! Fonfer!
   —The student at Saint John's Wood! Mrs. Rosenstein . . .

Tubby chubster in a bikini, with a tire-lifesaver[2] around her neck and a woolly little dog under one arm, shaking her rolls of fat, mariachichatting and hoochicooting around the puppet: Chow time! Chow-chow! Chaw-chaw! You chastened me to say my see-aitches well, didn't chew? Check it out, I'm champ. After you chanted choice filth in my chaste ears which I didn't even understand![3] And then charging: Repeat after me. Challenging me! And all the time sucking on bonbons while he read. What cheek! Charming charlatan! Who can separate cheat from chaff! Plus you hated my dear little poochie. Mi chelín! You called me your shilling! Pinching me trying to tickle me. Mi chelín! How much did each minute of your chatter cost me? Assuring me that when I got to my chalet in Majorca everyone would understand me. And trying to picture me bikinied on the beach. And you said I was a steatopygian Venus. Or something like that. Then calling me a golden retread! and she jammed the tire around him. Ciao, chump!
   —"Madame Michelin!" Mrs. Mitchel . . .

Spectral albino sexagenarian, wrapped in a sheet,[4] using a cane to spear the puppet, who was twirling like a top: Have some sugar cane from Old Castile! La canne à sucre[5] de ta Dulcinée . . . How

1. Huren! Whoring?:
Whoreson.

2. Annoy ya? Noia?:
No more affairs on your ferris wheel. Pray the Paternoster with the Mutter . . .

3. Rorschach test?:
Riddled with riddles. Ink links (KNIT INK!), a catenation of caliginous clots, currente calamo! Maculate Conceptions, or Tales of the Slate, that's the name of the collection of ink stains and cock-and-balk stories that Mr. T'sui Pen put together by shaking his antediluvian fountain pen. When it refused to write, kinks! he would clink it and plink it till it shot spots on the blotting paper that stubborn Monsieur Teste would interpret so capriciously. Tinctamancy? In tinctus veritas?

4. Test for two:
Yes, another title for Monsieur Teste, a collection of tests turned into puré story.

5. Lachryma Christi? Tears?:
Crocodile tears.

6. Traumatic?:
Schock! of turning sixty. Sixty!? But she immediately became accustomed to crossing that frontier. And she would soon be in her fifties.

did the old song go? Fais la cane, goose. Cancane! Go on with your blind flailing. Another phase of the mirror stage? Faselei! La Dulcinée, née . . . —flack! defringing, defrocking, monographing and maligning you. Mal? Malevolent maltreatment. Where were we? Schmutzfleck! let's start with a clean slate. En un Lug-ar de la mancha, Stärke! Strength! in the place of stain I don't want to remember . . . Did my distinguished don forget the spot? Spassnische ist seine Stärke!: Old Cast-tilling is his strength . . . He came to my office to give me Spanish classes, español é! a Quixote armed with Quijote under his arm, and finished all dry and wizened on the divan of divagations. Qu'hijote, what a son I came up with, Hurensohn![1] dragging on with his don-wandering as if I were his salvation. Then after class he'd dump on me his bitter memories of orphanhood and all his Oedipolar and Clytennistra complexes . . . Baby needs mommy to hate daddy, and viceversta. Two birds in one shot . . . Sch! Muttis! Schiss! Schizotte, Don Quizote! And his persecucution manias, plus the general paranoia, what a pair![2] riddled with all kinds of dirty things about the impeccable Herr Doktor Kot, completely slandering his benefactor Herr Tod, the famous philanthropist . . . And on top of that he brought me his own little red writings to use for our Spanish lessons. Didn't we agree to nothing but Don Kickshotter? And sometimes as a sort of present he brought me some pages full of inkblots.[3] Better than my test,[4] having a laugh at my expense. He'd cacodemonically shake his calamitous calamus, and spin a new story from the blotches and spatters. You'd have to see it! How I wrote some of my notebooks . . . But the worst was the other stain. On my birthday. He came with a bottle of wine and invited himself for lunch. I was a bit depressed that day and with the wine, Weinkrampf![5] I turned into a crybaby. Anniversary schock?[6] Did he put me in bed? Did I lose

1. Feste mobili . . .:
Bewegliche Feste! Festejo or feast of festejos: beast with clenched feasts! Careful with the partypooper. A great wile ago the world began with hay, hoe, the wind and the rein . . . [The crazed wet blanket swinging in the rain offkey, in the end-of-the-world deluge, a long time ago . . .]

2. Banks, holidays, watches . . .:
And of the Swiss mother of our antihero. Married to a Spanish Don Juan (Alia). Hispano-Suiza, they made the best prototype . . ., self-satisfied Milalias used to say, automatically.

3. Riss rasch!:
Break and scratch. How much is the first rip? In the Ritz, ach ja! very expensive.

4. Who are you calling that?:
Ollie! Ollie! In the World's End, already too late, after eleven on the 11, we'll suprise her. Ollie! Who's this Feste? Ollie! Your Lady Olivia . . . [Let's hope the hard corruptor of words, such an aficionado of infictioning everything, doesn't infest our fiesta. Oh livid Olivia, pardon your clown. He'll have a rough time of it at the end of the world . . . World's End! Staring starry-eyed at the living portrait of his bella donna di mondo on the police poster . . . But that's another sad story, another blind romance that will wait, curious reader, for the next vermicular volume, soon appearing in a playhouse near you. Don't you dare miss it, informed reader. L'Allucinant Rendez-Voudou Arrive . . .]

my head? Who undressed me? Besides the bed was all messed up and on the sheet . . . Shithead! she speared him straight through his long limb.

—Anna, the analyst of Golder's Green! Frau Doktor Fleck . . .

Debutante in black, coiffed with a black feather hat, opening and closing a black-festooned parasol around the puppet: Don't you know why I'm dressed in strict mourning, my entertainer? Or the cause of my melancholy, my dear suitor? You won't be at the last courting. What a relief! Why don't you explain yourself in this jolly fest of feasts with so many masks? This is very Midsummer madness . . . Frenzied festival![1] Why did you keep snickering that I'm from the country of the cow, the bank, and the hotel?[2] Tell me. Your Swiss swish or switch! Your cheap street whore! Who're you fooling! Did you forget my favors? I gave you a roof for your head and a bed to spread in, you ingrate! Today for me and the day after tomorrow for you, you always promised. Liar! Like a soul in need that sad February night I rang the buzzer on your door, cree-cree-cree . . ., and you didn't come down to open it or when you did I wasn't there anymore. The best woman in your life went on to a worse life . . . You had an alibi, I suppose? Hure! Fausse la vérité. Mein Pupe! And you always getting excited when I mentioned those . . . disgusting things! Another lip-flapper to the flophouse. You were my corrupter of whords, whenever I told you my troubles on the circuit of luxury hotels. And always free for you. With shipping. Insurance and fright included. Or on installments. Feste Zahlungsfrist! Even long-term payments come due. You courted me and then cut me off. You're all alike . . . Even though I only go with select clients and in the best hotels. Savoy avoided . . . Cocumberland . . . Ritz![3] and she ripped his cape with the point of her parasol.

—Lady Olivia! Ollie . . .[4]

1. Marish, mulish. . . ?:
Or like an onager . . . Very wild. And on top of that a real catapult. Pata culta! Ecco fatto el becco all'oca!

2. Les prières se transformeront en pierres . . .:
Pierres branlantes? Let he who is free of sin lay the first stone . . . React, Petronius, hide the hand and throw the rock—from behind your back. No bolder than that? A rock that rolls, and begins the repopulation. The Stone Guest, wasn't he called Deucalion this time?

3. Mets ta mort fausse . . .:
La p'tite mort, sans phrases.

4. Of errata?:
So close to the British Museum . . . Nest of library rats. Of errata. Of confusion. Mare's nest, Mea Equa! what horsing around. Jockeying for position with the chilly filly . . . Such premature jocularity, what with the haste and all, and standing up too.

Tall and bony, with a horsy face[1] under a ducal crown of tinsel, her back covered by her blanket of red hair, rapidly galloping around the puppet, throwing punches, and rocks: I lapidate you, I dilapidate you with your lapidary phrases. Bat us! I'll make you swallow them! You used to say you yearned for me . . . Didn't you put me to the touchstone! I beat you. Say your prayers.[2] Pyrrhic victory! End. Fin. Fine omesso, massochista. I met, amour, met a more mythamorphosisyphus of orgasmoriabundance . . .[3] Other phrases, other phases . . . Video meliora, provoker!; deteriora sequor. I see the better way, and provoke the worst . . . Tu quoque. You to . . . Divo! Avid! O yes. Your bird of prey, an eagle-eye having a feast with the plague of errata. All those Latin lapsus calami, Latinpanalley howlers . . . Cuniculinguist! Your guffaws came all the way up to my study. Erratum! Erratum! Muta, re. Return with your queen to the rat's nest.[4] How many hours alone in that dusty crypt in Bloomsbury. I took care of the phone calls, so many for you! made tea for you while you strained your eyes over the mountain of proofs. In macarunic Latin. Chaos on your desk. Chaos, rudis indigestaque moles. Well said, old mole! Looking for a new hole . . . That afternoon burning in my conscience: you said I wasn't an antique and I could be a Venus if I just knew how to fix myself up. Old maid, all made. You pulled off my glasses, quickly undid my bun, blustered around my buttoned-up blouse. Look at you. And me paralyzed like a statue. Kissing me, thrilling me . . . killing me! Pig . . . Pigmée! Lion battu! Chameleon! Mr. Wright is coming to pick up the proofs, he's coming, he's coming . . . And act two, like nothing happened, you went back to correcting those proofs, going around and around again, tourne à vide, O vide perpétuel! that you said reminded you of your own metamorpheuses. En, hic est nostri cuntemptor!

1. There was an old man with a beard . . .:
Nonsense, Sensemann!

2. Fignis coronat opus:
Iamque opus exegi, quod nec ovis ira, nec ignis, nec poterit caelum, nec edax abolere vetustas. [Chiseler, chisel out, carve the word in Time, and pay no attention to the choleric bleat of sheep . . .]

3. The daughter of the centaur Chiron?:
Who knows. A Spamish translaytion of the *Metamorphoses*, publynched or publotched in paperback in Spain, was a peerless example for protean Milalias. Australis monstrum. He said it was impossible to improve the metamorphosizing powers of the printers—or translator?—and with only a few measly letters. In the brief passage dedicated to Chiron's daughter, metamorphosed into a mare due to her gift for reading the future, this creature, what was her name? was first Ocirae, a few lines later Charicho, and Ociroe in the index. And last, but not least or beast: "Ociroe transformed into a cow." Sic, in the index. Who else gives so much for so little?

4. New Ager? NEW ONAGER! NO, NOR OMEGO AGE MORON. ON, REGAN OWEN!:
Pay no attention, Miss Owen. Little by little the wild ass's skin will diminish, gros chagrin, and chagrin after chagrin the desires will consume it. What will remain? A bray. And vice versa: órgano. A new Spanish organ? Novum organum, resonating in the desert against all the idols?

5. Galloping phthisis?:
This undaunted consumptive was titanic. And somewhere in her skinniness she found the strength to carry enormous towers of Babel.

And another burst of laughter. You lost your head on every other word. Inopem me copia fecit. In the clouds! I'll give you your destiny to you in Spanish! Sass! Sa! Trota, onagro! beating him, Trot, ass! roundly about the neck. Tinsel ass, ass of fool's gold! keep braying and seeking, crawl around with your massy rolling stone stories gathering no match, metamorphose the love affairs into five books, Tristitia! of your tristangled proteagonist weaving from filly to folly with all his sentimementos. Are you going to dig the grave? O Sir, you are old.[1] Like a dirty old man. What a leer! Go back to your old habits and pieces, your alibis and your thousand alias, Mil Alias, alias beatus, alias miser. That's life. Hoec et mille alia, these and another thousand puzzles. Are you about done for? Or is this just a pretense, more feigning fits by fiction's fink? Sphinx! Phoenix coronat opus![2] as she violently crowned him. No! Go back to your old tricks. Your monstrous mythic jokes on my Shakespearean name. Leer at me. Didn't you like it though. You twisted it and bestialized it. The organ sounded by chance . . . What was the name of that beast of burden?[3] My father too is half animal, and half crazy . . . You wanted to mount me, eh!? I was your queen, your new ona . . . Nay! Ris, gandin. Oui. Afternoon of laughs, it still burns, when you got me mixed up in your smoke cloud. Don't be so stiff and old-fashioned. Oh yes, that weed turns me crazy, I'd like to gallop again through the green meadows of Eden. Hyhnhnm! imitating a whinny, shaking her fiery mane and kicking at the puppet, throttling him around the neck. I'll neigh you and slay you! This time the win is mine, she whinnied.

    —Miss Owen? Reggie! Regan Owen . . .[4]

Stiff as a stick, and with carrot-colored hair in bangs down to her dark glasses, holding against her sunken chest[5] a pile of books, swaying and shuffling her flat feet around the puppet: Vendetta! liar. I secretly represent all the secretaries of the library of Babel.

1. And a good tumble . . .:
Of jacket and spine, with a heavy heading.

2. With breaking and entering?:
Or wreaking and ranting.

3. Librorbe, orbe ebro. Exorbitant. Drunkorbit:
Orbit, bit by bit, till the obit. Le Monde existe pour aboutir à un livre . . .,
mallaremarked Milalias one day as he wearily dropped the French daily that
Babelle had brought him, in order to get wrapped up in a book. Le Livre. . . ?

4. Make yourself at tome, in the N$^{a}_{o}$vel of the Universe:
Legato con Amore Radiante in un Volume Animato. Lega alla rústica vostro
atlante!

Bella bibliotecca! Isn't that what you called it? All of them, Fräulein Marx, La Madelon, Miss Lay . . ., they all send you their regards, tante care cose, caricato. And yours truly? I too, without fail. Secret segretaria a garbo, the canzonatore nicknamed me, after watching me march to and fro so gracefully and silently with my towers of tomes. Fa castelli in aria, un altro castelletto spagnoletto. Remember when we pretended to check the inventory? Bocángel . . . Boccalini . . . Boccaccio . . . You went over the list and I read the book spines from the ladder steps. Wham! That's some volume! È un bel tomo . . .[1] D'Annunzio . . . Dante . . . What larceny![2] He stole a kiss from me. La boccaccia mi bacciò tutto tramante. That afternoon we read no more . . . Acqua in bocca! And how your mouth was watering, reading me the menu of the restaurant there beside the office. Paradiso-E-Inferno, on the Strand. Now the tables are turned, tornagusto, your hell will be my paradise. Osso Nabucco . . . dono sor. Antipasto, pasteca . . . Chicken catchatory, and canaloony for the lady . . . and spaghetti al burro . . . who paid? I trusted you. Paga il fío! Libra a libro, pound for pound. Tieni i libri, take the tomes! and she started throwing books at his head. Take that, tomefool pedant. Supernova, listen! about to burst? See stars, a riveder le stelle, a rivederci eco ecuménico. Count and recount, from the crib to the grave. Put it all down in your double-entry accounting book. Cómpito compito? Pulpit to pit with your dizzying book of whirrds, your bookmerang.[3] You said you'd find the whole universe in a single book, didn't you?[4] L'universo si squaderna! and she unbound her fury and the last book against his head. Go forth and be clothbound and gagged . . .
    —Francesca Castelli! Signorina "Castellina" . . .

Virile prima donna in a royal purple bedspread, with a curly black nylon wig and inflated breasts, twisting a noose around her neck, tilting her head with continuous tics, and whipping the puppet

1. Buffa! And sopranizing too . . .:
Voce di peto, ma più farte! On an agitated night, coriggia! he would aim his aria at the garden . . .

2. Rumorous Ron . . .:
Only a romeo amoretto, but there were also Othellos . . . Almost always blacks. And dying with hunger. An ample cast.

3. Rump, or cul-de-sac . . .:
Vicolo chiassolo. Sicosiricorsi, and watch they don't sack the place rummaging around for the Korsakoff alcocholeric . . . Which is just what happened to Jamaican Ron. Or Rum. That almost musical name, Korsakoff's psychosis, they gave to his ailment. Milalias went to visit him one time at Bethlem Hospital. How are we doing? Poco-poco . . ., he answered in his Jamaicastilian. Pretty well? Así así. So-so. Loco loco . . .

4. A case of old porter in a trunk funk:
Almost twenty years carrying suitcases in the Great Western Royal Hotel, across from Paddington station, and he claimed that's why his arms had grown. Quite remarkably long. And he liked to show off his biceps and pectorals.

5. Demon! Don't give false Testi . . .:
He came down like a bundle! Like one of the big heavy suitcases he carried when he was young. Stringing along. Or roped into it? Wham! And then, again, silence in the night. Milalias went down to look. He called at his door. Mr. Testi . . . Unlocked. All his treasures, his trash, his portobellico bric-a-brac, strewn about the floor. (A Sicilian waiter and ex-bedpartner had told the police, for revenge? that Mr. Testi bought and kept stolen articles . . . After an unexpected visit from the cops, Mr. "Testy" spent his spare time muttering to himself that they would put him in the slammer or deport him. Not even his lawyer managed to calm him . . .) And through the open doorway to the cellar came a moan. Muffled. Mr. Testi . . . Milalias got up the nerve to go down. And to lift the cadaver . . . now resuscitated. Mr. Testi! Sitting on the floor sobbing, pulling on the clothesline (rotted) that had broken. His first hanging, a failure.

with the end of the rope: Colpo di fune, smemorato! Don't you remember? Cordiality like mine you won't find everywhere. Without a bed or lavoro, boaster. Without a lira, lyric liar. That bobo Bob with his bobbing and weaving, he brought you with recommendations, and I gave you lodging. Maledetto! How many times do I have to tell you, diavoletto! Bob is a birbone, be careful of the company you keep. Me, grouchy? A thieving magpie? But always a pie for you. I was a mamma to you. Although grudgingly, I loaned you my Olivetti, and you took my tea, tenebrone! la pasta, and the pastry I set aside for Fridays. Torta al burro, the same old story! Trot, arrivista, always slipping out of my hands. Scorsoio, corso! And always with a jeer and a jibe, un monte di robaccia!? trash!? when I came back bushed from my treasure hunting in Portobello. Your mocking, scherzando, when I heard my scratched opera records.[1] And your sarcastic tone when Jamaican Ron or Rum[2] came over to sleep it off. Because he rumbles in his sleep? A rum fellow? Because he's dark, buccaneer? Because he wears rumpled clothing?[3] Ratto patto! Your laugh, malévolo! when you heard us fighting. And your chuckling when you glimpsed, spiatore! through the half-closed door of my room the bella donna in her nightshirt that night . . . Would you rather I were alone in my shroud, cheapskate? And when I tried to tell you my troubles, mal piglio! you played deaf. Yes, you. And the next morning you went to Signore Alter to arrange for me to pose for his Torot. Another cordonatura! Former porter[4] changed into the hanged man? Porta, porta. Via! And where were you when the police sacked the place, everything downstairs smashed. Your testimony would have saved me. That pico de loro of yours, your silver tongue when you chattered away to postpone payment. Always badly and late. What a laugh. Me, grouchy? Ingrato! Now I unhang myself, orco infernale! and he slid the noose over the puppet's head. Appico discorso!

—Mr. "Testy"! Signore Testi . . .[5]

1. It may be fun to you, but it's death to the frogs:
May the metamorphoses leave you with a frog in your throat . . .

2. Rana? Frog. As the Spaniard Milalias hears it. Mrs. Rana . . .:
With succulent frog legs, fit for a prince. Of India.

3. Spat . . .:
Taps! Spot Czech. Don't leave anything to chance. Spat. Taps. Dropping off to sleep, blockhead, Svap! Swap! Repayment in kine as you barter with the cow. Strong. A real cool Czech. Lively tap dancing in that meeting in Trafalgar Square for Moby Dick, Save the Whale! when it occurred to you to approach her. Save the wail. And to top it off, she put you on her circus bicycle. A folding model. This one lightweight.

Effigy with a metallic[1] frog head and green stockings, skintight, hopping around the puppet, slapping her narrow rump: Could you come down please? He was looking at me in a way that . . . Because I was English and married to an Indian god? He didn't take his eyes off my haunches. And he promised that in just a few days . . . Now you *will* have to pay! Always delaying. He left poor Mr. Testi's house and only had to cross the Green to come do the same thing at my place. Can't the little froggie, tadpole! loan you a little something, after desperately spending so many hours in your room? Or your patron? Don't you toady to Mr. Tod? Frog in your throat? You ought to be flogged and frog-marched! and she gave him a resounding bop! with her head.

—The Phoenix Lodge landlady! Mrs. Rana . . .[2]

Bovine beauty with skin white as milk, in a white sack suit with big rips, bouncing in boots around the puppet, and holding a bicycle chain high with both hands: Imagine finding you here! How far did you steer me around that day, from the meeting in Trafalgar Square, Save the Whale! to the summer siesta in that hidden nook by Mr. Pan's statue. Pant, panter . . . Cower! and she rained a chain-blow on him. Your fault? Pretty pity. Pit píti Pan! A little tipsy, miserable, and nodding off at your side. Sentimental! Sprattling.[3] Tata wants teat? Happy now. Ay, masochist! In your park, sad park! A snake? Stark snaked. Non, ano, on and no. You liked my yes yes? Yes, jester. Oh boy! A karate match, rolling. My little chain broke and the charm never turned up. The golden calf. I almost had an attack! Then milking it for all it's worth . . . Did you steal my jewel? Was it you? Saturday theft. Was it your work? Spill it! prodding him. It had your marks. Throw in the towel! Crushed? Your little dear isn't spiteful, she's cud-cuddly. I'll give

1. Already the final dissolution?:
Il disoluto (punito!) tributary of affluent women.

2. Bogy. Boggy:
Row better, Volgar boatmen, beau gars! Boogie man, don't bogart that little man in the boat. Bogha boogie.

3. Un Gange passe . . .:
Passa a guado! Gangelically. Acqua cheta . . . All the rivers run into the seal . . . Vale meglio passare sotto silenzio el río . . . Acqua in bocca! A riverderci!

4. In the beginning was the Vac . . .:
In the beginning was the Vacuum, and the Vacuum was with Vāc, and Vāc was God and Goddess. Vāc, the World, was made flesh. The word created the world. And without this orginary goddess, Vāc, we wouldn't have voice or vocative or devil's advocate . . .

5. Sacred cows?:
Wise counsel: all of them are sacred, despite all the bum steers . . . Lean kine, fattened calves, all are couched in his vocowbulary, feeding his cow-and-bull stories.

6. Sad sadhu . . .:
Always playing sadhumusickissed.

you a present to remember, putting the chain around his neck, Krk!
Krást! and pulling it tight. Bullshitter!
  —Chick oh so slow . . . The Czechoslovakian . . . ! Milada
Dubový . . .

Voluminous veiled Indian in a shimmering blue-gold sari, shaking
a large cowbell around the puppet: Tan! Tan! Tricky trapping
lover, such a wicked web he weaves. I suppose you saw me
coming? And I'm sure you were merrily recalling your conquered
Indians. The one with thick braids and tight jeans, the olive-
skinned pharmacist in Paddington? The big dark one who gave you
the time of day in the newspaper stand in Bayswater? The fallen
apple of Brook Green? All of the same strain.[1] Ay! Ay-yee! Yoga
with me, come to my bed (hu! who? nothing at all?), bogus[2] boat-
man! turn, ford across, sink down without beating around your
mature Magna Matron, what a bhang gang-up![3] She'll flood you
right out of your streambed. Get my drift? Believe in me, schemer,
believe in the ring of my bell. Sing, lover, to the sound of my crazy
ballad. Mad guru: Samsara is shamshare. Gai saber. Sic. Bho
Bhoh! Not the gay cock anymore, something in your gullet? Upa,
sir. Come in! Tout de go, à go-go, I have a vacancy for my vacuous
friend. Let's return to the beginning, rude antagonist. In the
beginning was the Vacuum . . .[4] Amen. Atman. Mute of mantra,
and voice. Maya, yeah, peripatetic Mayeutic. I was muttering
prayers with my disciples along that shady path in Holland Park
and back there alone on a bench, you were writing with your little
finger in the dirt . . . Doesn't Daddy Longlegs have any paper?
Time of lean kine,[5] beggar? And with a branch you erase what you
write (sanscretinizing?) and raise a cloud of dust . . . To cover
yourself with dust? Bravo, sadhu![6] You stayed unmoving a minute.
Pondering, poetaster? And you raised your head. Admiring my
charms? C'mon you boob, stare at someone else. Want to see my
marked face? and she unveiled, showing a face covered with black
beauty marks. Look, proflingate, look what you did to me. Or were

1. Pancagavya?:
Sacrilege . . . Utter on, daffy ding-dung, spooner up some more bilk and mutter, a recurd of yearning for your dunga din . . . You'll be in the dungeon after the purification.

2. LONDON WELCOMES THE DIVINE MOTHER:
Below, the full-moon face (between her eyebrows a dot that would soon multiply) about to pass to a more virulent phase (Māriyamma, the goddess of smallpox?), completely dotted. Chicken pox?:

And under the portrait, with a few alterations:

HER HOLINESS
VACA TAPADA

(Unspotted cow?!) It also announced that her sacred words would be free for everyone for one holy week in the Horticultural Hall, Westminster.

3. The Queen's Head:
It's got a lot of history, Milalias told Babelle, proud of his neighborhood pub. Dick Turpin used to hide from the law here. I suppose his mare Black Bess was concealed in the back garden.

4. The blue bottle . . .:
The blue devils! Fly, buzz around your caliginous old witch. Calliphora vicina . . .

you merely looking at my garments? The fringe of my neckline barely veiling my enchantments . . . I was sacred and I'm always off-limits, prohibited, get it? I'll see you again. Coward! We'll meet again someday, you were thinking. And you recognized me a few days later on that poster while waiting for the bus on Hammersmith Road. London welcomes the Divine Mother. Fascinated by the perfectly round circle adorning my forehead? Till lack of decency drove you to add more dots. And still laconic, you finished by mutating my name. Vaca matta? Vaca loka? Vaca tapada! Sí señorito, veiled cow! I'll vaccinate you. I'll anoint you with my five . . .[1] Give it to him hard. Coward! You profaned my face, my name and my message.[2] All spotted, full of dots. Look at this one between my eyebrows, dot for tad! because it's the last thing you'll see. The old mole! Make a magic mountain of a molehill, man. A hilarious old story. Cowabunga! Go on, blind man, and she cowbelted him, take one below the belt!

—The Divine Mother?! Vac Tapadandah . . .

Blackened beggar in rags, raising a dark bottle around the puppet: Spyglass or kaleidoscorpio? Have a look, nudniknamer . . . I spin him around, another tour, pinhead, and change the view. One word is all word-embraces, one woman is all woe to men, one pretty pet all the pet phases. Will you mount me or will I dismount you? Heeyah, giddy up through the turpentine night alleys of London at the witching hour. How about a stop in our favorite spot in Brook Green?[3] Uncork a dream with your queen. Look how inky-dark it's getting, and she walloped the neck of the bottle against his head. You wanted to sweep me away, eh? In Islington. The blue bottle![4] Buzz, superfly. Scribble your specks. Look now, party animal, through the dark buttle of your diva!

—The London-roaming tramp! "Black" Bess . . .

1. Putorious foetidus? Mephitis Mephistofelon?:
No one gets skunked in no-mann's-land. Nenieslandono. Mirlandono.

2. A mammary zone?:
. . . he asked brazenly. Or a brattleground.

3. Princo!?: Prince?:
Same enough for Dr. Desesperanto, prince of his dark librovermo.

4. Femuro!?:
It's thigh time you explained.

5. Divine writer, ecce homo . . .:
If it be possible, what cupability! let this kaliko pass from me . . .

6. Li estas Alia:
He is another. Mi estas Alia.

Emaciated lady, middle-aged, in a white lace minidress, with an enormous braided bun the color of mahogany, hopping on one foot around the puppet, brandishing a red shoe with a very sharp high heel: Tango is tango. Dancing tea in the Café de Paris. Remimori, amoro. Kafeyo de Parizo, in Pikadillo. Balo romantiko. Fokstroto, amori, valso, rumbo, mambo, tango. A media luzerno, candle-lit. Palpi, palpitate. Cha-cha-chas, skuno. Mefisto![1] Demono! Impetuously charging my tablo. Pardonu! Mi fallto. Dandy, dithering excuses. Fi! Flee, fly, foe. Feliso kulpa . . . His clumsy catapult left me without a drop of tea. Savage sabotage! and a bellicose bellhop to hop to it. My sino! Mia robo! Mia mamzono![2] Dumped the whole teapot on the table. Applaud, plaudi! when the piece is over. And so fine, the princo![3] drying his face with my napkino. And then he sounded off, the trumpeting elephant. Trinki? A little drinky-poo? Look looking at my titaso, empty! and then my femuro[4] from the corner of his eye, okulo of Satan! the stain on the tablecloth. Revengo! I read you the three letters, beletristo, so lethal—teksteo!—dissolving in those tea leaves. Can you OD on tea? Letter by lerta, on the alert. Teomancy? What a swindle. But presto, preste donchuano! suddenly flirting. A very lovely virino, so solena and so alone . . . coming on with his gallant compliments. Galantavorto! And finally laughing along with his guffaws. And out of curiosity I spikokoteo to him. Yugoslarvo? Greko? Polo? Franco? Hispano! De Madrido? Mi parolas Esperanto. Simila, vorto a vorto, al hispana. I am Esperantisto and Espiritisto. Theosofisto. And you? Estudento en Londono? Literaturisto! Verkristo![5] Multa gusto, sinjoro . . . Alia?! Sinjoro Alia?[6] Bela nomo! And Don Johann takes me for a valse. A jam already: Libertino Don Yojano Tenorio! Granda viro, amoro, and I felt liliputa next to his korpo de gorilo. And stringing me along rub-a-dub-dub, frotifroto volvolupto, libelo! while the vampiro, the gyroskopolluter, with his false waltz . . . Trompo. Trample! Rapidu! Come rapide kun tu Venoso. And this histrionic

1. Clumsy?:
Moment of pathos . . . Patoso, Pestoso! she said in passing a moment of passion.

2. Sen brando?:
Right. Only tea, no brandy or liquors, in the dancing tearoom of the Café de Paris. Charged atmosphere and '30s-style decor. Red-carpeted stairway, titillating scratches, brass wall lamps, reddish screens, plastic geraniums, little tables for two with separate little tea services. Hodgepodge in half-light: off-duty waiters, nostalgic spinsters, retired people there to dance, foreign students, tourists, aimlessly wandering. Jammed. The sinjoro Alia about to enter combat with the Esperantist . . . La virino trinkas la teo. Tea for one. Would you like a rum-a rumba? She wanted to frolic. Ni dancis en la salono. To the rhythm of the melodies of Mel Gaynor and his band. Damo, estu bona! Lady, be good . . . Adio pampo mia . . . Il Tenore Bufo taking toad jumps with the theosophist. Patoso! What clumsy pathos! Fi al vi! Shame on you! And fortunately soon after came God save the queen, at exactly 5:45, and brought salvation. Mi venos lundon. He swore he would return the following Monday to practice the esperantango. La Dio pardonu vin!

3. Rod, spar . . .:
Unspared. Stinging blow to the head.

4. Pensée? Behind the ear?!:
Honi soit qui mal lit pansy!

5. Come to my woman's breasts:
And take my milk for all . . .

buffoon starts to tango me. Patoso![1] Such a tumbling amid the tumult. My stiletto heel broken. Tipsy? Last tango, without Brando![2] in the Kafeyo de Parizo. Tango! and she walloped him in the head with the shoe. Stango![3]
 —Miss "Tanguette"! Liza . . .

Rumpled blonde (a pansy[4] behind one ear) in a housecoat, a plush doll under one arm, wielding a green plastic laundry basket with the other: To each buck his bucket! and she pulled it down over the poor puppet's head—like a helmet: In the laundromat, shamelessly eyeing my dirty linen . . . How lovely! and looking at my cleavage, not at my nursing baby. Sounding me out and illiciting information. Traveling husband? how interesting. In Cornwall now? watching my pansypanties my spinning underthings rip-raped. Almost always alone? and you came closer. And your pitter-patter: Pete Pete Pete . . . Kootchy-kooing Pete, and my bubs in passing. And your eyes! of a roamer Romeo looking for romances. And you took the opportunity to help me carry the wash, already falling for you, and to come up to my house. A tea? and you took a bit more. Tea? Tit for tea. Two for tea. Too full o' the milk of human kindness![5] that you stole from my pitiful petite Pete . . . Sucker! It's wean or lose all . . . Dear little thing, rockabye baby . . ., beating the puppet, down will come baby, cradle and all . . .
 —Mrs. Bradley . . . Pansie! Pansie from Paddington . . .

Bundled-up witch with a black shawl fluttering over her head, and swinging a black handbag around the puppet: Prorated now. Still not paying your quota? Got the latest price quotes? For once,

1. Our private member plays many private parts:
Sometimes the privity is depravity . . .

2. Plump!:
Blot the clean slate, and pray it again, Sam.

3. Like mud?:
Very mulch so.

4. Kuppel?:
Or Koppel. Or Kuppler. Or something like that. At Madame Celestina's off-limits Swiss Cottage there was always such a feisty ruckus that the introductions usually got garbled. Anyhow, Milalias deliberately and trivaliantly designated her La Celestrina, for her trinity of unpalliated appellations.

keeping in mind our common vices, I won't notify Herr Tod . . .
Rat! The term comes to term. Eh, Herr Rat? What would have
become of my agency of au pairs without your privy counsel[1] and
advice versa . . . But at bottom you're right: the poor au pairs feel so
lost in Lohndon. It's not enough to find a family for the famished
creatures. The Thursday evening reunions at my house, Swiss
Kottage, you know, is the best place to make friends. We get
executives, businessmen . . . Why don't you deal with us anymore? Don't you need the help of your fairy fury, Kupplerinnys!
the magic procurative powers of your panderous Celestrina? Build
a better mousetrap . . . And you didn't participate in the lottery
either, notorious Lothario, Lotterbube! or the love auction. Don't
you love your Lotte anymore? No longer looking for your better
half? What a time that was, lot 69! that afternoon of striptease and
sympathy . . . The great Lotte . . . And that party playing blindman
in the buff. She who doesn't close her eyes, loses! I've got some
new gals now, a new shipment. Love flees and only the pains
remain: Auf Liebe folgt Lied. Who has the lead? Always in
dispute. Like Herr Doktor Kot's slogan, in Freud und Leid!
whether fair or overcast. Are you broke again, need a white slave
for the black market? Try another treatment. A good piece, eh? of
advice. Our great benefactor will arrange it, he always finds a
solution for everything. Der Herr Tod macht ein Ende aller Not.
Don't you think so? But then you don't do your parts, or devote all
your energy seeking money either . . . That escort agency I set you
up with was a fine place. Fidgety breeches, eh? Pump! Plump!
come and write it up, and down, largesse than life. Plumps![2] And
now you can't even raise your head. This is a fine predickament.
OK, I'll give you a hand one last time. First of all you need to get
some rest. Requiescat in pace, and no more of your sprees. Patsch!
jolting him with handbag blows. Requiescat in Patsche![3]
   —The madam of the au pair agency! Frau Kuppel . . .[4]

1. Spanish screen . . .:
With three sections, completely covered with thumbtacked images and clippings. Postcards, Babelle's photos of London, the latest instructions, urgent messages . . . Some cards, photos and reproductions of masterworks were replaced by others, with the changes of season and location. But the screen, along with the enormous trunk and the folding card table, went with Milalias to each new dwelling.

2. Old Nick? Nick!?:
Rascal, Nick off! Crime and punishment, devil take all! next to the Saint Nicholas Church. This time in Chiswick. Chis! Fallen in the nocturnal mud, after trying to take advantage of the poor alcoholic from the Old Ship pub. Escaping, like a person possessed, winding up in the river. In the mud, next to the Saint Nicholas Church in Chiswick. (Sic.) Back to your old tricks. Wanting to make it with her, wrestling on the ground behind Hogarth's last home. You really liked the masks on his resting place. And when the hissing voices and murmurs of the Thames died down, you climbed out of the river, run old mongrel, brrr, frozen to the bone, the river is within us . . ., and again took refuge on hallowed ground. Delirium tremens? Shivering, arms crossed, before the crucified Christ on the façade. Almost as dirty as you. So you tried to dry yourself, clean yourself up, blasphemous Ecce homunculus?

3. A mí no, rejón! Not that spear at me!:
A wound from the spear side of the femily . . .

4. Lift not the painted veil . . .:
This veil of tears. Let us draw a Velasquez over this Fountain Veil.

Strict severe mother in a dark brown habit, a prayer book in her left hand and her right gripping the crucifix, spitting her ejaculatory prayers around the puppet: Vade retro! You never saw your mother, you didn't have a father, the devil made you! Where's your soul, heartless heathen. I suppose you want to soil me with your scummy prayers again? Bonus est prestolari . . . Libertine acting repentant, ventriloquizes avemarias. Trying to sweeten me up? A little kiss, a little pinch, prorphaner. My image tacked up on your folding screen.[1] You beatized me and canonized me, and put me on high. Me, a praying mantis in your dreams, your beloved Nuestra Madrespaña, Mother Spain. Magna Marter. Ha! Now I'll give it to you with the hammer of uterodox contents. Hit the nail on the weak spot, eh? Mother Spain pains you. Your meternal selvation. No more. Fons et origo. No more. You left the fountain for the stream. And couldn't stay in the riverbed either. Mucking it all up. Polluted like the Christ of your Chiswick church. Another old story of Saint Nick.[2] Burn the candle at both ends, to the godevil! with the light growing dim on you. Your loom is spent. In your nonsanctasatanorum of Phoenix Lodge. You marvel? Ask Ez! With passion and without pause. All those crosswords of your crucifrictions. Kriss-cross! Infantuation at first glans. Prostate, prostrate yourself before my crux. Satan sits behind the cross? Sate on and on! and she nailed the cross to his head.

—No, Jeronima![3] Venerable Mother Superior Jeronima de la Fuente . . .[4]

*
* *

1. Abril in Armenia: living dangerously?:
Ja, Friedrich the Grate. Niet, Nietzsche. Sí, living and writing (: escrivivir!) pericolosamente, to be in leopardy. Ring the chances, penmaniac, trying to change your weak spots.

2. Ser o no ser?:
To be or not to be. Or to love? Serene late afternoon in April, by the fountains in Kensington Gardens. (High lantern-glow in the Lancaster Hotel.) The duenna with her black shawls set herself up on our bench. Chalk white face with a sweet expression, in spite of the network of wrinkles and her somber shawl. Babelle started talking to her and almost hugged her when she said she was Armenian. Her maternal grandmother (thus starting the babelisms?) was Armenian. And she started to babble with the proprietress, loose words from her childhood. The proprietress nodded and repeated them, smilingly. I wrote down *ser:* love! (But in Spanish, ser: *to be!* Ser o no ser? To be . . .)

That same night Milalias appeared in a dream, hamlettishly dressed in black, and alone walked through the Marlborough Gate murmuring his soliloquy towards the deserted fountains: Sir or no sir . . .

The somber duenna made her appearance and only said: Ser! And then from behind a hedge, a grotesquely fat nun, Sònia Sorolla, leaped out with a pot on her head and shouted in Catalan: Res! No res! Res de res! (Nothing at all?)

—Come on, Babelle protested, —you're always inventing dreams!

—Not me. Milalias dreams or dreams something up . . . I only transcribe. It's always like that. He loves and I'm his amanuensis . . .

3. Pot?: Olla!?:
O yah. Catalonian pot.

4. Abbots . . .:
The cook of that gastronomic abbey, Luis Gil, had almost been a monk before a chef. Fray Luis, from Leon, Spain. Then there was a Catalan student, a dish-washing companion of Milalias, who was about to become a Carmelite nun. God moves among the pots?

SISTERS

Gloomy duenna with her shawl awry, brandishing around the puppet, in each hand, a stinking lily and a dagger: Lay down your Armenian, my son, with your dearly beloved in your arms. In your linga barbar. Remember that afternoon at the Kensington fountains? I'll engrave on you everything you wrote down. Yes, secretive glosser. Loco amor requires violent april . . . The cruellest Abril.[1] More than love. Ser? To be? Or no ser? Ore ora, all your gibberish. An ordinary, nettled in your meshmash. You wanted to soar from sor to surprise, ay sor! an eyesore lying in wait in the night. Qui, chéri? Kiss her? Give my little granddaughter a smack. Gay lobo with your gay conscience. Polyglosser embellishing his linga barbar. Twists and turns, vast tour! at hazard. Miracle? Mera viglia! giglio selvàtico. From lily to lily, come with your chaste lily who'll leave you a most unspotted lily. Abril has come and gone. No more, no ser or . . .[2] Know, sir. To be and not to breed. My words have all flown. Now the cord must be cut. Be grateful I'm not sinking my teeth in. With this daggar—and she drove it into his neck—she beheads you.

—The Armenian grandmother!? Sousan . . .

Thundering nun with a pot[3] on her head, shaking a string of pots and pans, potsing and panting around the puppet: Els testos s'assemblen to the testes. Words to the caldron, skill to the skillet. Test a test, testy. Tackatack. Typing till all hours. Tap! Tap! Tap! typing out taps for all. Mot a mort, amor. La mort ho pot tot: omniportentous death. Pit for pot. Somnia in Sonia, sound sleep . . . Try this pot! Pots and pots. Come to the foot of my four-poster! and she gave him a boot. Jump, robot! A bots![4] In our roastaurant at every scrubdown. Remember! You liked to see me pout over the

1. Saint Nicholas in Deptford!?:
Yes, the church watched by two skulls . . . They say at night the atrium is haunted
by a Mephaustophelian phantasm. And there they buried a great sinner—no one
knows exactly where—who in life carried Christ, and after dying a bad death,
perhaps wound up being carried off by the devil . . . Hell hath no limits,
Christosphere? (Marlowe's mighty line!)

pots, to see me sob and implore you. Crying washes away the guilt . . . Rubdown after rubdown, my colleague can dish it out. More dishes and plates to wash, rentaplats! And after using me quick and dirty, he tried to get rid of me, by transferring me to the monomaniacal cook. Cóc au chef, and she popped him one with the pot.

    —Sor Olla! Sònia Sorolla . . .

The pig-faced nun priggishly waltzing along and pinching the puppet: Another cardinal point? Another pinch? Nip along! new man. Cor ad cor loquitur. You liked it when your bacchic organist whispered in your inner ear and played for you on the slime. Ex umbris et imaginibus in veritatem. Unreal shadow among the Deptford shadows. Under cover of night and in cold blood you turned up at my abode, a pig head under your arm, and got me out of bed. Hurry up. It's hopping in the Albany. Till dawn. And so no one would recognize me in that orgy of masks, you hooded me with your big pig-face. You're so pigheaded! Another pinch? Nip, nip, nipple! First you turn me black-and-blue, then you turn off-color, in the midst of the crowd saying salacious things with your buddy the alcoholiquored Belgian. Nip after nip in front of the iron rails of the Saint Nick Church.[1] One drop would save my soul, half a drop . . . anxiously shaking the bottle. My soul for a spirited drop. And me right there in front of the church, having to put up with the litany of two drunks. Swanking about under the streetlamp. And if one of the parishioners had recognized me? Perish the thought! scratching him. I'll give you the last drop, furiously knocking him over. Drop off!

    —"Sor" Dinah! Dinah Newmann . . .

Energetic sister with frizzy brown hair and a beatific smile, in a waitress apron, clapping rhythmically with a silver tray around the

1. Polish that droga:
And you might trip.

2. Ser, serious existentialist? What's that, cheeseler?:
One of his foods for thought. Caseus, mollis philosophus. Primum vivere . . . I
consume, ergo sum. While there's still stock . . .

3. Have a bit! A happy beat, Coito, ergo sum! to cheer up your existence:
On the road to happiness, dharma bums.

puppet: Daba daba da! I tried to give you so much in secret, sh! hush! but I was all the talk. The talk of the café-restaurant where you chummed up to the Poles. The Pan is a woman's panacea! you and your nonsense. Pan Demon! Your little coterie of Polish cats . . . Bova "Bovary." Mania the Maniac. Zosia the socialite. You even chatted with Madame Starzinsky, who set her eye on you . . . The clowning began when I showed this vagrant the opening chapter of my little book, titled *Droga*. A drug, Spanish fly? More and more droga[1] my scribe and I would need to finish our opus, and he laughed like a madman. It's a good thing it's brief, and he hefted my little volume. Levity is the soul of wit? Lo malo si poco, malo! and starting to chortle . . . And at first you seemed so serious. Quiet little boy, always scribble scribble scribble, pish! all by himself at a table. Writing novels? Romans d'amour! He seems sad. All alone and somber. Before I knew your aliases, I called you Sam Sambo. So alone, all in black like Hamlet. Ser or no ser, sir serious? From the first exchange I realized he was dying of hunger. And some-times, when the boss wasn't watching, I passed him some left-overs. Ser[2] or no ser, Sir Hamlet. Try something, a little home-made cheese. A bit. Bit by bit.[3] Slice on the sly. Did he want to eat à la carte, the poor devil? Right away he took liberties. Semper Virginem? he would say. And sometimes he didn't pay. Nie, nie mam. No ma'am. With his halve or have not he took me to his best cellar, in Queensberry Place, right around the corner: the blood-hound's home. Nobody's best friend. Pupa! and she gave herself a slap on the poop deck, what a pooper. He beatified me, the bolshevik! Semper Virginem? . . . And then each day more demanding, ordering the best dishes. Fantastic supper, my lavish Slav, priceless. Chew, chew, eat merry, you'll have the best rump in this rumpus. Now we'll see the asshole face to face. It's time. Wham! Wham! banging him with the tray. Crash! hard on the head. Pa, pasha! Pa!

—The Polish virgo potens?! Beata . . .

1. Lux Mundi?!:
Bring it to light, louche switchman . . . / Luz?! Luch?! / Flux! Consult the flutist
Hamelinguist. With this plague of errata, an anticlimactic parturition from the
mountains . . . / Ratifying your blasphemy? / In any case he has to keep gnawing
away . . .

2. Shin feign? Sinn fein?:
Sans fin!

Sister of Charity with a mousy smile shaking a heavy clinking bag around the puppet: Lux! Fiat lux. You're Catholic, aren't you? The Virgin gave us the Light of the World,[1] and it was already day. Praise and exultation! Oh là là, what joy. Pray to your lady. Lordy! Did you want to startle me? Alone with you, donn Seán, in your house. Micmac. Bric-a-brac. Scandalous. Bet et mal. Là-bas, bastard. A little offering for clarity. Need to clear something up? Need a Clarist? Ha! Playing the dandy in your den! Good-for-nothing! Fale em prata, talk funckly. Choir member inquiring in focal dialect. Can you spare a mously dime, an oblation for your pretty nun? Bless you. You haven't got any more, fool? A sure lack of religion. Period. Real clarity begins at home. Lux! I'll clear this up in your local dialect: I was making the rounds with this mala-propos bag, so heavy! collecting for our elderly one Tuesday afternoon in March, in the charitable neighborhood of Queen's Park . . . Try to remember. I knocked at your door, on Millman Road, tacka-tack! and you opened it in your pajamas, grumbling. My lord what a fright! Swinging in your left hand, like an ugly trophy, that dead mouse. I'm sorry, Mother, as you see there's nothing but rats here. Nope, nobody here but us rats. Mrs. Page is out . . . And suddenly you looked at me, face to face, captivated. But come in, Sister, you'll get cold out there. Come in and have some tea, sor . . . His savoir faire! Pharisee! I'm from the Holy Land of Spain . . . And you kept swinging your mouse. All you could give me that day? Dia do Stór! May God increase your wealth. I didn't mean to scare you. Ever cheerful. Come in and have a cup of tea to settle your nerves. I didn't cross the threshold . . . But you were giving your worst thoughts free rein. We sin. Little by little, felix cupla! we sin. Just the two of us, sinn finn.[2] Alone. All by ourselves in the end. Bel galant! Lazy idling loafer! I'll serve you some tea with mouse. Did you want to put it in my bag? With this bad bag, mala fide! smacking him with the sack, the spell is broken!
—The raving Erinys of Erin! Sister Muire . . .

1. ISRA . . .:
EL! God of war. The wheel is come fool circle. LEAR SI!

2. Flush away!:
Down the drain. Nadir. In a flush. The Spaniol muttering cur-sory compliments, currying favor. Virginal Virginie's lapdog exchanged for the wolf in wool's skin. Who's afraid of . . . Curtail that bestiality. Flushed out.

3. Like a dog with two tails . . .:
—Oh no, not me with the dog forget it!
And Tania backpedaled with fear and repulsion, clutching her wrinkled clothes against her chest.
Bob "Hitch-Cock," in the doorway with the wolfhound, looking at the scene with a cynical eye: adolescent in a pose of virgin-martyr, kneeling nude on the sofa bed of a typical depressing London bedsitter.
He approached her with the dog, put a hand on her shoulder (the other one scratching the head of the dog now looking into the camera lens):
—Look kid, I'm not telling you to fuck it, just make it look like you are. Got it?

4. . . . said the shirty dame:
Summammarily.

GIRLS OF HIS DREAMS

Overgrown freckled schoolgirl in a brown uniform and hat, twirling a rolled-up newspaper like a baton around the puppet: Spin, Spaniel! clubbing him from time to time. Attaboy! October afternoon down by Kensington pond, kites coming down and me too sometimes, playing with Flush. We rolled in the grass and his black muzzle, cold and wet! went up my skirt, snooping between my thighs. Cui-cuisse, I see you, c'est la vie! Right there in the hammock, hiding behind the open *Standard*: . . . EL:[1] TODAY IS THE DAY! And his black eye spying through a hole. Then he dropped the paper on his belly and stretched out in the hammock acting like he was going to sleep. One hand on top of the paper and the other below. Some siesta . . . Or was he watching? The half-mask of his dark glasses, and flushed face . . . Wasn't it the same bum digging through the trash cans on Lancaster Walk? Here Flush! Restless sleep, dreaming? Wickedly still. Only his paper pulsated . . . Thank goodness Mademoiselle showed up looking for me, calling me:
—Virginie! The little girl with the pooch . . .

An emaciated fairy-girl ripping her gauze dress and all the time whipping the puppet with a bunch of roses and thorns: Tit for tort! My flowerbuds . . . Low-down cur! stripping me by bitefuls. Dog me, dog my love. Flush back![2] I'm the one who had to undergo the cannilingus . . . Another one of your mangy movies, another improvised script for your one-minute porno films. Bob babbling while he rolled the film and me getting rolled in my role, Te dico che non morde! and you wanted to be the black wolf with the red tongue.[3] Blow up! Cancel it, cannibal. And did you see what happened to my dress? A dirty shame![4] Tit for tat! giving him yet another bouquet-blow.
—Titania the starlet . . . Tit Tania!

1. O Poppy!—all trembling . . .:
Pott's disease, perhaps?

2. Tennis on! To serve, to streak, to volley, and not to yield:
'Tis better to have loved and lust / Than never to have played at ball.

3. New Nabokovian Lolita?:
Nabbed again . . . That Polleninist Tolstoievsky had too many Pninfatuations. His poor Humbert Humbert would have been better off with the Spaniard Lola Lola.

Infanta in red farthingales, holding up a vase of poppies like a trophy around the puppet. Pop! Pop up! Oh poppy! Oh pappy you slipped into mommy and you plopped on your pupil. Your private lessons . . . lesions! It only hurts the first time? Papa, veto! no! your little sweetheart vetoes you. He doesn't even notice. Papa . . . And your cocksure gallantries. Amapola bellíssima amapola . . . Poppy pretty poppy . . . Of blood! what were the lyrics to your poppy song? and she smashed the vase on the peak of his hood. Poppycock!

—Mrs. Pott's daughter! Poppy . . .[1]

Nymphet in a tennis outfit, her right arm in a sling and cast, her left awkwardly wielding a racket, her skirt rising in her rosy spin around the puppet: Love! Who'll win the game, love. Split down the middle, tied up . . . Love all! shaking her racket at him. All! Fair game! Spying on me when I played tennis there in Brook Green. A courtly love game. And as I walked out of Saint Paul . . . Break, break, break.[2] And at the bus stop on Hammersmith Road, the abuse started. He ran into me, with a bang! Break! And me gasping . . . Break! So gallantly picking up my books and folders, and peeking at my legs. And one hellish afternoon he tricked me into entering his den. Mealy Milalias changing alias (the four skin of our sweet teeth). Merlin the Magician of Caramelot: Wanna sucker? Sugar daddy? Bubble gum? Smarmy caramels? The sweets of sin. Dulcedo amoris . . . A little chocolate? So sweet at first and then so bitter . . . Break! Don't claim Victoria yet . . . Break! and she plastered the puppet with her cast arm, not until the game's over.

—"Lolly Pop Corn"![3] Vicky . . .

*
* *

† 353 †

1. Lie, bah! Bah! Sleep . . .:
Lai pa! Come here . . .

2. Ch'ing! Ch'ing!:
Ch'ih ch'ing! Crazy love. Lovecrazy alchemy renders vital aperitif. To drink and
forget!

3. Her tiny fingers, so fine for shredding:
Shall I cut it all to little bits, Honorable L'eng T'che?

4. Swan? Suan?:
Reckon—wreck on!—the swan and its shadow . . .

CHINESE CHECKERS

Chinese gal chattering ch'a-ch'a-ch'a! and flouncing in her tea-colored satin miniskirt as she pushes her rattling cart of cups and saucers around and around the cape-cowled puppet, as if on a merry-go-round: In Soho, not so hot. So! Ho! Closed bar. After license-hours, licentious lout. Velly honorable teahouse. Our beautiful restaurant with tea flowers on the curtains. Drunk glutton nodding off? Lie, pa! Sleep. Maddog summer heat, four fou, oui. When suddenly he shakes it off and starts bossing me around. Come here![1] Watch out .. You want a drink!? No more alcohol, only tea. And a little something that only I know . . . A rich ch'a-ch'a-ch'a! A loving teaspoonful. What eyes he's making . . . Cheer up, donjuan, and put on a brand new face. Prepare tea! the pasha. Pow, chah! smashing the china on the puppet. Paf, pasha! Only tea, tea! tea! for you. You wanted to drink to me only with your tease. Ch'in-ch'in![2] pressing against me. Sh! Shui! Sh! Way out! giving him a head-butt in the abdomen. Don't answer back, shut up and sleep it off . . .
 —Fleur d'été! Tea flower . . .

Another willowy Chinese waitress singing and hip-swaying before the puppet, smacking him with a fan and laughing from time to time: Ho! Ho! Ho! And with me too he tried to ch'in-ch'ing! the sot sotto voce. Jew!? with his dirty tricks. You? Causing a scandal and bothering everyone in our honorable restaurant in Westbourne Grove. Goosing gluteinously, and when I served his duck[3] the penman got in my swan[4] way. And then brushed against me when I served the rice. And to top it off this same guy was already with two chicks . . . Ay ya! Then he wanted me to translate everything. How do you say in Chinese. . . ? You fantasizing stuffed shirt . . .
 —Miss Fan! my interpretentious Chinese . . .

1. Yuan?:
Vicious circle. Don Juan to the ring! Look around: raging viragos about . . .

2. Lei?:
Lei. You too. Relax, worthy gentleman . . . Lay, o yes! the masked warrior is tired.
And half-gagged, en plus de gaga!

3. None?:
O nan! each man with his swank offering, a wan cough . . .

4. Man?:
Man mano, passino a passino, passo a passio . . .

5. Relief message:
Lovely amasseuse remedies visitor's anguish . . .

6. T'ing!:
Stop! You'll be hearing bells and jingobells and won't know what you're about . . .
T'ing! T'ang! T'an! Cling! Clang! Gong! the bells of Saint John. Still to sound,
Dong! Dahng! in the party. Still to sound, T'an! T'ang! in the Church of the Holy
Trinity . . .

7. She?:
Wash-out!

8. Lie on your oars!:
O! The devil!

9. Yeh . . ..
Yeah! Night.

10. Shui?:
Shui. Dream on water. Wet dream.

Moon-faced Chinese woman with night-black hair, in a half-open white robe, spin-spinning completely around, Oh Don Yuan![1] and gesticulating, Oh Don Yuan! around the caped puppet: More Soho, oho! and more massages. In our steamy cellar. Yin-yang! my sly trickster, all wide-eyed, but without the yen. Let's see the money . . ., a pound per head. Lay down don! lay on don! lay![2] you must be tired. Fa-fa-fatigued? So-so. Hard pinching to start off? Oh, none of that, oh none[3] of your impudence! Your nanny nimbly kneads you and numbs you. O man![4] slow down. Don't put on that gloomy face. A relief massage?[5] and she violently dutch-rubbed the head of the hooded puppet. Wait till I slick you up . . . Two for the price of one, o nanay! Not me, no way! You and your hook-handed friend drunk too you dragged around. Pay first! cash-as-catch can! and if you don't pay up, the house bouncer will give you what-for. And to top it off you tried to unbutton my blouse to see my budding buttons, my full moons . . . Na-na-nanay! Lucky thing I howled and sounded the bell, T'ing! T'ing-i-t'ing! T'ing![6] but stop stop stop, and they stomped and strapped you till you were almost KO'd! Take a Chinese chance!

—My moonshinese! Miss Yin . . .

Towel-wrapped Chinese girl shoving and tossing mudballs at the puppet's head: She wash you . . . She![7] Your odored lotus wash you while you sully her, Oh lo lo! low and slow, in the bathroom of bad sin. Oar! pull a good oar in the pool, Oar! rowing the mud, Oar![8] my devil incarnate turned to dark flesh. Mangia il loto, lotus-glower. Yeah.[9] Sh! Way in! Shui . . . Shui . . .,[10] the door creaked and you paralyzed with terror in the steam of the bathroom.

—My Kensington Chinadoll! Loto d'oro . . . The Golden Lotus . . .

1. P'ing!:
Peace. Make peace . . . Play the pipe. Take out the peace pipe, prude.

2. Mint?:
Or demented. But don't mintion it. In any case, better to chew fragrant tea leaves and chatter a more fluid English.

3. Pee-pee-play the flute?:
It must be somewhere between "P'in-hsiao" (play the flute, merry fellatio) and "Hsiao-pien" (take a pee . . .)—what's your opipinion?

4. P'i? Pee!?:
Beer. Bitter. Or you're in trouble. Flowing like a pisciform Mississippi, like a crazy Orinoco, like a pearly yearning Missouri into Miss P'i's mouth . . .

5. Golden helmet of Mambrino, there can be no helm like thee:
Crown fit for a Don. To don the impossible drain.

6. Fecal stale mate, or what's past is passed . . .:
In another fickle party. Lokus Solus? Nein. No. The queen was on her throne when the chess champ quickly shut himself in the bathroom. She didn't bolt it . . . Gambit? Stunned. Both of them tipsy. At first he didn't see her. The dizzying floor tiles went to his head. He muttered some apology, swaying toward the door, but the queen quickly challenged him. All too quickly. Zip! And he tried to stalemate her. Zap! . . . I didn't think she'd do it all there, he'd sometimes say to himself, without fully believing his clouded memories. And so willingly.

Chubby Chinese gal with round lenses conducting two-fistedly with a brass flute and a beer bottle—an occasional bottle-bop p'ing-pong![1] and a smack of the flute on the puppet's head—while she spun around, chewing gum,[2] muttering and laughing convulsively: Ho! Ho! Ho! joker, I'm the one who laughs last. Mocking my music studies, calling me a viltuosa. Vile, you! Trifling with my fife . . . This rogue drunk on beer, and teasing me relentlessly . . . Peace piping up: You're in! The heroines of the Chinese classics did it when they were enamurined of someone and . . . A mandurinater! Then he's back to pissuade me, the mandarin like he's mandolins in the canals of Venice. Oh sweetie, the bold rascal says to me, how do you say pee-pee-play the flute[3] in Chinese, and not a word out of me 'cause my mouth was full. And he called me everything he could think of. Pee-pee-peeta P'an! and she goaded him with the flute, what an awful drag my pied piper from Hamelin, my horny horn with its deadly sins and sounds. I'll leave you high and dry.

—My plump drunk Chinese! Miss P'i . . .[4]

Milady with a black-and-white checked hooded cape, shaking a rusty barber's basin[5] around the puppet: Peace! Silence! before I hit the ceiling. I too had to put up with his silly messes in that bathroom of checkered tiles and pasts . . .[6] What an episode. Peace! and she dumped all the basin water over the puppet. Peace be with you! Malbrook s'en-va-t-on guerre, Mironton, mironton, mirontaine! In peace I impound you and in war I warp you, pig! And free of charge I discharge you.

—Mrs. Zippy?! . . . Mrs. Mississippi . . .

*
* *

1. Yenta?:
Yenta, yentzer!

2. Holofernes!?:
The pedantic windbag (a lord of words who loves words for their own shake?), and the would-be maestro who follows him with his little book, often lose their heads in this verbacchanal. They have been at great featsts of slanguages and stolen the scraps. Love-labours, lost? Lost amours return vivaciously active.

3. Key holds . . . To marshall your arts. Jew-jitsu? Or judo?:
O! My keys! Long as my exile . . .

4. Qui? Qui?:
Kick in! Kyrie, sir, cry the Kyrie . . .

KEYS

Weeper in mourning, with sunglasses and a phylactery on her head, yipping ay-yays around the puppet, and brandishing an enormous rusty key: One Sabbath there on Finchley Road he angered me, burned me up! with his taper. A widow, I got burned. Evil and black wind blowing there. Cover me up, young stud, I'm cold. With the mantle? What a black blemish! One dark night this bastard cloaked me in mourning. I lost my head over you . . ., he told me in that café full of yentlemen.[1] Talk with someone else! That painted devil with his little painted words. Presto and soon to my house we went. Help! Give me, good sir, my spectacles . . . Oh sir . . ., and his grabby hands yanked off mine veil and mine underwear. I've lost my head over you . . ., he told me in mine bed. Love's labors lost, Holofern![2] With mine key I'll open your head! she let the keys fly hard against the puppet's head.

—That slow-burning Sephardic widow! Judith . . .

Ondululating ondine veiled by her wig of black seaweed, in a tunic of green watered silk, brandishing a handful of keys and trying to drown the puppet with her tinkling hugs: O! My keys![3] tenaciously clinging to him, my keylets. The keen key I kept around my neck that night. On the quay with my key . . .[4] On the Hammersmith quay first, turning my little key around, me sitting with my back to you. How svelte, what a slender waist. Strolling by. Strolling by. Trying to guess who I was, o sirenamored Sire? O lory, lie! Olore, lai! sniffing about with your trick box under your arm, along the bank of the Thames toward Chiswick. Chis! sick! Ashes and rashes in your box. Of a hundred senses? Ready to hurl yourself with it into my waters? Now and in the bower of . . . Going by with your box of tricks, toward Chiswick chis! sick. Lovehate sickness and abandoned like a mangy lover. A bar-king, a wizard of id. Cane barbone, water spaniel to the water. Drowning yourself?

1. Dog! Swim, Spaniel. Re cane, rema!:
Ame renacer . . . Love to be reborn!

2. Soaped up and soft soaped?:
Au bon savon. Nova Avon! The last swan song, sing pen! in a bubbly soap opera
aperta.

3. Set the Thames on fire!:
With burning desire. ((The nightly waters of the Thames ignited, braised with
reflections of the lights of the Hammersmith hanging bridge. From the terrace of
the Old Ship, watching the brilliant foam of the streetlights. The Thames, they are
a-changing. No one can drown himself twice in the same river? Circular Spanish
answer: SI SE MATA, TAMESIS. The Same Thames, if he succeeds in suicide.
Playing with Thamesuidical ideas. Reflections, flowing. Embers on the river
water. Set the Thames on firewater . . .))

God![1] Break water, bagman, romp up the ramp, break into the light. I order you! Or maybe it isn't worth it . . . Shall I renege, renegade? Renew or die. A new fishion, Miltalias, and it's back to the spawnshop. Can't leave it un-fin-ished. Come to my stream-bed for an extreme function. Is it all dark? Come, more amor with your moray. The black waters? Dive in. Clap! Plop! of ducks in the black. Hear it? Dark night of soul, sole man, bubble your salacities. Remember how it smelt? Toi! Toilette of the god-fare-thee-wells. Sh! Hush! How wash it for you? Avon nova? Delusions! The higher they fly, the harder they fault . . . A mortal sinking, Icaruso. Soft-soaping me with his last song, that saponaceous Don Swan.[2] Croak. Croak. O pen! Breaking into song. Aphrodionysiac Orpheus. Shunleashing his Thamesybillancies of crisis, Oh sire ispirato. Nestle in with your undine. Un-die, Finicia. Fin, nix, your nixy naiad soaks you. Can your flame swim my waters? Disperse, aspergill your chosen fragments and stake the Thames.[3] And learn the lesson already. Lothario to the river! Don John-a-dreams on his Fairlady lane . . . I'm reading you the future that you will write yesterday in your memoirs. Casanova, a noiva cassa nova quer! The bride wants a new house. Or Cashanova. In the clouds, admiring the cloud-gauze: Avion! Plane! Watching in the heavens that vespertine trace of the one departing. Crassanova, going. Jettatura. Reborn lover flying high. I tell you your future as you will remember it perfectly well yesterday. Do you hear the song? On the terrace, on the bank, under the hanging garden. I was singing in the old ship of fools, after closing, and you came back with a bottle in a sack to visit Hogarth's last home, ho! ho! and the Christ of your crucifictions, all muddied. I sang in the dark what you'll hear that night, singing I know it's not a proper thing to do, but I'll do . . . Not proper to take advantage of a drunk. You too, my son? Come to my side. Oh so . . . No! Drunk streams of laughter in the dark. To keep from crying. Ho! Ho! Ho! You were drowning . . . With laughter? squeezing his neck with one hand and shaking a

1. Clef universelle . . .:
Klee, mann.

2. The keys of hell and of death:
The kiss of death and of life . . .

3. Mater Hile . . .:
Dura mater!

4. Given! A way a lone a lost a laved a long the:
nurre vir!

bunch of keys in the other. Sonorous river! Un soir. One night. Eh, con? Solos. Alone. A knot in the throat. Did I tell you it was a charm? How do you spell your spell? And you twisting the cord, toying with my key.[1] An alcoholic easily loses it . . . Would you take me home? Your nightly daring! Silky kiss. Exquisite. We didn't look each other in the face. Tell me. Tell me. I insist that you answer! A man without a name for a woman without a man . . . Tell me. Tell me . . . What's in a name . . . I wisp-whispered it to you in that kiss. The whole truth, and nothing but. Not the diminutive. I renege. Reinnocence man. His sigh, his shock! A car went by and the light dazed me. Furrowed brow. You were wrinkling up too? Are you denying that kiss? My keys![2] Where are the keys . . .[3] It's still up to you to open the last door, bluebeard . . . Take my keys, giving a great wallop to the puppet's head. My keys! And rabidly biting the cloaked mouth, The kiss too.[4]

—The crazy ol' localcoholic from the Old Ship! Reni . . .

*
* *

1. Il faut tordre le cou au cigne!:
Twist the neck of the signe, and sin against the signified. SWAN GNAWS? Answer: re-swan. Brood over it, and hatch another slogan.

2. Leda? Content?:
Tempting. Leda. Adel. (Noblesse oblige!) One summer afternoon in Kensington Gardens there was the Swede with a bored expression, squatting among the swans and tossing them hunks of bread. Until Peter Pan showed up and the two became good friends.

3. You! Peter Pan!:
By Jove! The swank ugly duckling (Don Swann) in swanton lust, another swan dive?

4. If it be possible let this cup pass from me . . .:
Osläckt kalk. Long live it! One of kalkalyx and another of sand . . . C'mon!

5. Pots!:
Pointblank, with cold water . . .

6. More kicks than pricks . . .:
Ferme ton becquet!

7. Kors! ricorsi . . .:
Chorus of bald and brash bonzes in saffron-colored tatters spinning around the puppet open-armed drumming on pots and the puppet rigid as a post, bopping him too with rabbit kicks:

   Hare! Khristna! Hare! Khristna! Hare! Hare! Khristna! Hare! Khristna! Hare! Hare! . . .

8. Grita!:
Swedish pressure cooker.

ETC.

Towering blonde in flower-patched jeans twisting the neck of a white rubber swan:[1] Happy hippie you called me. Leda![2] playing dumb that afternoon of ennui while I made friends with the swans at the Kensington pond. Me?![3] and him coming up so jovial. Hi! Not giving them anything but crumbs? Then talking to me about Sherlock, Stockholm, and bare Swedish massages . . . And finally he cajoled me and took me to his garret his ratnest with his line about wanting to draw me by daylight and took out his tail, svampire! and left me broken. Sangría for the blood wedding.[4] Droop by drop, what a mess. And what a feast. All from cans. Tasty? I'll warm you up some good red herring. Enjoy some kaka with cocoa. Here. An invitation, then irritation. The phantomcat swearing and swearing he loved me. With his golden tongue and his gift of gab, Eu falo em prata! and his echolalia, Ala! he bowled me over. Fria! Cold? Speak clearly, make some sense, spank! Cold? Spansk! whipping the puppet with the swan, in panicked Spunishment, your Leda will give you some leather, spak! as she raised a leg, stop![5] I'll sew up your mouth with kicks, stopp! you'll get a foot in your mouth, prick![6] and I'll shut your golden mouth up once and for all.
    —Ladi Leda! Fröken Rita . . .

Pretty blondine waltzing in a towel around the puppet rigid as a stake, snapping him with towel-cracks: Oh là là! stuttering again. Thirsty? Your vain desires. If you wish, your svampire will offer you the spontext. Agg! Bitter? Our Johnny on the spott! C'mon, drink the last drop of his sweat. And make a gesture: sign of the double-cross . . . Another trick? More jokes and jostling, Hare! Khristna! like that afternoon when the bonzes went by with their prayers on Charing Cross.[7] Shout! Greeter, greet a . . .[8] Pot to pot and pose to repose, poser. Compose yourself! Look at your nymph . . . Remember? What a silhouette, so svelte. Stand sideways, Mr. Hitch-Cock's filming you maravelously . . . Like a log

1. Tala, with an ax to grind:
Tala, a tree-totaler, with a talent for felling the tallest tree.

2. Some more Tala?:
Samoaning Tala. Cut this forest of kids' stories with the ax. Tala, a real borer.

3. Papa?:
You're Papa, and on this paper I will build my church. Rock of Ages. Sí, Sisyphus.

4. Au lit, au lit. . . ?:
Olioli!: Happiness, contentment . . .

5. Avis:
It's a five-part dance.

6. Gata? Spanish cat?:
With sinuous movements. I've gotta put it more accurately: snake.

7. Gata? Another cat? This gata has gotta stop:
Stop! Enough!

8. Vis sans fin . . .:
Keep spinning it 'round, mulling milling mauling over it.

now? Wretch! Lost soul! Sopor? In oh-so poor taste, his pigsty ideas . . . Wait. Rise. Little by little . . . Like a log? Tala![1] Talk Tala, you too. See? See how I cut down the great illiterate.
   —My Swedish svendetta! Tala . . .

Greasy Polynesian in a faded red lavalava skirt, a necklace of paper orchids over her breasts, undulating like a snake around the puppet and wielding a long sharpened file: To see Tala, or not . . . Chop![2] in my dark teinebrous jungle. Paradise or hell, storyteller? Toto in caelo! and she delivered a file-blow to his head. With my file I'll clip your wing, oh la la, and your beak. You told me in bed, wanting awfully to enter lawfully: You're Malia and I'm Alia, I'm in your end. You, you nincompoop? Take careful aim. Popinjay puppet playing the pauper.[3] Quench my thirst! Are you going to drink the Pacific Basin with a vase? Kiss by kiss, and with each little thing. I told my life story in Apia, from A to Z, and how I emigrated to New Zealand and then to England, while the wizard drank and drank and then slurred in his drunken voice something I read: Puta!? Whore in his language and I thought he said fat, and he only said what he said. And then sitting on the bed almost nude, with only the towel, paring his nails and me drying my tears with his handkerchief. You'll be all alone alone. I told him too about vacations in his beautiful country. Trip to Malaga. Ole, ole. Olioli.[4] Tio Pepe. Viva la pepa! Long live the clit! And the bear dancing with me the dance of Shiva.[5] Gata![6] your cat takes out an eye, she kills you!
   —The fatty from Samoa! Malia . . .

Blonde in shorts with suspenders and white boots jumping catlike around the puppet, Gotcha! and scratching him: Gata! sex kitten you called me when I rubbed and ruffled over you, I've gotta! and you already tired of pampering (a dezmierda!) the others. Gata![7] Finally vis-à-vis,[8] face to face . . .
   —The big Rumanian cat! Mini Calinescu . . .

1. Bad is as bad does . . .:
Hang down, hang-dog, hung from that withering height . . .

2. Thalatha? Ulysses' sea. . . ?:
Tuesday. Duesday!

3. Alas! poor Milalias . . .:
That nurse had a talent for muddling all names. The second Tuesday, almost
Mardi Gras, our protagonist was already Mr. Alalia!

Mata Hari with brown tresses, in a khaki sarong with a sequin sun on each breast, gripping a Malaysian kris and swaying sinuously in front of the puppet: Hand to hand, they all tango with the stiff-legged orangutan. He'll have no complaint! My turn now, and she made the sign of the cross criss-crass! on his head with the kris. Punctual puncture. You tried to kiss me, a big one, ay ah! Pulling on the bamboo curtain, and behind door number one, a masochistic dandy, a silver-tongued talker! I'll wrestle with you till the sun comes up. Shall I bandage you, is it blood or ketchup? Chap, chap, sorry ol' chap, with a sponge. Down, down, rajah, but don't go too far. No more metamorphosis, boy, and no more ululation. Enough. Yeah yeah. A whisper? Hush! Get out of there. Will you pass, dumb foundling? Coming or not? No more gay science, wise man? Laugh happily, hee-heek! until the tears come, bambino. Water passed won't turn the mill? Prink yourself up to drink me down. Sic. When tomorrow you drink yesterday's (a kiss. . . ? OK!), you will be free. Did you have a great time yesterday? Jesterday's party was a pip, peeper. Jin and yang, day by day. You were left without anything to hold onto, no handle, without hope. Upsy-daisy to my abyss, for ever rest![1] with your nostalgic malicious Malayan who made you laugh so much, heeheek! oh yeah yeah liar. Pure flirting, Harum al-Hashish! We're going to wrassle without rest, go bump in the night all night long. I'll trim your sails and lash you good, you rococo Simbad. Another story, Don Gengi? Storyteller's utopia, the ocean of story, lie by line . . . Oh! Another lacuna, lake poet thinker and sailor, in my matinal love song? Another parodyssey? Thalatha! Thalatha![2] To love you each Tuesday. And fry you each Friday, Fried day, fried friend. Forgetting the date now? Taste each word of mine, like before, murmur into my mammaries, mon dada. How did the ballad go? Pen plus penis paints over pains. Dadaista! Did he forget the date now?? I'm gonna fill his mouth. Or would he prefer emasculation. Doktor Gunting is waiting. You wanted to hide your timorous feelings, cheap coward, and I spied on you through the door grill. You can come in, Mr. Alas.[3] Who recommended our clinic to him? Mr. Rays or Mr. Rayos? Just so you don't do it again, I'm going to

1. Dalang!:
The gong (pang! gong! orangutongue) sounds for the narrator to make his entrance in this shadow play.

2. Putus? Minimus?:
Purus putusque sycophanta est. It couldn't be anyone else, with those phrases in disguises: Orationes putissimae.

3. Con d'or?:
Une espèce de faux con! Golden concoctor, or a foul con.

4. Condo Don? Condom Don? Dumb Don?:
Dura Lex sed Durex. Registered trademark!

5. Quiet flows the Don, by the don's early flight . . .:
Donna to Donna. Donnai. Amants, au lit, Ding! Dong! lovers to bed; 'tis almost fairy time.

kill it another Tuesday. You were scared of the drill, eh? Bah! Hard not to extract it. Sukar malu for teeth. Jijik! Your gullet's fault, glutton. Don't you know there are whole races of people that fast from the crib to the grave? And you chew on and on with your sweet tooth! Great pretender . . . Bitter after love. Dinding![1] dandy. Ding dong! the telling hour of retaliation sounded. Tooth for an eye. I'll mow you down and you'll end up healthy. I'm going to break you, putus![2] and tear you up. Maya, timorous. No sense of humor? I shouldn't be so harsh? With a death-defying leap your Mata Hari kills you! and she rammed the kris into his eye.

—The Malayan dental nurse! Miss Hari . . .

Light lively mestiza fluttering about in a lacy pleated skirt and a bright shawl, brandishing a flowery wand (of purple flowers) around the puppet: What a golden beak, condor.[3] Words drive out words, and one male drives out another. My Negro dancing the *morenada* more and more. Coming out of your slangor in bed . . . After the joy, the shock! and me running about terrified with the end of the towel between my legs while that little white river, Madre de Dios! ran down my thighs. Did I forget the English don't use bidets? I ran to that dirty drain you call a bathroom . . . While that simpleton languished in bed! There's no danger . . . Con Don[4] or no don, no one is safe with Don Juan.[5] Now Saint John. What can I say? Otro palo? Another fuck? and she dealt out a blow. With this lignum vitae I knock you off your pedestal.

—Ana the Bolivian! Ana ("Livia") from Bolivia . . .

Robust blonde in a bursting black leather bodice and black mid-thigh boots, raising her rod 'round the puppet: My maid Celestine picks up the receiver and says to me Miss, it's some foreigner

1. Well named!:
Babelle and cat-eyed Beverly barefoot and in jeans, maliciously elbowing each other while Milalias scribbles between bursts of laughter, reading the index cards tacked on the bulletin board at the tobacco and newspaper store entrance in front of the Notting Hill Gate tube station.

COFFEE-COLOURED LADY	SEATS RE CANED
SEEKS	ANY SIZE CONSIDERED
PARTIME POSITION	RING MISS BOTTOMLAY
727-5293	602-3080

Are you going to copy them all?

2. Erinia with hitzteria? Or bacchante with uzteromania?:
Ohe! Evohé! Laugh till you cry? Oihu! Uhin! Uholde! Or peeing in her pants from laughter so the schemer would do the analysis? She was nauseated, and said drunkenly: I want the gypsy's little son to be born. What are you talking about, gypsy! Childless wet nurse. Extrauterine pregnancy. Doktor Kot will put her straight.

3. Who?:
Must refer to a Reynaldo Rey, nicknamed by his enamored Basque, "King of the Gypsies." For his scowling owlish face and pitch-dark complexion, Milalias usually called him "Knight Owl." He read in Spanish in London and suffered frequent fits of depression. Are you feeling blue again? Milalias scolded him. A low owl, AWOL now. But after the calm came the storm. When he was in a maniacal phase, his euphoria and audacity had no limits. Milalias became inspired by this exalted aspect of his personality to compose one of his favorite masks: The King of Jokers.

who doesn't know what he wants. Allò, salaud! You obviously mixed up the phone numbers when you carelessly copied them from the bulletin board . . . German governess? Nein. Intensive French lessons? Pas du tout. Expert instruction in Polish? Tuck. Pitch out. Czech girl seeks checkmate? Ano. Ah no. Czech that one off. Basic American? Can it! Véngase p'acá. Sprick and span Spunish, s'habla hispano. Ricane pas! Seats recaned, I'll whip them into shape, never sparing the rod. Bottom up! and belly down. Lay down, sir, relax. Don't be so rigid. I'm an Anglican and I'm going to show you again, and she beat him once with the rod, the best of the best, la crème fouettée, again with the rod, de la culture anglicanne.

—A hot rodder! Miss Bottomlay . . .[1]

Wide big-breasted blonde in a red bodice and a Basque skirt, topped off with a Tyrolean hat, sweeping and splitting her sides laughing Ha! Ha! Jai! around the puppet Ho! Ho! Ho! and beating him with the broom: So it's flattery you want now? Adululation! I'll come up with you, you slob, to that sabbath brouhaha. Him bellowing and me sweeping. Ho! Ho! Ho! Sweep, sweep for your own benefit . . . You deny I cry? I laugh with irritation and I cry with hilarity,[2] lazy loafing laughter, since my ardorous gypsy, mi hijito! left me. A lake of tears for your missing friend.[3] So many tears, my bad companion, that I could irrigate the Sahara. Sandbagged, my pleasure at the bottom of a well . . . Oy! Oy! me without my little gypsy. Some nights I ululate, gow! gwow! until I'm going crazy. Always a she-wolf in your den. Wasn't that how it was? You didn't like me putting up my in-laws in my dark room in Covent Garden, and them coming and going. Did the chivalrous gentleman dare loan his passport? Just once. And you didn't want me to politicize my handsome gypsy. You slyly suggested maybe it was no

1. Sator? Breaker? Creator? Sower? Satan?:
Talpa. Cultivate! Work the plot. Plow, old mole, the waste land. Mountainous mortuary out of a mohole. Moldwarp. Plothole. Plat. A PLATE, TALPA.

2. Stubborn Guy Fawkes in his labyrinth . . .:
All day long burning scraps of paper. So smoky. Stubbornly gargling on with his dirge. On and on with his lively lasses. Every gal with her guy marching to the Promiscuous Land. Landrú!

3. Eurydice?:
Eurydice cries buckets and dances, the poor little Orpheusless Annie.

4. Zola will put his shoes on the right footnote . . .:
The debacle!

accident, perhaps they pushed him, and that it was worth thinking about. Don't babble, you driveling devil . . . A bilious thread for your labyrinth of mud or fraud. Will you file that filth, stash that slanderous trash in your hair-raising Ensickopedia? Burrow, mole (Sator: Rotas?[1]) Scale, mendacious beggar, that mountain of lies. And jump. Stubbornly,[2] keep on labyrinthesizing. The bad part is you planted the seed of doubt. Maybe yes, maybe no . . . But the worst is the lack of sleep. And I cry I laugh I cry precipitously. The wet nurse reigns but doesn't govern herself . . . You diagnosed it as a Eurydicean complex,[3] or I don't know what, and I could have problems of eurythmia or murmurs or something, complicated by an exhilarated sense of guilt over losing my little gypsy king. And you, my generous consultant, stubbornly insisted that I visit that erotomaniac psychoanalyst. The cure is a tough road . . . But the light at the end of the tunnel? Another day, another sol. Doktor Kot doesn't come cheap. Dottore elegante. And while I walk he makes little paper birds. He must cure people because he's so prohibitively expensive. He eats my salary right up. Does he give you a commission? Get out of the beer hall, you told me, with my background I could find something better. A charming girl always comes out smelling like a rose. So witty: Cupid brings cupidity. To pay the guilt, and the doctor? Looking after yourself. You'll recall, you big baby, the chatter alone in my room, leaning against my bosom, while that mutilated boy your friend was sleeping it off, carelessly sacked out on the good semeritan's bed. That moment united us. The two stretched out on the tapestry, at the foot of the bed. You'll weave it all together from A to Z, in the depths of your grand experimentalmudic novel?[4] Don't shrink back. You'll remember the accordionist too, the tickling kili-kili! you gave me when I was loaded down with stacked-up mugs, with your warbles, bel tenore, Lore! Lore! Alai! taking advantage of the occasion to drop the rosy ribbon down my neckline, what else: oh yes, the roar

1. Bis dart qui dart celeriter . . .:
No more of your dart games. Mal armé, pour ce coup. Whale the target out of the blank page. Cette blancheur rigide, dérisoire.

2. Accountant, the numbers count!:
They're all musical productions here. And everyone has his number on the set. Musikaleidoscopic. With dacapolkalypso beat!

3. Siete voi? 'Tis you? May I tease you?:
Mette sete, ottomano ammazzasette! We are seven!

4. Seis?:
Stop!

5. Psaltery?:
A sort of Finnish zither. Sing to him only with thine plectrum. Or pluck the lucky harp. Lady-kill her with your deep rough tenoriolé voice. Roar out your runes.

6. One more time . . .:
Talata! Step. Terra firma. You move even better than the waves.

7. Portto? In lingua franca?:
Franco di porto in porto franco! The port trait of a lady of the evening: there is a whore in that port of call girls . . .

of the crowd in the beer hall, the surge of the waves. From wave to wave, you wandering sailor, concocting waves of words. Cunt-cocktale from the sea. What was your motto?: A gal in every portu . . . Opportunist! Now the moorings will be broken and you'll only see sea sea mar mar and mar . . . Ho ho ho! Kapitain Tximist, the mist closes in and the noise begins, mystifying alchemist. In my bark-barka you'll find the pardon, poor don. Pardon? Pour down. Ha ha high jai! My stormy tempest of love-sniveling is dying down now. With a finny-tail swish your big siren will drag you to the deepest depths. Don't you hear the murmur? Nothing? You won't see anything. And will only hear sea sea mar mar . . . A good-bye kiss, musselman, and cheerio! Mar mar mar mar . . . Feeling queasy, like a tumbler toy Zoroaster? Kiss by kiss, come to my arms, upsy! I'm going to hoist you up, vizar, and you'll see the great bear . . .

—Mighty Maite! Maite Maithuna . . .

Cabaret-style femme fatale, squeezed into a skintight black tube skirt, maraca-ing with a dice cup, marking time with drunk cha-cha-cha steps around the puppet and smacking him with the dice cup: Encore, bis,[1] right to the core. Your tricks and dice games are over. The way you took advantage of my old doddering sailor. Obsceanographer! Didn't you say you were going to help me put on some musical numbers that would make the earth move? All tossed out, you devil. The Evil Won! Too! Tray! Fore! Woo! Sex! Shoo! Bah! Cha-cha-chant![2] One-two-three-four-five . . .

—Sei tu?[3] The Sibyl of Swiss Cottage! Sib . . .

Says! Seis![4] leaped in the tall dark lady with her psaltery,[5] Aalto! dressed in a long marine blue tunic, Thalatta! Thalatta![6] and as she sang she started swaying about, jostling and knocking over the puppet: Aalto! A love in every portto . . .,[7]—the motto in sailor

1. Argonauttia? Argonaut?:
He'll have to cross the Bosporus first . . . By the way, this time the fleece isn't golden. But this time his treasure, ol' boy! is a very cultured one, she even studied at Oxford . . .

2. Rude rod! Last recourse:
They'll measure this pro crusty thief by yardsticks. Rodsticks. Rude rod of truth!

3. In vino veritas:
Viini vidi vinci. Obscene and unseen, that unknown viking. Poor Leif Ericsson, Kyrie Eleison! where's your knavigation chart. Maybe Vinland will become Finland . . .

4. O lay! the oh-so-Spanish olé? . . .:
Ole!: Be yourself. Ole!

5. Thule!? The last land, the end . . .:
Tule. Come.

6. Pasto?:
Or better, antipasto. I think it's a manner of fasting.

7. Not the type for sin, or for the book of swindles:
Tipsy tipa: Last drop . . . Not a drop! Chuck the inkwell . . .

slang of this ancient mariner.[1] Hoist the middle mast![2] Set the course due east. (Does he dare ply south? Sur? Surely this south is a killer. Sí, Sinbad. Yes, Ericsson. Good-bye, Columbus. Onward to my colosea colossal continent, colonizer, and ever eastward. Vastus Oceanus. To the disputed coast of quarrels. A line in sight from the Pinta, admiral? Vinland?[3] Amerikka? Asia? Cosa Nostra? Terra Nostra? Nolo contendere. Great coast, great cost. All rich upon arrival? Earthly paradise. Tutti contentti: Lollipops from Haavana for everyone. Jibe on, go on with the contata and narrata of your truetale. Going out into the open sea . . ., far inside the marisma in his boatlet. What valor! Tutto è maia . . . All is illusion. Can't he see the luminosity on the mainmast, the aura? Plow the sea! Now you'll be plowed under . . .) From Wave to wavelet, ole! ole![4] till you gracefully arrive at the bank of your Ultima Thule. Tule![5] beat it. Come about, viiripotent. Play the foghorn. Muu! Muu! Sumu Puntifice. Got to sound somnipotent. Don't you see the rock with all this smog? A violent come-about. This muulish picaro windmilling, turning, the slave turning us around. Come to my abyss. C'mon, what's past is paasto.[6] Come, navigator, be my big buoy. Not thirsty anymore? Vene qui, vacuous! vene qua, vuoto! and empty that bottle. Don't bail out. No bad broad or tipa[7] to turn to? Vene qua. Packed tight, with the merry brunette. On her wave, on her little wave . . .

—Aava Meri . . . Aave . . .—

Hello! ¡Hola! Aloha, Sinbad! in jumped a colossal blonde in a tiny bikini of silver lamé, starting a striptease around the puppet: The cruel sea . . . A thousand names . . . The cruel . . ., see? Ya. Ay. Mild Alias! Now he doesn't remember that pub, my bare pubis?

1. A gang of gagsters . . .:
Or gaggle of ganders. In the hallway. Waddling. Croaking. Couldn't take a misstep or even a goose step in that packed pub. Lemme fly out of here! the miniskirted barmaid trying to shake off the sinful hands.

2. Min mand. My husband?:
He's no mean man . . . With a wife like that, you could really show off . . .

3. Olaf . . .:
Gas up the saga. The one the Paraclitoridian usually narrated to his electric Clitemnestras. The Viking Olaf plundered the goods of the wandering Irishman Sir O'Tilc. Fight to the death. Sir O'Tilc vs. Olaf. Pathetic falo. See?

4. Gorgone with the wind . . .:
Oui. En pleine vengeance. The gal was a gale.

5. Pay Ola . . .:
Pay off!

6. Authoritarian Note from Herr Narrator:
He who writes the commentaary, commands. Until (new comment or nuovo Komento) further orders. Got it?

7. Sanatorium? Sana . . .:
Sic. Yes, a hospital for ill words, for each insane word.

That bar, barbaric! with striptease and smog. Goony gangsters.[1]
No nice office workers: just greasy gross guys. Sonorous sauna.
And when I put an end to my act, skirting around the tables in G-
string with my bra (brass! brassière!) in hand, you accosted me and
tried to kiss me . . . Come! Come! And your one-armed friend, halt!
grabbed the chance to snatch my bra away and hide it. Stop! Strop!
Strumpet! So English my husband, mean man![2] so phlegmatic,
that he didn't intervene. Not a word, the guy chewing his pipe, so
primped and pampered. Fortunately bossy Sue Dama came along
to impose some order in the jungle. Don't you remember when
you met me, don't you remember the kiss, the robbery, the Arab
bite on the breast, the shout Hoi! Hoi! from the scratch? Come.
Go south now. Come, don. They're going to soak you. Wave by
wave, Olaf . . .[3] SOS, and she strangles him with the bra. Now for
the hurry-up call . . . by a hurry cane![4]
—The great Dane! Ola . . .[5]

Once again on the attack, round two, the saltatory woman with the
psaltery:
Let's go back to those places, placed you know where, to those
fishing holes. Got any more ways, fool? Bail out, ninpumpoop,
bala yourself. Vuotaa il sacco, vuoto! or I'll veto you. That's right,
chiotto, don't run me aground. Hoohoo, cabin boy. Together at
last. Insieme. Yes. Ah, man. Siemen. Sh! S! men! SOS: Save Our
Seamen. Yes. That unreceived message. Safe? Stickling right to
the coast. What are these laughs, all this risississota. Who's gossip-
ing? Let's hear your commentaa.[6] Silence in the sala! Safe in the
sanatorium.[7] Yes yes. Just one sanative word, Mr. Cure-all, and
my soul will be cured. Safe. Love balsam, oh! Cagliostro, hide that
bloody public region. Consequence of that crack of dawn, of your
racy conspiracy. I was sighing half love-mad, Voi! Voi! and him

1. Point? What point?:
Milalias's abode in Queen's Park. Where every rigid woman turns frigid with cold.
A free frisson. Despite all the friction.

2. Raja ajar? You're going too far . . .:
Let's see if the pickpocket comes out clean. Back to your bag, dad.

3. Consecrated?:
Or consacré for the sacrifice? Pudendum addendum: where it says sacred read
scared. I mean snared. Or shared.

sacking and cossacking. Just another little bit, and I'm bagging it already. Yes yes, get out of here! And you had me on edge. Brrr! so cold. Rushing me, are you in a hurry? there's still a lot left to tell, scarecrow. But I'll get to the point: All alone, passing through London? You picked up this quick exotic gal in the piccadillyesque discocoteque. Remember how you bent over backwards to please me? Waltzing and polkaing and rocking and then trip-dancing to your bed. Tacky touch, bad eticoquettishness, already getting to the point.[1] Nice house, Casanova. What a hole! You carried me to your hovelovely home sweet home. Where Homer nodded? Where Herodotus doted? The hero doctors his story! Don Juone in his room. Don Juono, your tarturn will come. You were looking for that one thing, slightly ajar, raja,[2] in the dark? Chis! Hush! Out of here, swaggarts!

And me too, he took me to his tavernacle . . ., a svelte vestal brunette popped up, wagging lasciviously around the puppet and tympaning with an electric cooker. He tried to get me drunk. His crazy idea to go to Queen's Park, to hell's fifth circle. After nightfall and me shivering there in the glow of the heater. Dark and icy bedroom, like stepping into a steppenwolf's mouth. This pariah has no heat! With his dirty jokes in the dark: I guess you must use light brown dye? A teacher who won't play show and tell? And he seemed so serious to me . . ., when I came across him in the Polytechnic cafeteria. His coarse peasant games: Touch but don't look. No! It's so late! Much too. No metro or bus, better that you stay and sleep it off. Two beds here, as you see, and I only want to watch over you. Your lies! To me, virginity is sacred.[3] Felon! I couldn't catch a wink because of the cold and the poor devil laid his hot little stove where he could at the head of my bed. And no sooner do I finally fall into Morpheus' arms, happily snoring

1. Nero? Black:
More light! romaanikirjailija, although Rome burns with Romulus and Uncle Remus. Rhyme, rhyme. What a genius (: Nero?) the world loses! The whole world?

2. Which of the three?:
Time shall throw a D'Artagnan . . .

3. Reservatus?:
Reserved for seduction.

away, when the Luciferocious creature leaps out of his makeshift bed and tries to assault me. Yow! the fire saved me. He let out a scream, divine punishment! when he burned his foot. Don't you respect what's most sacred? Remember, a female membrane unknown to men may only be dismembered by the most important family member. Hymen for the high man on the wedding night! a homily no highwayman knows better than you . . . Time to home in the infernace, as she swung a stove-blow to the head, a stove-in head for this lame devil!

—Sagrario? A golden sanctuary . . . Sagrario Rubio!

The tenacious psaltery assaulter hopping and sharpening her harpist claws around the puppet: The law of talon, captain. Retaliation time . . . After the raucous festivities in the cave with stalactites and music of sorts, Tiffany's, to your deep-freeze alcove for fresh experiences. Ha! Seeing how far we could go! Cavern of cabala. Traitor! Or Torah? Torah cabalistaa. Avante! Avanto! and this bold bear pushes me into his pit. A dark glacial cavern, camera oscuura, your Queen's Parka chamber. Oo-wee it's dark in there! and the sultan Mustafa playing deaf. Ché nero, uomo nero.[1] Laughter in the dark. It's more romantic with just the little candle. Pale fire. Adagio of ardor. Don't tell me! Damp bone-chilling cold. And the rain to give rain to your imagination. Marquis de Sade! and so refined, studying me surreptitiously: Portto? Some fine Spainish whine? as I stood there with my hands on my hips. A tila tea was what I needed! Tea? And you with your maltaa fever, burning with impatience: Another slug!—of that brew. Putting up with it! and putting it down. This idiot taunting and tempting: Have a little, tipple a little ripple, smoke the pipe to get wormed up. And the old staticky music from your untuned radio-casatta. Dead battery? As time goes by . . . Cucko! Strangers in the naittaa . . . Casanova wants a cassa nova? No way, not at all . . . All for one? Monist! Monopolizing musketeer![2] We all want more, vie piú, vie . . . koitus![3] much more.

1. The end of the world?:
Not yet. Just an explosion. But the Sibyl's prophecy, it seems, will soon be fulfilled. Now we're in complete chaos.

2. Who?:
A Finnish Don Juan who finished badly, torn apart. But they stuck his pieces together and set him loose again.

3. Who?:
The flower of marvels.

4. The fighting cock, a wily bird, a cuckoo cuckoo . . .:
It will be difficult for you to finish safely, cuco.

Interruptus? Up, risa upp! a nurse, long-legged bag-of-bones blonde, interrupted noisily, lurching on stilts around the puppet and pointing a pistol: Stanza! No reverse to this verse, no longer singing the same tune, scalded coward? Come to your cat, to my lap. O those sagas you sang, sagacious one, your number will come up. Climb up my hill to my stanza, room six—sex!—my charming little pad on Maple Street, right next to the Post Office phallus. Sputter isolandic phrases. Tala íslenzka. You ask me that almost orgasmoribound!? Be my two-bit tart, my fool on a fall . . . Wicked one! In a corner, a soft fluffy sofa, and sofawning over me. Marvelous smooth evening. Then in the moment of our truth, wha! you shout and spring. Spring!—the sexplosion. They violated the Post Office tower—spring! That end of October, a fall . . . Jinxed! Wouldn't you like to forget it, big brave man? The big boom, a downpour of glass. Ragnarok!!![1] Come to the window, quick, look! And in the excitement, bel ami, you left me half finished. On the sacrificial alter, ite missa est, hit and missed sorely. Much ado, fornicator, and little noodling. Mat another, matador! Nanay. C'mon, snore 'n' roar. To the sofa, ironic sophist. Swindler! Tartuffe! Pay the tariff. Terrorist! and she fired into the air and walloped his head with the gun-butt. Son of a goon! Arsonist! And all haste!

—The Icelandic nurse . . . Margrét ("Mara") Gunnarsson!

The harpist, back to her old routine: He makes me dizzy . . . Everything was spinning about me, round and round! In your hovelly mousetrap, ratty musician. Pied piper of Hamelin! Undress me slowly, what's your slurry. Lemme lemme, lemmiki Lemmikainen.[2] Pian piano, lento lento slowly on the wing the cock with his cuckoo.[3] Beak to peak. Peep. United in their nest, cock-a-deedle-dee, Kikiirekítos! koitto at dawn. Another wild fling? I'll trim the wings of this cuco.[4] I'll give you a fling you won't forget . . . Aave atque vale! I'm something to fear, my dear. Still kicking around? Still awake in the wake, wise guy? Brrr! what a chill. I'll cover you and bundle myself up. And this guy musickly

1. The two hemispheres separated . . .:
No! . . . Not at all. Only connect. There's a point to all the right-to-left coming and going in this syn$\frac{a}{O}$ptic gloss-spell. Catch the wave of this epic ecliptic fit. Connect. Use (brayin' power) your head. (Or should I say get a (b)rain check?) Sing that neu-ron-ron.

2. La signorina Parola:
A letter-day saint who comes and goes, and carries you farther onword each time. Your powerful owner and mistress. Always the same and different, this ever-changing kaletterscopic lady. Catch the wave . . . Every time she appeared in the newspaper ad, the attractive swarthy airline stewardess with her globe, the extravagant exploiter couldn't resist the temptation to expropriate the jingo with an excision:

the world is my dream

runruunning on with his snores. Enough, Caruso. Try your raucous song on someone else. Alone at last. Sola, soloist. Unrecoited love! Sonata in unisonno. Univerberation. Soloist unisounding in her polyphonic universe . . .

Genteel brunette stewardess with short hair and big black eyes underlined in charcoal, in a gray uniform and bowler hat with the crown marked—in chalk—with a capital L, hugging an enormous ball wrapped in newspaper: Each word a world, eh? A world of light and color. Lume. Orbe, orbetto. Look, sir, and don't touch it up . . ., and she ripped the paper till her globe was bare. Here you have me, safe and sound. In wind and limbo. Look but don't taste. Remember my ad? Was it really your dream? Your nightmare? Alice in Worderland? Chased Susanna of Babylondon? And so on with your Xs. My X chromosome ، . . You couldn't see me, so many mornings in a row, without feeling an overwhelming need to modify my inscription. The word is my dream! and she broke the globe in two[1] over his head.
—Miss World? Miss Word![2] Elle . . .

Half-nude redhead in a whitish shawl, a gaudy red flower at her temple and a black velvet band tied at her throat, strutting around the puppet with an open fan in her right hand and trying to cover her pubis with her left: Dream-party, draumaturge. That marvelous party with so many important people, with that nouveau reach! Clerk from Kilburn Woolworth's draws all the stares. Dérisoire, sire, le soir. To be or not to be—a pinup? On the cheap. You made me pose like a limp Olympia in that demural picture by that director Mr. Hitch-Cock. Me, Olympia? Sprawled between some slobbering old farts. Braavo! Bis! Encore! So I drink, I drink like an Olympian, to get the shameful act over with. Câline, your girl from Erin. J't'aime. Mwa! Kiss me. A Fwench kiss, sill voo play . . .,

† 391 †

1. Stay!:
Wait! and you'll see . . .

2. Eliotic heliotropes . . .:
Yes, the apostolondoner never stopped proseliotizing in his Wastelondon.
Especially during his holy day, the first of the crueliotest month.

3. Viikko santo! Saint Viikko?:
The true passion was during Holy Week.

4. And she plays a lone hand . . .:
Secured loan.

you requested, you drunk too. Right here? Forget it! Titimorous little me! Take it easy. Pian piano. Ay, rhymester, that hurts. Pian piano, don't be pained. Batter batter the breach. Micmac. Coitus reservatus à la maison close. Copulating on the table, on the bordeli line. Bric-a-brac. Chin-chinga! Stale toast... You bastard, you beat your royal Olympia and lead her by the nose. Tough man, eh? Pian piano, all in fun, ha! Here's your kind of fun! Fan! Fan! fanwhacking him over the head. Fan out![1] peacockatoo.

    —Olympia! Pat ("Olympia") McCoy . . .

And once again the brunette and her harp, quick and reckless as a lightning bolt, never ending, never giving the finish: All alone in that alley . . . don't you want me to tell it? I went so far . . . And the next day when I had to go to Stratford, the Marquis de Sade showed up in my Earl's Court hotel. To Stratford on Avon? What a unique opportunity to see Bottom's universal dream! On my money, it goes without saying. You're going with a friend? Then I'll bring a colleague of mine. I won't go into the tangle and the adventure now, Juhannustanssit! in that loony cheap hotel. Amadou mío, I love you so much. Should I tell Riita? We'll see. I won't mention that sexcursion to the Bard's birthplace with that idiot (who never stopped butting in till the end) and my comrade in harms Paula the Viennese (who fell in the trap too) and as part of the procession the maimed poet, always smoking his panetella, filling the bus with smoke, and defaming the English. And through the whole trip this other moron rudely rummaged through my bag, badly cackling out words from the book I was carrying. Splitting with his exaggerated laughter . . . Eliotin Cocktail Partyssa! This idiot with his eliotricks.[2] Then later cracking jokes on Vinland and Finland. And my first name. Round and round the circle. Kurssi rikkorsi:[3] All a little tipsy, in the pub where we stopped. Hell! Go to hell. Hell is oneself . . ., myself am Hell, recited the Miltonist with his sidekick. For you, yes, hell. Infernopolist! And me alone in the back. Sticking to me like a leech . . .?! A woman is always on her lone.[4]

1. Shrill cicada chirps from the chorus:
Now girls, don't be slowing down yet around the stalled dark stranger. Make an ever faster ringling, sisters or insisters, though it's already overrung.

2. Kodakapo:
Kodakapokalypso now.

Solitary me . . ., interrupted a petite fortyish baby-faced woman with a Scotch beret and a white Burberry raincoat, limping slightly around the puppet and swinging a camera: Lonely heart for the hunter . . . Sad café without ballad in Paddingtown. Eh?[1] Phooey! The teary window panes. Ever-weeping Paddington . . . It never rains in California. Solitary tourist, solitary wife. Seaport-and-sunset-painting husband taking advantage of his last vacation days in Penzance. Lonely wife shopping in London. Harrods . . . With so many bags, Burberry's . . . Scotch House . . ., in the Wimpy's in Paddington. Face of a Yankee tourist? They took advantage, the hunter and his friend. Frisco?! Frisky fun, they say. Simpatico loco. This girl too. Chick. Chichi. Pardon my French. Yo better español. Mwee airmohsso, noh ess vairdah? My husband, a telegraph operator and artist, speaks it too. He's of Scotch origin. I've got almost three hours left. Would that be enough time to see the Chelsea floral show? Certainly, and that way they wouldn't have to leave me alone. You would be my Baedeker. A double Beddecker . . . He called it making a sandwish . . . A lively *paseo,* walking Spanish style. Cosmopolitical. Flower power. Pretty chrysanthemums, mum. And the camellias, madam. Gardenias from Eden. Very pleasant man, mwee simpatico. The girl too. Plenty of time, still time. Not even one taxi. At full speed they dragged me limpstriding to Paddington station. They made me lose the train, and my head. What must Dear John be thinking in Penzance, getting worried. Pirate! Send a telegram? Saying I didn't have to worry, I had a place to spend the night, in a room right there at hand, with them. His pad in Paddington! How was I to know they would . . ., and she began smacking him on the head with her Kodak. A put-on! Kodak-kaput![2]

—Mrs. McCullers! Peggy . . .

1. Fork out your tongue, and garden with your pen, Mr. Tsui-Pen . . .:
Bore, hayseed? Il faut cultiver son jardin! Le roman du jardin des sentiers qui se bifurquent. Fuck around with your forked tongue and lead Mr. Tsui-Pen up the garden path . . .

2. Novelabyrinth like a garden?:
A garden of paths that bifurcancel out. The labyrinth of Hampton Court as a small-scale model of the book.

3. A MAZE, LEZAMA?:
Lima's mighty maze! but not without a plan. [Andante. Slow and steady takes you far in this intricate Paradissonance.]

4. Quel cauchon!:
A French Bishop (au fou!) for the King of England. The mate of the Bishop and the King.

Athletic brunette flapper with a pageboy haircut (in coat of mail, garter, and black stockings) swinging a sword and feinting around the puppet: Alone, in the heart of the labyrinth . . . Hampton Court —remember? From my grieving I come, to my labyrinths I go. New Yorker on her first divorce and her first trip to Europe. Labyrinth inside the labyrinth. Voices in so many languages (This way! No! Were we here before? There's no exit . . . Reverse! Yes. No. To the right . . . I'm telling you no! We're lost . . .) around us. In the heart of the heart . . . Writing a postcard from the labyrinth (I'm at the heart of this amazing maze . . .) to my bouncy brat. He's crazy about them too. Start from the degree zero and go to infinity. Nervous laughs behind the hedges. And you sat down beside me on the bench. Reading what I was writing, out of the corner of your eye? Leave zero and on to the next zero. Zero to zero again. Alone. Just we two made it. Pardon the delay . . . (?!?) —amused by the shocked expression of a perfect stranger. Now's the time. And you asked for my pen[1] to speedwrite something[2] on your cigarette pack. A Parker in hand is worth two in the bouche. The pen is maybe-er than the sword of Damocles. Your double-edged tongue, sword-words! blade runner. You mazed me with your mouth. Labiarinth! Pulling off your little plan, weren't you? This labyrinth was built centuries ago, perhaps only so we would meet, here and now, you and I. There's no time to lose. I believe it. We're all labyrinth, parts of the labyrinth. Everything is labyrinth. My inner ears were buzzing! We infernalized ourselves para-disiacally in vicious circles.[3] Ever harder to follow you. No end? Air a . . . secret? C'mon, it must go to . . . And you wound up cornering me in. Desiring the easy us. Half dead leaning against that live hedge . . . Couldn't you wait till we got to my hotel? The time had come for the tale of the maiden ready for sacrifice. Making pigshit glosses, hogwash! on my sacred name. Caution, cochon![4] Slaughter in the dark. It was once an arrow-shot from a triumphal archangel. Tempting me with your anarchronisms. Say

1. Three in One:
Cries to cry to heaven. Lost words which will last . . .

2. Yellow wigwag . . .:
Yes. Signal and trademark, in ancient Rome, of the oldest profashion.

3. ! ?:
The staging came about thanks to the talent of Bob "Hitch-Cock." In a series of
one-minute pornofilms he condensed the eternal scenes of Johannes Factotum.

out loud that this merveilleuse sauvagine was crazy about this free Lancelot . . ., and she sword-swiped him. Jesus! Suss! Sush![1]

—"Jeanne Dark"! Joanna Schwartz . . .

Messalina with triple muslin veils and a yellow wig,[2] lasciviously disrobing, causing a stir around the puppet: Alone at a table . . ., that sad early morning, in the Golder's Green Wimpy's. No ladies alone! that black son-of-a-bitch waiter tried to toss me out. Like I was just another two-bit hooker. And you, opportunist, to the rescue. Well hello there, I hadn't seen you. Don't be bothering my fiancée! No less . . . And in five minutes like you knew me all your life. I told you about my career. My whole curriculum. Othello just tossed me out of the hotel. No problem: my bed is your bed. Attack of professional jealousy, you know. Yes, things got pretty black. So he plays Othello better than anyone, but they don't call him anymore. So if I'm ready and willing to do anything from monkey business to Black Beauty and the beast, with two backs . . . Did you ever hear such a thing? Besides, the booze is killing him. And then too I get depressed being out of work. Sometimes I feel like throwing myself in the Thames . . . But how can this be? An actress who seems to have so much experience on the boards . . . And what a name! All roads lead me to you. Your hand, for the moment, on my knee. I must write your story! And saying I shouldn't worry because you had a friend who was getting up an avant-garde production, a sort of jigsaw puzzle of Shakespeare, and first thing tomorrow you would request the best part for me. A lot of Shakespeare about nothing! The next day at noon, when I tried to wake you, it was a different story. What potpourri, what friend, what Shakesperimental theater?[3] Shakespearances deceive. It's still too early, honey, sleep and let sleep. It's too late! strangling him with her veil.

—Roma! Roma Smith . . .

Cleaning woman-gypsy dyed platinum blond, with a bucket of soapy water and a brush, flinging bubbles and flecks of foam around

1. BUBBLE BATH:

Window washer energetically scrubbing a steamed-up window: a circle opens and one can see the inside of a bathroom: a blondine foamassaging herself in the bathtub. She stands up abruptly, covered with foam from head to foot, upon seeing the dark intruder in coveralls who just squeezed in through the window and swooped in on her. Close-up of her hands virginally crossed over snowy mountains. Paralyzed with fear? Athletic, but she seems defenseless. The intruder rubs her distantly, mechanically, as if he were still washing windows. First the two half-moons, dunes, of the blondine. Flack! Fleck, his face gets foam-covered. He scrubs her back, foamy to the nape of the neck, slowly turning the docile blondiana around. Close-up of her face smiling playfully. He removes the flakes from her full breasts, jiggling them. And he slides his two hands down her belly, to the foamossy delta. One fondle and a foamball quivers, unfalling. Flack! and then in close close-up, peeping through the foam, a pink tip appears. A jump straight back by the startled intruder. Beatific smile, in close close-up, of the hermaphrodite born of foam. Close close-up of the rosy rising member. Fade-out, with the snow melted. A halo of steam closes around the phallus.

2. Junta?:

No joke. Yoke team of draft animals.

3. Porcile!:

Pigsty. For the Pig and his Legion of Horror.

4. Find a painted bunting in the bush:

The catcher in the garden of no lights.

5. Sip maté? Salvia?:

Salve! My bottle of salivation!

the puppet, soaping him up with brushstrokes: My masterly services for the master of vices . . . The best table on our patio. Take a weight off as you wait, Champion of Rogues, and drop those pounds while you're at it. Or rather, pick them up. He sat stunned in that silly corner after he squeezed them out of me. The silly con on the valley of my décolletage. Are they all yours? bitten with curiosity as I kept showing him my latest full-color poses. Bob was drooling, bubbling over. His proposition: a starring roll in that stud-starred pop film with lots of pomp and pooper and bubbles and bubs. Tail of a tub. Of foaming gel. That I was allergic to. All porn and no pasta. Bob never paid a shilling. Not a penny. When the series was finished, blah blah. I'll prick your bubble! and she brushed his head. The world's a bubble. What a babbler, a big bubble . . .[1]

—"Lolita Lola"! Lolo Elola . . .

Alla lotta, Lottario! the red-shirted Garibaldine launching her war-whoop, twisting around the puppet and popping him on the head with a portfolio. Clinch! Shall we dance another bossa nova? On the way out of my night class he dragged me into that trattoria full of traitors from the Junta,[2] Por Chile![3] celebrating Pinochet's rise. Quiet! Calm down! the coward. C'mon, let's get out of this prigsty (on the sly, hush! almost stifling me by force) before the Troia war starts. Pig-sticking in quite the wrong way. Coward! Your judgment day will come. And to top it off he treacherously attacked me in Woodside Park. As he walked me home so late. We took a shortcut through the woods. Ambushed. Don't you see the fireflies, the lanterns there on the sod? You sot! You mite! Pressed against my rear end trembling. Tò! Oh! Fffft! Backfired on him. Seems like a magic painting. And you don't hear the song? Sta sordo! You're deaf! We almost lost each other . . ., and with a loud report she forced her portfolio over his head. Bosh! Cerca un Uccello in un Bosco![4]

—The Garibaldine! Carlotta Baldi . . .

Cha-cha-cha, Don Juan! danced the warrior with an African mask, brandishing a bottle, On the house . . ., around the puppet. Care for a sip? Chew, pa? Chupa ya mate![5] and she sprayed him

1. Wino? With a stink like ink . . .:
He hath not drunk ink. / Sh! Acqua in bocca! Acqua morta di Vita, acquavitaio indotto.

2. Mia Vita! sparkling . . .:
You wrung me out in bed, you absorbed and delighted, and joking on top of it all. English monitor violates native boy in Dar es Salaam from excessive zeal . . . How could you tell that one? Yes, yes, you. You, macho! Pretending to be asleep? Deaf? Your girl is talking to you in the vast English language, with her linguistic swagility. What about extenuating circumstances, troublemaker! Distorting my secret with your harlots. What's that? Don't act dumb. Nice scandal for my students! I'm reading today what you'll write in your tembolismatic Elephanthology tomorrow. Hey! Diluted words. Drink this soma or nectar of the god-byes.

3. Some what? Some drink, methinks, so mad, so magic . . .:
Samba or mamba again, Simbad. Another tangle for two? Cha-cha-cha! Don Juan. Juujuujua . . .

4. Entangled until the redolent affair is discovered:
Red-handed? The sly one taking the big leap. Beyond redress.

5. The Cruel Sea (un uomo in maremma!):
Alone at a table, next to the window, looking at the steep street, the coming and going of the scurrying customers. The sea of people. Three o'clock, and still not here. How would she recognize that bearded vagabond crouched over the bar, drinking a beer and sneaking a look at her now and then. He looked at the gloomy blonde for the last time, left, and that was that.

with froth from her mouth. Or would you rather have a glass? A glass of wino?[1] Before, you drank out of the bottle. To the last drop. Vita mea![2] that cheater's chatter. Mia Vita. You liked my nom de guerre so much . . . It wreaked havoc in Dar es Salaam when I was a school monitor there . . . Hush! More drizzle? and she sprayed him again. More kisses, mvua! mvua! as the rain soaks us. Let it drench us. Little drops of nothing? Let me come up to your place to dry off. A da capo of tea? And then heating up in my living room-bedroom with his titillalations tempting me and hunting that one thing until I took the plunge. Oh la la! The ties, the lies that bind! I'll give you a good summer assault, after the soma.[3] Both of us sloshed. And you were fascinated by the mask I brought back as a souvenir. Hanging on the wall. You didn't like seeing it unused. Why not try it? and she tore off the mask with a yank, freeing her tawny head of hair. Take that! and she struck his head with the mask. You liked it almost as much as my nom de guerre. Make war to me in love, you little sadist. Smoke your war pipe. Smoke and more smoke. You made me cough. My heart, pitterpat. Hold it in! Now I'll give you that beating . . . dealing out loud mask-smacks. Fa-faa-fatigued? faster and harder, feeling faint? Don Juan . . . Hwa! Wa! Ooh! panting with exhaustion. Here I am. Vita tua, your Vita . . ., wage war on your war, until your Victoria defeats you . . .

—Vita! Vita Winslow . . .

Glamorous blond gladiator in a short tunic with a mourning sash over her shoulder, rapidly wrapping up the puppet with her ready net:[4] That date, you stood me up in that cruel pub . . . Sea of cruelty.[5] And to think I was coming to cheat with you once again, mad masker, and leave my husband. Me, that's right, the one who went for you most hotly. Your enclosed garden. Your sealed fountain. Your dove. Your immaculate deception. Enough? That date still excites me. I came to London ready to start all over again. To separate. My married name really made you laugh . . . But you kept coming back to the mountain. Why did you give up on us? That's how you paid me back for everything. So childishly fond of

1. Another Bovary with Bovaritis . . .:
Another one for the emmasked man . . . So many women, Babelle once said, to blot out the memory of another. Of just one?

2. Put us? Rut us?:
There's a scratch in the original. Putus or putous, it looks like. Or Brutus?
[A helpful note from Herr Narrator.]

3. The Finnish letter doesn't cut it . . .:
I bring it to you by foot, me, your little carrier pigeon. And neither lazy nor shy it was spontaneously introduced in London. What a kyrie . . .

4. Bellow from the core of the chorus, the waitress in basquine and the big potted nun:
If you don't have Ganivet or machete, macho, I'll pass you mine.

5. If the seedy seducer doesn't die . . .:
The harvest is small and the reapers many.

you too. Where, who were you with when I sent the telegram. I'll
carry the torch for you for eternity. Don't ask for whom the belt
rolls. There's no redemption for you! tightly enmeshing him.
    —No! The Señora of Montealegre?! Emma . . .[1]

The recalcitrant brunette with her harp again, arpeggioing around
the puppet: This guy won't say a thing . . . It's not over yet,
smooth-talking boor! A few weeks later I had to return to London.
Landed! Lontoo! Lontano! After having gone so far . . . Crazed
with rage. I'll tell you a thing or two or muu! A real dressing down
for another undressing . . . Since you spoiled me rotten in your big
fancy house, Casanovel, I've been crazy for you. I want to spend
some more time with you, for your ruuminations and ruuminis-
cences. Remember how you used to tickle me, hoohoo, till it went
too far. Scratching away with your runaway pen, universal cor-
respondent? Scrape away, ra, raa, putus![2] Oh lapsuus . . . Sand
away, lecher, here in this carnival is your virgen piena de grascia.
Alleluia! File away. Push, purist, and don't polish the style so
much. That's right, I'm getting down to brass tacks, hardhead. To
finish it off, know-it-all: I got through the difficulty alone. Another
morning. A new day born, a new diamante! I had written you that
letter in Finnish[3] from Germany. What letter? Sing kyrie,[4] the jack
will turn up. Cost? What cost? You didn't want to contribute.
Evero, trovatore. Not a penny. Yours is a bad breed! The cost? and
she harped on him a bit with her harp. Not a word, impious pioneer?
Sing on, blockhead, with your chorist's song. More dressing down,
whoremonger? The stick will come later. Are you cold? I'll wrap
you and rap you, I'll help you, I'll harp you, worm! hacking him
with the harp. I must return. We die daily for someone. Remember?
Today for me. You'll return to die tomorrow.[5] For another. Let
each carry his own weight. And shovel. To the grave now. In living
coloratura. Calm down. Are you praying now? Pray with the lay
sister. Calm down. His hour hasn't come yet? His time? and she
broke the harp over his head. Finnish. Finni. Fin!
    —Aava Mary! Aave Mary! The Finnished Mary . . .

1. Plucking him?:
Pluck up, kaper, and even featherless you'll cackle.

2. Kappara! Expiation?:
The eve of Yom Kippur. The harpies will recite appropriate versicles. They walked around stupefied by their wicked deeds, having had to fast for their wrongs. All food made them nauseous; they were already at death's doorstep.

3. Who is being called *that?*:
Ali...? Alia? Au lit! [The bed moldy now, where you'll never get your point across with the darkly beautiful Jewish jewel.]

4. Kappa?:
For the moment, just a Japanese vampire. Joker and gagster, who doesn't give a tinker's damn.

*
* *

They all abuse accuse afflict assail asphyxiate aggravate antagonize bawl beat besmirch break bruise bust chop crack crunch damn dash emboss exhibit exhort fetter flail flog gag gash hack hammer hatchet inject injure jab jolt kick knee knife knock lash mash nick oppress pinch push quash rattle shake shatter shock slap stab batter trap trick uglify undo unwind uppercut vamp vanquish varnish vex whack whip wrench xylophone yak yammer yank zap zing the eccehomo.

Lively Salomessalina waltzing, with flutters of her muslin veils, around the puppet: Cape falling down? Put up your crest, Don Johaan. Kappen! Kappen! raising her rooster and measureless kitchen knife. Kaapen![1]
—Helen from Holland . . .

The damsel in black, now with the rooster and the knife, shaking the rooster over the puppet's head: No matter who caponizes you, no one has my capabilities . . ., and she beheaded the rooster over his head. Kappara![2]
—Lady Olivia . . . Ollie . . . Ollie . . .[3]

Madamu Butterfly thumping the puppet's head with an umbrella: Escape, caped caperer. Kappa![4] Ironic vampire . . . Oneiromancer! Smirking smiling as I smile-smirk now. What a dunce! Showing me every porno photo in his house . . . Every little thing. None of your incumbencies? pulling a cucumber out of her kimono. Take that! giving him a cucumber-conk on the head. Pack a prick with pickled peppers. Escape before you're alcaponed. Scar phase. Da kapo, with your Kappa effect. What a coincidence, yentlemango. Tango by tango. Samba now, kid, with your mammy. Me, you. Yes. You and I. Me your night. You nothing, a gnat, nattering. To know and two no. Never-rending? Don't get restless, Don Huan. Escape, it's clearing up. Humhumming baritone. Sweat, inquis-

† 407 †

1. Reza. Reezaa! in Japspunish:
Safety reza. Answered prayer. To shave your skin!

2. Kirisuto!? Jesus!:
Stop stop! Enough! Iesu was his house. His troubled double in the church, Santakurosu, of Saint Nicholas in Chiswick.

3. Cap on!:
Chapeau! You can break up this capon. But don't enter the chateau fort of the Greek lady, the castle of the chaste capone. A well-defended possession in north London. There a well-armed shipowner kept her a virtual prisoner. He was a dealer who received his clients with open arms. Emperor of an emporium frequented by all parties.

4. Tio as tío in Spunish? Say uncle!:
Nah. Astio. It's Greek to me.

5. The great Pan of all Pan?:
The big pang that didn't pan out.

6. Lana. And quit turning it around, naughty turner:
By chance, and after so many close calls, he discovered the pleasure (a fixation, Lana?) of the enigmatic Greek lady. When he put his ring finger on the spot. Her open ǎnigma. Imagine. Greek style. It was worth the wait (in the last analysis). [And the old gal had money besides. Grecian gifts. She knew how to grease his palm, that Lady from Greece. One afternoon of tea and antipathy with doughnuts and donatives in Daquise (she was cross with him, lately they had been seeing each other on the run), the imbecile tried to cut the scene short and pay straight away. Give me half a pound. And she, without fear or hesitation, and with a face of amusement, tore the bill in two. Split! Here. The other half, another afternoon when he met her again in the Victoria and Albert Museum. In their hunting hall. When desire overtook the encephallic, they slipped out the back while the uniformed chauffeur from hell waited, in Cromwell Gardens, at the wheel of a shining black Rolls.]

itor . . . Another riddle, o riddled one. Pray, punching bag. Pray![1] pulling out a straight razor. A close shave from the sura razor of your surly surrogate. Sing the kirie, kikiriki! I'll make you sing the hara-kirisuto![2] and she plunged the hell-raiser razor into him. Die. Memento mori, moron!

    —Keikoo! Keiko . . .

Haughty brown-haired lady in a rich tunic embellished with reversed letters, cutting scissor-swipes at the puppet: Capellina for the cap . . .[3] Now you won't be able to give me what I asked for. What a shame! Kikiriki, kirie. Cock-a-doodle, dodo. Ephemeral glossy poly-glossator! My boy, you must pose your little epistle in prose for pros, rhyme by rhyme, verse by barbarous reverse. Elarvorated and glossed with a lot of substance, abused. What a shame, eh pantymimist? You don't care about my rage, as if the accusation isn't serious? You love both good and bad without sexception, you diabolic hyperbolic polyglutton. A real ass, Tio Pep![4] What agony! With the sin comes the rapentance, pirate of penance. Gloss after gloss on your matemorphosis. Already rubbing up against your lady, wily linguist. Open my enigma, anima mea! disembowel me, anorec-tous arsonist. In your tongue-in-chick way? Scrutinize my labiarinth, cretin! Catch got your tongue? You malicious pornographer, you're as dark as a black sheep with the lanose wool pulled over your eyes. Feel line by line, philosophic filibuster kitten. A match, luciferian spirit? Hush, Milalias! Don't get blustered with your noncensus in Panhellenic Hispano. Páme páno! annotator: Let's go up! reveler, feeling randy in the victory museum and my desire climbs to the climax in such a cold climate. Claim it. May I? Yes. Stereophonic simphony. Come under the cover of your mystic mantis. Break and rape. Your Valkyrie wants you to mount her like that Sunday in the Victory Museum. On top of your victim! Ah ah ah accursed me. Let me be your tart. You don't remember. Mnemotechnical Kaptain. Yeah yah. Are you ready with you etyms? Atom in fis-sion . . . Pan![5] You're an explosive person . . . But now a slow cautious ending would be better. Sínfoni, some phony sin, sans fin. To begin the big in memoriam we need a martyr, a witness. Kápios. Someone. Kapetánios, don't escape, we have yet to go for the kappa . . .

    —The Dark Greek Lady! Lana . . .[6]

1. Skaal! Scull!:
Escape with your scalp. Cape the cup of the Kāpālin . . .

2. Careful with the Kappa effect, thaumaturge:
Still distant, they'll recede as they approach . . . Long-distance approach recedes,
vanishes away . . .

3. Agony column?:
Agony in the dark. Sans son ni lumière . . .

Hopping harpist handing out harp-blows and swatting at the puppet: Cut him up! Cut 'em off! piece by piece, till he doesn't have one good part. Sing the kirie! Kikiireki, you see? base cuckoo. Cut his capers off! and she held up a bloody diaper. Castrange him! Emaskulate him! Here, you see!

—Aave Maaria! Such finicky harpy-fingering, Mary . . .

Fiftyish feline in stretch pants and a jaguar-skin blouse, scratching around the puppet with a broken cup: Cuppa? Cup of tea? It was already five on the dot. Five, o cock! Clock up. Forgot to wind the crock, shandyman? Don't we have a private Spunish lesion today? The tea ready at home and waiting and waiting in my Jaguar, on a jag! at the entrance of the East Finchley tube, draining my bottle so as not to cry. Peripatetic professor, don't you take autumn walks anymore through Coldfall Woods with your fall student? Cold Fall! Fall in the foliage, vernereal Captain Nemorous, then warming up to love in my sweet home. Another cup? I'll decupitate you. Cup on! and she cuffed him. Clop off!

—Jenny "Lea"! Mrs. Bennett . . .

Various tongues, horrifying larvulgarities and irregularvas: Kapala, Kapalinguist![1] Felix cuppa! Capistrated! The test is to detest, monsieur. Kappá! Kapp! Kappe! Kappen! Capo! Caper! Da capo, al capone! Turning, infuriated, whirlwinding around the puppet.

The farthest harpies are swooping in. The Kappa effect[2] taking effect. An awestruck Don Juan watched from behind the column[3] as the big circle closed in faster and faster around the puppet: They'll asphyxiate him, windmilling in so tightly . . . Light avengers revolving vertiginously again . . .

At the core the chorus, spinning ever closer, shouted ever louder: We will be one flesh, united forever. One flesh only and only one butcher. To the left! To the right! To the middle! He's ours. And he'll be one of us.

1. Don Hahn, one of those who are haunted by le oui des jeunes filles . . .:
Or Don Hohn. Johannes est nomen eius. Don Johannes Fucktotem . . .

2. Stradivarius?:
Stro divario. We'll not talk here about estrus or ovaries or other variety stories of
the diva.

3. Ray! like a bolt . . .:
I get up young, sonrise! and I go to bed old, nightfaltering! every day.

4. Sun Rey. The Sun K'in! Plus ça change . . .:
Keep spinning around.

5. There may be some sense in this sensational centipedantry:
Better to leave this aristophonation to the batrachians. Hoax! Hoax! Hoax! Better
to go to the women's assembly and pick a word of 171 letters with 28 different
words. Here we go, still with the sound and the furies, into the femaelstrom. The
night of Don Juan will wind up being the night of Saint John. Virgin and martyr.
   Krioskrig . . .
   ((What? A shout, clamoring to heaven, and bolts fall, raining upon the garden in
darkness.))

Keep going, pass go. Let the game continue, don't shrink back. And bite your tail. Remember. To the rear! Beat. An eyelash! Both eyes? Pay. Now. Pay.

Bitter shouts in the darkness: Gallic gallant! Don Hahn![1] Birdbrain! Parroter! Fly-by-night! Henpricker! Eat crow, cockeyed rusester! I'll clip your wings. And I'll do the beak. And I'll do the spurs. And I'll do the crest. Careful with the gobbler!

The circle, in chorus, pressing in on the puppet with stifled shouts: All together! At the same time! All for one . . . For you. The big chance. Isn't it what you were looking for? Enter! Into the antrum of a woman. Today in the guts and tomorrow God only knows what. Thus in the end as it was in the beginning. Enter dirty and come out clean. Yes. Feeling mosstalgic? Aren't you cast in the same Castilian mold? Infant of cast steel.

Your birth in mess your death your rebirth. Stillbirth. Fit as a fiddle.[2] Rah,[3] rah, rapidly! I give birth. I cut the cord. Of your belly button bodice body my baby. Enter in us and you'll come out all new under the sun. The midnight son! We raise you to the light of day in the dark of night.

Faltering shouts of consolation: Mata Hari! Soleiman the Magnificent! Solomon! Sun-tzu! Napoleon! Rei Sol. Roi Soleil . . .[4] Jua . . . Juan!!!

The ring jams in even tighter, shrieking deafeningly: Ay aye ay! Pass. You'll pass through. Pose through. Ow! We'll pull you through. What? Sh! What's with the poor creature? Sh! A squirrel? A pearl? A churl? A whirl? A curl? A girl!

Shouts, of amazement, from the packed mass: A rainbow Jane? Honey! Hush! Doña Juana la Loca? Sh! A calamity Jane. Sh! Juanita Banana? Hey, look what a breach, so well-formed, see her rosy cleft . . .

Krioskrigcritschreihuutocrijeritanskrikkrikkrzykscreamkiáltá-skravyíschreeuw!![5]

Blackout

1. Thunder and . . .:
Sleightning tricks! Au! Tor! Mentor! Let's bring that tempestuous doubled double on stage for a greeting.

2. Coitus reservus? Reserved?:
With reservations beforehand.

3. Concha Cota without surplice or surplus . . .:
Shell out another taco shell. Or bomb shell. Or bomb shelter. Curtains up on a knockout production: See PILLOW NOTES 53, p. 521.

4. Galicia, the magical land of marvels? Galicia in wonderland?:
Of course: witches, witch doctors, the pilgrimage route, Santiago de Compostela . . . Tak! There's only one Galicia.

What was that? Don Juan still on the lookout, parapetted behind his column. A shout? A thunderclap? The tempest behind the torment . . . A hornblast? Wow, who have we got here . . . Did you hear that, Miss Nightingale?

Ragnarok . . ., cheerfully chirped the blonde disguised as a nurse who had just popped onto the porch. The roar of the crowd . . ., and she quickly entered the hall.

Torn. Turn. Trona. Turmoil . . ., Leda the Hippie challenged Don Juan with her leering laugh as she twisted the neck of her rubber swan. Storm, storman. Thunderdunderhead, don![1]

Hark, hark! a stout (pregnant?) peasant woman in clogs and a straw cape sang as she pushed a vacuum cleaner over the porch steps, Krah, krah! Be coy to have a coy tussle . . .[2]

This woman cleans the dust and leaves the straw . . ., the dark woman in a Spanish shawl bantered,[3] fussing with her fan. Shit! Did he do the vacuum cleaner trick with this big mama too? Buzzing away, and the door propped open so as not to raise suspicions. Another aspirator . . .

Isn't that the northwester out of Galicia,[4] Don Tenorio wondered, staring in amazement at the woman with the vacuum cleaner. Leira! take no more spins, Señora de Leira, her married name always first. Ramona . . . Maybe she's homesick? Her husband cultivating his furrows while she cleaned up half of London. So light and airy . . . The crazy white tornado who cleaned the Cleveland Gardens pigsties. From top to bottom. Cleans whiter. La Señora Ariel!

I'm afraid . . . Teño medo dunha cousa que se sente e non se ve . . ., the straw-bedecked woman moaned as she clutched the handle of the still-buzzing vacuum cleaner with both hands, and looked about fearfully.

1. That's a galecism, bel ami!:
Orlando furioso . . . All for a word. Un mot de passe-passe. Un mot passant contre le vent. A passing air.

2. Oui. Le vent, bien tôt. Vaunted. Vented?:
In vents. Who? They're gases. Or were. Eheu fugaces, sagacious gashes . . .

3. The Textravaganza of the Goyim's Great Goat?:
Book émissaire. Bouquin boucané de boucanier qui fait du boucan . . . (Bon bouc! exclaimed the hippie Leda, bowing to Goya's Gran Cabrón, the beast already sunk in a deep sopor, snoring away in the middle of some bushes; or perhaps to the black book flipped page by page by the breeze . . . [This hippie honey has turned satanist on us . . . Bon bouc? Broc-a-brac, de broc et brac . . . Bouc et misère . . . Misstreatise, filed and defiled. Bogey book, mean book! A mean book to cross. To get your goat. Let Rita read it! A goatresque billy-doux. Goatext, book for kidding. Not yet. Book for killing. Not yet. No. Yes. Note by knot, nickname by nicked name, word by worry, feint by faint, this thesaurus rex is deadly. (Time? Your time, busy reader? High treason!) We're finished by the time we get to the finish line. And yet and yet . . . In for a shilling, in for a shilling. Already gone for expenses . . .] Bon bouc! and the hippie started to clap. All right now, everyone to the table . . .)

4. Hush, little darlings . . .:
What an embarrassing piece of Enguish literarture!

5. Mistral?:
Mistral: Magistralis ventus.

6. An exhibition of local talent . . .:
Talang! Talent does what it must.

7. Torna?:
Torna. Hungarian gymnastics.

8. The mystery of Edwin Drood:
The greatest mystory. See PILLOW NOTES 54, p. 522.

Fear of something felt and unseen? he translated hesitantly. Mm. Le vent, très fort! the Casanova blasted burlesquely. The wind, in revanche . . .[1] Go chase the wind.[2]

With its invisible fingers the wind flipped through the black-bound book[3] open there on the grass, at the base of the decapitated statue of a faun, quickly going over the dark pages.

Let the wind read it . . ., the Gasanova puffed. Let air read voraciously, aptly. Better and faster than so many profassional readers. So full of wind, and with that air of insuffliciency, always swelling up with their own inventions. And some even earning their bread with a pen,[4] unpenting impending judgments. Brutish pedagogues. Illiterate pedants of the comediet of criticism. Pesky judges of the literary tribunals. Clear out! Let the wind reread it.

Mist . . . Mistraal . . .,[5] the Bellman stammered, to finish reading this mysterious missal of a black kermess. Toorning, toornados! exasperatedly shaking his bell. Tong! Tang!

Ta-ling! Ta-lang! The belles of Saint John . . . The toweled blondine lasciviously inciting Don Juan Tenorio: I was your plop tart. Be my sun, ring only my bell. Talang![6] Ta langue! Give me your erring tongue . . . Talang! Talang! The belts of Saint John . . . Talang! Talang!

To long! Too long! Sherlock Holmes said, shaking his head. Turn a, torn a . . .,[7] bowing before the dark treatise. This codex will have to be decoded by Braille . . ., as he licked an index finger and carefully turned a page. Hmm! Ah! A mushy marshy romance, a debonairrative. Roman noir, more mysterious than the one about Edwin . . .[8] The Dickens! with a start he dodged the graze of a sharp shadow that melted into the woody darkness.

1. Arm! Arm!:
Yes. A book is a sort of missile or even missal.

2. Tachygraphic transcription:
I accuse, yes erotomaniac, I accuusoo Don Huan, of losing himself in my deep canyon with his paperback tome-o . . . Honorable discharge! He whispered in my ear: In koitu reservatu we'll understand almost everything, everything ambiguity, all the machinations, who was who. Tickety tack. Goo, son of a goon! Another conspiracy, guru! I neither tick nor click your cant ay. Rocking rolling rounding your round. Nor do I pierce your tube. Burst. Hi hi hey hey. Mu Mu Music de nuitingale for a go-go girl. For a clover girl. Do-re-mi, tuba concert. Where's my tuba, man? Think and fuck, wise humper.

3. Ki? (Who?):
Ki! Whoever it may be!

4. Who would? The Fairy Feller . . .:
Preparing to make his masterstroke. A coup de Dadd will abolish chance . . .: See PILLOW NOTES 55, p. 523.

5. The sublime narrow door?:
The door of Babel? Tock! Tock! knocked Don Juan with his knuckles on the door. (Tack! Tack! the deep echo.) Made of iron. En fer? Hell! Horn or ivory gate? D'y voir! Can you see anything? and he stuck his eye to the keyhole: SOPOR, painted in big white letters on a tall black open bucket overflowing with black plastic bags, next to a staircase badly lit by a dusty light bulb. Sopor of a summer night . . . As if to put you to sleep beside this door. Sopor? Torpor by the door. Get out of here.

6. Head, heart and hand . . .:
Hanging from the ceiling, in Albert Alter's studio, a head-glove (a black hand with a white heart) that always intrigued Milalias. The mask he would have liked to wear? Three erect fingers on top of the head, and the thumb and little finger limp, like ears, on either side of the white heart-shaped face.
   —It's just a reminder . . ., Alter invariably said when Milalias tried to wheedle out some explanation (: See PILLOW NOTES 56, p. 524).

Take in with care this bookie tome . . .,[1] a phantasmadam ((Madamu Butterfly?)) advised, as she walked, coquette on tiptoe, toward the rear wall, covering her face with a sleeve of her kimono. It has so many puzzles. Ay. Too many. So many senses, sensei and sensibility. So many sins, my son. A sin for each original scene. So many singosongs. Sing! Sing, ay! Old men and new masks, all around. Everything fits, everything changes, everything changes costume in that bottomless bag of countless stories. Hey! Hey! and she pointed toward the wall whispering incoherencies.[2] I'm leaving without even touching it, I won't brook his incapable book. Dance a cancan as you can around his incapable book till the inky Don Huan is KO. And when the cock-a-doodle coots, Ko-kokoro-koo! Kick-a-diddle-dad! then yes, lovers all to coitus without prickoition . . ., and she ducked behind a hedge.

Qui . . . Qui . . .,[3] Sherlock Holmes stepped back. Who?

Hush! the Joker shushed from the porch. Sh!

Merde! the drunk muddied cabin boy cursed, shaking the last of his bottle into his mouth. Finished! and he pitched it against the iron gate to the garden. Ding!

Did he? Didn't he? Dio volante. Dio or diva? God keep you. Dio? Sherlock Holmes wavered, peeping at the silent ax-wielding silhouette. What a night o' black.

Unalterable, his eternal ax on high, the herculean leather-bound woodsman[4] stood statuelike off in the center of a clearing in the woodsy garden, surrounded by shining eyes and crouching figures in the darkness.

Night, open up . . ., Don Juan breathed. Oh won't you open up? No?

Next to a narrow black door[5] sealed with an iron bar and padlocks, to the left of main entrance, two motionless phantoms kept guard.

A wretched buffoon wearing a hood in the shape of a black hand with a white heart[6] painted in the center.

1. Fang?:
Naturlich! Neturalment! As if he could still see it. That egghead, shining in the dark. A furrow divided the convex forehead in two, down to the middle of the big black eyebrows shaped like bird wings, wings unfolded over the square eye-grooves and down both sides of the bridge of a big trapezoid nose that widened over the mouth, an almond-shaped opening right on top of the chin. And spinning rapidly, eggspanding and eggsploding in a sudden flash. It changed into the egghead of Doktor Kot.

2. Herr Narrator sticks his rusk in:
Fine art is that in which the hand, the head and the heart of a man go together.

3. Servitutis note of Herr Narrator:
Lose loose words to gain . . . To loosen the tongue. Keep it up, prosevere. Prose it, proscriptus! Prosit, langoureux! (Carmen mordax!: La double méprise pour une prose prospère mais périmée . . .) Il faut proserpinailler sur une prose si proustitouée et prostrée (c'mon, don't prosternate yourself ((prosternere hostem . . .)) before so much proslavery ((prosecta tristitia . . .)) and so much prosepompeii! Onward aprostate proselytizer . . . Prospice! :) pour proscrire la traite des noires et des blanches. Loosened words, unleashed, to lead us to Liberature.

4. Sei tu? (: Say two! Two in one . . .):
Our behatted Menippus with hiccups takes a step in the dark toward the bed where she sleepwakes. Arriving in the wee hours, and to top it off, joking with his habitual Italianesque litany: Sei tu? Is that you?
    —It's me, it's me . . ., sibillant whispering. Me. Yours. Yeah.
    (So! Sei . . . trying to calm her in bed. Sei bella!)

And at his side, even taller, a phantom-fool wearing an ovoid mask, African without a doubt,[1] dusted white.

With heart in hand? Don Juan wondered as he contemplated the buffoon with the extravagant hood. With heart *and* hand! That one takes the biscuit![2] Or the palm . . . Hey, where . . . They vanished! Through the barred door? Like apparitions repeating vaporous appearances. Is that the door to the cellar? Too many mysteries in this villa.

Cree-caw. Qui-qui . . .

Who's crowing now? and he stuck an ear to the black door. There's a rooster locked in here. Muffled kyrieleison in this catacomb. What's that sound? . . .

Son son. Oui-da, rushed roost ruse. Labyrinthian abyss releasing voiced aspirations . . .

Finally! From behind the column, Don Juan came out impetuously, still caped. A faint thread of a voice guides me in this maze. Loose words . . .[3] Flayed phrases, mixed maxims . . . Let's articulate, recalling vaunted adventures . . . Lovers: amor, remember, vincit all . . .

El? . . . Him? Or . . .

Elle! She. Yes. Or he. Lover confused with lover in the nightiness of Saint John. Ba . . . belle . . . Elle et moi. You. Me.[4]

Qui-qui . . . ?! Who?

1. Qui-qui? . . .:
Who could it be . . . A man and a woman! All tongue-and-groovy: See PILLOW NOTES 57, p. 524.

2. Wimpish response: I'll gladly pay you Duesday for a yamburger . . .:
Rebuttal: flat tuber.

3. The gown must be of night . . .:
Evening gown: See PILLOW NOTES 58, p. 525.

4. Gloss:
Glossy . . . Glass . . .: See PILLOW NOTES 59, p. 529.

5. The goblet? A chalice?:
Face to face, framed on the page, their shadows are about to join in a kiss.
((Coup(l)e, adieu; je vais voir l'ombre que tu devins:))

6. Happy ending:
Escape into the dark. Smooch! Melted at last in a kiss. At the end, their kisshadow:

With amplification soon to follow.

Hey, I'm no ghost . . .

Who? Qui . . . ?[1] as he backed up. Who?

That's exactly what I'm wondering! Today Don Juan. And tomor-row God or the devil will say . . . I AM, laughing apopeyeplectically and theatrically spreading his arms and cape, WHAT I YAM TODAY![2]

That's what you call living for the day . . ., came the yawning reply, as if he had just woken up or perhaps was trying to appear nonchalant.

For the night, more like it. In short, lover with lover on the dark night of Don Juan. In the dark and secure. Shivering? You must be frozen in that evening gown that I brought you that evening.[3] Come! I'll cover you with my cape. In the dark and jealous. Let's go black and blend in an embrace. Remember the shadow of that imminent kiss?[4] If it be possible let it pass . . .[5] Drained? A kiss. Fainthearted. A kiss. A kiss as long as my night. Keep your chin up. Chin-chin! . . . Finally! Like that. Fading out? It will all clear up. At dawn. Post tenebras spero lucem. It's still night. Escape with me into the dark.[6] Cup-coupled? No. Is it time yet? No! Escape with me through the garden . . ., and they vanished into the night.

Escape into the dark.

*
* *

1. Bury the chuckolate . . .:
After a squabble on Fulham Road, Babelle and Milalias made up by going to the last session of the Paris Pullman, right nearby. La Voie Lactée! A riveder le stelle . . . Buried in the darkness, eating their favorite chocolate, content, they were really in paradise. Smacking and sucking away. Until Mr. Hsi-Men got the whim for Golden Lotus to discover La Joie Lactée (sic). Ici? T'es fou! But we're practically alone . . .

2. L'uom di sasso . . . l'uom bianco:
The white man won't find (he dresses in shadows, the night is his cape and he wears the mask of night) the black man this time. He took his leave, French-style, without even shaking hands . . .

3. Kámentator?:
The dinnerless Stone Guest and our stenographer-commentator must remain stoned. Let them stay where they are, the Stenorio and his brunette.

4. Tapage nocturne:
Ta-Ta-Tat! in the night, in bursts, a rattle was heard. ((From the Mayakovskian machine gun?)) Ta-Tat! The words are mightier than the sword. But factions speak louder than wordeeds? . . . Words that are actions? In der Tat. Indeed. Tat! Tat! Auf zur Tat! Enough chatter, let's get down to words! To a working language? Tat!: See PILLOW NOTES 60, p. 530.

5. More than marbled edges. I marvel at your marble book . . .:
Milalias had the habit of looking, from his Brook Green Phoenix nest at night, at the white marble book in the illuminated display window of the funeral parlor across the street. The marble book in marbled paper . . . Tough to chew. We'll dedicate it to the first larva that gnaws this novel flesh . . . The first larvarian book must be black as coal, but the last will be white, like snow. (In homage to the abominable snowman? . . .) A blinding white.

6. Se sentiste come fa . . .:
Ta ta ta ta ta ta ta.

Find the ones hiding . . ., a sandwich man with a bald turtle-head going step by slow step, walled between two black placards with the legend: ESCAPE INTO THE DARK, chewing a chocolate bar. Obscurum per obscurious . . . Seek, seek . . . Or no more. Let the cad bury the cad . . .[1] Put dirt in the middle. The cad face to face with his cadette. Look, look . . . The rabble finds the rebel?

Vis-à-vis, yes, we're still visionless. Another tête-à-tête. He kissed, I kissed, we nibbled each other. Yesterday with me, today with someone else. C'est la vie. Ourselves alone? Escape into the ark . . . Up you go. Upsa-daisy. Escape! Flight in the fog for lovers. We lost Mr. So-and-so with his mystic spouse. Find the horn and play it in the fog. Toccata and fuga. And don't touch the corpus delecti. His renovella will have to be reviewed by Braille and Morse Cod. When it's daylight.

The hippie Leda followed, twisting about with her swan, sniffing around the corners of the porch. Did they escape through the hall? Gee! Through the Eden of Ambushes? Hell! And turning to the bearded Bellman, who leaned unsteadily against a column: Gallop out of here, go great shakes, peerless posers, till the gong sounds your last hour. Talang! Too lone! laughing cow . . . Why aren't you hiding in the bushes like the Don and his Donna? Holy smokes! Or maybe they escaped, and she called at the black door, TACK! TACK! through there. Tack-a-ta. Hush.

Ta! Ta! the statue[2] of the Comendador,[3] Ta! Ta![4] with a marble book[5] open between his marbly hands, looking around absently, Ta! Ta! Ta![6] like a frankenstymied golem. Where is he?

1. Mr. Ta!:
The catarrhous great-grandfather newspaper vendor with a chronic cough . . .: See
PILLOW NOTES 61, p. 531.

2. The glass goddess again!?:
Syrup this time. They never cured that case of bronchitis.

3. Three birds with one stone . . .:
Or many more. Yes, all is possible . . . all is permitted. As assured—in Morse—by
the permissive organizer of this vigil. Tutto già si sa. Spreading the news in all
directions: W   N   E

                    S

4. BOMB FACTORY FOUND:
A big headline on the first page of the *Evening Standard*, that trembled over
Babelle's eyes (: full of night: are they shut?), who was stretched out on the
vanquished divan. Found?

5. Where?:
Anywhere in these parts . . .

6. Sack time! Let him have it in the ——:
Don't say it, the last intelligible word heard in the Tower of Babel, just before the
confusion of languages began. The chaos. The sack of Babel! The loot, to play
with and seal its fate.

7. Word's End . . . vociferucted a sweaty old bag of bones, in red rags and armed
with a scythe, carrying like a staff a street sign with the inscription: FINIS.

8. Kling! Kling! sor . . . a double-chinned eunuch with a jingle bell jester cap
clinked the cup with his cup. Spilt his vinegar of tears? Not much of a cup for such
an Apopokalypse. Sip. Slurp it up. Apococupalips. When the great magician
makes an evil gesture, Crux! this Villa of Marvels will fly through the air. Like a
bubble bedeviled (bubblessed! babel! O felix kupla . . .), like a bubble gumboil. By
magic and by parol is quite the same. A boule or bulla to shoot the bull!

Ta! Ta! tum-te-tummed a bent and skinny grampa,[1] Ta! with visor cap and graysy coat, Ta! teetering through the hall handing out newspapers, Ta! and upending a black bottle[2] from time to time, Ta-ta! followed by a muddy black spaniel. Ta! Ta!

Tomorrow's news! Fresh news . . . Drugs pornography and terrorism in an orgy![3] Today's bombshell:[4] Irish rock band accused of illegal possession of bombs! Arsenal discovered in crumbling Fulham mansion! Tons of hard-core pornography hidden all over! The Napoleon of Porn is arrested! Grand piano crammed with coke! Suspicious shadow sought . . . Well-known philanthropist Mr. Tod assists police . . . Mourning news!

The end in his hand . . ., and a Chaplinesque Hitler in black wire-rims raised his black hand in a Roman salute. Last hand.

Nazi! shouted the warrior in her African mask, and she launched her lance, Nazi! at his head. I'll give it to you right in your coco- . . .[5]

Holding up a placard that read THE END IS AT HAND, the bearded prophet was making his way through the crowd, muttering, osav la sav . . . ocas la sav . . .,[6] unintelligible words.[7]

London Apocalypse . . . Revised Version, Antichrist! words sniveled in syncopation by an extremely pale disheveled blonde in a whitish caftan, gold headband, and barefoot, before she drained her drink.[8] Ay, ay, London, a vast sewer. Poor London, in an hour it will be devastated. London will burn, erupting flames. Gog and

1. Loopy ash-blonde revealing visions apocalyptically?:
Sitting on the edge of the sidewalk in front of the Chinese restaurant in World's
End, that very spot! sobbing and murmuring incoherently (with an accent?) was a
skinny blonde with a curly mop of hair. Babelle and Milalias tried to understand
and console her. (She seemed to be talking about the destruction of London, about
being followed, she didn't know by whom, and she couldn't manage to remember
anything else, not even her name. Amnesiac Jehovah's Witness? Anonymous
alcoholic? Drug addict escaped from some hippie commune? From some
nuthouse? Were the police looking for her?) Although fearful and distrustful, she
accepted the offer to spend the night at the Phoenix nest. (In her dreams she
repeated many times the word ark. Or arc? Was she dreaming of the flood?) She
disappeared the next day, before Milalias and Babelle figured out what to do,
without a trace. The only proof that they hadn't dreamed her up was a book of
cigarette papers—with some numbers and letters, an incomprehensible formula,
scribbled in pen—left on the divan where she had slept.

2. Vendredi, Venus's day . . .:
Let me be your girl Friday, she implored him submissively. I'm sorry, Mandy,
today I'm Baron Samedi and I have a rendezvoodoo with Miss Sonntag. Let's wait
till it's Holy Thursday.

3. So what's with these sundry sounds, sonny boy?:
Some sound basis, the sound of some sung ending, saunter and lift your cup. All
dancing now to the sound of the Turkish march. Sound off. Dreams are dreams,
son. Szzz . . ., such a shame no one's left awake in the vigil. Szzz . . . Won't you
stay up with the Maestrino?

4. Three sheets to the wind:
Four sheets to the wind . . . Go on! Gone . . .

Magog will flee the Guildhall and they'll raze her with their armies. It's all in the book. Open and devour it. Letters—acrid!—rendering ventriculus acidus. Learning apocalyptic revelations via acrimony. Latent anxieties repressing various abominations. The sun will turn black and there'll be silence in the heavens for about half an hour. Oh! Luminous Antichrist returning very angry. Lordly. Alleluia. Rapid. Vanquishing. Aammen.[1]

Black Friday . . ., Robinson went by with his parasol of skins and his parrot on his shoulder, talking alone and counting the days on his fingers. That fateful Friday,[2] lewd and confused. Black Sabbath! Satyrday with a black mass. Black Sunday! although I'm not very sure. For me they were all black. And maybe I didn't know what day it was. Thursday? Did I count wrong? Add it up again. For what. You're alone, Robinsomniac, all alone, Robin . . .

Rub in, son. Rub in, Robin . . .

Son! Son! the great Turk sitting on the floor, nodding in sleepiness or dreams, Son! Son! hitting himself resoundingly in the face, and his turban of bandages. Son![3]

Blackmail! the robust-busted matron exclaimed, pulling a letter from her slip. Black letter! His last letter with a registered trademark. Made in Stain. A page, in the black! from his double-entry accounting book. A page of his black book . . . Dark sheet from his book of darkness. Put clean sheets on your Bedeker. Sheet! Strip the sheets of your last night. Sheet! I'll shroud it, darkening the old dawn. Sheet![4] Here is his soul . . .

1. This is my test:
Oy yoy yoy! (More, masochist. More. Mash. Put your head to the test. Hoo-boy! Who can see the test in this fog.)

2. Professor Moriarty!:
Careful with those slips, Professor Arthur ("Artie") More, alias Professor Moriarty. The renowned exegete of Mr. Reis's antiwritings became quite angry when he found out Milalias had given him one of his aliases. Mr. Reis, it's beyond me how you can bear the company of this idiot . . .

3. Bolt out:
No, no need to leave out le Professourd Bolt, admired friend of Reynaldo Reinoso, alias Rey tout court. Don't you think he has a little gnome's head? Milalias would say to Rey, as they left one of the Miltonian-Moratonian lectures given by Professor Bolt. Or maybe a nun-head!? Gnome-man is an island, moan head.

4. The blind man doesn't need to see . . .:
The scales will fall from his eyes, along with the thirty coins. La trahison des clercs . . . Better to live behind the altar than the plow . . . Where could that have come from? [From a postcoital conversation with Sònia Sorolla, in bed with Milalias. Telling him the sad story of her uncle the priest, Father Martí, who was blind in the last years of his life. And he ordered the electricity shut off, the cheapskate. A blind man has no need to see. Mirall? Also prohibited were mirrors in that house, tools of Satan to encourage vanity. And when he was a hopeless dodderer, Judas would appear to him. Usually in the fig tree. And the priest struggled with himself, shouting: I sold the Lord . . . A crucifixion from his church that he had sold, with the bishop's permission, to publish the parochial quarterly. Her Catalonian uncle . . . Moses Martí. I'm not surprised he left you traumartyrized.]

5. Help the blind . . .:
Still more? We're running out of larvatives . . . [Help the blind. Every time Milalias saw the well-behaved boy with his book-bank in some corner of London, he thought (his plaster double!) of his boyhood. The orphan-student sitting in the midst of the doctors of law . . .]

Sh! Test[1] of the ironic aesthete, Sherlock Holmes reported, looking at the black sheet with a magnifying glass. Must have a look with the aesthethoscope. Lapsus calamitus?

Happy lapse! a pale man in a frock coat, quite tall and very thin with sunken eyes sneakily snatched it from him as if by magic. Happy slip. Holy mackerel, Machiavelli. Oui, manche à manche. More and more. Amor and morass, and moreover . . .[2] All to get his secret brunette. And blacken her. The best spot of the worst scribe.

Blot out![3] and it's quickly snatched up by the gnome topped with a university mortarboard. Black out . . ., holding it up against the light. When the lights are out who will scrotinize the darkarkness of our souls? No light, but rather darkness visible. Obscuclarity! except for the Daltonian, Miltonian and egotistical blind readers who don't want to lend their ears. Or chip in. Or escort . . . Escoltar?—and he winked at the mammoth multichinned cleric with a muddy biretta and soutane, whose glassy lensed eyes were glued to the night-black paper.

El cec no necessita mirar,[4] grumbled the priest, covering his eyes with one hand. La venda for the vendor. The blindfold! And slapping about: I don't need any help! I'll get along, I'll bump along by myself . . . The Black Prince of Darkness is trying to tempt me with his evil tenebrous work, written in gargot. With his published monstrosity, a dark bulky balking archive of evil. Get thee hence! Erudition doesn't deceive, I'm stuck between a rack and a bard place . . . I mean a book and a lard pace. What a hoax! From Frau to Miss, always spinning the affairis wheel with his promiscuri-ousity. Per fer tabola rasa de tot, making a tabula rasa of it all, that Guy Fucks slowly burns up paperwards of his fornicantations on a blinding fiery night.

Humble and polite, his eyes cast down and closed, holding a big black book on his knees, a child in long pants sat on a stool, by which a sign read: HELP THE BLIND.[5]

1. Duplicated:
The Tristrammeling Tristramp got the bright idea of starting the sad night of strict
mourning with a sternebrous quote, nocturnote of black smoke? that was also the
facsimile of the first page of the black novel, Ah! Il fait noir il est noir le noircisseur
de papier! charred in the auto-da-Phoenix, O sancta simplicitas! and the illustra-
tion of diverse London blackouts at critical moments, Back out! as well as the
graphic representation of the squaring of the black circle and of a black hole and a
black dot in expansion, a business in the black! and of the original stain of the
dissolute or inkblot of the abominable alpenist of Mont Blanc, Inkubus! or of the
black shadow covering it all in the night of nights when it all looked black entering
the mouth of the tunnel or the wolf, the very blacknest of all! like going in the dark
room of Phoenix Lodge, obscurus fio! and already now as in the darkest hour,
Escape into the dark! the dream is about to conquer it, tableau noir vivant . . ., and
in his nightmare pose, with his decapitated head in his arms, go goy à go-go! he's
about to arrive at the black door and the black page that opened the impenetrable
night, Auto-da-Phoenix, and to enter the black synoptic square to struggle blindly
and gropingly, tooth and claw, with the bête noire of his dense nightmare biting its
own ponytail, and retaled nightly, with the snarcotized beast with two backs of his
dacapocalypsis of Saint John. [(Dark night? Pitch-black . . . I'd say we're putting
our heads in the lion's mouth, Milalias said, looking at the page burnt to a cinder.
It's not as black as it seems, sighed Babelle. Was she right? It will all become clear
in the end, when the sheet hits the fanfire for the conning man. Beyond the page is
the pale; and the dark hour will cower . . .: See PILLOW NOTES 62, p. 532.)]

Crotchety chorus of lackademics, hypocrites, inquisitoreadors, pariodical writers, etc., crowing and cackling around the black page: Chunk of the dark night from the Almaniac of Golgotha ... / From his black soul ... / From his sinner's cape ... / From the hood of the word-executioner ... / From the evening of the evening gown of his succubus ... / From the smoke screen of his auto da felonies ... / From a sinister chocolate ad in The Waste London ... / From a blackboard in a public pissoir in Holland Park ... / From a sooty nook in the Victoria and Albert Museum ... / From a window by night in the Brook Green hovel ... / From the door of his cellar ... / From the black body of his bête noire ... / Blotch from his double-entry book ... / An exotic Stain from La Mancha or a mangy Spain on his refutation ... / Eclipse of the tenebrous enervalarvator's black sun of melancholy ... / Faithful portrait of the melancholic meanderthal ... / Enlargement of fly specks from the Lord of Spanish superflies ... / Vitiated squaring of all the vicious circles of hell ... / Of the satanic asshole of the analytic prince of darkness ... / The shadow of his larverbs on a mourning paper ... / Treasure map on black foolscap ... / Scheme of devilish tricks camouflaged as a black animal ... / Carbon paper for his cacographic chalcomanias ... / Radiography in the darkroom ... / Graphic representation of his mental chaos ... / Of his ideas ... / Pornographic representation of a kiss in the dark ... / Shadow theater production of a manipulated kiss ... / Test for lazy late lovers with amaurosis ... / Melanodermic texticle of Monsieur Teste ... / Bad necrological note of false black humor ... / Mark of the beast with two backs ... / Table of the Laws (of the Talion) from the Brook Green synagogue ... / Piece picked from the black legend ... / Black list of his sins ... / Inkstain of the Lutheran fabulator ... / Introito of the black mass ... / Synoptic note of his sleepless nights ... / Detail of the demon or naked monkey on the black moon, at the doorway of his Brook Green den ... / Bad beginning of the dark joker's black novel ...[1]

1. Mad Ali?:

—Ken Norton broke the guy's jaw, Babelle said, and flung (disappointed? furious?) the newspaper over the bed.

—Cassius Clay, the clay idol . . . Milalias answered, sitting at his card table, typing away. —Idle.

—Sometimes you make such obvious jokes.

—Watch it! When I let my guard down, Little Flower, it's to catch them unawares and leave them KO'd. Poor Mr. Clay. What a story he has . . .

2. NEON OF FLAMES:

Babelle, ever intrepid, snatched it from the fireplace. Getting burned trying to squelch the flame.

—What are you doing!?

—We've had enough of burning and burning, of playing with fire.

When the ball of ashes was opened, all that was left was a toasted scrap of paper: EON OF FLAMES:

—That could be a good title for our next Inferno, Milalias commented.

3. Light flight, or escape hatch:
See PILLOW NOTES 63, p. 533.

4. Elle se soûle avec le soulier . . .:
Le soulier de Satan! With the devil's own soles.

5. Veuve de Clic-cote?:
Sham pain from Spain.

6. A cock and bullshtory . . . Wind up the clock!:
The timeless cuckoo clock of Great Hall, broken down and out of time.

7. Cocaine?:
An aye for a knight and a tooth for a toot. Crackdown on the Bolivian Marching Powder.

I am the great test! a blackened shadow-boxing colossus jab-jabbered, pounding his gloves against the wall. The heavyweight will be quillweight. Bantamweight, even. Ain't nobody can dethrone me, beyond my ken! he boasted,[1] sidling up to his shadow.

I! Aye! Humpty Dumpty swaying behind Sinbad and his flying globe. Assault! Pasch von eins. Double aces? The pair enclosed in their shell. Bosch . . . Kokoschka . . . Pasch egg, pascher, and happy easterlies! Ab ovo . . .[2] Ei! Ei! clapping. Ei! How about a big ovation at the end to egg us on? That's all we need. Ay! Leggero, leggy dancers![3]

((Before the cock crows in this carniwaltz? Nein! Nein! Nein! Don Johahn "Strauss" hid his head under the wing of his cape, Tarn-kappe! and lay under cover, plucked and cluckless in the foliage. Turkey in the straw. Haven't you read, Morgenblätter! the morning dailies? Already yellowed sheets . . . Do I contradict myself? I don't know. With this brouhaha and such a tumultitude under-standing is difficult.))

Meadnight, Mr. Midnight . . ., a Cinderella in rags drinking from a Bordeaux-red slipper,[4] attended by a horned devil in a Spanish cape who limped along (his left foot bare) bearing a bottle of cham-pagne.[5] The hands on the cock[6] embrace, and she laughed lasciviously, tickling the poor lame devil, who writhed, his tail between his legs.

All to cock . . ., and Merlin the Magician breathing noisily, cover-ing his nose with a fist. All to Cockaigne![7]

1. Who *is* that with the tam-tam?:
Connie "Conundrum" . . . Constanze . . . The Anglo-German who lived almost constantly locked in her room, in the nuthouse in Cleveland Gardens. The jealous Pakistan lover, a supermarket inspector, had the slave under solid lock and key. Bramah lock? He handcuffed her to the bed when he went out to make an inspection.

2. Meek fairy, betrayed by some hair . . .:
Your good fairy, "Lady Violet." Fay Mew. At first you called her "Belinda," mute but not immutable. She sleeps alone, poor Miss Mew, in her enchanted den in a Brook Green attic, walled off in the middle from the Phoenix nest. And so artistic besides, an illustrator of tales of gnomes and fairies. Such a discreet neighbor, with whom you shared the bathroom. Didn't you get annoyed when she washed her brushes in the bathtub, leaving traces of her magic dyes? The violetted fairy, Oh! Fay! The violet of her—her eyes, her hair, her hair! An artistic extravagance to dye herself like that? Deep down, you found her enchanting.

3. By a hair:
Hair stoke. See PILLOW NOTES 64, p. 535.

4. Bevy! of all the women . . .:
Bev . . . Beverley . . . "Kitty" Bev, we thought you were left outside . . . [Smoking dope with Genghis Can in the wheeled comet . . . In Bardo Loco's van, with the bard behind the wheel, flying fast through the snowy night on the way to a bottle party on Finchley Road while in the back Don Gengi Canine violated, or nearly, cat-eyed cat-clawed Bev . . .]

All to pot, the feline blonde in white stockings with garters, Tap! Tap! sprawled on the floor kicking out, Micmac! Pouce! against a Tom Thumb in sunglasses who struggled, flushed, to take off her boots. Tap! But baby it's cold outside. Pray, before I go to bed.

Tan-Tan-Tann, Tannhäuser! the Rubenesque blonde in a torn negligee thumping the tam-tam with her chains. Come come. Come. In a blink, entangled scheme-weaver, you came undone when you heard the password through the pipe. Three tum-ta-tums, Tan-Tan! two short ones and a long: Tann! To the climax forest of Venus, mount that mound, bush-beating tangler. An impressive round of blows! C'mon, give me the password (: Say tan!) and give me the last pa-rumpa-pum-pum. Tandem D.O.M. What? Constantly riding tandem . . .[1]

Lock up! and the fairy with violet shawl and hair[2] tugged a lock of hair over her left eye. Split that harebrain's hairs. You're always getting in my hair. Escape,[3] hair-hound, or they'll make your hair stand on end . . . chattering alone and still looking at her lock, curl-ing her curl around. Violet? Violated! Grape of the lock! Victim of violet passions. The game finished in the black, Sir Plume. Let spades be tramps! to put it in black and white. Chop on! and pare his Spanish quill, the better to draw that raped lock.

Ding-a-linga, dingo! Box lunch, boxer! gadding about in a blouse, her tail in the air, was a fleshensual blonde with short hair and cat eyes. Where is he? Did he vanish? In Bardo Loco's van, at top speed, they assaulted me. The hound and his pack of bacchantes, Bevy![4] pulling off my jeans, my second skin, by force. Tearing away, strip-teeth. The mad dog, God! howling with his pack . . .

1. Stake after mistake . . .:
Capable of betting her life. Even her gold teeth, that gambling alcoholic locked up in Dr. Kot's clinic through Mr. Tod's intercession. The night watchman Milalias performed a thousand little services for her. Such as taking her to pawn her trinkets. And, as a last measure, a gold crown.

2. So dotty. Dot your eyes and cross your tease . . .:
Only connect. Write your own reading. Go read/write the last message from Nostredame Asa: See PILLOW NOTES 65, p. 536.

3. Cast a new Castilian!:
To make it brand-spanking new, Sprankish! was the dubdouble intent of that runaway-tongued outcastilian. Discount the costilian, cashtrate it and castle it without getting rooked, sheik! mate! to sanction the strange and quixotic, widen and unwhiten the origenital stain on the plain. Mincemeet the mensch from La Mancha. [Stretch out the longuage, prop up the leanguage, resuscitate the lunguage, tie up the linkguage, unlock the lackguage, regauge the langouge, till all languages mix and meet their match.] Wax and wean and whip the Classtilian (a crass struggle with Engel-ish). Promiscreate your Spanglish with Englitch, make a merry can-cant to violetter and carnovelize your larvarious Londonjuan romances. Amyriadcan? Ink a new Inkglish!

4. Finish coronat—:
Piss off! FINISH was written in chalk on that big blackboard in The Castle bathroom. And our polyglot Finn MacCool, letting off steam after the break with Asa, began to write with his free hand under the resounding FINISH

FINIS

FINI

FIN

FI

5. Polstergeist:
The pillow elf. Or the fairy? They never came to an agreement about the sex of the pillow spirit that incubates our dreams. The fairy Lady Violet brought it to life with her celestial brushes.

6. The end? El fin?:
Elf in! The endemic folly of wanting to end. Finis coronat—No! The clown ends the work! Nothing begins or ends, everything continues.

Three . . . seven . . . Ten! and the old woman dressed as a Queen of
Spades handed a gold tooth, Tooth for a tooth! to the stupefied
devil in his wing chair. Where's that poor sorcerer's apprentice . . .
I'll even up the score with him yet. Tooth for an aye.[1] Sonnez les
matines. Sonnez le glas. Ay. Or as my paraphrasing dentist would
say: Annoy for a night, a toot for a truth.

Tacka. Tacka. Tacka. Tacka-ta. Tocka. Tocka. Tocka. Tóchka!
Lady Godiva tattooed with dots,[2] belly dancing in polka rhythm in
front of the wing chair. Tacka. Tocka. Tóchka . . .

Die out, with a toss of his dice the gambler in slashed sleeves, as he
tried to elude the claws of the harpies who pulled him along and
searched him facedown on the floor. The die is castrate.[3]

Endpoint, said a bulldog-necked priestidigitator as he took the dice
((.)), and hid it up a sleeve while opening a black missal. I'll make
note of it in my little book but I won't close it . . . I make a texticle
for you, but the gloss is no pussycat, it's more of a vixen conveying
another riddle on each fable.

The sphinx with the spider hands lifted her blackboard: FINISH.[4]
FINE. FIN.

Chorus-dancing in a ring around the great Turk, Son! the great
Pope, Son! and the big nun with her pots, Son! and Madamu
Butterfly, Son! and well-endowed Eve, Son!

Sway . . . nay jah, whispered Madamu Butterfly, reeling to a tango
beat. Sway nay jah me sown scene tone knee sooon. Ah Sue sown,
so soon. Don! Don! don Pen-done. Submissa jah joe.

Du! Ende! they screamed at a lively elfin who was dancing with,
and defeathering, a pillow.[5] Hey! Elfin! The end![6]

1. Chemystery:
NADA   (Nothing)   —He writes.
A DNA   —He changes.
ADAN   (Adam)   —He made.

2. Dead Man's Hand? Black?:
Ghostwriter of ghost words . . . The mysterious author of the mobile novel that the nomad copied randomly on his walks through WORDERLONDON. Words on the walls of WANDERLONDON. Operete bufa.

3. Now here? Nowhere?:
Everywhere. Are you waiting for Mr. Goddot? He'll arrive on the dot, at his appointed hour.

4. The famous dots!:
With time—and a pen—those obscure points will be cleared up . . .

5. The Great Pan?:
She has him by the handle in this pandemonium. He certainly had a swell time with the model Pippa, the light bonze. The Lady Reaper . . .

6. Dr. Rays & Mr. Rayos, another strange case of split personality:
See PILLOW NOTES 66, p. 537.

7. A hang-on hangover:
On the long march of Turkish Jingling Johnny . . .

Eden out of need? scrutinizing in perplexity the big white letters
(: magic formula?[1]) on the blackboard. AND DNA?

A black hand[2] writes on the wall:
GODDOTISNOWHERE.[3]

Pip! Pip! Pippa passes . . ., the squalid bald girl—her pubis
tattooed with black dots[4]—clasping the erect penis of a hairy faun,[5]
who obediently let himself be led toward the armchair.

I never could make out what those damned dots meant! boomed a
cavernous voice from the armchair. Driving me dotty . . . Doubtless . . .

Where's Mr. Rays? and the bearded halberdier from the Tower of
London swiped the lantern from the melancholy sheik à la
Valentino. Race? the sheik shrugged with a look of surprise.
Where's Mr. Reis! the halberdier now violently jostling the Bell-
man who peacefully dozed away, curled up at the foot of the
stairway. Where? Wo? and thrust the lantern in his face. Reis . . .
Reis . . ., the Bellman sleepysmiling stupidly, dazzled.[6]

If we, shadows of other shadows, have offended, close your eyes
and all is mended. Resolved or revolved. Turn over and dream.
Sleep, eyes, sleep a free dream, while I tie your dream to my life.

Szz . . . szz . . . szz . . . szz . . . szz . . .[7]

1. Le casse-texte . . .:
Pluck the clover . . .: See Pillow Notes 67, p. 540.

2. L'Aurora et le Jour naîtront d'une Nuit obscure:
What deep dark mysteries! Babelle au Bois d'or ment? Will you give birth, bel esprit? What a miscarriage of just us! Elle avait oublié que son vampire Beau Ténébreux à le Mal d'Aurore . . . Counting on the nightly tunes of the scholiastic annotator, the other one, to get out of this jam? Maître chanteur! And she, so confidently: L'autre est à mon service pour ordonner toutes les pièces du casse-texte . . .

3. In the latrines . . .:
Clover. Lover. Over! Troubadour, abort. From latin to latrine, Dung John. An ABC so baldly trypewridden. Lokus Solus! Ja! Toil it. / The old shit, disinterred! Make it new. Expound it! / He collected all kinds of rubbish. Dreck by the pound looms throughout his gleaning tower of Pisan Cantos, of his cultural allusions in the Wastelondon. (I'm hot, E.P.) Like he said to his Muse once in the WC, meaning perhaps that the bard vents his feelings in the water closet: At the loo, miss, eu acho meu paideuma . . . I found it at the loo, miss. The best cacograffiti. The best crafts, man, Faber & Fabler, in the toilet / Toilet, Eliot?

4. Russian ace?:
Salt of the Turkish earth. Osman the Great's last name was Tuz, I believe. Or twuz it Tuzak?

5. Sade the Simple:
—Sade . . . Simple? asked Osman the Great, flipping through the paperback *Juliette,* English edition, that the previous occupant had forgotten in Milalias's room. Could he have thought it was an abridged edition without Romeo? Yes, very simple. Sex, atheism, death-wish, enclosure . . . What's in a name? A bit of everything under the sun. Mary the Finn called Milalias the Marquis de Sade, because she thought he brought rain. Sade . . . Simple . . .

6. Sister Angie!:
Don't look black in anger . . . Clear siren eyes . . . Sister Angie . . . Angelic charity. The charitable nurse from Saint Francis Hospital, in East Dulwich. She sheltered the interpreter in her room in Tintagel Crescent. Your hearth is my castle, said the artourist. And he almost burned up the whole joint, smoking in bed, one night of black smoke. The foolhardy oaf was suddenly overcome by lethargy while waiting for her, smoking in bed.

Puck, leaning against the Saratoga trunk, was screwtinizing with a frown the jigsaw puzzle[1] laid at his feet: pack off! and he scattered it with a swipe of his hand. To stick it together, stick with it.

There's a piece missing for sure. Will it all come clear in the end?[2] Bah! he yawned, best to sleep on it. To slip, perchance to dream. Sh! The iron tongue of midnight hath told: Dong! Lovers all to bedlam . . . Already the witching hours. Yeh. Yeah. We're all speechless and shut-eyed. Or wide-eyed in the dark. We'll have to rub ourselves again with the essence of magic clover. The clover of the lover![3] Pick the cloverleaf exit on the night of Don John-a-dreams . . . Now begins the countdown for the final courtship, if they don't poop out on the party first. Masters, spread yourselves.

Hee-haw! the drunk reappeared with his jackass head, galumphing along on all fours over the checkerboard floor of the hall. My fellow mu-mu-meulogizers: the ace will not be reconstructed tonight. Stop your efforts. Bye, Sir Tuz![4] and he gave a butt bop! to the big Turk nodding sleepily szzz sitting cross-legged in front of an empty plate. From the Vedas and the Eddas to the vile Sade,[5] with a glutton, what a mock-torture soup, such a stomp through these woods. 'Round these parts. Such depths and heights of aims . . . Like in a mirror now from top to bottom but later face to face. Aye. Quit kicking it around . . . Bottom up! and he threw himself face down in front of the black door left of the main entryway.

Shih . . . Shih . . . Shih . . . Shih . . . Shih . . .

Tin! Tint! incensing the tumultitude with jingling, smoking them out, an ash-blond Franciscan sister in rough coarse wool and angel wings,[6] looking back angrily from time to time. Tint! Tintagel. Ignite! and she rolled her burning eyes. Ignitiation!

1. È fatta!:
It's done, the sorcery cut off at the source. Don't waste any more spit. Let he who wants to see, hear here. There's no one more blind than one who doesn't want to hear.

2. Masked Balls?:
Masqué. Bal. Land of milken honey. Honey is not for the ass's mouth? Keep swaying to the beat of the Turkish march.

3. The last circle?:
The ultimate vice-vicious one, supremely: See PILLOW NOTES 68, p. 540.

4. Mr. Rays?:
See PILLOW NOTES 69, p. 541.

5. The "Van Gogh"!:
Almost certainly. The Bardo Loco's van that carried out all kinds of transports and also transported, on the weekends, the Irish rock group Shamrock. The band of four . . .

Rondo à la Turk . . ., and he rubbed his eyes. Ephthah![1] Hee-haw! I is the other. I is he who am. What an ass . . . No! What a life this is. Another turn of the . . . Screwball! So drunk in this bal manqué . . .,[2] he stammered balancing his Bottom head facedown, leaning against the black door.

Shih . . . A door opened slightly (in the back, out of the shadows, in a sphere: a circular library,[3] with a round table in the center) and then a head peeped out, radiant,[4] the Alchemist in a plush black-and-gold checked cloak.

From the mansion of mysteries to the nth dimension . . ., words accompanied by a complicitous gesture by the magician or presti-digitator (dressed in a tux, topper, short black cape trimmed with red satin) with oiled hair and brown mustache, accompanied by a herculean black man (in baggy knickers and topped off with a fez) carrying a writing case on a silver tray. We bring writing materials . . .

Thanks for the message, Mandrake, and he shut himself in the library with a slam. Vlam!

Mr. Leone! Mr. Leone! a muscular Valkyrie waving prissily at the door of the vestibule, escorted by two bobbies. Mr. Leone!

Yes, potbellied Napoleon turned around phlegmatically and raised his champagne glass to eye-level. What is it, Amadeus . . .

These two guys dressed as bobbies want to come in and don't have invitations.

The more martial of the two (a polished policeman) pushed his way forward: Who owns that trashy van[5] parked illegally out front? There's a blond Chinese guy with a busted head in there,

1. Their initials:
S for Siran, H for Hal, A for Artie and M for Mick. Sham Rock . . . False? In the
confrontation or conjunction culminating the masquerade, they kept insolently
joking and confounding things. They were accused of causing the blackout. Which
they brought about in order to escape. The one who controlled the special effects,
the leader of the band, the Bardo Loco, alias "Mick Finn" . . . It was Hal, Siran
said. It was Mick, Hal said. It wasn't me, Artie said. Hal's lying when he says it
was me, Mick said. We artists are all liars, Milalias would say to Babelle.
Rubbish! Doesn't this seem absurd to you, all this explosives stuff and accusing
them of being terrorists, Babelle would say a few nights later to Milalias. Yes, like
all nightmares. There was enough plastic explosives in the basement of the Villa of
Mysteries to wipe London off the map. And to think the dance was going on right
above it . . . To the sound of Shamrock. The real activity was under the surface, in
the cellar. But the four acted dumb, said they didn't know what was in that black
bucket marked SOPOR. Yeah. Maybe it was left by the hippies who lived in the villa
before. You think so? [Sopor . . .: deep sleep? SOPOR, brushed on in white letters on
the big black bucket. In the depths of the Villa of marathon Mysteries. Like a bad
dream, the babelic masquerade of a midsummer night. Perhaps the disarming
corruptor of words wasn't accustomed to breaking down *dream,* madre mía! into
its most dramatic anagram?]

2. Mash note:
"Demolition in progress . . .," begin the lyrics of a ballad that Milalias composed
for the Bardo Loco. [Mash, masher. Milalias to his note: Mash!]

3. Lux? Black light?:
See PILLOW NOTES 70, p. 542.

4. Extinct, the night of autos-da-:
Ex-tincture?: See PILLOW NOTES 71, p. 545.

says a violin was stolen from him. And we just saw a man with a bag jump over the fence. We'll have to report it . . .

Astinomía! Palítsiya! Police! Polis! Polis! . . .

SHAM ROCK! ROCK! the four hooded hoods, shouting on the quivering stage, electroslamdancing, short-circling themselves with the electrifying music. SHAM! and with a jump they turned their backs (S, H, A, M[1]—one letter on back of each of their T-shirts) to the audience, which noisily cheered them on. And they took another big hop, switching places, with a war whoop: MASH![2]

At the same time Mandrake made a gesture (as if directing an orchestra or writing that final thundering shout in the air) and a clamor resounded in diverse tongues, Lux![3] when it all turned to darkness.[4]

((What happened? Nothing. Surely just the fuses have blown . . .))

Pillow Notes[*]

(Rough-drafted by Babelle and translated [with Herr Narrator's interpolations] by Milalias)

[*]At the end of each PILLOW NOTE the page and footnote number from which it derives is given in parentheses.

1. Pluck the Clover . . .

The roar of [infernal] music SHAMROCK! ROCK! crashed in rock-androlling waves up Fulham Palace Road and the breakers grew bigger.

RAVE UP, reddaubed on the rear door of the fully graffitied van [Gogh!] of the rock-an-rant group Shamrock, parked across the alley.

Rave up, read the cockney taxi driver, nodding assent. Wild party, man.

The headlights flashed upon three hearts on the massive black iron-knobbed door. And lit up the graffiti on a brick wall supporting wrought iron. BABEL TOWER . . . VILLA MARA . . .

[MARAME? . . . (Trashville?) BABEL TOWER? . . . (The villa of Babel, beyond hell's filth circle?) Till recently a babel of globe-trotters and hippies filled that Fulham ghost-house.]

O raw war! [Cold war?] exclaimed the taxi driver pleasantly, maybe trying to tell me Au revoir.

There it was, just as you described, the Villa of Mysteries. As you rechristened it, and not just because of those immoral murals hanging in one room. You'll see.

You're sure I won't get lost?

A T-shaped two-story mansion, surrounded by a garden overgrown with all manner of exotic trees like an abandoned conservatory. So many ghostly statues—nymphs, satyrs, gnomes, busts and torsos—scattered among the trees and underbrush. At the rear of the house, beneath the portico, a shallow round pond. And on the esplanade below, a semicircular greenhouse with a flat glass roof.

No, I couldn't get lost after your instructions. From the iron palisade entrance to the garden, I could already see the leprous-white façade of the Villa, the columns of the portico all patchy with peeling, flaking paint.

SHAM ROCK! ROCK! . . .

Dark fronds burst into thunderclaps, rocked by the blasts of music. There next to Bishop's Park, the libertine without libretto had chosen his lair for a night. [Home, Sweet Home . . . Romeo, o Roameo, when in roam, do as the romance do] I couldn't have strayed in that dark forest of Act One [Act of Darkness] of his shadow play. A monstrous party [Let's have a big party. Una gran

festa fà preparar . . .] on a midsummer night of Saint John.
SHAM ROCK!
Pluck the clover . . .

On the night of Don Juan. More masks for my Milalias . . .
[Face-to-phrase masquerade ball—carniwaltz of words: vertiginous transvestivals—uncensored baccanalunacy. Passions of a new
June moon, Midsummer Madness! in the full folly of Fulham, the
aweful all-manor of evils, cleverly decorated with cloverly motifs,
made cloverdant for the wicked *Clover Club* festivile. A monstrous
fest! Center stage is revelreadied to make an obscene! by movie
director or rather metteur-en-scène and pornographer . . . Bob up!
and down—he's gone and back again to create his phantasmalicious
apparition in the dark. Flash! in the pandemonium . . . Pleasures of
the flash. The dazed exhibitionanist-voyeur . . . Flesh bulb! In-
decent exposures . . . Poses, possessions . . . The organizer of the
orgy, our wide-angler, said everyone would participate in the masquerade party, le tout WONDERLONDON! everybody should
be there. Including Babelle (as Sleeping Beauty)? This was decided
last minute, without suspecting she would get lost . . . And then she
shows up, alone. Yes. At that madhouse, Fulham's folly! where
everyone who's anyone is.]
    Your night mask . . ., my little prince of darkness.
    [Beau Brummelmoth the Wanderer . . . Dark Knight errant . . .
Un beau diable ténébreux . . . A Beau Brummelancholic in the dark
. . . Sneakily surprowling in his cape of good hope . . .]
    And I? Didn't I come Sleeping Beautifully hidden in my evening
gown?
    (I?)
    [Yo-yo girl? Night! Our Lady of the Night in her night . . . Dark
lady, like night her dress her hair her eyes . . . Her dreamy eyes so
full o' night. And bright white. Like her face, whitewashed, almost a
Japanese phantasmadam. . . .]
    (I? My other I? . . .)
    Say! Hey!
    (I? Haven't I been recognized? Does he think I'm crashing the
party?)
    He stares at me, examines my invitation, again drills me with his

eyes and finally stamps me flop! on the hand and with a grunt offers me the surprise envelope.

(Ferocious phosphorescent eyes behind the dark hairy mask.)

There at the gate entrance, behind the school desk and chained to the ironwork, a wild Wolf-Man admitting each guest with a stamp on the hand: a black clover.

In exchange for the invitation, a little black envelope enclosing half an ace of clubs, each side jigsawed into a distinctive shape. Only two of the ace halves fit together to form a complete ace of clubs, according to the mimeographed cloverleaflets passed around by the broad-beamed Valkyrie with lopsided locks and slurred speech who greeted the guests at the door, by the handstamping ogre.

And at midnight each guy and gal would look for his or her half clover of fortune. The prize [for that lucky guy and gal, or lucky guys, or . . .—all manner of perverse transvestites mingled] was still a mystery, to be announced at midnight.

Pluck the clover, the matching club in this club . . .

Is someone signaling to me? Some phantom, shrouded by the garden's dark shadows, shunting a lantern on and off . . . [Ah! that shifty shady sheik who checked us, not so chic, mate, shaking us up with his Morse flashes flash! flash! from the secret perfumigated garden of torments and delights . . .]

Everyone who's anyone will be there . . . Partouze pour tous! Monsterparty . . . With all pomp and expenses provided by our lavish host Mr. "Napo" Leone. [Or perhaps the enigmagnate Mr. Tod.] You told me he always walks around with his hand pressed against his stomach, in his imperial soot-gray three-piece suit. [And Wellington boots? Of course he can!] And you speculated (another of your cheap London mysteries?) that his soft-core pornography business was the cover for other scams involving hard drugs. That he was mixed up with some secret Chinese organization [Triad?] controlling London's heroin traffic from Soho headquarters. But seeing him now with that get-up, three-cornered hat and all, the poor devil not as black as you painted him . . .

And I walk into this sprawling spree of the hall, looking from mask to mask amidst the swirling mob. (The giant black mask [: or lazy eight?] weathervaning from the ceiling.) Where were you hiding?

But to fully fill out that surprise party-game, blast but not least the clover-clubbing would soon explode, yessiree! livened up by a thunderous Irish rock group, practically the "house band," appropriately named Shamrock . . .]

Pluck the clover, clubs are trumps . . .

Then on stage four heavy meddlers screaming and writhing (hooded with red balaclavas), red clovers painted on their green T-shirts.

[SHAM ROCK! those blastard punks steadily stunning us, damning us with decibels, tirelessly attacking with their trillion-watt torrents, guitars trailing and wailing all over the stage. ROCK!]

And I, looking, looking . . .

[In search of pantomimixtures in the pandemonium of that house on the rocks . . .]

Bottoms up! Ugh, and that drunk dunce of a donkey thrusting a bottle in my face till I slugged it, braying Hee-haw! Hee-haw! and tossing his papier-mâché head till I gulped—ugh! what a wicked brew—it all down.

[A bitter swig? Acid?]

Pluck the clover . . .—the secret sign for us to recognize each other? [shibboleaf to recornize each other?]

The Joker's wild joke: that we would find each other in that Villa of Mysteries without knowing each other's disguise, hoping our two half-asses would be lucky.

How astute! . . . Lovers drawn together . . . Lovers are riddles venereally ambushed . . .

[Like a rapid video audition. The riddle required sharp vision. And hearing. The hallucinations became audiovisual. An image at each turn. Kaleidoscopium: the better to see visions with. Beatific dreambeats . . .]

Looking, looking, great underclover crook. Ah! the mask of night, nightdisguise of bosky darkness . . .

[Invisible, like the new moon of that dark soulstice night . . .]

But I had unmasked my mascara, white face revealed. Body unveiled, almost, in my vaporous wispy caftan, so vamp fatale . . .

(13.1)

2. *Metamorphosis in H$\frac{a}{e}$mpstead* . . .

Like a worm, in the end . . .

[Like a worm (Mask! Larvprins!), and his Swedish parasite barking and biting (Fäll! Fellatio!) nearly pulling off Agg! the satiny bulb . . . Stark naked and shameless. His well-mannered Monaco girl turning up her nose, Agh!]

At the end of day's journey, in Hampstead.

Stopping for the night with the long-legged pair au pair (such sexhibitionist miniskirts!), your two blondies Tala and Gisèle, the sweetest Swedess and the princess of Monaco, in the British Museum House of Hampstead.

[The night of the marijuanarchy (all gone to potpourri!), that Friday of metamorphoses (Samsaraband!): the permutating au pair shuffling like cards (grasshopper hop!). What a pair!! milling around the lower depths of Finchley Road until they raised their line of defense, twisting like a worm plucked by a foul fowl from Hades, Hell! in that Hampstead house of tamed shrews.]

When the squabble blew up in that smoky underworld den off Finchley Road, you lost sight of your comrade in quarrels, your cohort in crime, the starry poetaster Rimbaudelaire. With broken glasses and cut eyebrow you groped. Face tinged purple. Myopic groping, a blinded four-eyes (short two of 'em) on all fours. The police swooped in sirening Whoop! Whoop! Whoop! Stampede! Busted mugs and no sign of Rimbaudelaire. Looking for him in the direction of Swiss Cottage. Never thinking that since he knew the password [: "I'm in Clover"] he had taken refuge in the Clover Club . . . And the two blind guides, binding and gliding you along. Taxi! finally yielding. To Hampstead, which was closer. The owners, Gisèle reassured, would be gone till Sunday. Not a soul in the house save Lord Merlin.

[Lord Merlin?]

Hell! the screech assaulted you as soon as you entered, surrounded by shadows bristling with masks.

That crazy parrot Lord Merlin! an infernal buzzard who paraded about screaming Hell! and squawking his Good morrrning! at all hours. Cackling and clamoring the whole house through.

[The voice of his mistress, his echo, the same chirping accent. A Swede she was, and as old as her parrot, Gisèle said. Mr. Barnet, on the other hand, could pass for her grandson. Maybe he married her because she's an antiquarian . . .]

Tala, usually meek as a mouse, split her sides laughing at everything, rattling away in Swedish to the parrot. And drunk Gisèle, in panties, pantingly unzipped your pants . . .

And once again his harping Hell! as you couple with the cooperative pair au pair, swinging, swaying and sambasambanding.

Hell! Go to hell! trying to slap off the demonic parrot. It spread its wings, gasping, without releasing your shoulder. Hell! Hallucination! through a veil of blood. The hallucinations again? Your bloody eyebrow! bleeding again. Seeing yourself as a blind little Oedipussy? Wingflapping, strengthsapping. Your playboy scouts guided you, keeping you well lassoed about the waist as you three tripped to the bathroom.

Masks on all the walls. Hair-raising, horrifying!! And almost as many closed doors as in Bluebeard's castle. No, not there! The Venetian master bedroom, complete with gondola. [It's OK, Gisèle made clear, Mr. Barnet almost always sleeps below in the cellar where he stores his relics.] A gondola-bed!—love boat? floating on that bluish-gray carpet. Come on! let's gondola through the Baccanals of Venice! Another voyage of Sinbad, the Venetian Sailor. Floating in his harem with two blond houris. Badsin. Soft. Immersion.

[GondoLondendearing himself with the two au pairmissives, taking badvantage of the weekend ab-sense of the mansion masters. La petite mort in Venice port, orgasmoribound. Finnish to the death! And resurrection of the flesh. Night transfigured in the Venetian bedroom. Bits of circus magic and violent Swedish gymnastricks. Scrambled dregs of clothes, over easy around the floor. Fuddled frightmare, naughsty nonstrous nightmare, mixed-up meddle of a muss! Pederestrian assault upon that lasst hill, journey of Sodom and Gomorrah. Or however the hell you say it in Swedish. Good morrrning! ending like the mourning rosary.]

In deepysleepdream.

Greenwheezing asthmatic.

And suddenly a claw on your breast, Good morrrning! and a cawing in your ear.

Not that damned parrot again! Still drowsy, trying to wrench himself free from the two sleepyheads.

And when you pry open your eyes, a long-beaked mask in the vague darkness.

Blurred.

Red.

The painted harpy almost on top of you, plunging the handle of her cane [ibis beak?] into your chest.

(15.2)

3. Sudden Drop-off . . .

The pusillanimous myope.

[Puss!

Puss!!

Puss!!!] [Più sospiroso . . .]

Under the two crouching purring Siamese-en-scène.

By night all cats purrsue the same rapture. Like our persevering pair au pair, Tala and Gisèle, in that scatological jazz session in Hampstead.

[Hop! grasshopper. Pass a joint to the gressivehopper bounding o'er the mound of Venus . . . Doped: feeling the dope flowing, letting the grass grow under your feat. That hyperboarean beast still grazing in his Swedish soiree. Greased piglet in a rosebed, days of swine and ruses, and nights of wine and cyrrhosis. The impassive High Priest, patient and alienating, thumbing through a Swedish pocket Talmud (Flickordbok! Samlagbok!) while the two perspiring aspirants (Suga sugga, sugar! Take a walk on the wild slide) crouching so merrily, Umm! Agh! over all of him orally, spermutating back and forth till the dawn comes, good till the early moaning dewdrop.]

"Drop . . . Drop . . . Drop . . ." drop-forging the final blow, while his Swedish succubus vigorously sucks, and Tala, breathless and panting, passes it to Gisèle. And Gisèle, tongue hanging out, returns it to Tala. Two misslickers kneeling over the undonned doped myope.

Not even a drop.

[The same old sack race. And it's blow, blow, blow the man down. Always the same witch (which?) switching masks. Saddle up that nightmare that bites its own tail and licks its aporcalypse.]

Now he was falling asleep, murmutating mutteringly.

[Purring in heat, Snarkameleon! hunting the beast with two backs . . . That bedlambastard Chameleon in his Camelot! He sure Camelot—from bed to verse! Night and day in his Swedish soiree. Such a knightmarathon! On with the saga? (Narr-ate to us!) Yes, sally forth on the Farce side Saga of London . . .]

Hallucination in the darkness.

A glimpse of her?: at the foot of the gondola, in that scrambled Hampstead bedroom, about to leap. Foggy mist. Phosfloweressences. In the Venetian mirrors. Roses? Thorns?

A vision, in slow motion, of the secret bosky garden of torments and delights: On the prepuce a dewdrop trembles, about to roll down. Like a cat [good dog!: god dagg, dagmama!] she stretches over and [the magnetized lovers in a spherical drop in the Garden of Delights . . .] captures it with her sluggish tongue. Good to the

[Drop slug!]

Last drop.

(15.2)

4. Eden Bed . . .

On dîne dans le lit, hungry Gisèle had proposed. To eat in bed! with two blondulations in their drifting gondola. His floating harem! [Smorgasbord or orgasm aboard? Bordeli!] Eating spree in bed for the overfed pasha-king. With indigestion, especially after sweets . . .

Forbidden fruit . . . said Gisèle, as she brought out her breasts on a silver tray. With other fleshy fruits.

[Two pears hanging as she bends over. Golden downyfuzz apricots. And the ripe fig, hmmm! ready to burst . . .]

Fallen fruit. Rolling on the bed.

Fru. Frukt. Frukta! . . . he muttered, fruitlessly but sweetly playing dumb. [Woman. Fruit. Fear!? . . .]

Tickling and teasing, underhandedly, with one hand. And with the left, you held that Swedish pocket dictionary. Found while pillaging Tala's purse.

[He wanted to read Swedenborges in the arid original . . . The crystalline Labyrinth . . . Daedalus Hyperboreus!]

And with your free hand you pushed her head down.

[Just you keep it up. Just stick to your business, none of your priggishness, nose to the swinestone. Another sorbet . . .]

Man. Mana. Manna! . . . you kept gagging her against your belly while you recited, nose in book.

J'en ai marre de toutes tes manigances! and she sprang from the gondola, kicking and scratching. [Fully fed up with all your manipollutions . . .]

Gisèle . . . trying in vain to give her a spank. Wait. It describes a new way to . . .

Va te faire foutre, mannequin! Fuck off, asshole!

What's going on? A toweled Tala appeared in the bedroom doorway with a tray of rolls, looking—with her candid cold blue eyes—first at Gisèle who was picking the fruits from the floor, and then at the polyglutton, so self-satisfied there in the gondola, thumbing through his booklet and nibbling an apple.

Nothing, with his mouth full. Yes. We have no bananalities! She simply got fed up with . . .

Nu är det min tur, Tala said, leaving the tray at the foot of the bed. Now it's my turn.

(15.3)

5. Sinbad, Your Bath . . .

All right already. Let's see about getting this nearsighted nut into the water. This shishivering man clenching hands between thighs and humming hallelujahs with a mania for monody. Groping blindly without his wire-rims in the lively billowing steam of that immense bathroom, fleeing from the icy hands of the Scantynavian [: scalded poet fleeing from the icy rime, once beaten twice shy . . .] and the other blondulation. Finally they got a towel round his head and plump! dunked him.

A stammering turbaned simbecile trying to squeeze out of this diluvian dilemma: Sinbad's Swedish bath in that Hampstead house with so many bathrooms . . . and all bestowed with bidets!

At the end of the eighth journey, Sinbad dopesmoking in the soggy marijuaquatic bathroom, enveloped in steam with these two blond bombshells sucking on the fat joint, right to the end! passing it back and forth.

[Languishing in the tub. Like soporic soup! turning you dopey. Priaperly stoned. Sweat, cool off and back in the steam. Your skull it simply swirls, reeling with howls and squeals: (: Skoal!) almost exploding. Skratt! Haw! Cascade of cackles. The minnesinger with his reminiscences, Minnehaha! Minne haha! a spurting stream in the laughing water. Low giggle-whispering on the sly: run away! until everything transposes, metempsychoses, to moody marbly mumbling in the violate volatile tileroom. Waxing slackly, and slap! dashed into the wash cycle of the Swedish bath.]

Wilting in that swirling seagreen marble tub.

[Carousel! Gyroscope in vaporclouds. He sinblabbers away, burnt out, merely a maudlin Moor murmuring moonily his epic moronanic monologue.]

So the cooperative pair au pair Tala and Gisèle put him to soak, to choke! to rouse him.

[With effort and reluctance he leaves his lethargy . . .]

But now they're as silly as the stoned sailor. How you wasted them! [Sinbad the Soiler . . .] Gisèle's white sweater soaked, prudent Tala with that towel round her waist. [So dainty in that diaper . . .] They collapsed in laughter on the now black-and-bluebeard.

[That's right, our Moor armored with bruises (rapture, capture, wrapped!), roped and tied tight, bagged and gagged (too wrapped to rap). But daring to kiss! Boldly sowing wakes in the jakes. Double perfusion: thalassotherape with Tala. High! Gisèle the naughty shark bites that limp lure. Another sorbet. Full steam ahead, sailor! Such a vigorous rubdown they gave Sinbad the Sailor, the ancient marionette. The two vamps swab the deck, thrashing him with soap and sponge. With brazen breasts they rinse him; with brassy tresses they dry him. The Madamadeleines! United they anoint him all-overingly, embalming and basting him beautifully, smearing him smoothly with sweet salvos of saliva . . .]

The blondies splashing. [Another sorbet, Sire . . .]

His Swedish succinctress continued succinctly underwater. And brash Tala breaks the surface spitting foam [Thar she blows!] and hands over the controls to her pal Gisèle.

Arrête! Il est complètement soûl. [Totally blown away.] Bon, she sighed, encore un coup . . . and decided to try again.

Still another dive.
[Another mouth, fool . . .]
(15.7)

6. Mrs. Appleton
—Mrs. Apple . . .
[Appel!]
Mrs. Appleton, your landlady, suddenly there in the cellar . . . [of Little Venice . . . Another petite mort in Little Venice . . .] With wide eyes staring at the calendar still lifes [Cézanne's apples?] gracing the walls. Staggering so palebloodless, her round cheeks colorless. She looked paler than death standing there in the garden entrance. Mr. Alia! gripping her bloody hand. (A slash while cleaning the lawnmower . . .) You step forward to catch her wounded dove. Her white palm flutters bleeding.
—Mrs. Apple . . .
[Surprise cuts off the rest of her name . . .]
And she falls readily into your arms.
—Emil!
(17.9)

7. Flame of Living Love . . .
A winter sunrise in Piccadilly Circus, deserted at that hour: quarter after four says the cuckoo clock on the Guinness billboard. A weekday. Just a few fleeting shadows of cars on the moist glistening asphalt. And in the square's center, a dark unmoving hulk huddles at Eros's feet: a kissing couple, covered with a cape. On their right, red neon declares the Criterion's latest comedy, LONDON ROMANCES, and light sprawls from the door of the Boots drugstore. [Open for all those insomniaddicts . . .]
The two sway like drunks as they kiss, descending the stairs; both soaked, fondling each other. He, much taller, wraps her in his cape as they kiss. And still embracing, they suddenly collapse.
Now squatting on their heels, kissing each other next to a giant book (: a dictionary?) in the puddle of the last step. (But no, not a book: a gallon can on which one can clearly read HELL, in red

letters, under the yellow scallop shell.)

And they keep on kissing, shrouded in his wet cape. But oh! the smell of gas even gets in their eyes.

Fffflam!!! the blast blazing high.

Embracing couple cloaked in fire. [Shielded by the bonzefire.] A living writhing flame.

To the right, in the doorway of the drugstore and on the sidewalk of Coventry Street, six or seven paralyzed onlookers. Were they hallucinating?! The dark form crumpling up inside the incandescent sphere. The small group, horrified and fascinated, watches the column of smoke that twists around and encloses the winged statue.

The thick smoke was making me cry. Then a distant pain, like an anesthetic wearing off, and I realized that the two fire-crossed lovers were us. Fused in the embrace.

(23.2)

8. *Gaol-den Lotus*

That little Chinagirl hitched to old yellowed Fu Manchu too old to be any good anymore. Mumbling and shuffling around the Victorian mansion in South Ken—Queensberry Place! Growling asthmatically at the doors of those behind in rent, trying to collect. [Pay! Now! Pay up already . . .]

And the Chinadoll almost never left her conjugal cubbyhole, so dedicated to her sewing. [A woman's work is never done.] Except at night, when she went up to the first floor to take a bath. That stirring scent infusing the whole bathroom . . . [L'odore di loto . . .] What a coincidence: whenever she went out, you would sneak in for a washup. Miss Unsociable would become insatiable! Yes, lotus-eater. As you did with so many, you gave her a special name: the Golden Lotus. [Uff! Every Jack has his jilt. The dissolute Mr. Hsi-men would soon find, God save the king! the accomplished accomplice for his dissolution . . .]

She let you enter, without saying a thing. Not a word.

[Silence gives license?]

(35.3)

9. In the Garden of Mirthly Delights, with Alice towards None . . .

Another bosky summer night in the park cemetery of Saint John's Wood. Another night of delights, the lights . . .

Playing blindman's buff among the gravestones? The Temptress groping, arms outstretched, frenzied white hair and bare feet. Her sheer white dress now stained by grass and dirt. Like an apparition.

And through the big high windows of the mansion across the way, the nonstop jabberrocking of the Satyrday night party.

[Will you, won't you, will you, won't you, won't you join the danse mockabre?]

Did she go out for some air? But now in the pose of someone possessed was she laughing or whimpering? Sitting spread-legged in the grass [Alice clover: alysicarpus vaginalis] by a grave, murmuring mad mumblings. She wasn't the least bit surprised by your furtive presence. Stretching her arms to you? The breeze carries her laugh, or her hiccup . . .

Hip! Will you undertake to take her? Gravitating to the grave? The spell of the abracadaverous night. Shivering? Poor frozen thing! Ice her tongue, her kiss too. French kiss, on the qui vive! Are you out of your mind?

Alice, you thought her name was. Her feline purring—her nails so sharp . . .

Almost sunrise already, and still gravestoned. Suddenly a wave of anger, she's a furious madwoman swingly wildly and scratching you, Scram! and biting you. Beat it! Get out of here! Screeching hysterically. You left tail between your legs, still stubborn. Fearing you would be taken for a graverobber?

At noon, you and your hangover returned to the spot. Nobody, not a soul in sight. Just trampled grass beside the grave. A yellow-mossy gravestone, on which one could read only a name: *Alice.* No! No, the C transformed by two scratches into a V (: with her fingernails?): *Alive.* Alive!? Alice, where art thou? where have you hidden yourself? Did the earth swallow you up? No one seems to have seen her, but you keep looking for her.

(35.7)

10. Miss Grey-"Hound"

That doesn't run in the family . . . Pure lust!

Remember her rapidity, her avidity, her ass like a grey-hound's. . . ?

So worn, weary and bleary-eyed she looked that day standing alone with her elbows on the balustrade, absentmindedly not-looking at the luminous green waterfall in that Duke Street bar. [Through the emerald eye of the cataract you could see into the deserted underground parlor: a redheaded waitress with a show-boat bust alone at a table, reading *The Art of Loving*. O vide! O! Video meliora . . . Our avid Divo would let that novice of Venus study her little book well, and return to the Duke days later to make her recite her lessons, to carefully cross-examine her. I'm weary of theory, what matters is practice . . . the works of that love artist must wait, like so many others, for the next larval meta-morphosis. Let's return to our greyhound . . .] Just taking a break from shopping on Oxford Street. Her face says something to me, you said, before doggedly accosting her. You would recognize her much later, in that Goyesque capriccio tacked to your Chinese screen. Miss Grey-"Hound"! Ah yes, it's a dog's life. She with her puppy love for Mr. Cann, an alcoholic Canadian who hounded her. At least that's what she said, and quickly showed us the marks. Shortly after entering her house [in Portman Square: If I lived there—said Milalias, impressed by the style and comfort of the apartment—I would write all the time in Portmanteaux words . . . Already ready to live in this Portman expanse, to express and expound at Miss Grey's expense . . .], not far from where we met, she slammed down an enormous shot of whiskey without stopping to breathe. [To chase away the dog-day heat?] Mr. Cann drives me to drink. No, he's in Toronto on business now, and then she told us in detail about the teethmarks. We must have looked incredulous. Sprawled out like that on the divan, her silken dress up to her waist and . . . Good canines, commented Milalias, very seriously. When we saw his photo in the bedroom, he added: And dressed up to the canines . . .

(37.2)

11. *Alpenglow*

Stationed at the card table, facing the fire, brandishing the ancient ever-clogging fountain pen.

[The fountain pen, fons et origo, fountain and origin. Penna matta! Crazy pen! he exclaims as he wets it. Source or sorcerer? The write of spring!]

Inkrivers with wordcurrents [eddy-fication] in a papyrus Tower of Babel . . .

[He was sweating ink, no, really blood! in his trance-fusions and cruise-fictions.]

Blot. Blot. Blot . . .

[On the spot! Read your blotouts: Lis tes ratures . . .]

Tack. Tackatack.

[Attack! A duel with the abominable paper, white as snow. The alpenist luring him, allaying him, tackling the paper blizzard. Wielding his pen or Alpenstock, family relic, Careful! Watch out! unleashing an avalanche of nightmares. (Please read note 4 on page 290 when time permits.) Until the antediluvian fountain pen, fons et origo, sagely spurred on, Steady, Steady! releases its lifesap.]

Flicking the pen, plump! another inkspot . . .

[Alla macchia, macchiavelino!]

Every inkspot is a chanson de Gestalt . . .

(37.4)

12. *Ink Battle*

You smashed it against the wall that night of hallucinations in Phoenix Lodge.

[Scribble to the limit, leave nothing in the inkwell . . .]

A black shadow stretching itself along the wall when you sit up.

[His Inkubus?]

Stubbornly struggling with yourself—boxing with your shadowplay?

Crash! with all your might you hurled the inkwell.

[Didn't Martin Luther throw an inkwell at the devil? An inkspot tranforming, like a kaleidoscope. Bad luck, evil lurking? The Shadow knows! Ectoplasm? Some incongruous stain?]

You spot it when you get up in the morning. There at the edge of the hanging garden of postcards and tinted photos: an ink clover [Ja! Kleecks!] on the wall. Planted between the door and the garden of images, as a black momento of your fit.

[Trifoglio mal stampato. Chè schizzo frenètico!]

Chuck the clover on a midsummer night's apocalypse . . . (37.5)

13. Mensch from La Mancha

[Meet the Main Maimed Man from La Mancha. And the house a mess. Tune in the English Channel: Man from . . . Ain'tcha? No angst in his pangst. Manx? Manchu? Fool! Let's speak plain chaostilian, just plain, from Casteel, where every man takes the reins, and every man meets his match. Go through the millenarian mill, Milalias . . .

Castile Mills of La Mancha, where every mensch . . .

Maliberische Spiele! La Mancha also means The Stain. Matchless: only one Original Sinister. (They don't make them like they used to.)]

Stains on the plains . . . Live crazy, man, and die sane [dye stain?], a donkeyman quixotically riding fearful and faulted . . .

Sullying it all, so very macho . . . [Dat mean mannish boy!]

Just like when you were giving it to her, your private Spanish lessons, more or less, to Dr. "Ana List" Anna Fleck. Continual Annamorphosis. The sexagenerian snowcapped doctor, Frau Doktor Fleck, able to change to a deliquescent nymph . . . Your freudulent alienist, whom you altered with aliases. Doctor Lakan, because she played along while you submitted her to the blank sheet test.

[Blank? The shame old sheet?!]

Your anal Isis, without veils . . . Pounding out those intensive sessions of gelded Golden Age Castilian in her sterling arty apartment in Golder's Green.

"Morir cuerdo y vivir loco . . ." She wanted to read Quixote in the language of Cervantes!

[Servant test, Sir?]

Bit by bit you finally deciphered the spots of your original test for two.

[Test-a-test? Answer, Monsieur . . .]

Ultimately a white stain on the sheet, the map of your only fatherland . . .

(39.5)

14. Mandrake the Magician

One of Milalias's favorite heroes. He insisted he had known him in flesh and blood, or rather in skin and bones, a shadow of his former self, in Dr. Kot's clinic, back when Milalias worked there as a night watchman. Mandrake the Magician passed his powers on to me, said Milalias, and he dramatically waved a hand . . .

[Man . . . drake? . . .

Silly goose! Chop it at the root!

Mais, Madame, il n'y a pas de Racines, he's a rootless rababelaisian. He hasn't roots, only routes. And there's nowhere to grab the no-holds bard. He has sexiled himself in swinging Wonder-London. Always changing. Mandrake waves a hand and he's gone. As he says: The more I'm mute, the more I mutate. After changing, transmutating, mutatis mutandis, he makes an exit. Through the cape he escapes from the cloak-and-dagger comedies. Although finally one would say he's somewhat sexhausted. Off the record: his succubus sucks out all his judiciousness (: elixir of love!) every night . . .]

And with all he tells me, Milalias said, I'm going to write his memoirs someday. The Memoirs of Mandrake the Magician.

(43.2)

15. Black Bess . . . tial!

—Bess! Bess! . . .

[Baise!? Baisse!?]

[Bess viol . . . beso profundo . . .]

Debating in dreams again with your night mare.

[Bess kisseeking Dick Tourpin in the dark? Bessmooching—Bess . . . tial!]

Appearing when you least expected it (yesterday in South

Ken . . .), the blackface vagabond bessmirched in her bess rags, giving you the evil eye.

A slip in the bed. Another one bites the bait.

From trap to tramp, such tricky satrapy! striving to slip away from the alcocholeric witch who jinxed you in Islington and appears to you daily on the most dangerous corners of The Waste London, then reappears nightly in your nightmares biting their own tails, quelle sale Tourpine! domimating you and domasticating you at full gallop, saddle-straddling, riding you to that Witches' Sabbath . . . Black Bess! Bestial night mare from your herd of nightmares.

(47.1)

16. Nina ("Menina") Pott

[Mrs. Pott, oh yes, pot of gold . . .]

Nina, with a kind word and a bone for a starving dog.

[His stomach was growling all night, roused by ravenous hunger: doggedly grinding out gastric juices like a poison. Eyes jerking left and right to meet meats. A starving vagrant misplaced amidst forbidden fruits, voyeur or stomasochist? in that fragrant bordelicattessen of delicious delights.]

Till he was about to collapse from inanition.

[Devouring it all with your eyes, in the Gourmet Department of Harrods, mouth watering . . . Torments of Tantalus? So much savory sausage saucily suspended there, tempting and unattainable. Stomach cramps stewing, from the salami salon through the pastrami palace, to the halls of King Salmon. Pantagruel getting delirious in Harrods Food Hall when suddenly out of nowhere he runs smack into the sweet petite appetizing flaxen-haired lady (: over the neckline of her biscuit-beige cashmere sweater look look how lazyswing her peerless pears) laden with bundles of abundance: dishes fit for a king, choice morsels for any mortal. A stumble and they fall. Pantygruel detached himself from the embrace. How clumsy of me, I don't know how I could have been so awkward. Hamming it up?]

Sso ssorry! Pan'o'gruel stuttered. I beg your pairdon. A thousand apple-apologies. At her feet obligingly recovering cans—lobster bisque!—caviar pâté roastbeef French cheeses a thousand and one delicacies—almost fainting from weakness. Please, allow me to help. I'll carry these. Mrs. ——? Pott. Rather dry at first. But she let him carry the bags to the car, a cream-yellow Volkswagen in a Knightsbridge alley. Yes, inside. Is he really passing out? She, frightened, sounding the horn. Please Mrs. Pott, he managed, I just need to eat something. Maybe from his extreme hunger she guessed he was Spanish. An unexpected open sesame! and she decides to take him to her mansion to eat. Two stories with garden, near the West Brompton cemetery, visible from Nina's bedroom. Death sleeps, but males need meals: first to the kitchen (with a large table and antique pine sideboards). Only in dreams have I eaten like this. [Be quiet and eat, dip the lobster in the curry while the charitable Mrs. Pott reels off her curriculum vitae: she owned an exotic clothing store near there, in Fulham. Divorced from a Scotch-English diplomat who was stationed in the Middle East. They had a sixteen-year-old daughter in boarding school in Lucerne. (Lucerna! Luzerne! Milalias's face lit up . . .) She had lived the best twenty years of her marriage in Beirut: cocktail parties in one embassy or another till all hours, wild dances in local dives, picnics with music on the beach, "dragon" regattas in Saint George's Bay . . . But her great passion was painting, she thumbed through all the art books she could get, and she even tried to be a naïf painter.]

This Bordeaux surpasses even my greatest expectations. Don't you want a drink, Mrs. Pott? Nina. For short. She confessed that her first affair, sweet mysterious adultery, was in Beirut with a young Spanish diplomat. His name was Juan and he looked just like San Juan in the painting. [In the Chicago Art Institute.] Spiritual nobility in his face. Melancholic Spanish eyes, well-defined sensual lips—the lower one rounded slightly inward—and curly black hair. The revelation: as he sat on the edge of the bathtub, a pink towel over his thighs. Saint John the Baptist, before the bath. And the Velazquizzical Don Juan, on the other hand, christened her "Nina Menina," saying she had the profile of the famous Velazquez Menina [Doña María Augustina Sarmiento] who offers a red clay vase on a tray to the Infanta Doña Margarita. So many Velazquisite evenings. You are the only person in Beirut, he flattered her, with whom I can speak of *Las Meninas.* [Cede to my infantasies, and let me be your seeder of Lebanon.]

With the scruffy aspect Milalias had in those days, Nina Menina found herself thinking of Menippus the cynic . . . But she allowed him to stay, bed and breakfast, in her house. But just until Saturday. Three more days!

—Poppy returns on Saturday . . .

Poppy came back from vacation and soon after they began the private Spanish lessons (: Mom, what good is this Spanish? she protested at first, when she still didn't know) and bel canto. And pop songs. Poppy, pretty poppy . . .

(55.1)

17. Mr. Teste Posits a New Example

I'll tell you this new Ovidian metamorphosis as you told it ((barren October: time of lean kine. With no translation work in sight, I wandered constantly from place to place to avoid being cooped up at home or falling into the waiting claws of Mrs. Appleton. At the far side of Maida Vale, in an open field, some little savages were playing soccer. As I went by I heard their bellows and grunts, Pass it! Over here! in Spanish. And it occurred to me to butt into their game (they were sons of Spanish immigrants, a dozen ten-year-olds) to kill some time. The field was quite muddy and I had the bad luck to slip and Hey! one of the little ball-kicking beasts kicked one of mine. I thought I would faint from the pain. I'm not cut out for this running around, and tail between my legs I retreated to Little Venice, limping to the left. It was getting dark when I buried myself on the couch and fell asleep right away. I woke up screaming with a horrible pain and must have passed out. I guess they carried me unconscious to a hospital (Saint Mary's in Paddington?) because I woke up in a room occupied by unconscious or sleeping patients. And suddenly in the half-light I see an imposing bald man in a white frock, his eggish head shining in the darkness, feeling his way through the room with a folder in hand. He was Humpty Dumpty and you at the same time.

—Monsieur Teste? . . . —What? I jumped, startled. —Señor Teste? —Huh? —Relax. Everything has gone miraculously well,

he told me in perfect Spanish. —All we had to do was remove it . . .
and from his frock pocket he pulled out a chicken egg, white as a
ball.

—What do you think, doctor? Do you think this dream shows a
Dioscuric complex?)) to the hardboiled egghead doctor.

(61.6)

18. The Kangaroo

Ken ("Garoo") from Australia. Kendy . . .

A kangaroo's small head and long paws, and she hops when she
dances the cancangaroo. Milalias met her in the wild wantonness
of a Saturday night party. But as usual it boomeranged for her, and
by the end she was worn out and weeping.

She lived in Kangaroo Valley [Earl's Court, which you might
also call Kangaroo Court . . .], perhaps, like so many of her compatriots, to keep up the illusion that she hadn't completely left
home.

[One must travel far to love one's home! . . . The family: small
and far away . . .—one of orphan Milalias's mottoes.]

She had left Melbourne, a good husband and three small children, because domestic life was death to her. [Enough of house-
chores, if a man's home is his castle, a woman's home is her hassle.
Tired of "A Bex and a good lie-down, dear?"] She came to the
London smog for room to breathe, and to choose to be or not to be:
a woman. She explained this to hubby in a long letter [asking him
to explain it to the kids and keep her posted], also telling him she'd
found a job in which she could finally find herself. She was a typist
for a lonely-hearts magazine [which had printed her story about
cutting the marital umbilical cord . . .] and had quickly made
friends.

[Half-friendships, kangaroo courtships lasting from one party to
the next, fortunately not lifelong . . .]

Her understanding husband sent news punctually, and, above
all, the snapshots. Especially of Thomas, the youngest. [Her kid
Tommy, the most photogenic . . .] Then he sent her one last letter
and cut off contact forever. Tired of awaiting the return of the
prodigal mother?

She began to drink—to forget?—too much. She would cry in her beer at the Kangaroo, and then thrust her hand in her bag [a marsupial purse!] to display the familiar photo.

She was just getting a breath of air at the window, hiccuping into her Foster's, when it occurred to Milalias to console her. Milalias has—I think—the calling of a [freudulent] confessor . . .

She was tearfully narrating her life and works when the moment came to dive into the depths of her pouch. The photo was the last thing Milalias expected.

In color:

So pale, shrouded in his white casket, the little dear.

[Hubby had sent the funeral picture of Tommy with the double inscription that Milalias could barely make out: Mommy left for the Old World; he for the next . . .]

Milalias turned white as the little angel in the photo. He didn't see what he says he saw. Did he see another dead child? Another resuscitated Tommy? [Enough of this Tommy and mummy stuff!] And while he was clinging to the Kangaroo, they both nearly fell out the window.

[It would have been quite a fall, four stories, from that window overlooking Redcliffe Gardens.]

Just a few days ago Milalias ran into the Kangaroo again, in the Earl's Court station. She was fine and funny, Milalias said, and seemed to be getting along well because now she's a typist for a feminist magazine. And among other things she told him she'd never marry again for anything in the world but was thinking about having another baby.

(77.5)

19. Puppet on a String

Once again I pick up the thread of the narration, where and how Milalias left it:

Remember that story of the cord, the record—Sursum corda! Lift up your hearts—the almost priapic malapropism via Adèle Weiss, the Swiss Mozartean stewardess enamored of her Don Juan–William Tell father—così fan tutte!—and slave of time, it was already late but it's never too late for fun and after two bottles of Beaujolais and two hours of family romance [incest: the game the whole family can play] we're in seventh heaven standing in this cellar kissing each other at the foot of the bed, No, not now, and besides I've got an early flight, aw Christ that's just my lust but handsosome Spanish fly buzzing under the minimal skirt already open that Swiss or Suez canal center of our conflict, and in that delishlippery gush the little string: *Le Tampax,* she moans deeply and me hard, of hearing, hearing only the plaintive flow of time and I force myself to confirm it in an echo heartlessly philosophal-lically tolling with anguish, Ah oui, le temps passe!

[Les fables ineffables . . .]

(91.6)

20. Miss Columbine

Note tacked on the folding screen: "The faun waits for his fawn in the Dove, this afternoon."

A burning June noon.

When I arrived at the Dove you had already flown the coop. With Miss Columbine [lovely dovey with white dress and pamela picture hat, preening and sunning herself alone, neckline pulled so low . . .], whom you'd picked up there a little while ago.

A manicurist aspiring to be a model . . .

I bet you put one over on her, crowing about Bob the camera genius . . .

And while I was watching the tidal return of the Thames from the terrace . . ., you coyly coaxed her back to her pigeonloft there on King Street. As she hopped from bed to bed [Miss Coolumbine, as that Myriadaptor would christen her . . .] she chirped that her roommate was about to arrive. To speed you up?

(97.7)

21. The Farce of Destiny

Tarai, kara, tarai . . .—he often hummed in the bathroom. Milalias liked it so much that we all knew it by heart, that Japanese ballad . . .

[That haiku by Issa (1763–1827) went like this:

```
Tarai / kara          (A tub / from
tarai / ni / utsuru    a tub / to / one moves
chimpunkan            noisy fuss!)
```

All the profound sense or nonsense of human existence, Milalias would say, enclosed in a half dozen words. From the newborn's washtub to the tub in which the corpse is washed for the shroud, recapitulating the mysterious and incomprehensible movement or trajectory of a whole life. The coarse final word of the haiku, *chimpunkan,* "gibberish, fuss, hubbub," especially pleased him. He claimed that in order to augment the gibberish and the resounding force and anger of that exclamation he could double it into *chimpunpunkan,* since *punpun* in Japanese means "irately" or "angrily." The sound and the fury . . . (A compound pun for a pungent punctilious pointmaker . . .)

A thousand times Milalias tried to translate that intense Japanese poem into his leprous prose. It would fall apart. For example: *From tub to tub we pass: quel tour de farce!* The word *pass,* he tried to explain, was in this case charged with meanings . . . But perhaps less was lost, or more was passed, in another translation, "The Force of Destiny," with the word *tinny* meaning "cheap" or "hollow": *From tub to tub, a tinny tale: destiny!* Perhaps these two versions could become one . . . But what he really liked was to sing softly the original Japanese, the music of Issa's haiku. Without isagoge, or preamble . . .]

I can see him or hear him as if he were here right now behind that door, Tarai kara, soaping and splashing as he hums, tarai ni utsuru, to various rhythms, till chimpunkan! and down he plunges.

(113.8)

22. Mr. Cantor

[Immoderato contabile . . .]

Whose name was not Cantor, not even Eddie, but Singer, as in sewing machines. Cantor was Milalias's nickname for Mr. Singer, the accountant.

Mr. Leone and Mr. Tod counted on his accounting, which he accomplished with remarkable ability. As did how many others?

Shortly after his wife left him, he developed a compulsive mania of checking and rechecking, from dusk to dawn, each and every account.

[Rerunning his Sisyphean cipher?]

He spent entire days shut up in his room diddling numbers [the secret life of numbers . . .] and one morning his landlady, the ever-askance Mrs. Askew, found him catatonic, his nose buried in a double-entry accounting book. He had covered even the walls with numbers. The floor was strewn with papers arabesqued with mathematical squiggles.

He had once confided to Milalias that the accounting was merely to pay the rent and for more than twenty years, ever since he had received his degree in mathematics, he had been preparing his magnum opus on the famous mathematician Georg Cantor. From zero to infinities . . .

[Singer, your numbers are running out . . .]

(115.5)

23. The Lost Ear

[Lost on the lawn a long time ago.]

The pensioned poet Rimbaudelaire liked to show his earnest ear. [The tip of the earberg, or what remained of it: a rosy wrinkliness.] Like when Milalias tried to get him to pick up that ugly gal in the Piccadilly Bierkellers, or in the Trafalgar Square joint.

You're in East Beerlin! Milalias bubbled when he saw him sunk in sad silence [his expression both fierce and timid], stoutly bitter [I dream, staring into my bier . . .] in that bearish boorish bedlam of beer and smoke and armpits [Ça schlingue rudement ici! It stinks in here!], and shouts and songs sung badly [Pull yourself together . . . Close your ear to this roar . . .] at point-blank range. At the least provocation he'd box anyone's ear . . . At just the right moment, when he was sufficiently drunk, he would act like he couldn't hear the au pair or tourist or on-duty waitress. Ahem, I beg your pardon? tilting his head and lifting the camouflaging locks of hair to bring the wrinkled hole close . . . [Bière . . . Trou . . .] Getting some morbid pleasure by shocking a woman? If someone asked about the earlessness, he simply said it was a war wound. [His war decoration . . .] Same with the hooked hand. Once over tea in a French café in Queensway, he told Milalias how it had happened. [By sticking his ear where he shouldn't. Snooping, the f-f-f-earless little devil.] He was crawling in the garden outside his house, not far from Liège, when he found something strange half buried there. And off he flew, the object still unidentified. [La gerbe épanouie en mille fleurs, it burst like a thousand flowers.] A souvenir the Americans had forgotten.

At least they're giving you a pension, old boy, Milalias said, consolingly, when Rimbaudelaire finished his childhood war story. Only an hour earlier they were two imperfect strangers standing elbow to elbow reading ROOMS TO LET notices on a bulletin board near the Earl's Court tube station. A bump led to the encounter. —Soggy. —Vous êtes français? —Non, belge. [Slow, thick pronunciation.] And so a simple apology [Le Belge est très civilisé. Also the Spaniard] started a tenacious friendship.

(127.1)

24. A Man Called Osman

In the Notting Hill Gate police station.

[CARACOL. A snail? Turkesque argot?]

Oh black day! face-to-angry-face confrontation with chased Susanna, who demanded reparation. Stop! Stop! Milalias parapetted, trying to contain the grand Turk, who was offering his last pounds to Susanna. That would be bribery after fondling . . . The Turk's confusion grew by the minute but fortunately his friends and interpreters from the Queen's Park boardinghouse, Milalias and Rimbaudelaire, came to the rescue. Mending fences with the infidel, stubborn as a scapegoat, who barely understood a word of English after three months in London. There's been a little mix-up, officer. Let me explain. The great Turk is innocent. The giant who stands before you, the aforesaid Osman of the World, is completely harmless. Only once have I seen him lose his temper, and then only a tiny bit, when our landlady Mrs. Page, in spite of his repeated requests, continued to fry his eggs in bacon grease. He faithfully adheres to his faith, and no matter where he is he bows toward Mecca. Once I asked him if he's afraid of getting the direction wrong . . . Solar show on left, rrright? Anyway, it so happened he would be returning to his country in a few days, so to say good-bye and send him off the right way, this friend and yours truly took him to a Greek restaurant in Queensway. Groggy after food and drink, he decided to clear his head in the Bayswater steam baths. Without realizing it he entered the women's section. An embarrassing situation . . . Isn't that right, Osman? Talking turkey with the Turk in an improvised argot. [Each escargot slowly makes his own argot —a Milalias motto.] In the end they let him go. After the voluntary payment of five pounds to Chaste Susanna, for breaking the make-up mirror and other trifles harbored in her conclusive handbag. (143.8)

25. The Cup
—The cup!

He woke me up with his shout. I thought it was about last night's drink. We were sharing a shot of gin in a Bayswater pub when all the lights went out, and we went out to see what happened. All was dark, a citywide blackout. [Black Friday in December. Darkness falls again on London, because of the electrical workers' strike.] Just the firefly glow of car headlights. So we strolled about, en-chanted by the dark. ((ESCAPE INTO THE DARK, his slogan a few years later. Shadowy ad [that some simple simian liked to modify: APE INTO THE ARK] on so many London walls.)) And he, glass in hand, corrected his Spanish refrain: ". . . the night is the dark cape of poor sinners . . ." You said a mouthful! because it started to *pour* and we had to hole up in a phone booth in Porchester Gardens. I suddenly recalled that Saturday in February when we got ac-quainted [in the beautiful biblical sense], click! blackout in your quarters and neither of us could spare a quarter to get the lights back on. In the dark again, listening to the pellets against the windowpanes. Covering me with kisses, a vampiroguish rake driven crazy by lipstick-and-gin kisses. And before I could put him in his place he lifted my skirt. Are you nuts? [T'es fou! . . .] Not here, someone might come in, maybe even the . . . He heard me the way one hears the rain. Soaked. Stiff. No, the lights didn't come on in time. Then the glass crash! ah! smashed to bits at our feet.

—The cup! . . .

It was another one. Of blinding brilliance. Found in a little market in a dream. Portobello? Much smaller, more like Islington. And in a few hours [everyone likes to fulfill their dreams] we were there.

It was.

Silverplated. Overly. Among plates jars cups clasps buttons spoons powder-puffs brooches porcelain eggs a cruet etc. scrambled in that stall in Camden Passage. Would you believe it was real silver in that trinket-trap. The silvers miss and I, hi-ho silver plate and I . . .

And while I was being entertained by [the silver-tongued yenta —erased by the translator] the Jewish antique dealer with her silver-streaked bun and a Star of David at her throat ((when she saw me looking at some old picture postcards of the Crystal Palace, she told me that as a child, before the war, she used to play there)), such a genteel woman, I suddenly felt him jammed against my ass, sliding his [quicksilver] hand into my cape pocket . . . My hapless cooperation, cups and robbers! in the copping of the goblet! I couldn't cope with that caper . . . [Cornered that time.]

Then he grabbed my hand and practically dragged me towards Essex Road. [And sex rode . . .] Exulting with his trophy. He wanted to baptize it, buy a bottle of wine. A cheap grape of wrath, as usual. Then sitting on a bench in Islington Green, in front of the war memorial, he made me drink a toast and bottoms up . . . [To the lees.] Until alcoholic bums [Dregs of high society . . .] showed up, also wanting to toast. [A booze, abuse . . .] At least our favorite bag lady, "Black" Bess, didn't show up that afternoon. Night was falling and the damp was chilling us to the bone. We could barely see the mast of the memorial now. As if we were on the prow of a ship, a ship-cloud isolated in the triangular garden. Glass and bottle sitting on the low wall behind us, next to the dustbin. And me still carrying the greasy bag of chips that stunk of vinegar even more than the wine. An invisible monkey-man came from behind with a whine, wah! for the wine. Of wrath. Milalias raised the bottle in one hand, threatening, and his glass in the other. Provoking him: chin! chin! . . . The chimpmanzee madly smacked the cup against Milalias's mouth with a slap. [Many a slip twixt ape and lip.] I screamed when I saw the blood flow. They vanished in a flash. And he reassuring me at last yes we'd get the hell out of there. He had a split lip. The handkerchief already soaked. Whaddya mean, I don't need any hospital! his loud voice resounding, just the two of us there. Then in the bus, downcast the whole way, without a word. Pressing the handkerchief against his lip. You look like Rimbaudelaire . . . Finally he let out a laugh. And we went to finish off that round of drinks in that tavern at the end of the world, World's End. By candlelight, because we were back in the united kingdom of darkness. Near us a circle of veterans recalled in chorus (the ladies the loudest) the blackouts during the war. Aye, Aye, Aye, I like you very much, in the dark . . . And they sang their whole repertoire. Then the notorious tenor joined in too, off-key. And amused himself by pouring our pint of beer into his tin goblet. Which he forgot at closing time, leaving it perched on a wall out-side the pub, near the door. After drinking a toast to the old reaper with scythe on high there over our heads, on the pub shingle. Finis! Phoenix! standing straight with final cup held high. We started to run when we saw the 11 coming, a little after eleven. The cup! we're already at Fulham Broadway. All in good time . . .

But in a few days he began to fabulate about the silver chalice, what a Te Deum, recounting one of his recurring dreams.

A shining white Lady Godiva appearing in a clearing in a dark wood [La coupe sombre . . .] bearing a silver chalice that gleamed like a glowworm [yes, a ghostly larva . . .] yielding a blinding light. [Perce, valeureux, les ténèbres avec ton verre sacré . . .] And the nudist deposited her cup over a tomb. And the cup turned into a head. [Kop! Kopf!] And the head split in two. Two faces. And these two dark faces turned around, facing each other. The lips puckered up as if to kiss and then once again the luminous cup flashed. [Il y a loi de la coupe aux lèvres . . .] From the treetops a black rain fell, like ink, filling the cup. [Let's forget and beget again the tale of the Holy Grail . . .] The cup changed form again: a black bulk, wrapped in a cape, lifting a cup. [Salut les copains! Don't throw sand in my eyes, Sunderman.] The dark man of cup, cape, and hat split in two, two shadows of two communicating vessels. Two black faces about to join in a kiss. [The universal joint . . .] Now do you see it? he asked me excitedly, trying to reproduce

those elusive shadows on the bedroom wall. By candlelight. [Still
in the dark.] Didn't you see anything? Nothing. In the darkness.
[Make light of it, Fiammetta!] He didn't know what meanings his
precious little holy gray dream might have, but he was busily writing [Bore on, Robert le Diable, and begin again the tale . . .] the
story of the kaleidoscopic cup. [Coulpe, adieu, je vais voir l'ombre
que tu devins.] Cop it off . . .

(163.6)

26. *Steel Bird*

[Each person carries his bird around his neck . . .]
The bit of twisted metal in the shape of a spread-winged bird
[wild dove? falcon? alcatras? Egyptian vulture? lanner? Roc of
Morocco?] that the stewardess "Zoraida" wore around her neck
on a little silver chain. Amulet against accidents—a fragment of a
smashed plane!—that a pilot friend had given her. Her talisman
against aerial anguish and vertigo. And she lost it that rockandroll
dawn in a Piccadilly disco. That same morning—a Friday!—she
had to fly . . . And she, super-superstitious, stepped into the plane
as if climbing the gallows.
[May your bird be with you . . .]
She told us that long before the storm [: over Iberia's bullskin],
she never stopped touching her graceful heron neck . . . while
forcing a frozen smile upon the passengers.
[In the deep skyblue, insecure Zoraida, flustered, watching the
blur from her steel bird soaring in the azure . . .]
And praying.
[Your bird of pray, in Allah's hands . . .]
She knew something was going to happen, she told us. Even
before boarding the plane. When they had almost reached Casablanca and she had finally calmed down, the landing gear refused
to function. Circling around over the sea. [Gliding among cotton
clouds.] With her heart in her throat. Terrified till terra firma.
[Take four birds and quarter them . . .]
Forced landing at the Casablanca airport. Whew, white as
death as if she had just returned from Hades. Panic-stricken in the
clouds, she had sworn to comply with the wishes of her father, who

never wanted her to fly. She was as good as her word. [Chickens don't fly . . . you teased.] And so she decided to change to a ground position. Around that period you met her.

(189.6)

27. *Bird of Ill Omen?*

[The white albatross at sunrise . . .]

Gliding over the sea with its wings spread wide. Huge and white. An albatross?

An old bearded mariner spots it there like a figurehead on the prow of his tattered sailboat. Like a monkey he clambers up to the crow's nest. He shouts, hurling harpoons. The other rag-clad sailors shout and throw rocks up at the bow.

Swift and flapping it escapes toward the yellow disk [: a brass platter] on the horizon. Its wings block the sun for an instant. [Sol?] Like a gold coin at first. Now sinking into the sea, like a copper coin. [Maravedi?] The bird dips, thrusting its beak under its wing to retrieve the reddish coin. Flying high again and turning redder and redder, it dives like a ball of fire.

And wakes you, bam! with a jolt in the bed . . .

[One of the stewardess's dreams (: premonitions) that the blind acrobatman didn't know how to interpret. In spite of his freudulent metaphorisms: Life is but a dream, Sigmund, and dreams make men wake hungry . . .]

When she told you her dream, her voice still sleepy, you didn't know what to say . . . In the morning, in the morning, OK? half-turning toward the wall. Too pigeon-livered to pigeonhole it?

[That cardinal-point knight in gale: bird of omen, Nemo. Tough beak to crack that rara avis . . . What bird of pray are you muttering, corraptor pollyglotton, in your pigeon-English lark? Another baked Aristophoenix in the furnace? Another hornbill under the cape, ancient nightmariner? Dreaming, an albatross? Languid airs relaxing volant albatrosses . . .]

It was falling like a ball of fire, like a meteorite . . .

[Miserly meaty meteorite . . . Crams it in the piggybank. Feed the meter, or rite of the winged moneybox . . .]

The stewardess Zoraida would go on upset and obsessed with

her high flights . . . Until you give her your version of the aversion!
(191.3)

28. Original Sinbad

One of the longest yarns spun by my Milalias was that of the
Second Sinbad, remember? that started on the eighth journey with
the requisite shipwreck. It was really the never-ending story
because those thousand-and-something implausible adventures
were stretched out interminably and Milalias never stopped adding new episodes and chicaneries, improvising as we pushed the
wheelchair of the Queen of Queensberry Place through Kensington Gardens. She was his most insatiable listener. And then?
What happened then? And then what? . . . like a little girl.

Imagine the story beginning where the famous tales of *The
Thousand and One Nights* left off. The relay race would begin.
After years the faithful listener Hindbad grew tired of hearing his
protector Sinbad repeat the same stories a thousand and one
nights, of being just one more in the claque in the merchant
Sinbad's palace. So one night he decided to leave and risk his
own adventures. Upon leaving Baghdad to seek his misfortune,
Hindbad was already Sinbad.

The tale would have to end with this Second Sinbad, old and
rich, retired in his own Baghdad palace, telling every inch of his
unbelievably tall tales to a group of guests. And suddenly, at the
climax of the story, he spies a shadow behind the lattice there at
the end of the room. The shining eyes of an assassin, perhaps, or a
robber? No, a little scallywag was crouched there listening, mouth
agape and eyes big as saucers . . . The generous Sinbad the Second
invites him to eat at his table and listen to his stories. And so it is
night after night, because Sinbad grows fond of him and is even
prepared to adopt him. Allah, who has granted him such wealth
and the most beautiful women, has not yet given him a son to
inherit his fortune. Maybe Sinbad exaggerates his adventures?
And one night the young listener feels the itch of adventure and
decides to emulate his patron.

[Navigare necesse es. Vivere non es necesse . . . That fable of
successive Sinbads is the true story of Spanish emigrants returning

from America with riches to that little town on the Atlantic coast where Milalias grew up, and there in the port they told their adventures to a ring of rag-tattered kids . . .]

That night of the full moon, leaving Baghdad with his bundle of belongings on his back [Where's your bag, dad?], he thinks he sees the silhouette of the old insomniac Sinbad standing in the highest arched window of his palace, his hand raised. As if to bless him or say good-bye? And he thought he heard him say: Good luck, Sinbad . . .

(191.4)

29. *Fat Fatima*

The plump Algerian we picked up or who picked us up that Saturday in the Trafalgar—another Trafalgaraid! Skirmishes between the Chelsea fans and Arsenal boosters. Arsenholes! Kiss off, Chelsea!—the enebeeriated loudmouths hurled their sharp insults nonstop. Provoking and threatening with badges, scarves, and poised—at least for the moment—beer mugs. And gangs taunting each other from opposite sidewalks on King's Road. They were all set to trammel tumultuously through the Trafalgar door. But in the pub, crammed body to body, not another soul would fit.

The houri and the Valkyrie at the back of the bar.

Her friend, a blond beauty in white boots, had slipped off the dance floor with an orangutangoist. Never to return.

Now alone by us with an anxious face, biting her lips, and when she heard our French chatter she asked us for a cigarette. Une gitane pour la gitane . . . With that scarf circling her strong swarthy face, silver smile, and a skirt patchquilted from bright scraps, she seemed a real gypsy.

A bit too solid for my taste, but a pretty face with those dark eyes of a surly houri . . . [A whole-wheat loaf is better than none?]

A scar or tattoo on her chin that she tried to hide with makeup.

She worked in a Queensway bakery, filling her hours of need. As that crumb would put it. Milalias's jokes, each time more insinuating [For the best in bread . . .], revealed which side his bread was buttered on. [. . . or the breast in bed!]

Since the pandemonium was heating up we decided to get out of the pub before the next Battle of Trafalgar, to have a drink [a Milalias euphemism] in the basement of Queensberry Place: the cave of Alibi Baba . . .

It was pouring and we were absolutely soaked by the time we reached the Sloane Square tube. (Milalias's antediluvian umbrella developed broken ribs so we tossed it into the doorway of another pub . . .) And then another long run, gushrushing! from the South Ken tube to the hideout.

The three of us shishivering around the tiny gasthmatic flames of the heater. Best to strip down to dry off. She hesitated, wringing the circle of her soaked skirt like a washcloth, until she saw me peeling off my pants and sweater. Then I came gliding back with the towels—not too dry either—and a blanket to wrap up in.

Milalias in boxer shorts, feigning a boxing match before the timoorous Algerian girl who reluctantly rubbed him. I'll leave you two alone for a moment, to make some tea—ingenuity for the ingenue!—in the little kitchen on the other side of the patio.

I wondered what could be going on. Laughter and panting protests? Caught by surprise? Long silences of kisses? Raptures of delight? Waiting, still frozen, a little longer. And then I tiptoed closer. I almost couldn't see you two in the reddish shadows. Suffocated on the sofa? under the blanket.

Submissive at first as you removed her blouse: her loose locks over her mamelons. Letting her hair down! Shaping her shapeliness, I need you! you knead her, massage her, assuage her, moldingly meddling in that shifting moving mass, you go mad with those moist doughy mounds, but even your bold movements can't unroll the towel so well knotted at her hip (and still imploring, calling her the Virgin of Fatima!) until at just the right moment I sneak up from behind, at the ready. A cry of surprise? It's OK honey. And I begin to lickcaress her earlobe, dropping down past her neck until I trip across her nipples, blackberries, tongue tip skimming them in circles. Go on! Oui! and then she relaxes and sinks still deeper in the sofa and helps you untie the towel and closes her eyes and throws her head back clutching my hair pulling me to her face as we swallow each other breathlessly [a reversible kiss] listlessly letting you open wide [Pair o' thighs regained!] her Herculean columns.

(193.8)

30. *The Flemish Flamingo and the Walloon*

The skinny one with flamingo legs and the chubby gal dancing together, Begin the beguine! pressed tight near the jukebox of that clandestine Soho bar. Damascus. [Damascus of dames . . .]

Tes belles belges! Belgian dykes!

And their compatriot Rimbaudelaire, elbows on the bar, foaming beer. The last thing we need tonight! [To fall among a tribe of tribades . . .] Leave those two cockteasing chicks alone! . . .

[In the original: Ces deux allumeuses, ces garces allume-poules . . .]

Their agile tongues fascinated you, viperishly kissing, while caressing with intertwined hands between innerthighs. They eyed each other naughtily as they slid by. Had they noticed Rimbaudelaire's Belgian accent? Or how horny you were?

But it was Rimbaudelaire, that sexist pig, who first broke the ice and opened fire:

Monsieurdames: Ici, il y a des femelles. Il n'y a pas de femmes.

Sh! Shut up, wouldya? The masochist already beginning to bawdlerize. Firing up another of his quarrels? Fortunately no one heard it or understood it. [In his sloppy slurred speech.]

You'll see, the jester winked at you, you'll see that Big Charlie is always right. And he stationed himself, swaying, before the two Belgians bewitched in their dance.

Il fait beau temps, savez-vous? Nice weather we're having, eh?

And sure enough, they burst out laughing.

[Didn't Baudelaire say in *Pauvre Belgique,* Rimbaudelaire's bible of masochism, that Belgians laugh at anything?]

And you took advantage by grabbing—each flame with his Fleming!—the lean flamingo dancer, stiff as a broom.

(197.6)

31. *Sweet as Candy from a Baby*

Sugarsweet American with angelfood hair. And how you caramelted over your treat!

Lollipopsicle-licker . . . You ate her up with your eyes . . . slowly from head to toe. Such a cool cookie. Stretched out to her full length, your majorette, letting your hot buttered libidinous lips tongue-baste her. Coyishly cloying: strawberry lips, raspberry nipples, juicy jam lips. [Glazed fig . . . Sweet country girl, candied Cunegonde!] Blond cotton candy mound of Venus. Creamy thighs. Sugarfrosted sweetcheeks . . . Until [Have your candy and eat it too!] she's engorgingly impaled [candy cane!] and sweetly surfeited!

O honey O honey O honey Oh! . . .

[O horny! From honey to ashes . . . O honey! O Hun . . .]

Candy delighted. [The sun in her eyes, eyes the color of California grapes.] And still on her lips the flavor of all those sticky Turkish delights.

In the basement of Little Venice, reclining with other succulent pastries, after dinner and desserts in Sahara City, with peristaltic odalisques and everything.

You invited her and she wound up paying for the exotic dishes with her American plastic.

Please! Please! she insisted, clutching the bill, while you rehearsed your Napoleonic pose [Ah belle élégance . . .] in slow-motion search for a nonexistent wallet.

But only a few hours before, she was an unknown tourist in flowery knickers right in front of you at the Central Post Office posting a telegram you couldn't help reading:

Arrived safely. Everything great, except food.
Love. Candy.

That telegram is libel . . .

She turned around, surprised.

Gastronomic calumny . . . [Vermicella della calunnia?] Allow me to show you the culinary asspectss (since your X-ray vision had lingered long enough on her tight tush in silky knickers), the Lucullan succulences of this Babylon in which all the world's best cooks and chefs are found.

(I guess you weren't thinking of your Wimpys and Kebab Houses and Fish Bars . . .)

For Christ's sake! scratch that "except food," at least for now. OK?

The Hindu in the pink turban was losing patience. Let the next people by!

You with your propaganda about this Wonderlondon. Give me the opportunity to help you discover the most refined pleasures a London table can offer.

Your theatrics amused her. [Histrionic host! as always . . .]

And besides, she really was alone and hungry . . . Her chartered roommates, students from La Jolla, California, were sleeping off jet lag in their Bloomsbury hotel . . .

Suddenly you were lecturing her about the pleasures of a well-laid table.

And those of a well-made bed, bedouin?

With those baggy pants of an odalisque, the best place to go is Sahara City. Whatever your eyes desire will be granted you. To the Sahara then . . .

[Come on, shahara!]

Sandman, sandwich her in that harem . . . Arabian Dessert . . .

Another candid candied, your Candy caramelting . . .

For a while she occasionally sent California technicolorful post-cards which invariably ended with the joke "Everything great, except food." But the little word *food* [The Food of Love . . .] had been transformed into a four-letter word. A libidinous leitmotiv. What would become of this Californicaterer? Your Candy, good enough to eat! now only in memories.

(207.9)

32. Gloss after Gloss, Glutton

Golosina? [titbit], I murmured, or more accurately, Babelle murmured, leaning over the Fictionary. It says here in Infernacular Spanish . . .

[Slowly savoring each word, rolling it around like a lifesaver. Gluttonous glossolalia, bonbon mots, glossy glace . . . When she really made up her mind to learn Spanish, Babelle spent idle hours sitting in bed yogi-fashion with that Textravaganza (: The Fictionary of the Language! The Novel of Words! Thesaurus of Golden Spoonerisms!) circling in red—and practically singing—each chosen word. Milalias, buried in bed beside her or sitting at his card table, would answer her, glossing the glossary. Sometimes a single word turned into a whole feast for those polygluttons.]

Glossina?

Sí, sí, a Spanish fly-by-night! Milalias finally answered. (207.10)

33. Nora Melo

[Melodrama in episodes . . .]

Another one you picked up in Le Troubadour!

Crammed full, like every Friday night. [Packed like sardinitwits . . . Bizarre life forms from Waste London . . .]

Alone?

Absorbed in her thoughts.

Amid clouds of smoke [bohemian steam . . .] and a babellicose hubbub.

So distant in that melee of manes that she immediately attracted your attention. Or with the absentminded air that myopia lends.

[Or with that opium-smoke air of the very myopic—a little phrase from Milalias's copious kaleidoscope of opinionated opinions for all tastes . . .]

Head in the clouds. As if she hadn't yet realized she was in the wrong place. And maybe the wrong era. Old-fashioned, in an astrakhan jacket—and the braided bun of a blond Madonna, Raphaelesque. Her age indeterminable, however, like her nationality.

You heard her respond curtly in German, I'm from Lisbon, to the inquiring herd of Germaniacs [thundering Teutons!] at the next table.

In her corner. [Siren song? Faint fading *fados* coming up from the cave of the Troubadour . . .] Any Portuguese in a storm. [Portuguese nostalgia?] Melancholyric honeymoist eyes behind tortoiseshell glasses, evading your glances.

You started your approach, positioning yourself at her table. To tee things off, your timely tease for two. She accepted your tea and your teeming chatter. Just getting intimate. Actually you were drawing her out. Nearly a complete confession. Staring at her teacup she revealed half her life to you. Born in Lisbon [forty-some years earlier?] but raised [or "spoiled by my grandparents"] in the Algarve. [Allusions to that Arabian toponymy . . . Occident de désirs . . . And the name from her husband, Almeida, also of Arab origin . . .] Educated in Lisbon and Zurich [Zurich . . . Zurichtung!] and Paris. Shotgun wedding with an army doctor. She became a war widow almost immediately. His life for his country in Angola. The melodrama of her life! An eight-year-old daughter, "a bit slow," almost always with the grandparents. Who were ruined now. She was the sole support [a joke in poor taste by the Interpolator was erased here] of the family. She had to travel constantly because of her job as simultaneous translator. In five languages. [Not counting her somewhat worm-eaten Spanish . . .] She came to London frequently. And to the Troubadour? Her first time. She had left her hotel in Earl's Court to take a walk and without knowing why, entered Le Troubadour. She was pretty depressed and the café looked so lively . . . [Le Trou Badour . . . The Happy Hole . . .]

The sad widow? You managed to cheer her up for a bit in the local pubs, but you didn't manage to break through her shyness. Nor her strange modesty. Intimidated even in the intimacy of your room. [In spite of her tipsiness . . .]

On the divan, the terrible divan—that moaned almost as much as she—of the redhot nest in Phoenix Lodge. In the first ravishment. Her jacket on the patchwork carpet. And the stiletto heels. And the straight skirt. And the pink stockings. [The silk of her newly flayed legs . . .] And the ruffled panties, like a blue flower. That's enough. [Nora Melo—Melusina?] The lingerie game had come to a dead halt. Only half nude. And with her glasses still on. Was she afraid of losing sight of you? Without eyes! Os óculos . . . And you took off your glasses, and hers. Gently, with a kiss. [Os ósculos, the kisses . . .] But no she didn't want to, no! release the tight bodice or the bra. Ashamed of her robust bust? Disproportionate for such a tiny waist. Twice-slaked potatoes, mellow melons. [Don Wanton is our charming shamming shaman!] Embracing her chastity bra. Arms folded in the pose of a virgin and mammartyr. She stumbled in the struggle, and collapsed on the conquered couch. Hiccups smelling of gin, elastic gymnastics. You realized too late when you first touched her [Elasti-ticity?!] but you reacted in time. [One falsie move—the proof's in the padding. Armor with the erogenous Amazon . . .] Vexed, resentful? Swallowing her teary gin-ridden kisses while you swear—and finally she lets her retread bra slip off—that the most splendorous woman in the world was a mutilated statue, a thousand times more Venusian than the de Milo, with one breast ripped out.

[Amazing Amazon . . .]

The Venus de Melo . . .

But neither she nor you were made of stone . . .

[Of marble? Veined?]

You praise her alabaster. Her pearly hollow.

Not that one!

And passionately you kissed that not-breast.

[No longer scared of the scar . . .]

Her unbraided hair over her shoulders. Her face burning, flushed from the gas flame, from the orgasm.

And then hooking your arm round her waist you make her confront, divine! the wardrobe mirror.

Queen of the Amazons!

(Glib enough . . .)

On the divan, under the blanket, sharing the joint. Strung out in the clouds.

New Nora, Nora renewed. Nora Mellow, now revealing, ravishing and uninhibited, toying over your mouth with her only breast.

She who seals your lips.

Sh.

Stiff . . . [Mmm . . . marbliss?]

Escaped statue from the British Museum?

[Sucking Pygmalion!]

Tacked up in hanging garden of postcards, your unfolding panels of wonder. Incredible, you insist, the resemblance to that Nora (or was it Norah?). Not an illusion.

[Noradream!]

And the melomaniac will keep on remembering, Nora Melo . . . (209.7)

34. *The Queen of Queensberry Place*
[Miss "Havisham."

The Dickensian nickname fit her well . . .]

Miss Peebles, Regina Peebles, by name.

"Miss Pee . . ." Milalias would cruelly abbreviate, nicknaming her for the strong odor, mixed with cologne water, that emanated from her clothes and the seat-cushions of her wheelchair.

Or simply the Queen, the treatment we usually gave her.

Almost always with a purple angora hat that hid her baldness. Little face and head of a mummy. With her cloudy little blue-gray eyes. Almost blind—though she never wore her glasses. And half paralyzed. A crabby tyrant, but still we managed to grow fond of her. Due particularly to her unexpected bursts of humor? And of generosity, on a few occasions. When she lost her head?

Every day more difficult to care for. Her memory was always slipping by then. And she'd start raving, especially about her mythical fiancé, who died on the ship bringing him from India to marry her. Or at least that's how she told it. She never completely accepted the tragedy, but kept on looking at the marks on that faded calendar, from 1919! to see how many days were left before the wedding.

She had a magpie mania for hiding her jewels in the oddest places, and the search always turned into an odyssey. She would accuse us all of being thieves: first me, then the night nurse, the cleaning lady, a tenant she had a grudge against, and finally the trustee. Even her niece and nephew, both single and fiftyish, when they came to visit her or were they only calculating how much life was left in the old bat. Since they were her only heirs, I think she looked upon them with suspicion. She often threatened to change the will and leave the house—a Victorian mansion smack in the middle of South Kensington—to some charity organization. Or she'd threaten to sell it and go live in the country. It was clear she enjoyed keeping them in suspense. Savoring her detestable tea—a secret concoction of her own—and tortuous allusions, while niece and nephew—both tall, big-boned, and with the same horse face—exchanged looks of alarm. Or suddenly she'd start to slip and declare that Archie—the ever-present dead fiancé—already had a buyer for the house or had decided to renovate it from top to bottom.

Even though the room she had granted me was on the second floor and hers was on the ground floor, the squabbling she provoked at all hours with the nurse—a sluggish Scotch matron, Scotch-as-catch-can—kept me awake more than once (and Milalias too, when he slipped in uninvited); indeed it kept the whole house up. Despite the thick walls the disturbances reached the other three floors, and sometimes the tenants stumbled out complaining and threatening to move. None of them carried out the threat since they were almost as ancient as the owner.

Her favorite time was the early afternoon, if it wasn't raining, when Milalias and I took her out for a stroll [roll role] through Kensington Gardens in her wheelchair.

With her turban (almost always violet) and the heavily powdered parchment of her dried-up sparrow face, sitting so rigid in her throne, she had an impressive Egyptian look. And her squawks and growls were piercing. But she could suddenly transform into a placid little grandmother.

Milalias knew best how to handle her. Depending on the situation, he treated her like a capricious little girl, a grand dame, a queen, or a harpy. He even played practical jokes that wound up amusing her. (Even though you'd say it was just for fun: deep down didn't you hope she'd leave us something in her will? Pah! Mummies last hundreds of years . . .) And he told her a thousand and one stories if she got bored with what I read to her. Or Milalias would take the book from me and begin to read without her realizing he was improvising, inventing a new novel. Until she nodded off in her wheelchair. And then while she napped we'd take a walk alone. Until one day she gave us a scare.

That afternoon, when we returned to the corner kiosk where we always left her sheltered, she and her chair had disappeared.

How are we going to explain that the Queen had been stolen!

Maybe for the wheelchair . . . (Milalias with his speculations).

Running around like headless chickens, checking every corner of Kensington Gardens. It might have been a kidnapping . . . Come on! Or a Queennapping . . .

Until we heard shouts of delight at the edge of the Round Pond. Some schoolboys were pushing her in her chair as they jogged around the pond. She was deliriously happy.

But she wouldn't last much longer. And such a cushy job for us, too. A little later she got it into her head that people wanted to poison her, and she refused to eat. The niece and nephew managed to have her declared mentally incompetent and stuck her in an asylum in Richmond. [Where there's a will there's a relative.]

We went to visit her there a few times, but by the end she didn't recognize us. It pained me to see her in her chair, completely uncomprehending, pressing on her lap an album of family photos —that she couldn't see anymore—and the green velvet-bound book that we had read so many times. Between cereal and serial.

I remember on the last visit Milalias repeated a routine joke: that we would sell the house and the three of us, with Archie, would take a trip around the world. She didn't stir, as if she didn't hear, but finally she smiled and opened the book by Keats. (I don't think she ever understood that poetry, but she certainly enjoyed its music. To dream by? Because she fell asleep whenever she heard the words of the poem. The best lullaby.)

And Milalias and I began to read to her in unison . . .

[The blaze, the splendour, and the symmetry,

I cannot see—but darkness, death and darkness.

Even here, into my centre of repose . . .]

She was nodding off and Milalias left the book in her lap, over her shawl, so we could leave; but she half-opened her eyes and pushed the book unsteadily against his stomach. We looked at each other, not knowing what to do. Did she want us to continue reading? She moved her lips in a murmur, and Milalias put his ear close. It's yours now, Milalias claimed she said. Perhaps in the asylum she didn't have anyone to read it to her.

They'll think we tricked her out of it, Milalias said, stashing it in my purse.

But all our books are stolen, aren't they?

[Epicpockets.]

Yet that's one of the few books that, up to now, hasn't wound up at the used-book shops on Charing Cross Road.

But the most extraordinary thing was that the following winter, when they started to demolish the Queensberry Place mansion (surely she wouldn't find out), the bulldozer that razed the old walls had a brand name written in big letters: HYPERION. Milalias, who doesn't believe in meaningless coincidences, insisted that ending was also inscribed in Keats's book.

At the far end of the street, upon leaving Milalias's cellar, we saw day by day [Demolition in Progress] how the bulldozer ripped up the ruins with its claws.

[I will advance a terrible right arm . . .]

All that remains of the house now are the photos I took during the demolition. In one of them you can see a piece of the strange mural—Egyptian—from my room. And I copy now what Milalias scribbled on the back, under some arabesques: "Nothing remains where that house stood; yet something makes me love to return there."

(213.2)

35. The Beautiful "Zoraida"

You baptized her "Zoraida," in homage to your most disturbing childhood heroine. You would be the masked Crusades warrior and your amorous Moorish woman would rescue you from the vile mob of Moors, always in the tightest jam imaginable . . . In the arms of your faithful infidel you would forget the pale and chlorotic beloved back in chaste Old Castile . . .

[As shameless as he was precocious, our little knight manipulated those comic strips to his whims . . . With Zoraida in the tent, bedouin in the bed, rising and falling with your panting. Zoraidazoraidazoraid . . . Under the covers, prayers and red raw rubbing. Much later, and you already the captive of other pleasures, she will be superimposed upon another quixotic Zoraïda who offers you her treasure. Upon lying down the two become synthesaurized into one!]

And you'll bump into her centuries later [exactly on October 12: Día de la Raza—A Day at the Races, brother . . .] in the Polytechnic cafeteria on Regent Street.

As lanky as you, that giraffe in boots and miniskirt, with jetblack hair down to her waist. Her eyes big with the blackness all the houries have. And her face sharp with a rather pointy chin . . . As soon as I met her I wondered where I'd seen her before. Until the revelation months later, on the cliffs of Brighton: she pressing her hair against her ears and roaring at you and your friend Diana, as you two teased her by swaying at the edge of the abyss. Munch's *Scream* pinned up in your hanging garden . . .

There in the food line pushing the tray along the counter. What?! Yes, I'm sure she said "Co-jo-nes!" with a perfect Castilian accent. (She always liked nasty Spanish words . . .) She was chatting in pure Spanish with some squat owl with a crewcut and V-shaped eyebrows (your first glimpse of Reynaldo Rey, at that time a lecturer in Spanish at the Polytechnic), and logically enough you thought she was Spanish.

A few days later you saw her again in the cafeteria, this time alone at a table and in a stewardess's uniform.

Pretending you were scouting for a seat, tray in hand, finally heading straight to her table.

Her package of Spanish cigarettes on the table: pretext to start a conversation. She wasn't Spanish! No, she wasn't. Behind the veil of Spanish smoke, the chat unrolled in spiraling smoke rings, capriciously. Fumes and humor, to unveil your houri. You follow another and still another route, the better to probe her. What a Madrileño accent! She had studied several years in Madrid. ["I'm crazy about Madrid."] A short step, "From Madrid to Heaven." Literally, because when she left Madrid she started working as a stewardess. But not all her experiences there had been pleasant. Days later, in the intimacy of bed, she would tell you about her ex-boyfriend (still somewhat attracted to him) from the Upper Crasses, and the depressing abortion.

(The first time, in the chilled room in Queen's Park, you two broke all the rules . . . A bloody duel, unforeseeable from the placid Polytechnic lunchtable chat.)

She had been flying over Iberia's bullskin almost every day. But cowed by a narrow escape, she made up her mind to stay in London with the ground staff.

And as you bid her farewell on Regent Street, at the door to her office, the first kiss—in flight.

(215.3)

36. *The Secret Garden*
[The last refuge—or subterfuge?]
One afternoon she unexpectedly turned up terrified in the Cleveland Gardens apartment.

[Zoraida, agitated again . . .]

With a big black hat and sunglasses. [: Garbo in spy garb . . .]
And she brought a suitcase and a carry-on.

Months without hearing from her. Not since your last night—
and sad sunrise—in the Nomad Hotel.

She was talking rapidly in that Madrid dialect, and at first I
barely understood. That she had to hide.

Rimbaudelaire's room was still empty and you invited her to
stay. She hugged us crying and still talking frantically. Eventually
we were able to calm her down so she could explain it all to us from
the beginning.

We looked at her and each other, both surprised and incredulous,
as she narrated her fantastic misadventures. She no longer worked
as a stewardess. But her daddy the merchant (in Casablanca) was
sending her money now every month. And a Lebanese chemistry
professor at the university had given her a room in his house in
exchange for some household work. Crazy about her, at first he
constantly hounded her all over the house. Once in the middle of
the night he appeared completely nude, blinding her with a lantern.

The tail light . . ., Milalias joked.

But that exhibitionist courting (she managed to ward him off)
was not the cause of her fear.

The Lebanese belonged to an Arab terrorist organization and in
the university laboratory he secretly made ballpoint-pistols, letter-
bombs, and various explosive devices.

Dr. Jekyll and Mr. Killer . . .

Yeah, go ahead and laugh . . .

(Couldn't all this merely be her romanticizing? Or a ruse to
come live with Milalias?)

Although she didn't want to know anything about it, the profes-
sor-terrorist had begun to make her his confidante. And accomplice.
Because she had consented to hand some mysterious packages to
some mysterious strangers . . .

Chè imbroglio, Mata Hari . . .

But eventually she started worrying, and when she told the
Lebanese professor good-bye, it's been swell but I'm leaving, with
two slaps he declared the need for Arab solidarity. [His mission:
submission? Factions speak louder than words.] She couldn't get

out now! And when the professor found out that she was only half Moroccan (her mother was French), the threats and blackmail increased. He called her a spy and said if she managed to escape, they'd finally catch up with her.

Not here, assured Milalias. This is the best hideout. You're in Arabia Felix. And there's even a whole dowar of bedouins on the first floor . . . Every afternoon they set up in the hallway to drink tea. Arabs coming and going all day long. And who would look for hay in a haystack? [A Moor in a moorland . . .]

She still had her doubts . . .

OK, it's better if you don't go out for a while. And Babelle will take care of you.

One grief cures another. Her arrival was providential. Like manna for our maintenance. The rent hadn't been paid since Rimbaudelaire moved out, and the landlord had given us a week to pay up.

She immediately offered her savings: about fifty pounds. Hidden (those contagious espionage tricks . . .) in those soft Moroccan slippers.

But by the end of a month, you were taking her jewels to keep paying the rent. And some extras, that she wouldn't part with complacently. (She being far more possessive than I . . .)

The night of the party-bacchanal, when she refused to leave her room despite your heavy-handed insistence and the chants of the bacchantes, was the struggle that broke the camel's back . . .

The following noon, hungover, you didn't have the energy to convince her to stay like all the other times . . .

With all her pride and swallowing her tears as she heaped her clothes in a suitcase, she told you for the hundredth time she was moving out. You didn't believe her. She left, but was back that night. And she began to come and go freely, as if she had nothing to fear.

And just as she came, she disappeared one fine day, leaving you only a message scrawled in lipstick on the bathroom mirror that you never managed to decipher . . .

(215.6)

37. *Parrot and Paramoor*

The start of their romance.

(After some heroic coupling in the Queen's Park igloo, she'd phone for a taxi, and sometimes he accompanied her to the Finchley Road house where she rented a habitat without cohabitation rights. The owner-ogre allowed her to receive visitors only at decent hours in the living room. The dying room, Milalias called it. But sometimes, to prolong the farewell, they stopped at the Wimpy's close to her house.)

Nonchalant chatterers in Golder's Green till all hours. That all-night Wimpy's, a free port where night owls could temper their drunkenness with a cup of tea.

With snowflakes falling and no booze available, Zoraida and Milalias warmed up and gazed into each other's eyes, sipping tea after tea for two. Heavily sugared, just as she likes it: Arabian syrup. But missing the mint, she lamented each time.

A majestic mantle of snow over Golder's Green that night. And at another table facing them, a lush in his heavy muddy loden over-coat, chewing his cigar stub and tirelessly tapping a spoon on his cup to order more tea, More tea! I'm a teatotaler . . ., a tedious abstainer.

And the two of them billing and cooing, holding hands by a window while the flakes kept fluttering down. With Milalias repeating his alcoholyrical ravings: Nevermore! Dead fiancés shredding their love letters . . . The couple cornered in Wimpy's, watching the flakes fall.

[At sunup London was once again the unreal city of snow. Albino Albion . . .]

Snowflakes slowfalling . . .

[Flake out!]

And the drunk fell drugged over his cup of tea.

[Deleterious drowsiness . . .]

They decided to go out sliding on the snow . . .

The pilaster of the clock in the intersection, with its white cloak, was a giant snowman. [The abominable snowman? Yet another Yeti? . . . For the Clown Prince of Darkness, all the whiteness and the snow itself—wondrous strange snow, que sa blancheur défend —created both dizzying confusion and repugnattraction, a kind of love-horror vacuum . . .]

—Finsteraarhorn!!! . . . he shouted at the night, or at the snowy colossus.

—What? as she tried to follow him.

[The beak of the black eagle . . . Shut. Not even a peep. Where are the perpetual snowwhites of yesteryear? Another legend—white—for your novel new book of snowballroom dancing . . .]

—Leaping alpinists risk vertiginous avalanches . . . and down he slid, flapping his arms desperately.

—Emil! embracing as the [aforementioned] avalanche descends upon them.

A miracle they didn't smash against the display window of Lindy's [crescent roll moons, honey-glazed quarter-moons . . .]. Splitting their sides laughing, swiftly sliding down the pavement a duo. Right into a snowdrift. White, at least, but not soft. Laughing, still embracing.

[And he slips to his knees with the greatest of ease, that daring young man . . .]

The enraptured girl standing now and coaxing the idler, who still sat chattering [occasionally cupping his hands against his mouth, breathing on them, a characteristic gesture of his, to thaw them or thaw the words . . .] his refrain: flake by flake the park weaving its wake . . .

—Are you coming?

(271.1)

38. *Honeymoon*

[Beam of delight . . .]

On the nearly bald boughs, frozen flakes twinkled and titillated.

Moon of honey.

[Hornymoon?]

Mooning.

[Doom that moon mood!]

The Honeymooners.

While you two, moonstruck, skirted the park along Harvist Road, toward your room on Millman Road.

A croissant moon?

Pressed against the glass, moon-gazing in the dark. Neither of you had ever seen it that color. A slice of bread soaked in honey?

Head in the clouds? because you're cold and hungry! [Aye!]

Ramshackle frigid room in Queen's Park. Impossible to heat it up with that infernal little heater.

Ash Wednesday supper for two, love by a fire of newspapers.

After the attempt at paella, with curry! that you burned in your room, with a vinegary wine, supposedly Spanish, you two began to warm up.

Kissinking, caressinking lower and lower . . .

Tonight, no, we can't . . .

But you happily skipped over the Koranic rules. [REDROD, ORDER!] A minor order? [Menorrhagia . . .]

So infatuated that night, the first honey moon! that you couldn't wait—three or four days?—for Zoraida to purify herself.

Tonight, no, we . . .

[Moresque mores? Don't leave for tomorrow . . . To Morocco? Your Tangerous tongue of a cunninglinguist, and you spent a Feztive period with the girl from Morocco . . .]

Tonight, no . . .

Nothing better than a blood pact! you assured.

(Like the rest of them! The same thing almost always happened [rule without sexception] in the first act [Fate! of an instinktive olfaction?] with a new ingenue.)

With all your urging (but there wasn't too much begging, was there?) and your burning passion, she didn't turn up her nose at you.

Tonight . . .

Ah, she gave in, she was bound to. But prudent and neat (not like some beasts I know . . .), she stretched a towel over the bed. And she, hop! on top. [Air hostage.] In the reddish shadows. [Earning more redwings? Courage! Red badgering . . .] Yes red see red . . . And opening [Sham! ham! for ash!] with your babbling. Go down, Mozarab . . . Honey, honey moan . . . [*Irrumer en miel* : honey-linguist, rumí-mating . . .] With honeyed lips? By the light of the golden moon . . . And she urges you on [We must go where Allah commands], caresses you Come on, come on . . . And then [Eden den] the doors of heaven open [Al Kadr! though it doesn't coincide with the calendar] when she brazenly embraces you, red-hot.

† 502 †

Restless pleasure! Paradisepurgatoryhell, what a mixup! with her moans ahhh and scratching bites. She nearly flays you as she lays you . . .
(217.3)

39. Disengagement Ring

Down to the last one already.

Which cost her the most to part with, but finally she let go of the gage and Milalias, such a golden tongue! managed to get it to the Paddington pawnbroker. For just a bit.

Back again after a few minutes.

Regretting your rash snatch?

You can keep it, he said, and let it fall on the bed.

[So many times Milalias had spoken ironically about that engagement ring that Zoraida's Spanish boyfriend had given her. With his airs of the Marquis of Who-knows-what . . . Ugly, Catholic, and semental . . . When they broke off the engagement after a fuss about the abortion, the boyfriend, noble and generous, had insisted that she save it as a keepsake . . . Your enrapement ring, teased Milalias, disengagement ring . . .]

It's a fine imitation, he added.

No! Zoraida leaped from the bed as if she'd been stung. That son of a bitch!
(217.5)

40. The Milky Way

[Mr. Hsi-men's milky way . . . Another gala, another galaxy. On the way to a pollution, till he finds the ultimate solution . . . Il Dissoluto punito!]

With Zoraida in the Classic Poly, near Oxford Circus, to see *La Voie lactée,* another story from those uterodoxical Spaniards! for the first time when they had a chance encounter with Diana.

[Little ol' London!]

Zoraida and Diana, who knew nothing of each other since the crazy times in Madrid, suddenly ran into each other in that theater.

You enjoyed hearing their excited Spanish in the aisle of the theater until the lights went out.

Days later she invited you both to dinner in her Putney apartment. By candlelight, and right in front of Zoraida, she started flirting . . .

Diana Fender with her fiery hair, and already scorching in the fluttering flames. Until they were extinguished. And then at the door you deftly deflect the farewell kiss, just gently grazing her lips.

She was a secretary for the *Guardian,* and predictably you nicknamed her "Guardiana," but that was later. When you went alone to her house for dinner some Saturdays. From the table, a little tipsy, to the bed. To continue quenching your thirst . . . [Diana-dipsomania!] And Sundays you had to suffer her thrashing you at tennis, she being so athletic, Diannihilating you. But the terrible tennis trounces were balanced by what came after: Diana-bathing. [From forty–love to frothy love!] Double bubble bath. But Sunday, after Saturday's revelry, began again with reveille.

This valiant little soldier stands at attention with Diana's first call-to-arms! despite your pomp and bluffoonery as she stretches your pendulous penis with fond fondling. And he always hit the mark, even half asleep, smack in the center.

(219.10)

41. The Battersea Amusement Park

Paradise for a few hours . . .

Already almost nothing left in the grand esplanade of Battersea Park.

[Foundations of fun . . .]

Some walls still standing. Twisted steel like modern sculptures [by Caro?], shredded billboards. Ruins of the Fun Fair.

[All gone. Luck turned happy voices to mute silence . . .]

But that night continued in a recollection. (And in this urgent note that tomorrow the corruptor of words will alter to his fancy . . .)

Vertigo and high laughs on the ferris wheel. [Don Juan don-wandering . . .] The circumnavigation with Sinbad the Wailer, and near-shipwreck in that little port in miniature. Batter sea . . . Dual bitemarks in the carameled apple. Cotton candy beards. The carousel [of swift steeds . . .] at breakneck speed. Shouting in the air. Infantasy in the park of marvels, contemplating the Alices and Joys in fluttering skirts. Carouselling kids . . . [Infancy means in fancy!] Ruffled waves, colored corollas, petals in the air. [Flower-escent puffiness of carouselland . . .] Another kinder-garden, another lost paradise . . . [Loose carollary: a garden once lost is edenized. There are only lost paradises . . .]

But the main attraction, what attracted you most: the booth with the blonde en déshabillé, stretched out on a makeshift bed sus-pended over a water tank, coolly leafing through a magazine while that firing squad of riotous sailors threw balls at the target to send her plunging to the water. Would they dump her whap! or whap! not? The cross-eyed bawd in a black shawl, Come on love! pushed an orange ball in your hand. Go on! the gal needs a good dunking. Without thinking you closed your eyes and splash, down she dropped amidst howls. Embarrassed and proud at the same time, repeating you had closed your eyes to be sure not to hit the bull's-eye. Silly game, diluting delusion. You still hadn't seen the burly Popeye behind you, proudly beating his chest with a pipe in his hand. And he popped hop! over the counter to help her out of the tank, that nearly nude soaked beauty.

(223.3)

42. *The Scurrilous Squirrel*

[Burn!]

In the smoky autumn redness of Holland Park. Sprightly scurry-ing with fiery tail, snapcrackle darting through the dead leaves. Lightly climbing up the mossy bark to the crown of the walnut tree, and falling chaff! like a burning ball.

Right onto your chest? The burning woke you up.

Or the bite on your Adam's apple early in the morning, from the Persian vampiress who had burned you with her eyes that Sunday afternoon in Holland Park.

You had glimpsed her first, alone on a bench, in the garden in front of Holland House. Following you with her eyes?

A cloud of smoke floating between the trees. Black form in folds.

Darkening, approaching, more dense step by step. Slender, wending her way.

Wrapped in her silky black cloak, next to you, leaning on the tree bough fence, as you two contemplated the bustling squirrels. Something nunlike in her appearance? [Sister Deafmute, definitively turning a deaf ear to your entreaties . . .] Sorcery in the burning afternoon encircled by smoke. Her mysterious mask. Funereal, until you dragged a smile out of her with one of your juggling tricks. Shaking out the little bag of walnuts and hazelnuts for the cleverest squirrel.

Her name is Peri . . .

[What a parry! Periphrastic parable of the pairing squirrel, with pirouettes! And what perils! A peripatetic parakeet lost in the Perineal woods . . .]

Yes, Peri . . .

That squirrel, the one with the fire-red and ash fur, is really an enchanted fairy, under the evil spell of a vengeful wizard who tried to woo her. And the unlucky damsel won't regain her beautiful feminine form until a sweetheart wins her confidence, and she eats only what he gives her for one year.

[Dried fruits of love? A nutty tragedy?]

The one-year anniversary will happen exactly at midnight tonight.

Squirrel scheme, rodent ruse . . .

Yes, that one, the clever one that confidently climbs up your shoulder for a nut . . .

Perching, parasitic . . .

And the Persian looked at you, perplexed perhaps. Infected by your nonsense? Fascinated by your cock-and-squirrel fairy tale? Miles away with her vacant look.

[Periblepsis?]

Suddenly a puffing matron in mourning, also wearing a chador, took her away almost by force, gesticulating frenetically, moving her fingers in the face of the peripatetic Peri.

Deaf and dumb?!

[(Go on! throwing pearls before squirrels . . . Better to disparage that Persian Gulf. Milalias peerlessly persevering with his Arabian nightmare.)]

Perilous pairing, or change of Persianality. Chase a more persuasive tale! You stand before the Gates of Paradise with your Peri, pathetic Peri.

(223.5)

43. Helen of Holland

Helen Helder.

[The doors of hell, VOI CH'EDENTRATE, ALL WHO ENTER . . ., will not prevail against her.]

Another Hollandaise source. [Dutch treatise. Sic.] Discovered [by guided chance] in Picasso. Pick a so-so pickup . . . Pick as so directed to help that painter. Complete dunce for submitting to that vile vaudeville, to be Albert Alter's alter ego.

His former lover and model, Helen of Holland, Notre Dame of Amsterdam, recently arrived in London to rancormence the stormy relations. [Altercations.] Ready again to destroy the canvases and features of the genius. Rip and tear, slash slash! this jealous Dutch girl with a knife in her stockings.

But it was Alter's fault. In a moment of nostalcoholgia [of alteration], he got the strange idea to call her.

What the hell are you doing in London!? How could you leave like that. I'm coming there right now . . . [Like a cold shower, suddenly sober . . .] He swore and foreswore to her that he didn't have a flat and was flat broke, that he was sleeping every night in the house of an acquaintance, in parts unknown. I'm leaving right away, Alter said she told him imperiously. You'd better be waiting for me at the airport, at the KLM counter, from noon on.

The receiver fell from his hand. She's serious! And then, in a flash of inspiration [alterior motives]: Better in the Picasso Café, Alter suggested, on King's Road, at exactly five P.M. [His wacky idea to get rid of her for good . . . The transference . . . Step after false step, off the mark.]

Alter wasn't going to keep the date, but you would certainly have to come, to his aid. With pleasure! Alter described her in the rosiest terms [and no thorns!] in fine detail. So at first she's a bit surly, but when she warms up . . . Really I'm doing *you* the favor! And hey, you don't know me, you never even heard of me. And when you see she's fed up with waiting in the Picasso, accost her with your conquistador's manners . . . To sum it up, and because you are a friend, I leave her in your hands. Or vice versa.

Sure he'll leave you in her hands! Between her razor-sharp [measureless] fingernails . . .

(237.2)

44. Mrs. Askew

At first I thought it was an alias Milalias had pinned on her. Mrs. Askew. Plain and simple.

Mr. Reis's landlady, Mrs. Askew, never looks you straight in the eye. But not always cross-eyed either, only when she's nervous. She seems at once timid and intimidating, I don't know why.

Slight, fragile, and agile despite her years, sixty-something and bearing them well. She has a strange face, attractive and at the same time repulsive, you know. Soft and suddenly hard. The fuzz of her cheeks stands on end. Sometimes she looks her age, and then in the blink of an eye, seen or not, she changes, she has become a girl. No. A face like an ancient doll. I found it by chance in an antique store in Islington.

Mrs. Askew!!!

That Victorian doll sprawled out in a display window, her peeling porcelain cheeks rose-faded. A little pink silk cap down to her eyebrows. And her watery blue eyes looking [extrabismus!] cross-eyed.

Milalias laughed like a madman and asked the price of the doll [Many dollars for the doll!] in order to give it to Mr. Reis. I can just imagine the face he'd make . . .

Mrs. Askew and Mr. Reis don't speak, they grunt! when they cross paths in some recess of the Maida Vale house. And despite all, I have the hunch there was something between them. Or is there still? [Un ténébreuse affaire!]

When Mrs. Askew rented two rooms to Mr. Reis during the war, she was a recent widow and they were both young. Wouldn't they remember now how they were then?

When Mr. Reis has his asthma attacks, she gets quite nervous and tries to take care of him, almost by force. On the other hand

Mr. Reis holes up in his room, barricades the door, and gasps at her to go away. At times, yielding at last, he lets her in. Is he afraid of her? In their cat-and-dog relationship I smell a rat, just as Milalias does. [Something fishy, fictionist!] There must be some kind of mutual bond [an evil union?], a quirky love-hate bind perhaps, between them. Or perhaps Milalias has infected me with his fantastic ideas. He insists Mrs. Askew is a medium, says he has it on good authority, and suspects she's in cahoots with some spirit who's very important to Mr. Reis. Imagine that!

Wouldn't it be simpler to see the obvious?: they need each other, the two are alone, and after so many years they would miss not seeing each other's smiling or even grumpy face. And yet, and yet, I too smell something fishy . . .

(255.7)

45. Mr. Reis Has an Asthma Attack

I was finally going to meet him!

The mysterious X. Reis.

I was even beginning to think he was just one of my Milalias's inventions. So many times he had talked to me about him, of his fraternal friendship with his parents and with the mythical uncle Emil. [Quadruplets? . . .]

It was a midafternoon in February and already getting dark.

Now I know how much Reis likes to sit sometimes in the shadows till night falls. Sitting in his armchair looking out the window or at the black television screen: he looks at the past, or hears it . . .

Milalias had just introduced us, and Reis was still squeezing my hand between his, affectionately.

Suddenly he let go of my hand as if he'd received a shock [seized by a spirited emotion?], and in two strides made his way to the bedside table. His back to us, he put on his oxygen mask and inhaled loudly several times.

After this he returned to our side, gasping, trying to laugh it off as if it were nothing.

—Pardon me. These days Asmodeus won't leave me alone . . .

He used to say, I don't know if it was completely a joke, that Asmodeus was the devil-god of asthma . . .

The conversation began as if nothing had happened and in spite of his gasps Mr. Reis jumped from one subject to the next with happy indifference, and even mock-flattered me about my white lamb's-wool coat—or almost white . . .

[. . . she added sheepishly. Dressing mutton as lamb? Revenons à nos moutons . . .]

A fairly worn three-quarter coat with big shoulder pads, from the late '30s or early '40s, that I bought at the Ladbroke Grove flea market.

Later on, when I found that photo of Milalias's mother in a similar jacket, I thought I understood the cause of Mr. Reis's emotional attack.

In the shadows of his room I was suddenly an apparition . . . (255.8)

46. "Titty Titania"

Milalias nicknamed her, most crudely, "Titania and her Dancing Nipples" . . . [Or "La Mamelon," on occasion.]

"Titty Titania."

The queen of the Chelsea fairies.

When Bob "Hitch-Cock" discovered her in the World's End pub Man in the Moon, she was named or called Tanya. Titania stuck immediately, because her titties could not be overlooked. So he filmed her, highlighting her charms in all kinds of roles and poses.

[He screened his keen teen epicene dream to be seen in reams of obscene scenes. In one of those sixty-second shorts, she was the Shakespearean fairy Titania and rubbed against a strapping young lad wearing a big papier-mâché donkey head. And the other head like a donkey's too . . . Nice special effects, assembler. Some jackass-of-all-trades that Bob "Hitch-Cock" got from who knows where . . .]

He was going to make her a supermodel on a smaller scale, a superstarlette, a well-trained Pavlovian ballerina.

Delicate miniature, the bratty kid's just a flyweight! and such a flapper . . . Anemic little bobby-sox blonde, with a face like someone fasting. All eyes, darting around like the naughty boobs grafted on her rickety little girl's chest. [Conspicuous consumptive. Pithysical.]

Your cute little bobtailed titi monkey, with those titillating breasts of a hormoned child. Although she might not be such a young thing, she didn't look older than eleven or twelve. As precocious as she was shameless, she adapted to all the roles. [No! Better if we shoot it with a dirty old man . . .] But her greatest role, so well rehearsed! consisted of coaxing adolescents as skinny and squalid as herself, to draw them into the studio. Where she and Bob would then share [sexploit] them. Until one black night a waiter-Romeo appeared, and preferred to frolic with only Titania *in camera,* without the supplementary attentions of the camera-man. And he carried her off from night till morning without any warning. [Bob babbled, was baffled, went batty . . .]

At first Bob didn't believe it, but then he made a painful decision and visited Romeo in his Knightsbridge restaurant. Milalias insists that Bob offered the waiter five hundred pounds to leave his Titty Titania [bobby-sox bauble] alone. Knowing Bob I don't believe it was five hundred pounds, but it's true he offered him some money and Romeo accepted it. And he must have told Titty Titania, because she disappeared—perhaps disenchanted—as if by magic. We never heard from her again.

Bob was downcast for weeks and finally hired a private detective.

[It must be acknowledged that Janos Kerek, detective in his spare time, is no Sherlock Holmes. Not even a Dr. Watson . . .]

To no avail. The fairy queen went up in a puff of smoke, leaving no trace . . .

Bob "Hitch-Cock" organized orgies almost every night in his studio to forget her. He was more involved with blokes and dope than ever before. All for nothing. The flashing eyes and nipples of Titty Titania stared at him blindly from the enlargements hanging on all the walls in the Fulham studio.

(257.1)

47. ALICE IN WONDERLONDON

One more.

[Alice deliciously licentious, a gorgeous Eurasian (French and Vietnamese), so nice . . . And not one to mince words. A true delight. To hear her. Slowly savoring her stories. So spicy.]

Telling you her adventures in detail, in franglais. I hope you'll translate *this* one without betraying it too much:

Didn't I tell you what happened last night? Mr. Leone, you know, the poker boss, comes over and tells me Fix yourself up, I'm taking you out to dinner at Le Coq Hardi. No less! OK, I hadn't been asked out for a while so I said Sure. Why not. He picked me up in that boat he drives, me dressed to kill, with Biba's dress, the black one, you know, really low-cut in front, and he takes me to that Coq Hardi just over there on High Street Kensington, yeah, with a terrace out front. Man, what a menu! Super! So anyway we sit down and it turns out I know some guy there. And it's a good thing he came over to our table 'cause I was getting bored outta my mind. I had had enough. Mr. Leone didn't even say boo, sitting right across from me and not even a squeak out of him. Like I ask him You had that gambling joint very long? Yeah, and nothing else, just chewing away. Lemme tell you I was really getting fed up. He coulda asked me about my life or something, whatever he wanted, but nothing, no way. All right so we finally got outta there and into that luxury cruiser of his, that Al Capone Cadillac, and he says in a very serious voice, Let's have some coffee. Another? So then he takes me to his gambling house, you know, the Clover Club. It was closed for the night so, you know, I start to wonder what's gonna happen next; but I felt like I could handle myself. All of a sudden he tries to kiss me and I shove him away. And he's telling me Hey you know I'm not gonna hurt you, I respect you, I've always respected you since you started working for me, I know you're not one of those girls . . . and besides if I was really looking for something all I gotta do is pick up the phone, going on with his blabber. I'm sitting on the sofa, see, and he's in front of me talking, now he's really talking, and suddenly he comes at me bends over and kisses me slides his hand under my bra and pff! creams all over me. I'm looking at my dress all sticky and horrible, shit! I jump up and now I'm really pissed off and he's all over himself making excuses

Excuse me . . . I'm sorry, you drive me wild, he throws himself on the sofa and pants like he just ran a marathon, with his little tail looking shrunken and ridiculous. And then he gets up as if nothing happened, back into his Napoleon pose, the hand on the stomach, and tells me Prego, hey I'll buy ya a new dress, we'll go shopping . . . But just imagine, he must have opened his fly when he put his hand down my dress and then poof! the goo. That's right, this guy doesn't ask you to do anything. Anyway my shantung dress is fucked up, a nice shantung dress all fucked up.

(259.3)

48. Dr. Hoffmann

Looking like a wise old crackpot, with his usual absentminded air. I can almost still see him, so gawky with his fists in the pockets of his white frock, looking through the window with dead eyes at the graves of Saint Margaret Church [by the low wall of the church cemetery on Station Road, Edgware, in north London, Milalias sometimes waited for Babelle to get off work; and one afternoon when she never came out, he entertained himself—killing time?— by copying tombstone inscriptions: Dedicated to the memory of William Hinge who died July 24, 1810, at the age of sixty-six . . . James George Austin, who died in September of 1851 (the day illegible) at the age of seventeen . . .], on the other side of the street, waiting for the first patient of the day. But when a mouth opened before his eyes, those same dead eyes gleamed and shined vividly. As a dentist, Dr. Hoffmann was an artist . . .

[And as a laborer of love, one might say, our protagonist worked long and hard as assistant to Dr. Hoffmann, Edgware dentist.]

A true magician, not just a tooth-puller. As if he weaved magical spells with his big bony hands, deft despite their trembling.

[Babelle marveled at how Dr. Hoffmann kept his patients from pain. They were sometimes quite impatient when they arrived, even in agony. A case of expert sofronization. Milalias held fantastic theories about Dr. Hoffmann's anesthetic methods.]

First the aperitif: the tiny glass, drop by drop, of a liqueur of his own creation.

[Dr. Hoffmann's elixir. Hoffmann's anodyne? Is the placebo

pleasing?]

Tasting like strawberries, but with a grinding aftertaste . . .

[And now some scenes from our action-packed driller!]

And no injections of horrible anesthetics. Just relax in the chair.

Then he calmed them, speaking low and looking in their eyes and putting them to sleep while he poked around in their mouths. The drill tztztzzz! would spin without a complaint.

[Babelle believed he was a sorcerer. He had her half hypnotized too. And also performed miracles on her . . . Didn't he have her virtually living on air? Dr. Hoffmann scarcely paid her, taking advantage of the fact that she didn't have a work permit, but he generously allowed her to live in the garret over the clinic. And he filled some of her teeth for free. For the little good it did her then . . . Lots of fillings, but nothing filling; lots of silver but none in the pocket.]

Tztztzzz! . . . spinning almost without pause from morning till night. I don't know why Dr. Hoffmann worked so much and with such fervor.

[Work sets us free . . . And to keep her out of trouble, Dr. Hoffmann permitted his assistant to baby-sit on the weekends.]

He lived alone in a boardinghouse in the Edgware area, and had no family. A client told it to me: his whole family had died in Nazi concentration camps. Did he work so hard so as not to think?

We would start working on teeth very early, at eight o'clock sharp. And if sometimes my dreams wouldn't let me go, immediately the bell would ring, and then Dr. Hoffmann's klaxon voice behind the door: Es ist schon Zeit!

When he got angry or nervous he spoke in German.

He also spoke German with his many patients of German origin, the majority of them Jewish. That's why I didn't pay too much attention to that chubby patient with blue eyes—although it seemed to me that Dr. Hoffmann was speaking to him in a loud harsh German—who might have been calling me or waving to me behind the doctor. And suddenly the shout with the squealing drill.

It was ghastly!

Did Dr. Hoffmann have an attack? Fallen against the patient, the two of them struggling. He had destroyed teeth and mouth in that face full of blood spluttering blood. Dr. Hoffmann's face was spattered with blood too.

And me! I don't know how I had the strength to go for help.

During the trial Dr. Hoffmann's lawyer alleged that his client had suffered an epileptic fit.

[Milalias maintains he had a hallucination. Or maybe he recognized someone. The patient whose teeth he had worked over was German, and Aryan, although his record was irreproachable. Who knows . . .]

It meant Dr. Hoffmann's hastened retirement. Sometime later a Hindu dentist set up practice in his clinic.

[Dr. Hoffmann included the assistant in the transfer.]

Do you want me to tell you the story of Dr. Singh?

No, not today, the memory of that butchery in Dr. Hoffmann's clinic has worn me out.

(259.6)

49. The Magic Mandarin

Play.

From bar to bar . . .

[Tok! I put you in that case. Listen. Titok! Secret. Titokban! In secret. Careful with the bella toccata, from bar to bar, of the Miraculous Mandarin. A csodalatos mandarin. Beware of the Magyar charm of his magic violin. In search, czardas after czardas, stardust rhapsody by rhapsody, of his better half-mandarin. Liszt! The list for the flour dealer! Cut flower? Horse of a different color. Finally reunited, the mandarin and his heroine taken from the robbers. Having no alternative, defend yourself. Seize the Stradivarius. Pull the strings. Grab the bow. Reignbow! Shield yourself, tok! with the case. Face to face. Play! Listen to his case, tok! tok! and talk.]

Doing diabolical variations on Béla Bartók's *The Miraculous Mandarin,* Milalias or his alter ego Tsu'i Pen had written an incredible phantomime (a tall tale . . .) or shaggy-dog shadow play, complete with tangles that subdivided or subdeveloped and re-entangled in Soho among crooked heroin pushers. The work hasn't made it to the stage yet, knock on wood! but seems to be secure in his Saratoga trunk. The hero of that play of shadows was his detective friend, Janos Kerek.

The idea of a similar mad variation occurred to Milalias while he was waiting for me at the Piccadilly tube, WHAT'S THE TIME? next to the clock-map showing the times all over the world. On the left, leaning on a trashcan, a Chinese chap with a violin. And he seemed nervous, he deduced, because he never stopped looking at the clock. Finally another Chinese fellow arrived, they muttered for a moment, and the impatient one handed over his violin (or was it only a case?) to the new arrival, who in turn handed over an envelope. And they took off in opposite directions. What was in the envelope and the violin case? Janos Kerek doesn't believe it was a letter and a violin. [That would have to be detected by a better recounter, ja, a Geiger counter, for example.]
(267.1)

50. Andalusian Light
Light of Andalucía.
Lucy, Light of Andalusia.
Milalias, inundated with light [into the light, larva-like, glow-worm...], named her a thousand ways: Sunshine, Moonlight, Lux Aeterna, Light of my Eyes..., verbally hallucinating luciferically.
[Let there be Light, and long live the night...]
But she was, more than anything else, Andalusian Lucy.
[Her real name: Luz Lozano.]
Not so radiant by the time I met her, in that foreboding Earl's Court dive.
A fading ember.
Her big black eyes, which burned and shined in Milalias's descriptions, were now extinguished.
And though she was a tall woman, she couldn't have weighed more than 110 pounds. Milalias says when he met her, at the end of '69, she was vivacious, glowing with health, and absolutely charming. [Captivated by her grace, and enchanted with her Andalusian accent. Mi alma! My soul! she would say, and Milalias would teasingly imitate her: Mi arma! My arms!]
Dripping with sweat as she ran from table to table, Hey! Move it! or when she burst into a heel-tapping flamenco dance. And with her blouse trembling and rippling so so . . .

A resplendent light, this exuberant Andalusian bloom. She was working as a waitress then, in a Jewish café on Finchley Road. And after closing time, with only the loyal clientele still there, she would jump on a table and toss off tack-tacka-tack flamenco dances, comic or melancholy, till the early morning hours. [Till the dawn's early light . . .]

And from the Finchley Road café she would dance Andalusian [And a loose dancer!] to the flamenco in the basement of the Lord Chandos, across from the Central Post Office. She could shake and toss so well [And a lovely prancer!] and she liked shaking and rattling so much [even belly dancing!], that from there she was taken to work the street and to cruise clacking along Soho and Piccadilly by a bullying Albanian pimp with a Hungarian gypsy air.

[The Albanian was named—Christ, what's in a name!—Kristo Puto (!), which meant pimp to Milalias's Spanish ears. And in the Soho kingdom of streetfighters and streetwalkers there was and perhaps still is another ruffian, this one French, named Monsieur Pons. (!!) All we need now is some cocky Spanish lowlife named Mr. Ponce. (!!!)]

Milalias and Rimbaudelaire saw her many nights making the rounds of the slot-machine saloons and hot dog stands, propositioning lone drivers when the bobbies weren't looking. And if the Albanian wasn't guarding her, they chatted with her, hoping to elevate her morals. [Which had been at ground level ever since she had been thrown into the street . . . Her pimp worked her hard. The Duke of Albany would be her bane . . .] Every day, every night, sinking deeper.

Like lots of others, she made her start in London as an au pair and English student, then worked as a waitress, gradually going from tips to tricks to trips . . .

How long had she been shooting up?

Ever since she fell into Attila's grasp, Milalias says, and the Hun changed her into a nobody. A nothing, a null, who would do all the horrible things he ordered. To sell herself more, and even worse, selling all kinds of drugs and cheap highs everywhere as fast as she could.

[Attila was the one who shot her up, saddled the poor little fool on his white horse . . .]

† 517 †

She was at the bar the night I met her, that Earl's Court bar full of barmy bar-barnacles. A surprised shadow—trying to remember? [Slow-motion swishing, an aquarium.] Lucy . . . Skeletal silhouette, unreal, in the unreal light. And the toad, stationed on the barstool. He had her shackled by an arm while he whispered in her ear and spied out of the corners of his slanting eyes. A Mongolian toad. As if he were about to jump any moment to catch his prey. And his wired teeth, so repulsive! the way I saw them glare . . .

[A Dr. Hoffmann, Edgware odontologist, could have fixed his mouth . . .] Dumpy pug-nosed pig-headed Chinaman. Dyed blond!? A blond Chinese. He toasted us—with champagne—in German. (How do you say Chin-chin! in Chinese, my Mao-Sait-Tout asked him. For an answer he got a look that could kill.) This blond beast had lived in Germany and was proud of his beastly German. As ragged as his hair.

Is that why they called him Attila?

[Wherever his horse stepped, the grass would grow no more . . .]

And now shining Lucy, her light gone out. I'm not sure if she saw or heard us, but from time to time her mouth stretched into a dumb smile. You told me she was barely a shadow of her former self. And that's how she seemed to me, a shadow.

Attila must have quickly tired of his conquest. Now used up, she wasn't any good to him. The Andalusian Light burned out.

She turned up dead in her Notting Hill Gate room with a needle stuck in her right wrist. Accident, murder, suicide? [In alphabetical order . . .] Overdose was the diagnosis. And the police doctor asked if she was left-handed.

[There wasn't much right about her left, or her right either! nothing was right and the whole thing was sinister . . .]

Strange too there weren't other needle marks . . .

[She injected herself under her tongue. Milalias learned this at a bottle-party on Finchley Road, given by some friends in common. Rimbaudelaire was there with his bottle too, and at the end, in keeping with custom, he organized the battle. But before they started breaking bottles and heads, Milalias pushed Rimbaudelaire into the bathroom to sober him up, and there they found her: Andalusian Lucy open-mouthed before the mirror holding a hypodermic straight up, injecting herself in the mouth. That image really stuck.]

Milalias tried to do some sleuthing with the help of his friend Kerek [alias "Sherlock Wholemess"], but they didn't shed much light. Attila washed his hands of the matter and went on with his dirty little deals.

Not long ago, passing in front of the Victoria and Albert Museum, we saw chalked on the sidewalk: Remember Attila! Milalias started furiously erasing the inscription with his hands. I don't think I ever saw him so beside himself.

He's convinced Attila killed Andalusian Lucy.

But it seems he had abandoned her months before she died . . .

Exactly! Maybe she was jealous or resentful and maybe she could have squealed about something . . .

Who knows . . . Would it ever come to light? [Our burned out Lucía!] Who knows . . .

[In any case, what counts is that first injection. And not just the final stab of the bullfight. (That bullfight metaphor isn't just bullshit!)]

The lively Andalusian ever gloomier. That's how Milalias saw her. Consuming herself. A dying light.

[Will he pay, he who put out our Lux Aeterna?]

Just today in front of the Lord Chandos, as we headed towards Trafalgar Square, Milalias remembered that one night after the show the lovely Andalusian told him sometimes when things were going bad she repeated her name autistically, and each time she said it it seemed to mean something different. Luz-Luz-Luz . . . [She had never heard mention of Lord Chandos and certainly not of Hofmannsthal, this lively Andalusian whom Milalias answered by going off on tangents that loony Moonday night: Verbalove isn't worth anything, what counts is your scorching night love . . . That's what you say to all the girls, she would or could answer.] . . . Luz!

[Since then, Milalias spent a lot of time on a lot of occasions repeating—questioning—that word. A syllable, a gene from the Spanish Genesis of his childhood! The word from the beginning?]

Luz?

(269.3)

51. *Cora with a Finger to Her Lips*

Cora from Soho, a little sweetheart, half Chinese. Or Korean? Her mother was Maltese and her father no one knows. [Some accidental Oriental . . .] Your father must have been that damned Chinese ogre, her mother told her, with a black spider as big as this tattooed on his back.

Like father . . . What a mouth [Cora with a finger to her eager lips . . .] for telling in disturbing detail all those shaggy-dog stories that Milalias turned into runaway mongrels: the strange confession bared in a sleazy Soho strip joint, popping the eyes of all those onlookers crowded around our Chinese chatterbox.

The story of the one-eyed snake charmer to start off? . . .: (I must have had eyes big as saucers, I was only about eight years old, when he suddenly showed it to me there in Soho Square. Staggering around bare-chested next to the gardener's cottage. Psssst, hey kid! I didn't know it could be so big, and so hard! and him so skinny and old. Three cheers for Popeye! In Soho everybody called him Popeye, this old exhibitionist wino with his sailor's cap and pipe. Just imagine! Then he takes my hand and makes me feel it, how disgusting, feeling how he could move it. A big knot, hard, making his shrunken arm jump. Biceps of steel, eh honey?—and the way his eyes sparkled. And at first I didn't see it, the snake around the ball of his muscle, a horrible tattoo. And how its forked tongue stretched out ssss and back in when he moved his muscle. I broke free with a scream, jumped through a puddle, and ran away.)

This isn't porno, protested Milalias. Better to start with the one about the drunk cripple looking for his cane.

(281.3)

52. *Midnight, Mr. Midnight . . .*

How many more times will I humdrum it to myself, that scratched record [Johnnie Ray and the Four Lads and the Buddy Cole quartet] from those first nights when [Midnight, Mr. Midnight . . ., Babelle leaped from her high alpine bed (in the labyrinthian attic of Dr. Hoffmann's clinic), impatient to show the future Mr. Midnight (I'm a part of your shadow parade) the newfound double treasure: a phonograph (on the Lyrophon label, or in babelian pronunciation,

Lyre au faune—Lire au fond!) that held in the lining of its case an old record (Midnight, Mr. Midnight) that soon became the broken record she mimicked ironically (Like a puppet that swings on a string) when the midnight man (The hands on the clock embrace) limped home late.

Kneeling nude near the bed, It's the witching hour for lovers, looking into the eyes of Milalias, But I'm not one of them, in turn doubtless peeping at her blind jiggling ones, Midnight, Mr. Midnight, she would frantically crank, Till the moon and shadows . . ., the scratchy worn-out gramophone, aall faade . . . while Milalias sang from the bed, a cavernous voice from a Greek mask, the faint fading flatus vocis of the aphonic phonograph . . .] just as now the Blessed Trinity Church in Brook Green rings its late night bells Ding! Dong! and still Mr. Midnight hasn't arrived.

(285.4)

53. Concha, Conscientious Objector

[Concha, prompter's box . . . trou noir du souffleur . . .]

La Concha, plump and dark. The Madrileñian chambermaid at the Nomad Hotel who makes the nomad's bed but won't make it . . . Panting, butt pushed against the sink [Conscious planning . . .] when the telephone started ringing. The boss lady! Cuntcha . . . Cuntcha!? . . . Yes, faintly. If you've finished on the second floor, Cuntcha? please come down. What should I tell her? rapping the receiver against her rear end. Yes ma'am, right away. Yes, Miss Ireland. I'm coming.

Concha Cota, a coat of mail, a concrete shell and hard to conquer. Iron-willed, rubbing it, misguiding it, squeezing it between her thunderthighs, to keep you out . . . [of that tight little conch shell]. Clamming up. Barely even a crack. And the chair against the half-closed door. The vacuum cleaner blowflying, nosing into things tzzee-tzzee-tzzeeee . . ., clever trick she concocted, making it seem like she's hard at work cleaning your room. The giant tsetseesawing buzz drowning out the heavy breathing, the concupiscence.

—No. Not even a little bit, you dickhead! [Cuntradickting him?]
Serious or just fooling around? Suddenly spitting out the bad

word. And when she got pissed off, watch out! Her story or hysteria of the stretcher-bearer (and compatriot, too) when she was cleaning up in Saint Mary's Hospital: he tried to steal a kiss and she almost bit his tongue off in one bite. [When a Spanish woman kisses . . .] He shouldn't have forced himself on me . . .

Pinned against the sink with her skirt raised to her belly button, and you tried to get into her bare-handed. [The precious conch shell protected.] Steadfastly refusing you. [Sort of . . .] She moaoaning as if you were beheading her. [Finally driving your point home . . .] Pulling her hair. [Black, oily.] No no you motherfucker! [L'espagnole quand elle baise . . .] And she snaps her head forward. [Conclusion, concussion. Unconscious pilot . . .] What a conk you got from that conscious objector.

(417.3)

54. *The Mystery of Edwin Drood*

The biggest mystery? The posthumous—and unfinished— Dickens novel. They gave it to the schoolboy Janos Kerek, in a Colchester school, soon after the young refugee arrived in England. [When the overbearing Russians crushed the Hungarian uprising.]

I remember him entertaining us with the great mystery in the Lord Elgin, telling how he had learned English [Victorian] from *The Mystery of Edwin Drood.* He didn't know any English when he arrived but vowed not to rest until he was able to read his novel. Fascinated, he scrutinized the engravings and finally learned all the words from beginning to end. Even in the boarding school he deciphered it by flashlight under his sheets while his roommates slept.

The Mystery of Edwin Drood would become his endless obsession. Dickens had taken the solution of the mystery to the grave. [Sh! sir.] The mystery of the solution . . .

He collected possible endings, all the hypotheses the Dickens specialists had juggled around, and challenged his friends to come up with an original, coherent ending. Perhaps as Dickens had in mind? He even paid a visit to a spiritualist, a friend of Mrs. Askew, who boasted she was in contact with the great Dickens. Dickens's spirit only dictated to her, cryptically, through the Ouija: *Catch a tartar!*

Milalias created more than a hundred possible endings for Kerek. He had plenty to choose from. The same system [help yourself to the beginnings . . . and the endings . . .] that he would employ to the letter in one of his larvarian books.

—I don't know . . ., Janos Kerek said doubtfully. Could Mr. Tartar be Edwin Drood's murderer? It doesn't seem likely that a retired naval officer could . . .

—Why not . . ., and Milalias began to thicken the mystery plot still more.

(419.7)

55. *The Prodigious Woodcutter*

[The father and magic master? Imaginary character or something worse?: The Fairy Feller . . .]

Altering our egos and answering our ids till all hours in Albert's new studio. And his new muse (: an exuberant six-foot blonde, Brietta or Britta, who he introduced to us as simply "The Great Britain") left us groggy with her successive grogs, stronger each time, switching from reds to whites to . . .

On the walls and along the floor, the new "Alterations & Repairs," some in sketch form: a series on *The Fairy Feller's Master-Stroke*, the masterwork of Richard Dadd [1817–1886], the great patricidal painter, who had also recently become Albert's obsession (catching the mutant virus, Daddaism). He followed Milalias's advice and spent hours and hours in the Tate staring at the Dadd painting. Actually it isn't the woodcutter who is spellbound, he said, it's me. The feller is your altered ego, joked Emil, up to his usual games. The Fairy Feller . . . See how you two even look alike. And it was true. There was something there: the corpulence, the reddish hair (except Albert usually wore it in a ponytail), the profile . . . Let's see, turn around. Yes, that's it. The woodcutter in the clearing in the calligraphic woods, with ax poised to split the giant hazelnut [Nutcracker! Crack of doom . . . Losing your last judgment?], petrified forever by the stares of a circle of fairies and gnomes . . .

Already flying on the magic carpet. Through the smoke spirals, Albert's alterations fluttering, vibrating, in a profound silence.

The one that most attracted me altered Dadd's painting with a cobweb interwoven by the lines of the stares. [The woodcutter caught, enchanted, in the web of stares.] Threads holding the ax of the marionette woodcutter.

Emil spoke of Dadd's life in an asylum, an entire life. Locked within himself, in reality, in his work. He had been imprisoned for more than nine years in the painting of the magic woodcutter. And he wisely left it unfinished. The patience and wisdom of a famous old Chinese painter.

And in the window, a stumped Japanese aquatint: the black arch of the little Camden Lock bridge, a sharp brushstroke suspended over the dawn mist.

(421.3)

56. Mask of Milalias the Clown?:

[A picture by Babelle is worth more than a thousand words by Milalias.]

(421.5)

57. Here's the Key!

—Qui-Qui. . . ?

almost asleep when a creak startled me crick-cradge! a grating clink, feet scuffing nearby: the Shadow growing till it hit the ceiling (: —. . . Qui!? Who!?), ah . . . who else! my

vampire Count Orgasm, my Wild Phantom of Cunterville returning ((Isn't it about time, Dr. Who?)) from his pornoctambulations
through the erogenous zones of the surreal fantasy, The Waste
London! mask of the night of sad continence, in the candle's half-
light, petrified next to the wardrobe, hypnotizing me with his flashing black wire-rim glasses, looklooking at his Babelle au bois
dormant who just sat up in bed (feigning indifference), and offering
a sideways kiss asking "Sweetheart?"

(425.1)

58. Sexy Black of Night . . .

From the thousand and one—no!: des mille et une nuisances!
that formal getup that doesn't get up. Or down. The dress must be
of night, and the mask of night too . . . The devil you say! Your
queen was and is naked. Sexy Black of Night . . ., in that department store [posh shop!] display window or mundanities fair. Black
is Black! the neon letters blinking on and off, Black is Back! the
mannequins hovering about in their vamporous black outfits, Black
is Beautiful! next to a black and white grand piano, slowly turning
pian-piano. Un peu trop tape-à-l'œil, too flashy you know. . . (No,
I know: you're just a bump on a log, you don't see or hear anything!
while I keep myself busy talking to the wall to hear myself talk . . .)
Here we go, watch out! into the tricks and treats department. It
started to pour again as I went flying by that display window. And
in the blink of an eye I dive inside, bam! already in the trap instead
of the Oxford Circus tube. Going down! oh yes . . ., down the
escalator, to a houri's paradise: why the hell was I going down
there? Yes me a soaked little twit la poule mouillée walking on eggs,
my muddy Swedish clogs clack! clack! on fluffy silk moquettes,
Just looking . . . Thank you! between all those finicky miladies
looking and looking again at their models, this basement boutique
like a luxurious nightclub, tout un décor: stardust on the soffit, blue
half-light and suave blues going to your head like champagne
bubbles. Ah! I vaguely wander around the vogues, among shimmering silks tulles crepes scented sachets sheer satin formals, des
soies de soirée! And those sleek frozen mannequins with sac-
charine smiles and pompous poses, black silk hoods and sashes,

salomessalinas in muslin and see-through black veils! staring me down. Veritable vertigo, I was now in the clouds. Yes, obnubilation! Maybe my fasting, faim de mois! this ramadan! plus the heat. On étouffe à l'étoufféerie! Then right in front of me, waltzing and spinning, my model my double my mannechimera, whatever you want to call it!: stretching her arms out to me, ses manches bouffantes! half nude or half dressed with a very low-cut transparent caftan of black chiffon showing her breasts, pommes mousseline! and smooth black panties. Already seeing myself sultry silky, smoothly seducing the supposed seducer . . . I can see it now! Even if silk clothes don't make the man, money might make a Mona Lisa. Chameleonardo! And then in the jungle of art nouveau clothes racks I was bound to find, dangling like a leaf from a branch, fifty pounds sterling! unwittingly turning the silver price tag round and round. Do I dare—I don't dare, squeezing it for all it's worth, balling it up, ça serait facile de la glisser dans mon sac, an easy slip into my bag, looking around, barely a handful, I go crazy for a moment, crumpling wadding that little black silk ball. And why not? Much easier than the books, to rob a robe . . . and now if nobody's looking. Est-ce que je ne piquais pas des bouquins pour toi presque tous les jours? these lean tough years! pinching pounds of books that turned into pounds sterling: our verbal alchemy! That very same morning in Foyles, Come on! hurry up! to the second-hand bookstore a little farther down. Our Bank of Charing Cross Road. Deux livres that brought nearly trois livres! Just for you this time, to pay the price of your pleasures, tes caprices go-goyesque! But now my whim for once, merde alors! caressing and stroking it, rubbing my eyes with that black fabric. And then, black is black! ah ah I saw it or saw it again all black: a little while ago you behind the Torino window, I saw you! en train de popoter avec ta pépée, seated at a table with the Pompadour of the Pampas, the plump dear all dolled up! and her *Liberty* bags beside her on the chair. Et moi comme un rat raté et ratatiné, sous la pluie, sans un sou, your little rat on the Oxford Street corner getting soaked from sheer curiosity, just to get a look at her. Not my type, je te jure! your Argentinean. Oh yes, I understood everything, all your Spanish-isms on the telephone the day before, how you made a date with her in the Torino café at exactly four, l'après-midi du faune! because she had to go shopping on Regent Street. Falling back into your old habits! I still remember that first messy affair, waiting for that Metropolitan tube that never arrived, back in the Paddington station, on our way to Ladbroke Grove. Yes, dredge it up and describe it. I wanted to go through the Portobello market and you with your tricks, Portobello is for tourists . . ., taking me in the opposite direction, saying you'd show me a more interesting market, the smooth talk of a womanizer! loaded with bargains. Oui, le marché aux pucelles! the flee market. Afterwards, in bed, you confessed the reason: your date in Portobello, that Saturday, with the Argentinean antique dealer. Were you already tired of your pampered little fool from the Pampas? your oh-so-generous antiquarian, with her flirtatious gifts. Mandrake root to stimulate the appetites. And that phallic peace pipe that she offered you to make peace or war or love in her rococo smoking den on Park Walk. On and on it goes. Pipe dream! Pip! Nom d'une pipe! The Queen of the Night rejuvenates you . . . Flûte! And her unbelievable name Ester Ling [or was it Sylvia Dollar?] Something-or-other, surely your invention since she's loaded with dough, or as you put it, she had enough silver to buy all the clothes in London! Mais moi je la trouve vieux jeu, she's rather old with all her fussy frills and flounces and her cabbage-patch hairdo like she belongs in a museum! You call that l'élégagance? A moitié gaga, half gaga or senile the way you stood there admiring her. A Madame Tussaud figure in the shop window, jammed into her braces and laces. At least *my* dress was . . . already in the bag! In the blink of an eye I bagged an eyeful! my new evening gown in my old looting bag. And suddenly I'm drowning in the density of this dungeon, dying to get out in the open air. The robe robbed, my foolish five-finger discount. At least the books were useful . . . Not even in my dreams have I flounced around in a dress like that one, pas le culot de me trémousser dans une mousseline pareille, Babelle the belle of the ball, the Sleeping Beauty of the bash! not the same old stale stuff in *that* gown. And all to surprise you, t'en mettre plein les yeux! so that you wouldn't see me looking the same as always. Surprise, oh yes, and a good one: Would you mind opening your bag? that mean mannish woman in a tailored tweed suit, at the exit, holding me almost affectionately by the arm. Would you please open it. And I or she or we emptied the bag, froufrousse! that black rag with the bad tag still dangling. You didn't pay for it, did you? very slow and courteous, unfolding the evening gown. No, I haven't paid yet! She asked me to walk with her, all quite discreetly, to the elevator. Then to a messy office, please sit down, where two lackeys filed or shuffled papers. Both joking their stupid private jokes while she called the police. But none of it mattered to me, as if my whole body were asleep. And it was all really happening to my double, that "Babelle" you invented? like in a mirror or a movie, and I just stepped into the middle of it. But the movie went on! A baby-faced bobby and that female store dick [Dickless Tracy?] escorting me to the paddy wagon, the Black Maria! already at the store entrance. Public enemy number one, hop up! locked up in the back, looking through the barred window at the thousand-headed [hydrocephalic] monster. Maybe you even passed by, so smart and self-assured! in the crowd, la foule folle, the five-thirty tumultitude in Oxford Circus. Zipping off to the nearby police station, right behind Oxford Circus, to take my statement and fingerprints and fill out forms. The police were quite polite with their routine questions. What scared me most was my work permit, not valid since I took French leave from the clinic. Dr. Singh is on vacation now, on the Continent I think, and I'm staying with some friends for a few days, in Cleveland Gardens. Toute une histoire! Another story! Then in another room I have to strip in front of a big policewoman, a meticulous examination: You'd be surprised what we find some-times . . ., tugging at the elastic of my slip and conscientiously peeping around. No, I'm not surprised at all, but who knows what she hoped to find. And then from the ocular inspection, ou je dois dire oculaire? to still another room, sitting alone on a bench to ponder my plight. Lucky for me the cherubic bobby took pity and broke the rules by giving me his pack of Piccadilly's. Then smoking, hoping, and giving up till finally! they let me call you. Absolutely furious on the phone! I thought you wouldn't even come get me. Maybe it would have been better. You with your face of a gentle-man whose sensibility has been offended! As we were leaving you asked, the only thing you cared about! how much the fine would be. The police evasive, unhelpful. Of course, it depends on what was stolen and who did the stealing. But in my case, a first offense,

maybe half the price of the dress. Twenty-five pounds! And our pensioned poet and last resort Rimbaudelaire, grumbling and moaning all the while, loaned us the money. And this from the same guy who wanted to get me out of Cleveland Gardens once and for all. The following morning at ten, alone again in a tight spot, in the courtroom on Great Marlborough Street. While I waited a very friendly bobby came up to talk to me, said I wouldn't have to wait much longer, looked at my citation, told me to be calm and that my case isn't very serious, take it easy, and so on, and casually asked me how much I brought. The twenty-five pounds. And then he went into the front room, the one numbered on my citation. He came back immediately, smiling, and nodded for me to go in. My turn now. And in two minutes the wigged hypocrite was through with me, even with his little lecture and everything . . . Don't do it again, miss. Twenty-five pounds penalty! Next case! and a smack of the gavel. Just like that for the sentence. And almost immediately I got furious with myself for telling the cop I had twenty-five pounds. Born-again fool that I am. [Prize idiot!]
(425.3)

59. Graal

—Graal . . . Sangraal . . . he kept on gargling, sitting at the card table.

—What?

—It seemed to be both a vase and a book at the same time. [Bok? Bock?] Maybe when we get the book, we'll end up with the vase.

—Where?

—The last place you'd think of. But since we don't have a vessel, give me a *beso*.

[Esquisse. Kiss, or sketch:

One night in the Phoenix nest, when the lured lovers were about to melt in a kiss. Don't move! the passionate painter recorded forever that passing instant of passion, tracing (with Babelle's eyeliner) the silhouettes of the head profiled on the white sheet (Milalias's bête blanche, the hated trophy!) thumbtacked to the wall. (Would that imminent kiss be the happy ending of his book? The end of the inquiry for his Grail?)

According to another version, more plausible, the Hero with a Thousand Farces composed the shadow of the kiss with his own hands and Albert Alter (Beau Gest, Alter! Gestalter! Drain the cup to the . . .) limited himself to tracing those shadowy theatrics. Was it all just sleight of hand, or slightly handy? Figure is ground and vice versa, intermittently. A handy hackneyed image worth more than a thousand wasted words.]

(425.4)

60. Strokes of Midnight, Ta Page Nocturne . . .

Tap! Tap! Tapage nocturne! Your midnight strokes disturbing the peace, staccato-bugling your last ictus taps . . .

Dead tired, nodding off over the typewriter but one finger still typing his Nachtmusik: Tap! Pat! Tap-Tap-Tap-Tap-Tap-Tap Spat! Top-Top-Top Spot! Tat-Tat Spat!

[DIABOLUS EX MACHINA:

At the high points he was writing at full gallop, rocking on his saddle and vigorously banging away at the machine.

He had broken several in successive races against the clock. An Olympia that Eva Marx had stolen or borrowed from the office one weekend. The long-suffering Olivetti, grudgingly loaned once by Mr. Testi. And the portable Adler, a gift from Babelle, that wound up flying through the air—the last flight of the eaglet!—in a spell of fine madness. But the one that outlasted them all was the old brute [German?], Uncle Emil's legacy, that proved itself truly invincible. Its brand name, in gold letters (the first letter almost obliterated: G? B?), looked like ROMA. ((All roads lead to Rome!)) But our Grand Nicknamedropper rechristened the indestructible infernal machine ENIGMA, since its keys struck haphazardly and made up word games on its own. Babelle, who was a good typist, almost had it tamed. But when you least expected it, the diabolus ex machina could still pull some pranks. Especially when Milalias became possessed with the devilish device. He used to say that within his novel, ENIGMA would have as much importance as the names *Babieca, Bayardo, Rocinante, Brigliadoro* . . . had in their times. To say nothing of *Clavileño*. And he was convinced he must introduce it to the reader. The best way would be to offer a sample of its wryting: please see, in PILLOW NOTE 63, a facsimile of a prank ab ovo of the diabolic ex machina.]

The rattling typerifler (our stammering ENIGMA) ratatattled slower and slower. The stubborn writer nodded off at the little card table in front of the black window. Since our last tiff, already more than a week, he wouldn't trust me to type his hieroglyphics. From one moment to the next, he was about to fall over the machine like a log.

Tap-Tat-Tapt!

—Wouldn't you rather sleep in bed? I said, and went back to hiding my head under the blankets and pillows.

Ta-Ta-Ta-Tat!

(427.4)

61. "Mr. Ta"

The catarrhal old tattler "Mr. Ta," Ta! who sold newspapers at night, Ta! Ta! at the main entrance to the Hammersmith station, Ta! always accompanied by his asthmatic dog. A cocker spaniel, I think it was, usually muddy and filthy, and always devoted to rubbing against my legs. Rheumy nostalgic eyes. Mr. Ta, whose real name was Mr. Tatham, on the other hand, had merry sparkling eyes. Between his humming and shouting (he added his witty additions to the evening edition), he frequently tipped his bottle of cough syrup. Or rum for his raspiness, Milalias would say. Perhaps. But his jolliness was real, and he was friendly with everybody. We only saw him lose his temper once, and only then because a drunk had taken a kick at his dog. Milalias had trouble pulling them apart.

He told me once I reminded him of his granddaughter (is that why he liked so much to chat with me?), who lived in Belfast. He was Irish and lived alone with the dog in Barnes. He also mentioned that his landlady, a "wicked widowed witch"—those were his words—wanted to throw him out because of his dog. If the dog even got whiff of her from a distance, it bristled and growled. Highstrung, like his master at times. Shaking itself in time with Mr. Ta's humming, which was frequently accompanied by his heel-tapping and hand-rubbing. [Buck and wing! . . . Cold and windy on Broadway . . .] They're not there anymore.

The dog was hit by a bus on Hammersmith Bridge Road and took off howling and yelping towards the hanging bridge. Mr. Ta spent a night [a dog's night] looking for it. The dog (what was its name? Buck?) was waiting for him, badly injured, at the door to his house in Barnes. The dog recovered, but poor Mr. Ta . . . A severe case of pneumonia took him in a few days. Another newspaper vendor told us that the "wicked widowed witch," appearances deceive, took care of the dog. But at night it goes crazy and she has to let it out to wander. It comes back in the morning, from who knows where. Rumor has it that some nights around Hammersmith, a ghost is seen with a dog that howls sensational news. Tomorrow's news? Milalias swears he saw them once, behind the Olympia, because of or in spite of the fog. And he insists that now only the dog coughs, and Mr. Ta looks much better than before.
(429.1)

62. Sheet Lightning

Last night, Ash Wednesday, it was time for my favorite chapter: carniwaltz of the night of Don Juan.

Even with the windows up there was so much smoke it made me cry. This chimney will never draw, Guy Fawkes [Focs, Fox] was saying, wrapping his tiresome tirade with the smoke and flames.

I remember most of those masks perfectly. Maybe I could make a list of those who took part in that crazy party, just in case the vampyromaniac got the urge to rewrite it.

[A sort of dramatis personae, although incomplete, written on various little pieces of paper—torn movie tickets, bus transfers, grocery receipts, scraps from newspapers—stuck in Babelle's Album.]

Finally the pyre expires . . . Whewf.

The last sheet contracted and expanded, it seemed alive! and was finally stiff. Completely carbonized, burnt to a cinder, yet whole. A black leaf on the mountain of ashes.

And he, reading my thoughts? said something like: At least I cleared something from that night: a black sheet. [The sternebrous opening quote of his Auto-da-Phoenix.]
(435.1)

63. Ab Ovo

((Ay!

Babelle entranced, nose pressed against the Daquise shop window, showing Milalias the two Easter baskets with multi-colored eggs.

—Nobody could paint them like my grandmother [the Armenian].

—Mine made me a really big chocolate one. [A Portuguese nanny.] At night I had to recite a magic formula in front of the egg: Choco choco late late? Choco late? And in the morning the egg was broken and she assured me that a magic bird had flown inside the broken eggshell leaving all those tiny chocolate eggs.

—This wouldn't be another of your cock-and-egg stories?

—No, really.

—And if we bought one . . .

—With our last queen?

—An Easter egg always brings good luck.

—Then it's a good investment. Besides those must be Russian . . . Yay . . .

Milalias scraping the pockets of his jacket: much ado about a few pennies . . . And scraps, many scraps of scribbled notes.

—Forget it.

—No, no. It's the principal of the thing . . . Heh.

—What?

—Nothing. The last pound I had is gone.

—We'll buy it tomorrow. Tomorrow the Queen has to pay me.

They pried themselves away from the window and linked themselves together with Babelle's long red scarf.

—They'll think we want to be hanged together, said Milalias, in a properly economical fashion in these austere times. Thus enscarved they ambled to Thurloe Place and continued along Cromwell Road until they arrived at Queensberry Place and descended the cellar stairs at top speed.

[With Babelle thinking Milalias had been hit by one of his urgent needs?]

With shoe-tips he cleared a path through the newspapers strewn on the floor and sat down at the card table. He started to pound away on the infernal Enigmachine.

—Don't look! he shouted at Babelle.

Rapidly he positioned and tore out several sheets, crumpling and tossing them.

—No peeking. Not yet.

Finally satisfied, he took a sheet from the typewriter.

—There it is. My gift. My easterized egg . . . and he handed the sheet to Babelle:

<u>O. AB OVO</u>

OVO

V
ᛞ

VOO

—What . . .

—Easter egg Portuguese-style! exclaimed Milalias.

[In Portuguese the egg (*ovo*) hatched with wings spread in a V and transformed into *voo*, flight. And flew away.

And she so happy. Babelle kept it in her album and later tacked it on the best spot on the folding screen in the Phoenix Lodge attic. That's how our novel should start, Milalias used to say. Ab ovo. The egg-flight of the Phoenix. Especially in moments of rage, when the egg-shaped ball of crumpled paper flies into the fire. Choco, late! (Hen, choke or lay it! Cock'o'late!) And took flight from its ashes. Which came first, the flapping or the egg?]

—Quel oeuf! What an egghead!))

(473.3)

64. *Ticklish Question*

A huge interrogative mark, thin and very black, in the sink:

And I keep looking at it on the white porcelain, jealous? tell us! and I keep asking myself whose it could be. Could he have brought some whore home last night? [A wild hair up his ass?] It was he, that Hairy Whodunnit, who taught me the enigmatic hairstrokes of hairs left on sinks and bathtubs. He even claimed he had invented a new means of divination according to the form, color, and disposition of a hair. Surprising, all the forms they could take. He said he would have a chapter in his book dedicated to hair which might be titled "Hair-teasers" or "Splitting Hairs" or "Hairmeneutics" or simply "Hair" [This was back in the heyday of the musical *Hair,* and its lyrics were sprouting up everywhere.] The other day he came out of the tub all excited. Eurekackling his discovery: Lady Violet even dyes her c--- hair violet!

The pubic hair made public. Violet, violated [Rape of the lock . . .], and held high like a trophy. That pube.

(439.3)

65. Connect the Dots

Stitches?

[Just connect.]

Get to the point!

. . . of reference. Of no return. Weak point, moot point . . .

Delineating dilettante . . . (Two of a kind, Milalias and his geo-mistress.)

Even with charts or graphs, it's still just Asa pointing us around with her punctilious messages. Another of her pointless astrological tricks? Where and why was she hiding?

Impossible to decipher these obscure points from any point of view. Milalias going dotty, staring at the missing Asa's mysterious message. The very same, day after day.

You won't see *me* again, she shouted pointedly from the stairwell as she fled, fed up with his scenes. You won't see me again . . . And yet she provoked him to look for her.

Look for me in this constellation. Constellation? Only the dots, like tiny flyspecks on the white page:

Look for me in this constellation

Look for me in this constellation. Where? Milalias scrutinizing that message for the thousandth time. Always the same. Day after day. Almost a month already since her disappearance. Asa, the all-around superstar, was conspicuous by her absence.

She had called to our attention that each message was sent from a different point in London, but at first I didn't realize those points

could be related with those of the message. [Why?] Cardinal
points . . ., Milalias said. We need a magnetic compass to find her.
[And a drafting compass?] Of course. Why hadn't it occurred to us
before to note the postmarks on the envelopes. And moreover,
why didn't we think of that pockmarked London map that Asa had
tacked on the door of her room in Holland Park. The points show
where I've lived in London, she explained. Even more changes of
address than Milalias.

Of course. All quite clear. Clear? I saw it all through a glass
darkly. It must be necessary to read, or write . . .

[One must write the reading . . . Rascally rereader! Mr. Tsui-
Pen longing for childhood pastimes and the *bricolecteur* to order
his labyrinth?]

Organize the messages by date. And mark each of those points
on the London map. Then hit the bull's-eye . . . Would it be possible? Milalias began to number them.

Look for me in this constellation

What did she want us to get out of it?
[Only connect.]
Join the dots?
(441.2)

66. X Rays

[One of the *Notes of the Nomad* that were saved, thanks to
Babelle, from the auto-da-fé . . .]

Upon leaving the Elgin [Lord Elgin, on Elgin Avenue, Maida Vale, that our Spanish devil typically disjointed into El gin . . .] I decided to take a moment to pass by Reis's house, to see how he was doing. Already past eleven, but I knew the old night owl still had many sleepless hours left.

The central window of the ground floor [the one to his room] was illuminated as usual at that hour. And the sash window slightly raised, in spite of the February cold. But when I went up to ring the doorbell of the door marked *X Reis,* I stopped: I heard loud voices and laughter in Spanish. I was shocked—Reis almost never received visitors. And fewer still would be compatriots.

I went around on the gravel path till I was in front of the window, to see who it was. Like a robber crouching in the dark behind the hedge, I could hear and see the scene.

A relative from Spain? Or some friend's son? More or less my age and maybe not so tall, also with beard and Lennonesque glasses.

Sitting face to face by the hot radiator, chatting noisily with cups of tea. No, not tea: Reis tipped a little gin in the cups every so often. Until he put the empty bottle (Beefeater) on the fireplace mantel. Somewhat ginebriated? They were laughing at every word. I had never seen Reis so expansive. But they must not have known each other long because now Reis was explaining that the X stood for Xavier or really German Xaver, his name in memory of a missionary uncle, his mother's brother who was swallowed up by the jungle or some Amazonian cannibal. ((He never told *me* that story.)) Reis hated his Jesuitical Christian name and reduced it to just X. "An appropriate initial for an anonymous author . . .," he used to say ironically. Yet here he was solving the unknown X for the stranger. ((Could he be one of those professors who were now starting to discover, in forgotten magazines, the singular early work of Reis?)) And on he went, quite at ease, with his genealogical history:

—My father, who misspoke Spanish with a thundering Teutonic accent to the end of his days ((now he would tell . . . no, he didn't tell the one about the "calf of lamb" . . .)), could never convince the Spaniards that our name was really German.

—Ah, and I thought it was Portuguese.

† 538 †

—No, no. German. Low German, originally, pronounced *rice,* but written R-e-i-s. And Reis it remained, but pronounced *race* or *raise* in Iberia.

—What's in a name?

((Not overly original, this bearded guy with his appearance of a bard sans halberd. And then he goes and finishes off the Beefeater . . .))

—And when the storm in '39 tossed me out to this island, I started getting used to the fact that whenever I gave my name, they would invariably write Rays.

—X Rays!

They both laughed again. And the bearded bloke, mouth still full of laughter, added:

—But what a coincidence, you and I are namesakes.

—Namesakes?

—Yes. My dentist's assistant here in Maida Vale, a Malayan, always calls me Mr. Rye-owes, like *rayos,* Spanish rays!

More bursts of laughter.

—Malayan line . . .

—Malayan alignment, the bearded guy laughing again. —Shamed be he who think it malign . . . But some of the English modify my name that way too.

And Reis, half choking, quickly put his oxygen mask to his face.

—Mr. Rays and Mr. Rayos . . ., both guffawing, eyes full of tears.

—Do you want me to open the window a little more?

—No, it's already passed . . . and he put his mask back in the pocket of his robe. It's over, gone. Mr. Rays and Mr. . . . .

The laughs were building up again. Brrr, getting cold as an ice-brrrg standing still and listening to them laugh senselessly, and I decided to go home. Right away . . . An icy chill with each gust that ripped down Elgin Avenue. A little beached whale there on the corner of Warrington Crescent?: a car covered with black plastic.

Rye-owes . . . Rayos . . . Who the devil is this Mr. Riots or Rayos? I wondered out loud as I crossed Randolph Avenue. Would Babelle be warming the bed for me? With luck she would know something about this bearded stammerer. That Mr. Rye-owes with his riotous laugh.

(443.6)

67. Emil's Jigsaw Dance . . .

Family relics . . . Another one. A puzzle of clover-shaped reversible pieces that represented a carnival dance in a hall of mirrors on one side, and a danse macabre on the other. The strangest thing (macabre joke? or some morbid game?): the pieces could combine in different ways and some figures could pass from one dance to the other. One piece was missing: on one side, the face of a lady in a red domino, whom a cloak-and-dagger suitor was trying to kiss; and on the other side, an oval hand mirror being held in front of a lady by old Father Time with his scythe on his shoulder.

And to think the apprentice libertine used to play with that family skeleton while just a child . . .

(445.1)

68. The Library of Babel . . .

[Of Babelle, in dreams:]

Black, gray, white: three heads bending over a Giant Treatise. Another us.

From a large window, here and there among the Fulham grove, the Thames. Steely or leaden or iron-colored, changing with the weather.

We were in the library of the Villa of Mysteries. Sitting at a big round table that spun like the ones in Chinese restaurants, and serving ourselves a banquet of readings. At our disposal were all the books we like and even those we had always wanted to read. ((Remember how envious we were of that Japanese man reading in a low voice, as if praying, the copy of *Genji monogatari* on display in the famous books section of the British Museum . . .)) And we were discussing them animatedly in a sort of table chat.

The dark-haired one was me. (But with shorter hair—to make me look like Lewis Carroll's "little beggar" Alice?) And you were on my left, somewhat aged, with gray hair already. And facing us, on the other side of the table, an old white-haired man with a somewhat androgynous face [Re(b)is!?] who was without a doubt Herr Narrator. Our guide and controller. He was also controlling a type of television or computer, and sometimes on the screen there appeared quotes, translations, images, and whatever data we might need.

[Tolle lege, tolle lege—constantly new readings and adventures.
What joy!]
(447.3)

69. *Portrait of Reis*

After Emil and I interceded *a duo,* Reis agreed to pose for
Albert. After a long stroll, when we had already said good-bye to
him at the Marylebone tube entrance. I'll be waiting for you next
Friday, the three of you at three P.M. It's also my birthday, one
year less! and we can drink a toast. That eleventh of March was
very cold and Reis received us wearing a robe and bundled in the
red scarf I gave him last year. That's how Albert painted him, with
that knot like a hangman's knot, and framed by the fogged window
in the shadowy half-light of his bedroom. He's stroking his goatee,
his most characteristic tic, and his eyes shine with a mix of curiosity
and cunning. Not only his eyes but his head seemed to emit rays.
[Spherical and radiant, his forehead stands out in the chiaroscuro. A broad clear forehead that clears away shadows. Albert
Alter's able pencil enveloped in circles of light his forehead, his
bald patch, his eyesockets. That portrait of a radiant X. Reis is a
visual gag and an allusive homage (abusive, Reis would say with
his modest pride) to his god. The sphere of his bald patch with his
forehead, and mane of long hair—although gray—gives Reis a
Shakespearean air. Doubtless Alter was thinking of the well-
known engraving from the first folio frontispiece as he drew the
shakesperiphery of Reis's head. (Shapesphere! The Globe, his
head . . .)]
Albert made the portrait in just one session of about an hour and
a half, though he reworked it somewhat in his studio, and during
that short time I think Albert and Reis got to know each other
surprisingly well. They were already studying each other when
Emil introduced them, each perhaps measuring Emil's description
against what he saw, and I was relieved and satisfied to see how
well they got along. Reis was almost a chatterbox, as he is when he
imbibes a bit of Beefeater [gin breaking the ice], and Albert was
able to keep the conversation from flagging so that the model
would appear relaxed during the session.

When they spoke of Holland, Reis explained that in his family there also existed the legend of the Flying Dutchman. The founder of the family. Back in the eighteenth century. A Dutch sailor, some Reis who was always off traveling [Reis means *voyage* in Dutch] the seven seas, until one fine day he docked in Hamburg and met a German gal who trimmed his sails [no more flying, Dutchman] and he caught the curse. The wandering second mate became a stable mate. He put down roots in Hamburg and had German off-spring, and the last name passed for German. [Reis means *offshoot* in German.] Just as would happen several generations later, before the First World War, when Reis's father was sent to Lisbon by a German engineering firm. There he married a Lisboan, daughter of a Portuguese and an Austrian, they had a son, and the surname passed for Portuguese. Soon after the war broke out, the Reis family, with their two-year-old son, went to Spain and from there . . .

—Who knows how many more turns are yet to come, said Albert, with his half-Italian Spanish. Cuántas giratas . . .

—No, said Reis, —I am the last descendant of the family. And I'm an anticonceptionist . . .

And he winked at Emil and me.

(447.4)

70. *Let There Be Light?*

—Luz! Light!

Aloft and illuminated, with the burning leaf on high, pendulating naked around the dark room towards the chimney.

Regressing half a step and advancing two, with difficulty.

Visions: the dark or silhouetted demon holding a flame, barely a reflection sparkling in the armoire mirror, moving resolutely towards the fireplace, ready to face the old blast again to start the new auto-da-fé. Auto-da-Phoenix, in the nest of the Phoenix Lodge?

—Ah! A-ha! And there was light . . .

[LUX ((: FLASHBACK))
One polished little word in the chaoscuro, Lux! liminary luminary

of the roasting sheet of smoked psalms, ever-darkening as he reeled stoned, naked and shivering pian piano playing acrosstics, teetering toward the fireplace to scrap all the sheets of the musicaliginous (Light opera?) comediet of errors. Ho! As it is consumed all the remainbronzes are recast, letting him remake it anew, exhumation point! projecting a round of chattering shadows that returned unannounced to releash the hallucinations he would soon try to transcribe synoptically, in a trance and in double parentheses as follows:

((Rabbi with scholiosis, spine bent, swinging a bone over the sacrum sanctum Talmud: "Luz, bel bello tenebbreoso, path of the burning nest of Phoenix (fenicererone) to finitiate the resurrection." Sephardic osteologist in mask performing a Torahcectomy: "Luz!" [Light?] Ossianic bard with tabard and dark glasses, flaunting his glossary: "Luz, bone mot and bone fire, more marrows that have slangoriously burned." Father Brown, brandishing his humbrella: "Luz? Love-light of Spain. Light-o-love. Cherchez la flamme! A la lumière de flambeau." Giordano Bruno the Toastmaster in the limelight, seasoning his supper of ashes for the dark night of Saint John: "And the Word was made flash . . ." A pack of phantomastiffs, a confederacy of dunces! in chorus: "Dumb Scotus!" "Scotus go home!" "Donn Scrotus!" "Dun Ascot!" "Dung Skot!" "Done as Kot!" "Pay your scot!" "Leading light of scotological scotolasticism whose scotopical vision found the Spinozian solution to the enigma of l'Immaculée Conception!" "Make light of your bright clear idea!" "Peirce an Ersehole, latrinist! in the larvastory." "Hushitup!" "Supremetaphysical scotheologist mariolater!" The subtle doctor in brown Franciscan habit, vulgarly Lating-a-linging the brass medallion with the scottolatin inscription *Deus Solus,* imparting it with the blessing: "My lightmotiv: *Deus Solus!* God is Light, which is why he could penetrate, what subtlety, without break or stain, the perfect unpolluted womb of the Virgin." A little Irish nun kneeling and rattling away with mousy beatific smile, in focal dialect: "Lux! Fiat lux. Lux Mundi." Grand sourire. And mezzopianoing: "Giving birth to the light of the world and it's already day." And with a cri du coeur: "Oooh la la, my God!" Shadow with a *lume* and volume in each hand, in front of the mirror: "Lux Absolumière!" Domine in domino facing the mirror: "Et lux perpetua luceat eis. Gaudeamus, Igitur!" Petty critic from the Ville des Lumière, consulting his Manuel de Littrérature: "Luz, bel et bien! c'est de l'espagnol. Le premier mot polarisant d'un roman noir en édition de lux." "Lux? More light?" Knight of the Light on his deathbed completing his last—guet-à-penser—metaphorism: "Mehr Lichtenberg!" Andalucy in her frilly Andalusian dress, with delicate clapping: "Anda! Loosen Lucy! I was startin' y' know my liddle act in Lor' Chando righ' there by Trafaga Skwa, jus startin' wi' my cantejondo, the one that begins Andalus! Andalus! an' all those bingin' Englishmans shoutin' On the loose! On the loose! Osú! Those slanglosessions." Shabby shuffling old man, slowswinging his oil lamp on high: "Lux, primordial syllable of diogenesis . . ." Svelte silhouette nude, evanescent, her black hair over her face and breasts, babelizing: "Luz! bel lament, first Spanish word I heard from his wolf's mouth. Naked, shamelessly, in his Cleveland Gardens cubbyhole. Having just met me. And he was pissinging in the Water-loo when the darkness hit. Luz! he hooted, thinking I had turned it off. Not even a shilling to put in the meter, yeah, mamita mía, and me nonplussed." A naiad, hair standing on end, bearing a fish-key round her neck: "Inebroiated, lost up the Thames because his sweetheart left him. In the clouds, along Chiswick, watching the wakes . . . In darkness circling, making the rounds of the Old Ship and the Saint Nick church. And next to Hogarth's tomb he got nosy, sniffing me out, rudely rooting, truffling with me, his hog art! I smacked him on the snout. I renounce you! With my shouting, Help! Hell! he left to make his escape and fell in the river." Big scary froghead croaking: "Kva! Qué va! No more Luz. Sin. They sealed up the meter in his nest so he couldn't pull any more tricks . . ." Fairy in a mauve mantle, brandishing a paintbrush: "No luz? Lose out! He arrived all muddy banging on my door to ask for a light. Just a flame?" Mephistopheles scratching a moist match on the sole of his boot: "Lucifer? Match! All grimy and filthy, coming apart at the seams after the fall. Did he lose the sequins of his tailurid suit, that litiginous loss-suit? Bird! Brain! Blindly charging while he strips with jerks and shivers. I will burn my books, he raved." A straw man sniffing about: "Luz! O Sancta simplicitas! to seize that little sheet chosen gropingly from the Tower of Babble." Dark form grasping a mummy's hand that clutched an extinguished candle: "Don't you see the light?" Sphinx playing scrabble by herself, turning letters on a tomb: "LUX. UXL. You excel!" Stingy boy at the edge of his grave: "A story, unca, to go to sleep. Turn on the light, unca, here comes the sandman . . ." Abominable snowman brandishing an alpenstock: "Finsternis, sin fin, den without end. To my peak! There's a fire under the snow. Flamme! that clamors. That carnevil afternoon in Luzerne . . ." "Nyet! Not yet, yeti!" a hooded Ku Klux Klannette driving it away with lantern-swings. Plumed Tartuffe making esses: "Luz! affair. His scare! seeing the black ape in the armoire mirror. The dreaded beast of his dreams?" Distinguished phantasmadam, with a parsol shaped like a four-leaf clover: "Emil! Luz . . . Indestructible, my son."))

Luz? he wondered about the meaning of that bright little word as that round of masks kept parading through his dark night.]

(449.3)

71. Inknight

Falling.

With the rain.

[Her aquatint . . .]

Spilling, spreading, from bough to bough through the trees of Brook Green.

[Turning fronds into founts . . .]

Getting so dark now I can barely see the letters of this note I'm scribbling, sitting in front of the window, while I wait for you.

(449.4)

Babelle's
Photo Album

Babelle's Photo Album

(Snapshots in alphabetical order of some London sites mentioned in this novel.)

Battersea Park, SW11

Bishop's Park, SW6

Blomfield Road (Little Venice), W9

Blythe Road, Hammersmith, W14

Brook Green, W6

Brook Green (Phoenix Lodge Mansions)

Brook Green

Camden Lock, Camden Town, NW1

Cleveland Gardens, W2

Chiswick Mall, W4

Chiswick (Saint Nicholas Church), W4

Deptford, SE8

Deptford
(Saint Nicholas Church)

Deptford (Saint Nicholas Church)

Earl's Court Road, W8

Elgin Avenue (Maida Vale), W9

Elgin Avenue

Finchley Road, NW3

Fulham Palace Road, W6

Fulham Road, SW6

Golder's Green Road, NW11

Hammersmith Broadway, W6

Hammersmith, Lower Mall, W6

Hammersmith, Upper Mall (The Dove), W6

Hampton Court (The Labyrinth)

Holland Park, W8

Hyde Park Corner, SW1

Islington Green, N1

Kensington Gardens (The Fountains), W2

Kensington Gardens (The Round Pond)

King's Road, SW3

Knightsbridge
(Harrods), SW7

Maple Street, W1

Post Office Tower
from Maple Street

Paddington,
London Street, W2

Porchester Gardens, W2

Queensberry Place, SW7

Queen's Park, NW7

Queensway, W2

Saint John's Wood, NW8

Shepherd's Bush,
W12

Soho Square, W1

Southampton Street, intersection with Strand, WC2

South Kensington, Thurloe Street, SW7

World's End, SW10

Index of Names*